DREAMS OF AN AVERAGE MAN

DREAMS OF

Also by Dyan Sheldon

VICTIM OF LOVE

AN AVERAGE MAN

DYAN SHELDON

Crown Publishers, Inc., New York

Grateful acknowledgment is hereby given for the following:
Song lyrics on pages 11, 12, 59, and 138 are taken from
"Life Is Just a Bowl of Cherries" by Lou Brown and Ray
Henderson, copyright 1931, © renewed 1959 by Chappell &
Company, Inc. All rights reserved.
Excerpts on pages 86 and 87 from the poem "El Cántaro
Roto" from *Libertad Bajo Palabra* (1949, 1960), by
Octavio Paz, Fondo de Cultura Económica, Mexico City.
Excerpt on page 303 from the poem "Sueño Despierto" by
José Martí, first published in the collection *Ismaelillo*
(1882, New York).

Published in the United States in 1986 by Crown Publishers, Inc., 225 Park
Avenue South, New York, New York 10003

Originally published in Great Britain by William Heinemann Ltd., 10 Upper
Grosvenor Street, London W1X 9PA

CROWN is a trademark of Crown Publishers, Inc.

Manufactured in the United States of America

Design by Lauren Dong

Library of Congress Cataloging-in-Publication Data

Sheldon, Dyan.
    Dreams of an average man.

    I. Title.
PS3569.H39265D7 1986   813'.54   85-26965
ISBN 0-517-56139-5

10 9 8 7 6 5 4 3 2 1

First American Edition

DREAMS OF AN AVERAGE MAN

O N E

Already, this has been a year for dying. Air crashes in the middles of cities, busloads of children blown off the highways, young couples mutilated by madmen, mown down for doing something so simple as stopping to steal a kiss. What once were people are instantly bodies. Infants drowned in toilet bowls, fried in Teflon-coated pans, eaten by the family python. Sandy's colleague having a stroke as he swam across an Olympic-size pool, only thirty-three and in perfect health; the waiter from El Flor del Broadway stabbed to death on his way home from the hospital; a guy Tony used to work with falling from a ladder while changing a light bulb, breaking his neck as he thumped down the stairs; one of Parker's clients found dead just this morning, dead from unknown causes for three missing days. A year for dying.

And when hasn't it been?

Oh, never, he thinks. Never. But it didn't seem so close before, so malignly personal. As though Death itself is stalking him, cool and untroubled, waving at him from between baskets of plants in the windows of trendy bars, winking at him from across the subway tracks, laughing at him as he bends to remove a half-pound package of peas from the swirling depths of a supermarket freezer, "Gettin' kinda cold in here, doncha think?" Sometimes Death looks like a Hollywood version of a Harlem pimp, and sometimes it looks like Doris Day with that I'm-*really*-a-nice-girl grin. But always Death is saying, the words just gliding through those bright-as-a-polar-ice-cap teeth, "You, too, Rivera. You, too." From windows and doorways, from cabs and cars and belching buses; on crowded streets, in cafés filled with steam and noise, under the dignified awnings of the more expensive buildings, "Hey! Rivera! You, too!"

Only this morning, as he was adjusting his bicycle clips, Death, a six-foot-tall black man, his hair in dreadlocks, a black toga wrapped around his massive body, sandaled, wild-eyed, and not without a certain majesty, appeared from around the corner as though on a morning stroll through the wilderness, one small, green apple in one large, brown hand. Jesus Christ, he'd thought, now it's moved into my street.

If only he could be sure (as everyone else seems to be) that he is losing his mind. It wouldn't be so bad, really, a pale blue, padlocked room in some private sanatorium set in tranquil surroundings. Nothing to do but sit out on the sun porch in your old clothes (we don't like to make them feel like prisoners here), reading *War and Peace* or making models of exploding H-bombs out of clay, concocting enough stories to keep the staff in pocket and amused. On the weekends, the visitors would come, rigid with normality, bringing his favorite foods and news from the outside, laughing and chatting, how are you feeling? how are they treating you? the doctor said we could go to town and see a movie if you felt like it. Nobody would expect anything from him; if he did nothing they would probably be relieved. What could be bad about that?

Bent forward over the bars of his bike, wearing a faded denim jacket and a green and faintly luminescent hard hat—relic of his brief if painful career as a construction worker one long-ago summer—Tony Rivera rides home into the wind. Cutting cabs, racing around buses, whirring suddenly across the paths of preoccupied pedestrians, he imagines himself as of old, Rivera 9, the number drawn in felt-tip on a square of paper pinned to his shirt, racing through the colors of a softened world, man and bike one creature. He can smell the smells and hear the sounds, as though still humped over the Peugeot, nose to metal, a perfect being in control of its own time and space, winning winning winning as the wheels go squish and the gears go clack click.

Easily, he navigates a young woman, in cape and sombrero, dragging two small children across an intersection; devilishly, he rounds a drunkard, and a dusty Cadillac, horn groaning. He imagines sun and wind, tiny insects sucked into oblivion as the bike bowls on; can hear the stillness of the earth and the stillness of the universe as he climbs ancient hills and slides down time-mauled slopes of unknown ancestry, his bicycle's chrome glinting wickedly in the relentless sun.

In reality, though, it is an abnormally gray and grizzly June night, a spectacular break in the early heat wave that has threatened to evacuate the city ahead of time this year. A fine, cool rain nips at his face and hands.

In the shops along the streets, everything proclaims that it is summertime and the living, if neither really free nor exactly easy, is fun-filled and frivolous. Electric fans and ice chests, canvas caps and imitation Panama hats, fishing poles and folding chairs, teeny bikinis and gypsy skirts all hang and plop and lean in gay profusion. Towers of bottles of suntan lotion, towers of fun sunglasses, towers of boxes of crackers and party snacks all sing their peculiar good-time songs. Pyramids of bottles of gin and cheap wine, pyramids of insulated jugs, and pyramids of plastic plates and cups all mutely shout their promises of rest and recreation, pleasure and well-being beyond, or, perhaps, despite, the city's seamy dreams.

But Tony Rivera pedals on, oblivious. Death takes no vacation, and nor can he. At the bus stop on the corner, two Puerto Rican girls in tight shorts and strap T-shirts huddle together out of the rain, pulling dime-store jewelry from paper bags; this is to go with the pink top, these are for the dance on Friday, oh, look at this, don't you think it's really cute?

Maggie Kelly comes around the corner in the ash and neon night, carrying a four-foot-wide red satin heart with black lace trimming loosely in her arms. Inscribed upon the heart in velvet appliqué are the words *I Surrender*. Maggie reaches the corner just in time to see a huddled figure on an old girl's bicycle, black and rust, his head green and his face looking frozen, screech through the last fraction-of-a-second of yellow. Jesus, thinks

Maggie, that bastard's going to get himself killed. And pulls the heart more tightly to her chest.

It is not a small world, no matter what rumors to the contrary you might hear. Limitless are the vistas and the visions; unfathomable the logistics and the means; continuous and invisible the interweavings and coincidences; dark and magical as oceanic depths, the workings of the world and, in particular, of the human heart. As impossible to appreciate as God, the possibilities and limits of this world. Not small, but it sometimes seems so. It seems so to Maggie Kelly, who is determined to have it so. And it seems so to Tony Rivera, who desperately wishes that it weren't.

On this evening especially, ending a day that has been rife with familiarity, as Maggie recognizes the wino on the corner and the old man in the faded fedora who waits at this stop every Thursday night to be taken south for borscht and canasta, and Tony maneuvers the well-worn trail that takes him home, the world indeed seems small. Small and unpleasant to him. Small and comforting to her. Tiny, predictable, and threatening to him. Tiny, knowable, and malleable to her. The only thing they might agree upon at this point in their separate lives is that surviving in it requires a certain amount of luck.

Each of them has had a bad day. Maggie has been felt up on the subway, and loudly accused of shoplifting in one of the larger supermarkets. Tony has had everyone on his back: Parker, the hospital, the students, and the uncorporeal presence of Sandy, not nagging, exactly, but certainly reminding. Maggie, today, has lost two crucial accounts, has had words with the buyer for one of the better shops (a fierce, thin woman clearly accustomed to being right); and, four months after St. Valentine's Day, is stuck with one large heart. Tony, today, has fought with everyone unfortunate or insensitive enough to have come within range; has been warned three different times to mind his own fuckin' business; and has been knocked off his bike twice, the first time this morning by some cowboy in a cab, and the second time just as he was leaving the staff parking lot by the car coasting beside him which had been signaling left but which had meant to turn right all along. It has been the sort of day that gives life a bad name. The sort of day that confirms the darkest suspicions and bleakest opinions of what living is all about: the trivial and the treacherous; humiliation and futility. The difference between Tony Rivera and Maggie Kelly, though, is that she doesn't believe that she has to live like this, and he can see no other way.

Tony Rivera is looking for a little meaning and magic. Though he would be likely to call it depth or justice or triumph, were he likely to call it anything. Likely to put some name to this sense of loss that haunts his heart. He wants something above and beyond the muck and the melancholy through which he daily, yearly, wades. Something immutably good and filled with hope. Something he once thought he had (though what it was and why it had gone would be difficult to say). Sandy says, in her relentlessly clear and honest way, that he is getting soft. Soft and sentimental. Thank God, she says, that he wasn't in Nam or they'd be listening to his stories about that for the next twenty years. Thank God, she says, that he grew up in the city or she'd still be hearing about the time he caught his first big fish, it was just me and him and the fat old sun. Thank God, even more, that he was never a junkie or a fugitive youth, surviving by stealing handbags from old ladies in the Bronx, their voices screeching after him like sirens, whaa whaa whaa, or she would be lullabyed into old age by the repetition of those words, you can't imagine what it was like, you can't have any idea at all. It's a minor miracle, she says, that he hasn't taken to raising pigeons on the roof. She calls it character flab. Sometimes, though, he thinks that she might actually prefer it if he were like her imaginings—his medals framed in the hallway, his nightmares making him cry and punch her in his sleep, ending every social occasion with a tear for some real buddy splattered like mud against a wall in Phnom Penh, oh, poor Tony, she would whisper, he's never really gotten over the war. Would like him better if he did keep pigeons up on the roof in padlocked cages, champions all, each one named, that's Zeke, that's Bob, that's Betty Lou, his weekends spent at pigeon meets and pigeon shows and among other pigeon men, oh, Tony, he's up on the roof, you know how he loves those birds. Might find him more acceptable, made harmless by the standard obsessions, a sideshow lion, toothless and declawed, roar for the kids, you old king of the beasts.

It is bad enough, she said, that he is approaching middle

age not with renewed vigor and the commitment of wisdom and maturity, but with no view in end but to privatize his soul. He hadn't understood what she meant, and she had taken that as another sign of his degenerative state. "Privatize?" he'd repeated. "You mean like in pirate?" And she had thrown him that smirk of hers—the one he has always found so beguiling when directed at someone else—Jesus, it's worse than I thought. "Well," she'd said, nearly steaming up the sides of her juice glass with the heat from her hands, "I suppose that's close enough." He had meant pirate, as in barrels of run, smuggled guns, and the hot, angry breath of the law. She had been thinking more along the lines of bootleg video tapes and illegal CB radios.

But that was long ago last winter, before things began to get worse. Now she just says that he's becoming—become—a cynical romantic, childish and insensitive and neurotically suspicious, looking as though her heart will snap.

Maggie Kelly wants nothing to do with meaning or magic, and even less with triumph or depth. What she wants are safety and security, some tangible reward for staying on the planet for more than a day or a year or a decade or two; some small but not insignificant prize for still being—against all odds and with only sporadic and minimal encouragement—alive. Maggie finally knows that there is no meaning and no magic. Finally knows that what she once thought she had—that power and that insight— were nothing more than the illusions of ignorance, and of age, or the lack of it. She has finally come to accept that there are other things to be had: things to make life comfortable and passing pleasant; things to make it all go by like someone else's dream instead of her own nightmare. Things like a home and a job and a family and someone else's toothbrush dropping gop onto yours from the next slot in the real-pine holder. Winter vacations on paradisiacal islands, where lean young men rest against palm trees, guitars and not guns cradled on their laps. Summer vacations by the shimmering sea, far from the restless drumbeats and languid violence of Manhattan. Well-stocked larders and well-padded lives. There is no real dignity in dying in some subway lavatory with a hole in your arm, or in your head, or in your heart, and your boots on. Finally, at thirty-eight, she knows all this. Thinks she knows almost everything.

The earth is an oblate spheroid with an approximate polar

diameter of 7,883 miles, but the worlds of the majority of us are considerably smaller. Maggie's own world, for instance, stretches no farther than one hundred miles in any direction—not counting her cousin in Los Angeles, two old friends to whom she still writes, one in Canada and one in Brazil, and her past. Once there was nothing she wanted more than to emigrate from this nation of immigrants, but now she just wants to stay still. So still that her feet grow long, knobbly, brown roots. Surrounded by people wanting to go back to nature, or back to Detroit, or back to Belfast for a look at the ancestral slum, Maggie has decided to pitch her tent more or less along the banks of the historic Hudson, and is ready to stake her last claim. Maggie has had it with the temptations of the exotic, the new, and the flesh. Let her old mother constantly go off on daylong explorations of domesticated waterfronts, overnight excursions to Atlantic City or Hershey, Pennsylvania. Let her old mother go off on vacations in the bosom of the Catskills, major expeditions requiring vast quantities of unguents, ointments, and aspirins into the foreign hearts of Hawaii, Egypt, and Arkansas. Maggie no longer responds to the lure and the excitement of the unknown and the unknowable. Now turns a blind, unblinking eye on the challenge of all that has been, once was, or yet might be. She returned to this old New World not for reasons of freedom, liberty, equality, or fraternity but because there was nowhere else to go. But now she sees just what it might offer: the manageability and protection she craves. A small, small world, her own, plotted not by imaginary lines of latitude and longitude but by concrete, specific people, places, and plans; foreseeable happenings and reachable goals. A world where even death is just another numbered item.

Where else could she have gone?

Crossing the intersection, Maggie passes teenage lovers, arms around waists, he saying, "That's what I call wearing your heart on your sleeve," the girl laughing, thickly and warmly like a tropical breeze. Maggie frowns and pushes the heart down just a little in her arms, so that its message isn't quite so easily seen.

Tony Rivera's world also has a polar diameter significantly less than 7,883 miles. It is a world run on motives and urges that, lately especially, have become depressingly obvious. A world governed by forces and laws that he once thought were mutable, but that he now sees are numbingly predictable. A world easily analyzed and dissected from a variety of perspectives—and even more easily and depressingly understood. No god or demon tampers with the world of Tony Rivera's reality. No personal passions or foolish delusions cloud the clarity of his thoughts. He knows (though there are those who remain unconvinced) just what is what and what isn't; what can be done and what can't; what should be done and what never will be. A simple universe, straightforward in its way, man-made and, therefore, man-controlled, where reason and logic, science and theory no longer divide the wise men from the fools. And one in which only the things he hates the most ever seem to come out on top.

Stopped at a light, he quickly removes his glasses, blurred with slop from the road and slop from the sky, and slides them into their black imitation-leather case. Now he is nearly legally blind. He knows that the lights have changed only because the vehicles around him all leave him behind, and several horns blow. Eyes straining to see the bumper in front of him, brain silently marking the passage of blocks, Tony Rivera rides home on automatic.

And Maggie Kelly boards the uptown bus with her garish, unsold heart.

It has been one of those days, faded and intrinsically uninteresting, sluggish and perversely disquieting, a cuckoo in the nest of time, looking, at a glance, just like any other day, but empty of elemental promise and low on even the most basic energy. The planet itself has moved along solely on its own momentum. A perfect day for either suicide or murder. Why not? One of those days, and now it is one of those nights. A night on which the weave of the universe is somehow loose and open; the colors and patterns, pale and indistinct, capable of being changed or even blown apart by just a tug or tiny shove. The sort of night on which the rise or fall of empires (and the more important rise or fall of individuals) begins. From just a simple twist of fate. From just the completion or incompletion of the most trivial incident. The sort of night on which God might have had the idea for Jesus, or on which Mr. Himmler might have caught the scent of Mrs. Himmler as she laid the supper on the table and decided not to go out for a beer after all.

◇   ◇   ◇

The elevator isn't working. Mrs. Burkowsky greets Tony on the stoop with the news, her old black umbrella held above her head like a balloon, her expression one of doom triumphant. "I called the lousy super," she tells him as he starts to hoist the bike up the stone stairs. "I told him this sort of thing can't keep going on. I told him, 'You got old people and young mothers with carriages and shopping, what do you expect them to do, fly up?' Don't they think people got a right to what they pay for?"

"And what did he say?" he asks, trying not to sound as though he's out of breath.

She makes a gesture that could mean several different things, none of them good, and pulls the umbrella a little closer to her head. "What do you think? He says it's none of his business, it'll have to wait till the morning. I told him. I said, 'You're the superintendent, aren't you? If it's not your business, then whose business is it?' I ask you, Mr. Rivera, if it doesn't concern him, then who does it concern? That rotten landlord?" pausing for breath. "He's always around when you don't want him," she adds rather cryptically, fixing Rivera through the steady rain with the same look that has terrorized the local shopkeepers for decades. "Have you ever noticed," she continues, oblivious to the night and the weather and the battered body of his bike threatening to drag him back down the stoop, "that nothing ever breaks down around here before five o'clock, when suddenly nobody can do nothing about it till the morning? But he's always sneaking around the building when he should be home with his family. Have you noticed that?" Oh, yes, he's noticed. She stares past him so intently that for a second he thinks that someone more interesting or more sympathetic has come up behind him. "He thinks I don't know what he's up to, but I know." She touches one black-gloved hand to her forehead with authority. Mrs. Burkowsky has her own ideas about dressing for the weather. "I'm not stupid, you know. I see what goes on around here. They think because I'm an old lady that I don't understand, but I do. I'm not stupid."

Sandy says that Mrs. Burkowsky is crazy. Of course, you have to feel sorry for the poor old thing (you can just imagine the sort of life she's probably had), but that doesn't alter the facts. No matter what sort of hell the young Mrs. Burkowsky might have lived through in Poland or Hungary or Michigan; no matter what the struggles, sacrifices, and disappointments of her youth and middle age; no matter what the deprivations and loneliness of her old age, she's still a crazy old bitch. Tony Rivera's sentimentality won't change that. Complaining and demanding, moaning and stirring up trouble, always accusing everyone of being out to get her, shuffling through the hallways like a very large black bird in orthopedic shoes and surgical stockings, Mrs. Burkowsky is symbolic of the self-indulgent flab of American society in decay. "Self-indulgent flab?" he'd repeated. "She's lucky if she weighs a hundred pounds. She's lucky if she's got a couple of bucks over at the end of the month to buy herself a bottle of root beer or a decent piece of meat. What are you talking about, self-indulgent flab?" And Sandy had leaned across the table on her slim, strong arms, mouthing her words with precision, as though her only chance of being understood depended on his ability to read lips. "I didn't mean literally. I meant metaphorically. I meant her head. I've heard things." Should he have guessed from whom? "If you weren't so busy bleeding all over the place all the time, you'd see what a reactionary old racist she really is. If you weren't always skulking around like there was some insidious conspiracy going on, you'd realize what a real old cow she is." So he didn't have to guess, after all, Jerry Vega, the phantom super of 45, strikes again. "Not just Vega," she'd countered, reading his mind, always two steps ahead of him and two steps behind at the same time, ready to go whoomp with her metaphorical net at the slightest rustle in the grass. "I was on that committee with the social worker she had last time she was hospitalized. She told me things." Should he have asked what? He'd made some crack about the testimony of social workers and psychopaths not being held as admissible evidence in any court of law, not even in Louisiana, and she'd told him, quite convincingly, to drop dead. If Mrs. Burkowksy's so miserable, why doesn't she do something to change her life? Why doesn't she get herself a bike and do some political canvassing? Join a senior citizens' lobby? Volunteer for Meals-on-Wheels, or to push a trolley of books around the corridors of Bellevue on Thursday afternoons? What about the city day-care centers, aren't they all understaffed? couldn't they use a volunteer aide with the superb credentials of having raised eight children, four of whom still sometimes talk to her? Why can't she be as Sandy herself will be when she's eighty-three, fierce and formidable, still marching off to demonstrations and rallies, her placard held high, I may be old but I'm not dead yet? Who but a fool would believe that a half-senile old woman like that, with nothing but time on her hands and delusions in her mind, was the victim of a plot to expel her from her apartment so that the rent can be exorbitantly raised? She should be in a home. "She's got a home," he said. "Second floor, front." And why would Vega want to get her out, what would he stand to gain? "He'll get a kickback from the landlord, like he always does," he explained, once more. It happens all the time. But Sandy says that it only happens in his paranoid imagination—just another example.

"How are your legs?" he asks, trying to move the left pedal out of his calf without actually letting go of the bike.

"My legs?" She wrinkles her forehead, shrugs her shoulders, shivers just a little in the dim circle of light from the doorway. "They're still there," and starts to slide toward him, for an embrace he thinks for one fearful second, but she has only decided to descend and needs the railing against which he is propped for support. "What was that song you were singing the other morning?" she asks, just as he finally rests the bike on the top step.

"Song?"

"Yeah," she says, almost smiling. "That song. You came thundering down the stairs early in the morning and you were singing . . ."

He manages to look blank and bewildered. It never occurs to him that he might be heard.

Mrs. Burkowsky purses her lips and stares at the handle of the door. "Something with fruit in it. Berries? Was it blueberries?"

"Cherries," he sighs. "Life is just a bowl of cherries."

"That's it," she says, as though he has been especially clever. "I haven't heard that song in years. I thought there was something in the hall and I went to the door to check and there you were, running down the stairs, singing." She looks at him, but in the poor light and with his bad eyes he can't be sure if her expression is one of pity or of admiration. "And that's what it's like to be young, I thought. Five-thirty in the morning and you can run through the building singing about fruit."

He wheels the bike over the tiny white and black tiles of the entrance and stands at the bottom of the staircase, wondering how long it would take before his body was discovered if he were to collapse on the third-floor landing. So this is what it's like to be young. But even as his foot falls on the first step, and he remembers again Parker's words over lunch, "Just remember, Tony, if you need to talk to someone, that's what I'm here for," and the feeling of incomparable futility with which they filled him, another part of his brain has already begun to sing, *you work, you slave, you worry so, but you can't take it with you when you go go go* ... Little old Mrs. Burkowsky, stirring it up again.

He is hours later than he should have been. He told Sandy he had one stop to make on the way home, and instead he made several, spent over an hour before the rains began sitting on a bench on an island parklet, practicing for when he's an old man and nobody wants or even needs him anymore. Which shouldn't be all that far in the future, the way things are going. It's a habit he got into in the spring, when the first warm weather began to draw the old folks and the vagrants out of their uneasy winter retreats. He was just going to do it once, sit on the splintered old wood as though he had nowhere else to go, no one to meet, nothing in particular to do, just watch the first springtime lovers kissing at the other end of the bench, the mothers marshaling their short but recalcitrant troops across the dangerous thoroughfares, and he, an old man, stranded without home or love, sitting on the sidelines, dropped from the team, with no claim on life but the past, I used to be something in my day. Just once. But now he stops most evenings (sometimes at one place, sometimes at another; sometimes to talk, sometimes to be alone), drawn to the streets like a gambler to a casino, I'll only go in for a minute, I can stop whenever I want, I'm only killing some time. Or is it time that's killing him?

For a man who—these days—is almost always late, and often simply missing, he actually pays a great deal of attention to time. More and more now, he is noticing its slow but determined passage, a passage that has brought with it none of the things he had always expected. For time, unlike most other natural phenomena—glaciers or tornadoes, hurricanes or hordes of hungry locusts, plagues or volcanoes—which in the passing change or rearrange, just passes and makes everything older, suns and moons and myopic community workers, but no different. No matter what the promises of love or good intentions. Time passes, and the poor are still poor, the lonely lonelier still; the possessed and the dispossessed still tear away at the edges of the world's fabric. A man's time may grow shorter, but the sufferings and miseries of the world grow no smaller and no softer with the using of its days. Only the hearts of some are caused to change, to warp and shrink, the minds of some mangled in some trap of the transit, smaller and smaller and smaller yet. The heart and mind of Tony Rivera, for one. Who was once so young and so brave and so uncompromisingly strong that the entire planet lay before him like fresh tar on a sunburst August day in Mississippi, warm and malleable beneath his feet. Tony Rivera, who was once so knowing, so caring, and so certain that the whole universe spread out at his feet like a paint-by-numbers picture, frame included, and all he would ever have to do would be color it in.

And thus can ignorance be confused with bliss.

Huffing and puffing and wondering, with no real curiosity, if everyone's life is like his, an obstacle course with a mine field waiting at the end, he finally reaches his floor, approaching carefully like an advance scout. Will Sandy be home? Will she be angry? Will she wonder why it has taken him over four hours to bike a distance that a troop of Brownies could have walked in two?

Meredith's little boy is running loose in the hallway, dressed in too-small red ski pajamas, a red bath towel pinned to the shoulders of the shirt. "Hi ya, Tony," shouts Will. "I'm Batman. Watch!" and runs at him full speed, voom woom woom.

"I thought you were Spiderman," says Tony, surprisingly agile in his avoidance of being butted in the balls. "Yesterday you told me you were Spiderman. What happened?"

And the small boy gives him a look he recognizes instantaneously, he has seen it so often before, that fine mixture of exasperation and contempt. "Tch," says Will, just like his mother, his face in a scowl. "I changed my cape," and, flapping it behind him, woom-vooms away.

The door opens and the apartment is dark. The bike rolls over his right foot, and the left pedal bangs him in the shin. He can almost hear the dog leap from the bed to come rushing into the hall, so that by the time the light does go on he is standing before him as though he's been there all the time, man's very best friend. In the living room, the plant lights have failed to go on, but that is no less than expected. He wired it up himself to impress Sandy, who was insistent that they get someone qualified and competent to do it, one of her friends, but though he carefully followed the instructions that came with the time switch with excruciating patience, this to this and that to that, the damn thing has never worked as it should. Sometimes it comes on when you want it to, but at other times it doesn't and comes on when you don't want it to instead. It seems especially partial to noon and three in the morning.

He stands for an instant in the hallway, listening for a clue. Probably Sandy herself has not come home yet. Probably she is at a meeting, heatedly debating the future of the peace movement, or the past of the American Left, or the present state of the social services in this thriving metropolis. Or maybe she is sitting on the faded oriental carpet of some homey living room, drinking espresso out of mismatched cups with people as intensely concerned as she with the city's educational system and its inability to deal honestly and pragmatically with the realities of contemporary urban life. Or having a meal down in Chinatown with Mrs. Burkowsky's ex-social worker, spareribs, giant prawns, and shoptalk, and then what did she do, the old cow? Or sipping wine from imitation fruit jars and smoking dope around the rustic oak table of some valued woman friend who can't stand the sight of him, whose white or black or dusky skin still bears the rough deep scars of the tribal rituals of a sexist society and its tyrannical, if often subtle, male domination, when are we really going to wise up? Or fucking some anarchistic computer genius who after they have unglued their bodies challenges her to a game of life on his home system.

He parks the bike and pets the dog, plays with the timer until it says 2:00 A.M. and the lights go on, turns on the television for the news, and, while Zorro waits impatiently in the kitchen, sitting by his bowl, his tail going thump slap thump on the linoleum, races down the hallway and into the bedroom to see if his pillow is still warm. That goddamndog. He stands motionless by his side of the bed for a minute or two, just looking, almost touched that the room is exactly as they left it this morning, yesterday's underwear lying on top of the book he was reading in bed last night, which lies, open and face down, on top of his sneakers, Sandy's Victorian nightgown neatly folded at the foot of the bed. Across from the bed is the dresser and the oval mirror and the picture of Sandy in her well-spent youth, marching in an anti-Nam demonstration, her head back and her eyes half-closed, her chin lifted, waiting for a punch. On the left side of the room is Sandy's desk and the armchair she likes to sit in when she is reading, fondly draped with the afghan she crocheted two Christmases ago when she spent a week with her parents to take a break from him. And in the opposite corner is his slightly broken bentwood hat stand, from which hangs the collection of hats in which he used to look so wild and dashing, but which now make him look merely foolish. Everything just the same as it has been for months, for years, our room. If it is all right, then he must be, too.

He fluffs up the pillow on his side of the bed, and tucks in and smoothes over the old Indian print spread, then changes into his worn jeans and his Marilyn Monroe sweatshirt, a joke Christmas present from his father-in-law, the artist and adorer of womankind who has barely a functional sense of humor. Oh, Norma Jean, they keep doing it to you, too. The apartment is so quiet—as it never used to be, so long was it a meeting place for the crusading and the concerned, a stopover for the passing traveler, a haven for the homeless and the hysterical. But now the crusading and the concerned meet elsewhere, where he can't interrupt them with his jokes and his stupid questions, if insomnia can be caused by a guilty conscience, how many people do you think are awake through the night on a regular basis? And Sandy has put her foot down on all passing travelers, unless they are friends of hers, since the time he put up a refugee fireman, a quiet man with pictures of his wife and children on the bureau in the spare room, I thought when you said fireman you meant someone who puts out fires. Even the homeless and the hysterical seem to have found more congenial havens recently, places where no one is liable to wake them up at three in the morning, crashing drunkenly into the bicycle, who the hell put that there? liable to wake them up with a moving rendition of "FDR in Trinidad" at 4:33 A.M. The apartment is so quiet, only the quartz alarm clock in the bedroom beating away like a boxed heart and the tap in the bathroom dripping like a giant's tears.

Zorro pads into the room, a quizzical expression in his big brown eyes, and with one swift leap is back on the bed, tail wagging, your time is up. "Get the hell off the bed," Tony orders, face to face, eye contact direct, and is rewarded with a warm, wet lick across his lips. Someone still likes him.

He scoops the dog into his arms, and trots through the hallway singing, *nobody knows you when you're down and out*, Zorro hanging on to his shoulders with a total lack of confidence.

What was it he once thought he knew that he no longer knows? What was it he thought he understood that he no longer understands? Why doesn't he seem to care?

Sandy would like to know, too. Sandy would like to know how someone she once thought so tough and so strong, so sure and so true, could turn out to be just another underachiever. "You used to be so smart," she has said on more than one occasion, looking at him as though there were something familiar about him, but she can't quite place the face. "Even Jack always admired your logical mind. Everybody thought you'd go far." But he has gone far. Far far away from the Rivera of yore, so fiendishly sharp and so effortlessly clever that there was no one who could trick him, nothing that could delude him. Only now does he understand that it was himself all along, stacking the cards, manipulating the scenes, staging the lies, blowing great clouds of smoke before his own eyes in a perfect, impenetrable screen. Belligerently brilliant (or so they used to say) in his youthful prime, he is now, as Sandy so neatly puts it, simply foolish. A burlesque quixotic figure draped over a rickety old bike that isn't really his (his was blow-torched off the stair railings one night last March) but one he bought for ten dollars and a half dozen old albums from his wife's friend's daughter who'd outgrown it—the legs of his trousers always getting caught in the chain, bike clips or no bike clips.

A good psychotherapist, or even a not-so-good psychotherapist, would rightly deduce that he is depressed. And then go on to point out—in the detached, explicitly reasonable way of men, be they priests or politicians, who are paid for knowing what is best for everyone else—that that is not an exceptional condition, things being as they are, he being who he is. They would talk. Tony would tell the therapist about his dreams (which are increasing) and about his fantasies (which aren't); about his fears and sense of failure, both fierce and fecund; about his obsessions and malignant memories, his maundering thoughts and apocalyptic visions. And about his new good friend, Death, trailing him like a peyote hallucination, come to me come to me come to me now. The therapist wouldn't let him get away with anything just because he knows the game so well himself. The therapist would ask to meet with Sandy. He would ask her what she thought was happening. He would ask her to fill in some of the details. It's always good to have more than one point of view. He might even ask to see them together, family session, group rates. Sandy and the therapist, with such similar sorts of minds, such sympathetic outlooks, would get on well, it's obvious with whom the problems lay. Sandy and the space-age guru would get on so well, in fact, that his feelings would go beyond professional empathy and concern; hers beyond professional respect and trust and relief-filled admiration, gee, mister, thanks for saving my dog. They would have an affair. It happens every day. Tony would be coming in one door, weaving under the weight of his own madness, thrusting his anxiety and vulnerability, at fifty dollars an hour, into the hands of this genial, mellow wiseman, while Sandy would be scurrying out the other door, zipping up her jeans.

His mother says that the only thing wrong with him—more or less—is that he's finally reached forty, a well-known dangerous age. "Oh, forty," said Sophie, waving her hand in the air, stirring up the spirits of all the fortyish men she has ever known and probably wishes she hadn't. "Oh, forty," exactly as, when her sons were small, she could watch them from across the room, her glasses precariously perched on the end of her nose, and judge, "Oh, German measles," "Oh, pink-eye," "Oh, for God's sake, it's only a sprain."

Tony sits at the kitchen table, Zorro, full now and happy, dozing at his feet, staring at the pattern made on the cracked, yellow oilcloth by the wicker shade of the hanging light. The bike stands just outside the door in the long, narrow hallway, beneath the coathooks, like some garden creature brought in for the night, just waiting to catch unwary visitors with its chromium horns, liable to open its single, battery-operated eye if only jostled, likely to wail if disturbed by man or beast or haunting shade, *arooarooaroo.*

"*¿Qué piensas?*" he asks the dog. But Zorro doesn't speak Spanish, was raised by the Mahoneys who had to leave him behind when they moved to Seattle to start anew, and rescued by Sandy who was certain her mother would take him to live in the country. "Sandra always was one for bringing home strays," said Edith, giving her son-in-law what might have been a significant smile. But she wasn't taking any dogs, not even one that could do three tricks (roll over, sit up, fetch his own leash) pretty much on cue.

"*¿Qué piensas?*" About what? urban renewal? nuclear disarmament? military intervention in Latin America? the dog food that's on special this week in the bodega across the street? Zorro opens his eyes, sits back on his haunches, and gazes up, looking patient and intelligent, as though it were he who asked the question and Tony who must supply the answer. "I don't know, either," says Rivera, scratching behind the floppy brown ears, and gets up himself. If Sandy does come home suddenly, it would be unwise for her to find him brooding.

Maybe Edith was right, and he is just another of her daughter's strays, rescued from a life on the streets or a quick, societally beneficial death through the goodness of Sandy's large and socially conscious heart. She was the little girl who wrote to President Kennedy and begged him not ever to use the bomb. She is the woman who has donated all of her major organs to be distributed to the needy upon her death. ("What's the difference?" she keeps asking. "You'll be dead. Wouldn't it be nice to think that your kidney was still going on, letting someone else live?" "Ah, ha!" he has countered. "But what if they gave it to a child molester or a Mafia lawyer? Then how would you feel?") She is the lover who took him in and permitted him up on the furniture and into the rich and energetic mainstream of American life. Good boy.

In the living room, he sits in the old, upholstered rocker by the window, headset on and Zorro once more at his feet, listening to his favorite rendition of "Columbus Stockade," wondering how it is, with Death hammering away at his door, that he feels doubly haunted by his life—and all the questions implicit in it about which he has managed not to think for so many years.

It is life itself, he is beginning to realize, that has always made him feel that he was born with the wrong ticket clutched in his blotchy little hand. Life itself that has baffled and eluded him, run him down one path only to turn around immediately and start tearing up another. Life—which to others seems such a simple and straightforward thing, or at least to make some sense—to him has seemed like an expensive stereo system with the instruction booklet written in a foreign language (or several foreign languages), he in the middle of a stranger's living-room floor, diagrams and wires and lethal-looking plugs all about him, little holes and tiny screws and voltage warnings staring at him from the backs of several components, speaker wire threaded through his teeth, trying to guess how big the explosion would be if he put L2 where R1 was meant to go. Boom. No good saying you couldn't read the manual. No good stammering apologies in English and two dialects of Spanish.

Of course, as far as he is concerned the entire world is in a foreign language, and none more foreign than the ones he knows. He is an impostor no matter what accent he employs, a pretender no matter which words he might choose, he with his Italian-black mother and his Scots-Argentinian father and his brothers Puerto Rican. It's a wonder, he thinks, absentmindedly slapping Zorro on the head in what is intended as an affectionate gesture, that he can speak anything at all. That he has managed to bluff his way through forty years of life, acting as though he knew what he was doing, knew what he was saying, knew where he belonged—doing such a good job that he even convinced himself.

A dying man, just before the switch is thrown, just before the bullet hits his heart, just before the roof falls in on top of him, may see his entire life going whooshing before his horrified eyes, whoosh his childhood and whoosh his youth, whoosh his teeny triumphs and whoosh whoosh his unchangeable defeats; all his mistakes and misconceptions, losses and unspoken longings spangled across the blackening sky like shooting stars, flaming one last good-bye. And so may a man who feels he is in danger of dying, who needs no doctor's solemn sympathy, no hearty handshake and orders to the front to understand that his running time has almost run out. As surely as though he is standing against the whitewashed mud wall of some remote village, forgotten by the whirling world, staring into the barrels of half a dozen GI foreign-aid rifles, he sees his life in moments so vivid that they are more relived than remembered. Sees his life with all its frailties and deceptions so clearly now. Now that it is liable to be blown away.

The chains on my legs are makin' sores . . .

When he was twelve, short and plump and having difficulties with Sister Regina Jean, who wanted him to play a leprechaun in the St. Patrick's Day play, he flushed his goldfish, Diablo and Loco, down the toilet. "Well, that was smart, wasn't it?" said Sophie, that expression on her face, half longing and half stupefaction, staring at the empty bowl as though it contained his future. He'd thought, with logic that seemed irrefutable at the time, that they would go out to sea. "To see what?" asked Sophie, her grasp on the language always tenuous at best. "Out to sea," he'd repeated. Thinking they would swim into the sewers, past the alligators and the turtles, and into open water, bound for home. He had watched them—by daylight, by lamplight, and by flashlight—nudging determinedly against the sides of their glass globe, fins beating and eyes bulging, knowing, somehow, that they were not where they really should be, not where they would have wanted to be had anyone given them a choice, not home. Every time Diablo swam purposefully over to the front of the bowl and spat gravel at him, he took it as a sign, two fingers and an angry fist, fuck you, you little cocksucker. Every time Loco swam in futile circles for what seemed like hours, he imagined him looking for the way out. Like his grandmother (who was always going back to Tuscany), and his grandfather (who had quickly gone back to Jamaica), and his mother (who left every place she ever went, even leaving Señor Rivera and his island paradise for the more solid shores of Manhattan), Diablo and Loco had known where they belonged and where they didn't. Unlike he. Oh, sure, he had thought himself safe with—at home with—Señor Rivera, Sophie, and Sophie's little Riveras until the fateful stirrings of revolution, when political differences split the family once and for all. "Don't give me your true man of the people shit," screamed Sophie, her voice frantic against the tranquil, languid night. "That's what they said about

Peron." And Señor Rivera (Carlos *querido* in better times) had replied in his impeccable English, "You are an extraordinary woman, Sofia, but you are a political moron." "Don't call me Sofia," raged Sophie, hurling something heavy at a wall. "My name is Sophie. S-o-p-h-i-e." "You are an extraordinary woman, Sofeee," repeated Señor Rivera in a voice that slid through the night like crème de menthe sliding over ice, "but you are a political moron." "No," said Sophie, teeth in all her consonants, "I'm just a moron. You're the one who's political." Then, for a while, he had felt himself safe, at least, with Grandma Maria on the Upper West Side, a shrine in the bedroom and chicken blood in the sink. It was only when he was shipped to the Bronx to live with Sophie's sister, the youngest widow in the neighborhood, while his mother "found her feet" (and where had they gone? he wondered, what kept her shoes from caving in?), and he was made to go to a Catholic school that was half-Italian, half-Irish, that it became clear just where he didn't belong. His brothers, still judged too young to be separated from their mother while she searched, were never called Spic or Puncho or Chili Breath. Never had the shit beaten out of them in the schoolyard by a gang of choirboys, doncha know, fardha, he musta fallen down the stairs, he don't speak English so good. Never had to sit at the end of the untouchables' table in the school cafeteria, praying that no one would pick on them, wot's dat you're eatin', Puncho? a bean sandwich? hey, Pudgeo, is it true all you people got fleas? Forever banned from normal intercourse, social or otherwise. Never allowed to play in any of their boyish games unless half of the class was out with chickenpox. "Why doncha go back to where you come from?" they asked him at every conceivable opportunity. But where was that? So he flushed the goldfish down the pink bowl in the upstairs bathroom, and Sophie, summoned especially, I just want you to see what he's done this time, had stood in the doorway, hands on hips and lip on lip, I don't know, it must be hereditary. Angela, clucking, had thrown a second bottle of bleach after them, this time in front of a witness, I told you a hundred times, you don't know where those things have been. That night he heard Sophie on Angela's daily disinfected telephone, talking with Señor Rivera's successor in her affections, laughing herself to tears, "Jesus, Mary and Joseph, have you ever heard anything to beat that? He thought he'd flush them out to sea." Choking to a halt and adding, "And he's really good in school, too. I don't understand it."

Zorro gets up, stretches his bony little legs and his long, pink tongue, and looks at him half-expectantly. How can it be that things have never really changed? What made him think they had? He got taller and he got thinner; he became a biking fool with a row of brightly colored ribbons and shining trophies on his dresser; brains began to count for something and there even began to be advantages in being bilingual. He met people who didn't remember him from St. Anthony's, weren't you the one who cried when McNamara scored a basket with your glasses?, and girls who found him forbiddenly exotic, gee, I've never kissed a boy who wasn't really white before. People stopped calling him Anthony. He moved back in with Sophie after nearly three years in the nightmare world of the Calavetta Bronx, plastic saints on the mantelpiece and plastic covers on the furniture. He began to figure things out. Or thought he did. Began to see rhymes and reasons. Thought he could see a direction that would take him home. For his fourteenth birthday, Señor Rivera (in sunnier times Papa) sent him, as mysteriously as miraculously, his old guitar, with a simple note, immediately ripped into strips by Sophie, "Play a song for your mother for me." None of his brothers, all sons of a revolutionary, albeit a minor one, ever showed the slightest bit of interest in political or economic theories—unless you counted purely personal ones like how to score some easy cash, how to get laid with little cost and less postcoital bother, where to get a car for the weekend with no money up front—but he did. None of his brothers, all sons of a passionate musician, albeit an amateur one, ever showed the slightest bit of interest in playing anything but the numbers or a hi-fi—but he did. "You're just like Señor Rivera," screamed Sophie (never again to call him Carlos or the more rare and more randy Charlie). "Thank God your brothers are normal." Did he think people didn't commit suicide in China? Did he think nobody in East Germany had any problems? What about all those poor people in Russia? She encouraged his guitar playing, even managing to find enough money for him to have lessons once a week, but she didn't want to hear any song she'd heard before. Did he think that being able to explain something was the same as being able to understand it? "I don't know what you're talking about," he'd shouted back. "That's exactly what I mean."

But now he knows.

Maybe.

With those small advances, all meant to give him a sense of belonging, has he ever felt truly comfortable? Ever felt completely in residence? Even though he'd been good at basketball. Even though he really liked hot dogs and hamburgers and Breyers ice cream. Even though he was one of the best racers in three boroughs, a sure bet, a neighborhood hero. Even though he could walk through Harlem blindfolded, developed a street sense second to none, not even Gene's, and got a college education. Even though he didn't lose a leg or a liver or a life like a lot of the sons of Sophie's friends, have a bullet explode in his ankle like Frankie. Even though *The Village Voice* once described him as "one of the best session men in New York." Even though he was invited into homes that did not feature a wizened grandmother praying in tongues and burning things in the back bedroom, or coasters printed with seaside scenes on the coffee tables and Latino music on the record player. Even though, through some strange and inexplicable process, he was eventually popular, liked by almost everyone, even the local hoods and his brothers' friends with their sleeveless sweatshirts, homemade tattoos, and eat-shit grins, ey, mahn, what's the *qué pas*? Even though.

It is not a problem that he has seen afflict anyone else he has known.

Not even Zorro, now flat on the floor and soundly asleep, who must surely know somewhere inside his small, canine heart that he doesn't really belong on the sixth floor of a salvaged tenement, eating canned food flavored like meat from a red plastic bowl labeled DOG and going to the park on weekends with a red bandanna tied around his neck. Must know that he isn't anything like either a fox or a *criollo* Robin Hood. Tony sighs and pulls the headsets down around his neck. He should never have let Sandy talk him out of renaming Zorro Pete.

Who will paint your future over, while I'm behind these prison bars?

He met Sandy during one of those intoxicating phases when he knew he knew exactly who he was, where he was going, why he was going there, and what would most probably happen when he arrived. She was, if anything, the proof. He was the intellectual-revolutionary-who-was-going-to-change-things-from-inside, and she was the New-World woman, raised on liberal politics and sexual equality ("My mother always worked." "My father always did a lot of the cooking." "You can't liberate the proletariat without liberating women as well."), who would never pluck her eyebrows, shave under her arms, or be caught without her diaphragm. After over a decade of comfortable affairs that didn't so much fizz out as never fizz up in the first place, affairs with girls and women whom he liked or admired or wanted at the time, but whom he easily forgot, meeting Sandy was like being raised on boiled potatoes and then being introduced to hot and sour soup. She laughed at his jokes, she agreed with his ideas, she played the flute all through high school, she didn't believe in Love. She wasn't dismayed by Sophie's many moods and phases and tendency to start drinking whenever anyone mentioned the struggling masses. "You listen to me, honey," said Sophie the first time he brought Sandy home to have a meal with Mom. "Forget all this politics shit and stick by your heart. When it comes to the crunch, one son-of-a-bitch is pretty much like another," knocking back a tumbler of gin and orange juice without wasting a breath. Brought up to be polite and to win the hearts of adults, Sandy had smiled a minute smile, and said, "Oh. Ah." Had taken another sip of her own drink and gone on courageously, her parents' child, "I do feel that it's important for every individual to have a personal commitment beyond his or her immediate needs." "Oh, yeah?" said Sophie, at an uncustomary loss for words. And Julio, the dancer, still at home at twenty-one, had looked up from the book he was reading while he ate his salad with his fingers, and smiled broadly. "Jesus Christ," he grinned at Tony, the only other of Sophie's sons to inherit her astounding good looks, "this chick's too much." "Tony and I," continued Sandy, sticking to her guns, "believe that a marriage should be based not only on mutual trust and respect, but on shared goals and ideals as well," on something more permanent and reliable than the tilt of a smile or the sparkle in an eye; on something larger and less self-indulgent than lust or desire or the need to be loved. "That's nice," smiled Sophie, and poured herself another double. Sophie has always been a woman of passing passions. But women of Sophie's background and manifest attractions often are. And women of Sandy's background and manifest attractions often are not. Sophie, despite her nursing degree and her four sons, has had the sort of past that would seem improbable in a novel, though fascinating to read, described on the paperback as "A Sweeping Saga of Adventure, Spirit, and Love." Sandy's past, such as it has been, would more likely be included in a documentary study of second-generation Americans cast out of suburbia by the earnest churnings of the sixties, Where Will They Go from Here? "So your father's a painter," Sophie continued after a silence in which it was possible to count the number of times Julio chewed his lettuce. "Yes," said Sandra Sosha Grossman, eager as a child asked something by an adult that she can actually answer. "He's an artist," not sure that Sophie might not think she meant houses; naïvely assuming that a woman like Sophie, who was once held a prisoner of love on a private island by a brilliant, wealthy, and irredeemably berserk poet, would consider this a point in her favor. "What's he paint?" asked Julio, surfacing for another glass of juice, dancing is like being in training, something of an artist himself. "Well . . ." hummed Sandy, not sure which part of the question might hold the trick, ". . . pictures . . ." surprised that she seemed to have given the right answer, only Tony burying his smile in his glass. "Does he make a living at it?" Sandy's silk shirt and perfect teeth had not escaped Sophie's notice. "He's an illustrator as well," replied Sandy in the slightly apologetic tone she always used—still uses—when admitting where the money really originates, everyone has to eat. "You know, books and things," implying by her shy vagueness and the shrugging of her lovely shoulders that she knew about hard times and struggle, her heart was with the malnourished poor even if her body seemed to be with the affluent middle class. "And what's your mother do?" Sophie moved her arm and her silver bracelets jangled. "Oh," beamed Sandra, getting interested once she was getting some interest, "my mother's an amazing woman. You'll like her," leaning forward into the light so that the gold chain around her neck seemed almost alive. "She sells houses." Slowly, slowly, like a cat burglar moving across the rooftops, Julio's head moved from down to up. Looking only at his brother, he said, in his always-soft voice, so incongruous among the bellowings of the rest of his family, "You mean your father deals in the unreal and your mother deals in the real?" Provoking Sandy into a seven-minute monologue on the responsibilities of the artist in contemporary society, and her father's lifelong commitment to socialism, democracy, and racial and sexual equality, it's people like you whom he's always championed.

Sandy's only comment on his family (then) had been to say, as they hurried into the subway arm in arm, "How did your mother get off that island?" He had pushed her through the turnstile before him. "She swam."

Oh, Sandy. She had seemed a combination of everything he had most feared and most wanted, all his dreams, both sleeping and waking, packed into a small but attractive body with big eyes, a sharp tongue, and an aggressive mind. The best of all worlds.

Days after that first meeting, Sophie said, sitting with him in her living room, sharing a six-pack and watching the "Late Show," seemingly speaking to Marlon Brando, "What you need is a plain, ordinary woman who likes to cook and wants to have children. Someone who'll put up with all your shit." Was this the woman who once threw a pot of stew all over the table in front of Señor Rivera because he asked where his supper was? He looked over quickly to make sure her lips were moving. "Are you talking to me?" to me, the liberator of the enslaved, the defender of the oppressed? to me, with my wild dreams and raging uniqueness? "No," said Sophie, popping a top. "I'm talking to Marlon Brando."

He gets up, turns off the stereo, and stands by the window, looking down at the street, which is both dismal and deserted, trash cans lined up along the curb like dead bodies, a plastic streamer from some forgotten sale or celebration, broken and faded, flapping from the awning of the candy store. And there, sitting in the doorway like a doll in a box is Death, poorly disguised as the black prophet, looking neither wet nor chilled, reading a book by streetlight, his toga (though, surely, it can't really be a toga, must be an old remnant of cloth snatched from some rubbish) modestly wrapped around him, as though he is both at peace and at home. Probably, in reality, he is just another street lunatic. That's what Sandy would say. "For God's sake, can't you tell a bum when you see one?" Quietly, he raises the window and squints out into the night. As he does, the large black head, haloed in hair, turns toward him, expressionless and disinterested, and slowly turns away.

But death he can, in fact, handle. Death he can at least understand. There aren't any tricks or subtleties with death. No patches of exclusivity, no chance of getting it wrong. *Finito*. Or *infinito*, as you choose. No rude awakenings or slow-fuse shocks. No more hot flashes of ecstasy, how fucking incredible to be walking by the fruit store with its terraces of grapes and oranges, avocados and mangoes, mushrooms and onions and fat tomatoes, the sun hot on your head, the kids squealing and grunting and laughing, just like kids, as they wrestle and run under the frantic water of a busted hydrant, a girl in a green dress stopping on a stoop to adjust her shoe, someone shouting "Oh, shit" from an upstairs window. No more the slap that makes you remember to breathe, or the kiss that makes you forget. No more the look that makes you wonder, or the word that doesn't. No more pounding heart, or steady pulse, or undefinable flip-flopping in ventricle, stomach, or groin. No more more.

Though a man who worries as much as Tony Rivera would not miss the possibility that death, like everything else, might not necessarily turn out to be as simple as it seems. In which case it could easily mean more Parkers, more clever-but-sincere politicians, more hustlers, pimps, fascists, shrinks, and sociobiologists. More dyings. Eternity spent at a department meeting, the administrators snapping their cuffs and everyone else snapping the plastic spoons that come with the coffee, each second passing as slowly as a night spent in the Greyhound terminal in Scranton during a blizzard. The interlude marked by them taking it in turn to each do his or her own specialty: Parker reading his poems about battered babies and the lights going out over Atlantic City; Audrey, the chief administrator, doing her monologue on efficiency and the slackening of standards in every aspect of modern life, and the difficulty of finding a reliable housekeeper; Rose, the doctor, and Marti, the art therapist, doing their double-act on the soul-depleting problems to be faced by the single, middle-aged professional woman; Tony himself doing his unique and highly personal version of "Guantanamera" and

"Desolation Row" (both rarely performed in public anymore, and never before two in the morning and a combination of drugs), following that with a few of his old Groucho Marxist routines, it's not finding a cause to die for that's the problem, it's finding one to live for that's got me stumped.

Eternity spent on the checkout line in the supermarket, a raving junkie with a frozen chicken in front of you and an old lady with a shopping bag filled with stolen light bulbs behind. Eternity spent listening to his brothers argue about whether Puerto Rico should be made a state or an independent country, about whether wrestling or boxing is the more corrupt sport. Eternity spent eating dinner one night a month with Jack and Edith in authentic ethnic restaurants, usually Chinese, while Jack talks out loud to himself about art, politics, and young women, and Edith thinks of ways of improving the restaurant's food, service, décor, and location in between detailed descriptions of the failings of all her friends. Eternity spent on the D train, going from the Bronx to Brooklyn and back again, watching the stations flash past, this train don't stop nowhere. Eternity spent with Sandy, doing all the things there are to do, reaping all the rewards there are to reap from living with a sense of purpose and rightness; sleeping each eternal night the sleep of the eternally just.

And then, of course, there is always the possibility of coming back again. In which event, there is no doubt in his mind that he would come back as himself.

The street light in front of 45, controlled by some greater intelligence, switches off. Two late-night, all-weather joggers in twin track suits bounce by, weaving past the prophet who doesn't give them a glance, and in and out of the trickle of pedestrians hurrying home to their domestic sanctuaries or their nights of unbridled lust or drug abuse, and past the local boys, ready for the night, swaggering up the street, hands in pockets, keys dangling, looking for trouble or looking for relief. Directly below him, the barmaid and her boyfriend begin a fight that will go on for the next two hours; directly above him, a couple who have been brought together by a computer clink together glasses of sparkling wine. Tony Rivera stands at the window, waiting—without seeming to, not even to himself—for his wife to come home. Wondering what she would do if she were to come in and find him dead, poker chips of blood spilled all over the woven carpet; what she would do were she to return and find him gone, a handwritten note propped up against the bowl of polished stones on the kitchen table, Dear Sandra . . . ; what she would do were she to come back and find him naked and hard, tangoing by himself in the hall, a rose between his teeth and lust simmering in his eyes.

Below him Meredith and Will come out of the bodega, holding hands, and Meredith looks right up at him, standing in the window, looking down. And though she is too far away for him really to see her expression, he knows immediately, from the way she pretends that he isn't there, that Sandy won't be coming home.

Maggie, too, even as she climbs aboard the packed and oddly smelling bus, has had enough. Enough death and dying, enough madness and melodrama, enough sadness and loss to sink a thousand ships of dreams. Enough enough. Only she doesn't think that she may be losing her mind. She thinks that she is coming to her senses.

Maggie's life, so far, would also make a good book. It has been the kind of life that women like to point out to men, to illustrate how women can live when given the opportunity (when not shackled by mere survival or by that bastard love); that men like to point out to women, to illustrate how women can live when they choose (when not tying down or competing with men); that everyone likes to bring to the attention of everyone else because it shows that romance and adventure are possible, if not actually necessary nor necessarily desirable. The kind of life that is often seen as independent, exciting, and remarkable, filmable even. The kind of life that Maggie's own mother has often described as "no way for a person to live when they've had all the advantages you've had." In other days, she might have been burned as a witch or stoned as a whore. Might have run the local saloon and a house of perfumed girls with melt-your-heart eyes and suck-your-cock smiles. Might have been the kind of woman a man could really trust. It is not another time, though, it is now, and she is simply the sort of woman who never really settled down. She has had various jobs and a couple of careers, has survived on wits, chutzpah, and luck, the times were with her. She has lived alone and in paranoically busy communes with principles and values. She has traveled from coast to coast and continent to continent, all the while thinking she was searching for freedom, truth, meaning, and a girl named Maggie Kelly. And now she knows for sure that there was no one to be found, nothing to be discovered. She has searched along the ancient banks of the Ganges and along the mythical shores of Mexico, in chattering forest and on ghost-ridden plain, in hotel and hut and beneath the hallowed sky, bangles on her ankles and a pack on her back. But she found no timeless roots, no memories of truth, no revelation, and no balm. She has been hippy, hustler, gypsy, gypster, activist, action-woman, freedom-lover and freak, but she has left all that behind her now. At long last, and against all of her mother's predictions, Maggie is going to settle down. Firmly and more or less permanently, like in cement. This time she is going to become one of the most formidable creatures the world has ever seen: a couple. With matched sheets and a joint bank account. With a fixed address, credit cards, shared bills, and plans. There will be things to do and things to be done. There will be purpose, profit, and protection. Safety from her nightmares and sanctuary from her memories. Finally, Maggie Kelly is stilling the siren within her, the she-demon who has perpetually lured her away from all sure ports and sleepy harbors, who has howled through her bones and sung through her blood, calling her away from the shores of her birthing and into the dark dark dawn of dreams, always looking for something more and something better. Now she knows that this is not a world in which true love or true commitment, true passion or true freedom were ever serious contenders. This is a world of survival and compromise. A world where everything is neatly tied to profit. Where prophets are honored only after they are dead and safely out of the way. Where heroes are quickly domesticated, commemorated by a poster or a T-shirt, or ignored. Where heroines end up half-senile and arthritic in filthy, cheap apartments crammed with junk and cats, their scrapbooks wrapped up in tissue in a drawer of the dresser, do you want to see how I used to be? She who once thought that there must be more to life than her mother's predictable cycles, her father's predictable patterns, and the boring peace of her sister, married to a telephone repairman in Denver, now knows better. Safety first. No dream and no illusion is worth the risks of pain and aloneness to which it might expose you. Take no chances. It is impossible to calculate just how much grief or how many tears the human heart will be expected to surrender.

Yesterday, Maggie came to a decision. She was standing against a small ledge attached to the wall under an old travel poster of Rome in a pizza parlor on Broadway, eating her lunch, her bag gripped under arm, her samples in a case between her feet. It was her first day standing in for Meredith. Meredith usually does most of the selling, but Meredith's son is just getting over the flu and Meredith is afraid he will be barred from the day care center for the rest of the year if she sends him back too soon. Meredith is better at dealing with people. Meredith doesn't get into fights or lose precious accounts. Not so easily, at any rate. Trying to eat her slice of pie without burning her mouth, dripping sauce down her chin, or tangling the rubbery strands of cheese in her hair, Maggie looked around at the other lunchers, at the phlegm-yellow tinge from grease and smoke that coated the ceiling and walls, at the monotonous, mindless movement of the street outside, unrolling like the projected background of an old Western, look, there's the Grand Canyon, don't it look real?, thinking about the defeats of the day, and about the defeats of her years, and wondering how she would continue to pay the rent if things kept going the way they've been going, and some small, fragile thing in her heart went ping. Though, perhaps, it wasn't her heart at all, that worn-out, much abused organ. Perhaps it was something in her head, some last sliver of pride, some final, shimmery, faery-image of the lies she believed when she was still so young, went poof. And all the world was the dingy pizzeria and the gray and multicolored street, so full with strangers, so fraught with dangers, and Maggie Kelly, left behind and all alone by the dreams she no longer will remember, eating her lunch from a piece of waxed paper, steeling herself for the rebuffs and humiliations of the afternoon. The young man who slid the pies in and out of the oven while humming along with the radio was wearing a black T-shirt that announced in white print: JESUS SEES YOU. If God does exist, wondered Maggie, would he really need to advertise? And in those few moments, so unstartling and so un-new, she decided. Though all she remembers thinking was that she wasn't going to take any shit from Meredith about anything.

Maggie's mother would say that Maggie's present state of gloomy, joyless realism is all because she is thirty-eight and has (later than most) reached that age when she finally understands what is, and what isn't important in this life—and how little time there is in which to do it all. Which is another way of saying that Maggie, too, is pushing forty.

The world is small after all.

But on the bus, so crowded and so uncompanionable, sitting between a thin, tense woman who is having a running and somewhat impassioned conversation with someone who isn't there, and a fat man in a suit who holds his briefcase on his lap as though it contains a bomb, there lurks no song in Maggie Kelly's mind. Instead, she is thinking of a hot bath and a strong drink, a cold meal and a light book. Her heart lies on her lap, her arms across it, and her eyes stare at it blindly. Just let me get home. Where it is dark and stuffy, but not unfriendly. Where there are two Yale locks and a chain on the door. Where her cat sits waiting, banging its head against the cupboard door, impatient for its supper. Home. Please. Don't let anybody mug me or proposition me. Don't let anybody try to tell me their life story while we're stuck in traffic, and then one day I realized, hey, you're over forty, it's time you started doing something for yourself, it's time you started having some fun, too. Please don't let anybody try to hustle me or hurt me, just let me get home, and looks up and out of the window at the passing buildings and the passing people, each one a part of the great and throbbing whole, being pumped through the city's avenues and streets like blood cells. She is in one of those moods where she will scream if anyone speaks to her, will burst into tears if anyone touches her. So much for the wisdom and maturity of nearly four decades of human experience. At least she is on a bus and, therefore, not likely to be hit by one so that no one is likely to discover either the shoddy state of her underwear or the shoddy state of her soul.

Maggie Kelly has her specter, too. Unlike Tony Rivera's (which is a master of all disguises), hers is short and thin and his hair is never combed very well. From time to time she sees him, walking down the street holding someone else's hand, being wheeled through the supermarket in some other mother's cart, a bag of potato chips on his lap, let's get this, let's get that. Now and then she even comes upon him, riding no-hands through the park, testing the charm and gum machines for forgotten coins and prizes, the back of him in his plaid flannel shirt and cowboy boots just turning the corner out of sight, yelling, "Mom! Hey, Mom! Wait up!"—but not to her. She has seen him no matter where she has been, but especially here. Here where his body has left his shade behind. Here where all her memories of him end and begin. Here in rooms that are always still and slightly cold. Sometimes, if the light is right and the landscape is just so, she sees him yet, standing in the playground off the park, around him his pail and empty cans and the box with his cowboys and Indians and misshapen animals, all small and plastic and in unlikely colors, moaning, "But Maggie. Maggie, I didn't enjoy carrying them here. But Mom . . ." And then come all the memories which that memory drags along behind it like chains: the wasted years and wrong decisions; the bad starts and disastrous endings; the mistaken notions and the willful mistakes.

Maggie once knew a girl who tried to kill herself fifteen times, though not, like Manny Mazocca, Maggie's first true love, all in the course of one long night. Manny tried aspirins, cold capsules, hitting a bullet with a hammer, electrocuting himself with the living-room lamp, and, finally, gassing himself, and would probably have gone on to even more imaginative means if the stench hadn't awoken his brother. She tried overdoses, slit wrists, walking into traffic, and, the last resort, jumping from the bedroom window, bye-bye, Dave, her arms up, her blouse making angel wings as she jumped from the tenth-floor window and down down down into the alley below. But it isn't that difficult for everyone, dying. It wasn't that difficult for Maggie's son. All he had to do was leave, for thirty-three seconds, the free zone of the pavement. All he had to do was step lightly on his miniature, just-like-real-people's feet from the gray of that sidewalk onto the blue of that road, and into those few pure moments of suspended time, his body stopped and the world still moving. There were seconds when someone might have done something: might have thrown the dice and spun the wheel a different way. Seconds when a million things casually could have intervened—a racing hero, a grasped steering wheel, a faithful dog leaping from the roof of the van across the street, an act of God—but didn't. And just that easily was he dead. Healthy, normal, a burden, and a pain in the neck one minute. Dead the next, his perpetual present a clipping from one of the dailies: BOY KILLED AS MOTHER LOOKS ON IN HELPLESS HORROR. And in the simplicity and ease with which he took to death making living all that much harder for some. That much harder for his mother, a part of whom would be forever standing in that liquid afternoon of that July day, holding a melting Fudgsicle in her left hand, making thin brown, vein-like trails all down her arm, and a collection of change in her right, pennies for the dead child's eyes, screaming no no no, nonononono. As though she might still be able to will time to stop and backpedal, to begin again with everything as it should have been.

Maggie Kelly has been to hell and back. Or so they said, her mother, her mother's friends, and her aunts with their fevered Celtic imaginations, rose rouge and peach-tone powder on their faces and platitudes in their hearts. To hell and back, poor thing. What she had needed, they had all agreed, was to get out of herself for a while. What she had needed was a month in Nantucket or a week in Florida. What she had needed was to get her mind off things: take one of those interesting courses at NYU; find herself a new man; have another child. If you've nearly drowned, the best thing to do is to get right back in the water. Tripping through hell, and then staggering back. We know how you feel. Or so they said, her friends and acquaintances, her doctor and her doctor's receptionist, the man in the corner store, and the super with the gold tooth and the silver crucifix, what a shame.

But the trip to hell is not a cheap excursion, booked in advance through your aunt's son-in-law, with special extras in the off-season, I bet you wish you were here. Hell is a one-way ticket, and once there there is no real return. You can visit the pyramids, or the Taj Mahal, or the Great Wall of China, and then go back to Oklahoma and paint the shutters green. You can walk among the beggars of Bombay, or the Bangkok whores, or the bloody streets of Belfast, and still go back to Great Neck and mix yourself a gin and tonic while you decide what to do with the evening, go to a movie or henna your hair. But hell is not like that. Once seen, not ever forgotten. Once experienced, not ever ignored. She has needed no brightly painted pottery pitchers, no intricate pieces of silver jewelry to remind her. No photograph to recall those sepulchral nights of frozen despair, the wind blowing hard across the wasted plains, the only other sounds the silence and the wailing of her heart. No souvenir to relive those embalmed days of frantic hopelessness, the soft, slight breeze disturbing every single leaf of memory, the only other sounds the noises of the traffic and the weeping within. A person could go mad. Or just go.

So she sold most of her possessions, from the convertible sofa to the electric toaster, packed her books into boxes to be stored in Mrs. Kelly's garage, and moved to California. She would never have to stop. Freed by grief from all the old excuses and older restraints, there was nothing to stop her, no reasons for hesitation or retreat. She could do anything at all. And almost did. To urgent prophecies of disaster and dissipation, of tragic endings with her half-clad body washed up on some lonely shore or found, dismembered, in a cheap suitcase in a Holiday Inn in Duluth, she had only to say: So what? To stories of amoebic dysentery, syphilis, hepatitis, drug addiction, and white slavery, she had only to say: So you think that's something? You think that's bad? You think any of that could hurt me? To her mother's emotional admonitions to think about the future ("But the future," Kate would scream into the receiver in her long-distance voice. "What about the future? What's going to happen to you in ten or twenty years?"), she had only to throw up the hobgoblin of the past ("Future?" she would snap back. "What's that?").

First she moved from man to man and then she moved from woman to woman. First she moved from apartment to apartment and job to job, from one great idea to another even greater—and then she began simply to move. She hitchhiked down to hungry Mexico; cashed in her savings for a ticket to India, never mind how she would get back. She lived in caves in Crete, in huts in Goa, in a van in Tasmania. She drifted first one way and then the next, back and forth and to and fro, plotting her moves on the moods of the moon and the utterances of the *I Ching*, what difference could it make? She was going to taste life before death tasted her. Who could argue? Even Kate couldn't argue, though she tried. From England to Israel, from Amsterdam to

Athens—everything and everyone constantly changing, always renewed, and always about to be left—traveled Maggie. Two months ahead of her mother's letters and only seconds ahead of her own mad memories. She did all that, moving as fast as a jet-age desperado could, but, eventually, she had to come back, her mother was right. There are dead children in India, too.

To illustrate the omnipresence of *dukkha*, or suffering, the Buddha told the story of a woman wracked with grief, who went to the All-Compassionate One with her dead child in her arms, begging that its life be returned. After he had listened to her, the All-Compassionate One sent her back to her village to fetch a grain of mustard seed from a house that had never known death. Obedient, the woman went from door to door, to the homes of the wealthy and the hovels of the poor, but at each the answer was the same. Don't cry no tears around me.

Nor has this lesson been lost on Maggie Kelly. When it comes to the gathering of mustard seeds, the world is not quite large enough. Not large enough to allow one small corner of grace that might permit some earthly hope of release from all this lousy suffering. Not large enough to allow even one small corner where a person might forget the meaning of misery. Resignation, it would seem, and not redemption, was the message.

And so she has come back. Come back to sit on a bus in rush-hour traffic with a satin heart on her lap and her mind half-stoned on the smells of sweat and stale breath. Come back to all the things she left.

But can she return?

Maggie is convinced that she can, having tried just about everything else. Lying in her sleeping bag in a field in Israel, listening to the guns going off not that far in the distance, she finally decided that she was ready to stop. Was she becoming a voyeur of other people's anguish? Was there nothing to be said for security? And suddenly it seemed obvious that she had one last chance to avoid the future she had been building for herself for over thirty years. The future in which she is forever alone. One last chance to alter that image she sees on insomniac nights, her older self gone to fat and to seed, dressed in an old floral kimono, stained and held together by a safety pin, her once-beautiful hair bleached and thinning, her eyes shrunken and bleary, a whisky glass, half-filled, always in one hand. The one in which her only friends are an old canary and the one-eyed tomcat that comes to the back door for his meals. The one in which the only people who feel even pity for her are the homosexual social worker who visits since the heart attack, and the little girl in the wheelchair who lives across the street with her three brothers and her alcoholic stepfather since her mother ran off with a gambler. Only one chance. To start brand new. She will never again be that woman, the one who vanished at 3:17 on that muggy afternoon nearly six earth years ago, but she can still be someone else. Someone less demanding and less willful. Someone more easily pleased. Someone more flexible. Someone whose dreams can be satisfied. She can do it all over, but do it all differently. Enter through another door and into a world where survival is uncomplicated, where there is nothing that can't be handled or bought, where the questions are all kept simple and the answers simpler still. A world that she has come to think of as Skip's world.

She trudges up the street, looking in through the windows of strangers' homes, tucked into the darkness of the buildings like campfires, all of them always seeming more inviting than her own. Everyone comfortable and safe in their well-lighted apartments with plants on the windowsills and food in the freezer. Everyone snug and settled, shoes off, shades half down, speeding along in their separate compartments of their private trains, the world zipping by, its treacheries distanced, its details remote. Maggie's heel just misses missing a puddle of vomit congealed on the pavement. Oh, typical, she thinks. Oh, sure.

It was Meredith—who knows about things like good gyne-cologists and inexpensive restaurants, feminist lawyers, and truly international cheese stores—who recommended Skip, a dentist you could trust. And Maggie had known, even that first time over a year ago, tilted backwards in his chair, avoiding the light beaming down on her, and staring, instead, at the mobile of small silver dolphins dangling from its neck, her thoughts frozen with the pain in her lower molar, that here was a man with whom she could build an alternative life. She watched him fit on his plastic earthman's goggles and his disposable mask, and said, before he became engrossed in the private world of her teeth, "Did you always want to be a dentist?" "Huh?" "Did you always want to be a dentist? Even when you were a little boy?"

With his clear plastic eyeshields and his paper mask he looked like a bemused bandit owl. "I don't know what you mean," he said, and meant it. "You know," trying to shift her mouth out of range and stall the putting into it of metal objects. "Is it something you always dreamed of being?" When all the other boys could think of nothing but football or cars or female sexual organs, were you driven mad by thoughts of teeth? "Open wide, please." "It just seems like a strange thing to do." That stopped him. "Helping people?" he asked, sounding shy. "Is that strange?" and moved in with the probe. Here was a man who worried about what sort of toothbrush you used and whether or not you flossed after every meal, who charged the day's wages of a secretary for twenty minutes in the gunk of your mouth and believed that he did it as a public service. She rolled her eyes over to see if she could see a ring.

She jiggles the key in the temperamental outside lock, every cell of her body sighing, here we are again, and finally pushes her way into the dimness and restless quiet of the lobby. The floor is tracked with dirt and water, the elevator moans like a dying dragon as it climbs its shaft. Maggie stands in front of its dull black doors, chiseled with graffiti, wondering if it is possible that the draft is coming from all directions. She has never formally met any of her neighbors, but guesses that they are largely small-time hustlers and illegal immigrants, lying low. Somewhere above her, a heavy object falls, a child screams, a door slams. People who have never visited her before always think that they must have the wrong address.

The light has been left on in the living room; the pillows on the couch look as though someone has only just left them. In the tiny kitchen, two wine glasses stand heads down in the yellow dish drainer, a copper bowl tilting forward in its slot beside them. Maggie tosses the heart into the wicker throne and throws herself onto the sofa, relieved to have made it, happy to be at last alone, her three locks locked, her cat asleep on a pillow that itself looks like a cat in the chair by the window that stares out on to another window.

Once or twice she has returned home too early on a Thursday night and found Sandy still here, alone but looking kissed, making coffee for her as a gesture of the goodwill, a token of the sisterhood neither of them feels. Then they sit across from one another, the foot locker between them, making routine conversation about public transport and street crimes, new movies and old rock groups, pretending that they don't (instinctively and for no apparent reason, or for no good apparent reason) dislike each other. Like God, Maggie doesn't mind lending a hand when she can, but, also like God, she doesn't like to get personally involved. If Sandy wants to film group orgies in the apartment on Thursday afternoons, she is free to do so—as long as she cleans up after her, remakes the bed, and doesn't upset the cat. But Maggie wants no confidences or conspiratorial chat. No explanations or soul-bared excuses. She has no energy left to expend on understanding. She just wants to be left alone. It is part of her new philosophy of life, keep clean.

The cat stretches first one paw and then the other, its claws catching on the canvas of the chair, its eyes just gashes in the continuity of its fur. Maggie pulls off first one shoe and then the other.

Meredith says that women have to stick together. It isn't enough to get on with your own life, mind your own business, do your own thing. It is not sufficient, says Meredith, to protect just yourself. Women must protect one another. Meredith did the cards and they agreed. Conspiracy, said Meredith, is one of the most important tools of any oppressed minority—though it took very little to perceive that this was a borrowed line. Would Maggie have refused to help in the Underground Railroad? Would she have stood on the stoop in the black-and-white morning, the passing footsteps echoing the beating of her heart, shouting at the soldiers with their rifles over their shoulders and no expressions in their eyes, "In here! In here! They're hiding the Jews in the basement"? Would she eat a South African orange?

Probably not.

Maggie does understand that all women are congenital outlaws. Excluded by an accident of birth from the clubs that count, the assemblies that decide, the meetings that matter, and educated to believe that in both the realities and the dreams of mankind they are always the ones pushing the wrong way, either fucking up the wheels of progress with their sentimental irrelevancies or blowing down the fragile visions of the poets with their petty complaints and niggling demands. Women always exist on the fringe. Neither soldiers nor saviors, neither destroy-

ers nor builders, they are permitted only the illusion of partici-
pation, the leavings of power. Always suspect and fatally flawed,
the original hosts of original sin, they must huddle around their
own secret fires, poking at the flames with bent sticks, muttering
to one another in a language all their own, their expressions
guarded, their bodies expectant, their hats pulled low. Living
outside the law by circumstance rather than chance, they must
band together in their own small and squabbling groups, or steal
silently alone along the edges of the towns with their important
doings and even more important machines, irrationally clinging
to some outmoded code, clutching at their quaint and battered
sense of honesty, given to dying in their own beds with their
shoes off and the sound of relief in the next room. Maggie knows
that, as when man plays with God, when woman plays with man
it is his ballgame, and his balls.

And so, way back last year, before they had so much as
seen one another, she agreed to let Sandy use her apartment on
one afternoon a week for her clandestine trysts and passionate
purposes. Meredith thanked her from the bottom of her heart.
Sandy thanked her too, she was a lifesaver. Meredith, who claims
to believe in neither men nor in love (and for whom inconsis-
tency has never been a problem), thinks that it is all wonderfully
romantic, a sensual adventure. After all, everyone needs some
sort of romance. Didn't Maggie agree? And so Maggie, who has
had her fill both of romance and of love, said "Okay." Meredith
swears that she'll never regret it.

Maggie goes "Tch tch tch" to attract the cat's attention, but
the cat, dreaming its sweet cat dreams, doesn't ever so slightly
stir. Maggie looks at the small black cat, refuses to look at the
small black hole where once her own heart lay, and then looks
warily at the small black phone on its carved and inlaid table.

Should she call him to make sure that his excitement of the
night before, when she accepted his fifth proposal of marriage,
and his excitement of this morning, when he remembered that
she had accepted, have not yet evaporated? Should she call him
to tell him she loves him, that she's been thinking of him all day,
that she can't wait to see him again? She leans her head against
the pillows and looks up at the ceiling. Yes, she should.

Maggie has never met Sandy's lover, has found not so much
as a cigar butt in an ashtray or a few unfamiliar hairs in the

bathroom sink. She has never passed him in the hall, has never smelled him on the sheets or on the towels. A demon lover, here one hour and gone the next. A dream lover, riding through the girded gates of this wonderful city one day a week to sweep into his strong muscular arms the woman he so endlessly desires, and to take from her all precious drops of love, her body like a flower, his heart a hungry sun. From where does he come? Meredith doesn't know. What does he do? Meredith doesn't know that either. Doesn't he have a name? Of course he does, but Meredith doesn't know what it is. Neither of them can quite bring herself to try to extract information from Sandy, whose business is it, anyway? Is he tall? Is he short? Is he handsome, or just oddly attractive? Is he smart? Is he stupid? Has he been genuinely swept over and beyond the shores of reason by some unparalleled passion that could only have been engendered by a high school guidance counselor with straight eyebrows, strong views on everything from peanut butter to masturbation, and a rapidly failing sense of humor? Or is he merely extending good will? "For Chrissake," said Meredith, "if you don't want to help, just say no." Is he married, then, the obvious answer? But no, that was the one thing Meredith did seem to know. "Why not?" asked Maggie. "I suppose," said Meredith, managing to look both innocent and shrewd, "that he never found the right woman," before.

Maggie has never met Tony, either, but of him she knows a lot more than she wants to know, probably more than he knows himself. He drinks too much, smokes too much, and likes to sit in cheap cafés talking to men who read the *Daily News* and the *National Inquirer*. He is antisocial, unambitious, insensitive, self-indulgent, and probably marginally manic-depressive as well. He is cynical and uncommitted, mediocre at a job he loathes, and he has always had a chip on his shoulder, though, somehow, it was never annoying before. He is not violent, but he is unreliable, saying he will do things, go places, meet people, when all along he never intended doing any such thing. He is not overtly rude or crudely aggressive, unless very drunk, but he makes people uneasy, as a retarded child does. She also knows that he hates health foods, is a careless if fetishistic dresser ("He's got all these ridiculous hats he won't let me get rid of"), and ridicules all of his wife's family, friends, casual acquaintances, and dreams indiscriminately. More importantly, he is, tiny chip by tiny chip, breaking Sandra Grossman's large and largely good-natured heart. Maggie knows all this because Meredith has told her. None the less, and despite the fact that she is certain he isn't worth half the trouble he seems to be causing, Maggie can't help feeling slightly sympathetic toward the poor bastard. She certainly wouldn't want to be married to Sandy.

Sitting in her own stillness, old thoughts and old fears whizzing through her mind, Maggie wonders if Tony Rivera knows what is going on and, if he knows, whether or not he cares. But this, of course, is simply a distraction maneuver, designed to keep her from thinking about what is really on her mind.

Next door, the opera singer, a thin, young girl who works part-time in a department store selling baby clothes, begins to practice. In the alley, someone shouts for Jesus. The cat stretches and yawns, flexing the tip of its tail. Maggie gets up and goes over to the stereo to put on a record, still standing, minutes later, looking down at the red and black and shop-damaged heart, thinking of Skip, My Real Name Is Nelson. For all his perfection, his tailor-made suitability for the role of rescuer, there has always been something catching her back. Some little thing. Not the fact that she doesn't love him or that he is, often, wildly boring. Who isn't? she would like to know. Not even the fact that his experience of life is such that if he were let loose on the streets he'd be dead or completely mad within an hour. Absentmindedly, she fluffs up the intricate edging of the heart. Like a small child being carried home crying from the Firemen's Fair—the stuffed toys all unwon, the rides all over, the popcorn all eaten—she can't believe that there really isn't something more. One last shower of fireworks like a fountain in the blue-black, smoky sky. One last manic spin, her number revolving, click-clack, click-clacking to a miraculous win, anything from the top shelf. Just whom is she trying to kid?

She has just decided that, yes, she will call him, after her bath, and after she's eaten, and after she's had a drink or two, after she's sure he's back from his Thursday night squash game and meal with the guys downtown and she won't be forced into another short but not-so-sweet conversation with Mother Ellis, oh, Skip's father and I were in the West Indies once, but of course we never got off the yacht, when a sudden noise or movement behind her causes her to jump. There, in the doorway to the bedroom, stands Sandra Grossman Rivera, looking like the ghost of someone who had a bad death. Her skin is white as moonlight and her clothes are rumpled; her eyes are swollen and all cried out.

"Jesus," sighs Maggie, feeling foolish with relief. "You scared the shit out of me. I thought you'd gone."

"No," says Sandy, in a voice she rarely uses. "No, I'm still here."

Some people are liked for their charm, or for their looks, or for their infectious warmth. Some for their lively minds, unique sense of humor, or genuine kindness. Some people trail happiness behind them the way a toddler will pull a wagonload of dolls and stuffed animals, look what I've got. Some people come dressed for all occasions in calm, effortlessly shedding off layers to disperse among the poor of spirit. Some people are just nice. And some people are just likeable.

People have always liked Sandy because of her competence and because she has always known what she is doing. Orderly at the best of times (she never gets lost, never leaves the meat behind at the checkout, never forgets to call when she's promised), she really hits her stride in a crisis, any kind of crisis (the soufflé falls, the ceiling collapses, a life caves in), able to organize the lifeboats or grab the gun or pound the button from a choking child. Where others are born with a spoon of silver or a spoon of shit in their mouths, the spoon that came gripped between her infant gums was made of confidence, I have every right to be here, I know exactly who I am. She never loses her head, never acts illogically, is never at a loss for an explanation, always knows exactly what should be done.

If all that is true, though, what is she doing here now, folded up like a carpenter's ruler, her arms around her legs, her mouth a graph of unhappiness, bloop bloop bloop bloop bloop...?

Maggie is in the other room, talking to Skip on the telephone, her voice at a simmer, only occasionally a word bursting through the not-quite-shut door, oh ... of course ... I know ... not nowww.

Sandy swallows a sob, runs her fingers through her hair, and leans her forehead against her knees as though this might clear her head. She looks like someone in a state of shock, like someone whose heart has been rolled over by a tank.

Sandy is confused. She doesn't know what she's doing here, either. Only this morning, she left her apartment with a spring in her step and a slogan in her heart. Only this morning, she felt strong and invincible, more than capable of dealing with her present life, its complications and their possible ramifications, and with her problems, which, though not insoluble, have required some premeditation and time. At the moment, however, she feels like a small child confronted with death, what do you mean he's not coming back? She can only think of crying, crying as she cried as a teenager, stretched out, face down, on the yellow, cotton spread, her sobbing making the bed twitch, her mother hovering around her, why don't you wash your face and come out and have a nice cup of tea? More often than not, her mother would bring the tea in to her—the tea or the cocoa or the coffee—resting cup and saucer on the bedside table, resting her bottom on the edge of the bed, resting one hand tentatively on a scrunched-up shoulder, would you like to talk about it, dear?

This time, though, although she does, in fact, have a cup of tea, provided by Maggie (this will make you feel better, it's got lots of B_{12}), there is no one to whom she could talk, even if she would. Not Tony, not Meredith, not even her own mother who likes nothing better than a disaster in which she can throw her maternal weight around. And especially not Maggie.

Sandy's lover has given her the boot, has given her the old heave-ho, this is the point at which it all stops. It's been fun, it's been terrific, it's been a very satisfactory and worthwhile relationship, we'll always be friends, be pals, we won't get out of touch, but now we must bid a fond adieu. She can hear Tony singing in her mind, *so long, it's been good to know you*, and it makes her want to scream.

Sandy's lover is getting married. He told her this afternoon, before they made love (he is not callous, not a cad), you know how we've always said this was a temporary thing ... But he'd said that before. So had she. "I know," she'd said, stopped in the middle of a story about this reactionary gym teacher who won't let the kids spray paint their hair in shades of pink and neon blue, her glass in the air. He looked like Cain, caught by God.

"She hasn't found out, has she?" "Oh, no, no ... she hasn't found out," and then looked at her as though she should finish the sentence. "Well, what's wrong then?" Sometimes it's been that he's feeling guilty, sometimes it's been that she's feeling if not actually guilty a little contrite, often it's been just nerves. They have been ending it for months, since the close call last winter. (It really was silly to keep it going, it had almost been over before it began, it was only an affair of convenience and friendship, an impermanent matching of needs. He was so lonely, she so fed up. It was unwise and stressful to continue, they could end it any time, they should.) But somehow it never quite finished, somehow they always agreed to meet just one more time, usually to talk things through, again. But this time when she asked "what's wrong?" he said none of the things she expected him to say. His nerves weren't shot, he wasn't losing sleep from worrying, from feeling like such a shit, he wasn't concerned about her husband ("But what if he finds out? What if he tries to kill me?" "Oh, for God's sake, I told you he's not violent. He's never thrown the first punch."), or his newer girlfriend ("You don't understand. She'll never forgive me. She's not like that." "Of course she'll understand, if she loves you. I'm not a threat."), or what his clients would say if they ever found out ("Imagine, one of his own patients. I've heard about doctors, but dentists ..."). This time he is getting married. "She said 'yes.'" "Well," said Sandy. "Well." "I was beginning to think she'd never say yes." He wasn't the only one. "Well, I guess congratulations are in order. I would have bought champagne, if I'd known it was going to be a special occasion."

Only after he'd gone—after he'd asked her six times was she sure there were no hard feelings, after he'd asked her twice if she could find out from her mother whether or not that place he saw last autumn was still for sale—did she cry. Only after the door was locked behind him, after the glasses had been washed and the bed freshly made (she studied sociology, she knows about ritual), only then did she collapse on the couch like someone who has just staggered from the wreckage.

Nobody likes to be unpleasantly surprised. Nobody enjoys losing something any more when they know they're going to lose it or when they think they wouldn't mind if they lost it than when they don't. Nobody likes to be rejected, though some people have more practice at it than others. It is almost always better to leave than to be left. Politics again.

She huddled on the couch for a while, unable to stop her own tears, or to make herself reclaim the motions of an ordinary day, as though it were time and not she who refused to move. Then she went into the bathroom, washed her face and brushed her hair, stared at herself in the defective mirror—a still-young woman, not yet near her prime, attractive, intelligent, having a bad day—and then went into the bedroom and threw herself across the spread. She might not know what she was doing, but she knew that she couldn't go home, couldn't stand the sight of Rivera, asking her one of his Thought for the Day questions. If you were at a Washington cocktail party talking to the Secretary of Health, Education and Welfare about the creativity of slum kids, and one of the waiters pulled you aside, but instead of showing you where the phone was told you that he was an alien looking for specimens of human life to bring back to his planet, to save for posterity, because in five and a half minutes the whole earth was going to blow (nobody's fault but your own), would you go with him? She might not be completely sure of what she was feeling (was it just shock? was it Tony's fault? had she depended on Skip more than she thought? more than she ought?), but she was sure that things would have to change. And then she fell asleep.

Maggie's voice becomes even less audible, they must be talking about her. Sandy gets up and tiptoes to the door. But she can't hear Skip say, "Are you sure she's all right? Would you like me to talk to her?" She can hear Maggie say "... you?" She can't hear Skip say, "Well, I am her dentist."

Sandy goes back inside and sits down. She will stay here for the night, and in the morning she will decide what's best to do. In the morning she will not be feeling so disoriented, or so distressed. She will be able to think more clearly, more rationally. In the morning, she will know, once more, what she wants to do, just what she is doing.

Maggie appears in the doorway, obviously trying not to look too pleased with herself, trying to spare Sandy's feelings. Earlier, over a drink, she had said, "Well, it's not so bad, really. Everyone gets walked out on one time or another." "Do they?" asked Sandy, always aware of when she's being handed a line.

"How're you feeling?" asks Maggie, unable to think of anything else to say. The sight of Sandy, bunched up like a bear in a cage, has not made her like her any more, but it has made her feel more kindly toward her. Suffering may not ennoble, but it does make everyone the same. Sandy, however, doesn't seem to want her kindness, cries wordlessly, or sits like a blind woman, staring straight at you but unseeing. All Sandy would say was what was fairly obvious, her lover has left her and she's rather upset, she couldn't go home in this state, could she? She has resisted all attempts to draw her out, to cheer her up, or to get things off her chest. Every time Maggie makes some move toward her (to lay a sympathetic hand on a heaving shoulder, to touch a fist with friendly fingertips), Sandy looks like a fundamentalist being introduced to Charles Darwin, this is the man who says you're a monkey.

"Oh, yes," says Sandy, smiling wanly. "Much better. I could eat something now."

"Right," says Maggie. "I'll go see what I've got."

To her back, Sandy says, "I really do appreciate everything, Maggie. It's really nice of you to help me out."

"Don't mention it," says Maggie, and, stopping at the entrance of the kitchen, swings around suddenly and adds, "Oh, yeah. Skip said to say hello. He's worried about you."

"Is he?" whispers Sandy, moved almost to tears, it would seem, by this unexpected kindness.

T W O

The people across the hall have gone off to Martha's Vineyard for the summer. Henry, the scientific masseur on the first floor, has gone off to Fire Island. Mrs. Burkowsky's arthritis is killing her, the department secretary's hay fever is driving her mad, and people are constantly passing out in the subway from the heat. Street crimes are thriving. Since the great rain, the weather has been aggressively hot and sunny, this part of the planet and all its creatures moving tortoise-like from one day to the next. Air-conditioned buses, behind whose tinted windows intrepid tourists gawk, drive through Brooklyn and Harlem, the Upper West Side, the Lower East Side, and Greenwich Village, wow, there's a real drug addict, isn't the city great in the summer? And the vagrant's name is Richard. López, who runs the bodega like a Spanish garrison, says that he's been around for years, he just travels slow. López thinks he comes from Boston. "From Boston?" hooted Rivera. "You're confusing him with that white guy who dresses like a court jester. He comes from Boston." Boston? Angola, maybe, but not Boston. "I'm not confusing him with nobody," López screamed back. "Ain't we talking about the tall guy with that black thing wrapped around him? The one who never says nothing? Someone told me he comes from Boston." Boston, Angola. López also says that the small stores all let him help himself to pieces of fruit, cartons of expired milk and juice, and stale bread. "You do?" "Sure," said López. "There ain't no point in arguing, is there?" though he sees the point with everyone else. Aside from such incidental, though-invigorating-in-their-way conversations, he has spoken to no one for days and days.

He has been alone for nearly three weeks.

Meredith came to the door the night after the night Sandy never came home, her ticket of admission a plain white envelope with his name written unfamiliarly—Anthony—in an all-too-familiar hand.

While he sat in the living room, reading the letter, letter-by-letter, she went into the bedroom and packed Sandy's suitcase with just a few things from an immaculately legible list. No one has ever had any trouble reading Sandy's notes or letters. No one has ever had to puzzle, turning the paper first this way and then that, stopping passersby to get their opinions on whether the word in question was naturalization or maturation, the letter *e* or *i* or *n*, over something she wrote. Unlike, for example, Tony, whose handwriting, even when he's trying, resembles nothing so much as the ECG of someone who has just died. He certainly had no trouble reading what she had to say.

"Well, that's that, then," called Meredith, lingering in the hall, wobbling between diplomatic sympathy and ghoulish delight. "If there's anything you need ..." From some new hole in hell, with benefit of neither mind nor heart, he managed to call back, "Yeah, Meredith. Thanks." Thanks? "Look, Tony ..." inching toward him from behind (though he refused to raise his head or look at her), coming closer (though it should have been clear that she had already come close enough). "I'm sure that everything's going to be all right. I'm sure she just ... you know ..." By simply moving his eyes he could see the note still open in her hand: red skirt, denim skirt, blue floral print dress with heart-shaped buttons ... "Where is she?" But Meredith wouldn't budge. "I don't know." "Where is she?" "I told you, I don't know." "Then what are you going to do with her things? Leave them in a locker at the bus station?" With impeccable calm and awesome care, he refolded the letter and replaced it in its envelope. "Get out, Meredith." "I'm only trying to help," sounding very much like the injured party. "Well try not helping for a while. Try minding your own fucking business for a change." "Now listen here, Tony," said Meredith (and he knew, even before he finally raised his head and faced her, that she would have the suitcase on the floor and her hands on her hips, just like when she lays down the law to Will), "I only came over because Sandy asked me to. If you don't want my help, just say so." "Right. I don't want your help." "Fine," she snapped, and slammed out, but not before telling him that she'd left a bowl of homemade gazpacho on the kitchen table, in case he got hungry later on.

He may never be hungry again.

As always, Sandy's communication was succinct and to the point. If she doesn't get away from him for a while, she will go insane. Things are too confused, there is too much pressure on her. Things are worse than they were last winter. She has to have some time to herself. She has to be alone to think. She knows that she can trust him not to bother her when she asks him not to, but just in case she will be staying with someone he doesn't know until school ends and she goes up to visit her parents. She will call him then—if not before. He is not to hassle Meredith, who is only being a friend. She is sure this is the best way. "After all," she wrote, "we have been separated before, and it has always helped us sort out our priorities. I know you'll probably feel angry that I did it this way, but I don't feel that I could go through even one more argument with you." And, PS, "Don't forget to change Zorro's water in this heat."

But he feels neither angry nor brokenhearted. He feels like a hermit crab suddenly poked out of its shell, desperate to find some place to hide.

That second night, after Meredith banged out the door and he had bought himself a bottle of whisky and fed the soup to Zorro, he sat on the sofa, not doing anything, really, while in his heart a strong, small squall blew about the debris of forty years; ticket stubs and unpaid bills, torn checks and discarded designs, balled-up plans and busted dreams, dust and crap and hoarded treasures, schwump swoosh woooo. Leaving the surface barren and black, so that looking into it was like looking into the deepest gap in the galaxy. So that, looking into it, there was nothing to be seen. Nothing to be felt. It was not the same as freedom; it was the same as nothing.

Tony has known several people who have been saved. Just when things seemed as bad as they could get, when there seemed no point in hoping or wishing or making yourself any more promises. Just when there seemed nothing to expect, no reason to go on, no reason for having gone on at all. One minute despair or resignation, the next minute hallelujah. His grandmother Maria—who, during her prime, which encompassed the years between nineteen and fifty, led a life that could be called either shocking or misdirected—discovered Jesus (though not the Pope's Jesus) (and not, to Sophie's temporary confusion, Mrs. Sotomayor's son, Jesus) in the basement as she was emptying the garbage, one stinking August night. Charlie Guzman—at one time one of the best dealers in the city as well as one of its finest drummers—woke up one afternoon in his all-black bedroom, reborn, redeemed, his heart and mind completely renovated, now I see where I've gone wrong. Sandy's cousin, the nurse; Susan Lethbridge, the fastest typist the department has ever had; Mrs. Cardona, who lives next door to Sophie and who always has a light bulb that needs replacing or a plug that needs repairing. All of them have been saved. And each of them has described to him, simply and without elaborate exclamations, the instant of awareness, the moment of the falling of salvation and the rising of the soul. I am saved. Lifted from the polluted sea of human experience, mucky with all the vices and virtues of tellurian life, and on to some peak of existence where none of it could touch them anymore. Reborn without having first to die.

But that night, sitting in the dark on the old Salvation Army sofa, the last Apache left alive after the massacre, he understood that he cannot get in, yet alone rise above. Can neither succumb nor surpass. Cannot even imagine what it is like to have faith, not in anything, not anymore. And—though she has left him before, will almost inevitably return, probably—he finally understood what it really means to be alone. Alone like a bum, with no past, no present, and no future, no direction and no home. Without Sandy to cover for him, to intercede, distract, and protect, to bear the burden of what were once his dreams, the world will know the secret he has always kept—even from himself—that he is dead already. Sophie Rivera's changeling child, slipped into her womb by antediluvian gods teasing for attention, let's see what you make of this one; gone to the dustlessness of eternity, only waiting for his body to catch up.

Many are saved, but he is lost.

And so have they gone, the minutes and the hours, the days and the weeks. Before when she left him, he either spent the time pursuing her (answering her letters, calling her up, meeting her for dinner, exhibiting his good intentions), or drawing her after him, in and out, frantic with work, endlessly busy, let her hear that he'd been seen in Rochester or New Platz or Southhampton, working so hard he barely noticed she was gone, Sandy impressed by both his diligence and his obvious grief. This time, in all this time, he has done nothing. He has not been to a favorite bar, a favorite café, a favorite old movie, or to visit an old friend, favorite or not. He has not hung around in the office, stayed late at meetings, or donated extra time to the pathologically voracious students. Has not stopped at his usual stops, made his customary appearances, or haunted his normal haunts, merely going to work and home again, locking himself in each evening, and locking himself out each morning, going forth only to buy necessary provisions and to take Zorro for his walks. When driven to answer the telephone at home, it has never been as Tony Rivera, the middle-aged boy wonder of the Greater Metropolitan Area, but as Tony's Pizzeria, or Father Anthony of the Church of Latter Day Martyrs, or Rocky Rivera, ex-failed boxer and well-liked janitor, if punchy, or Kid Rivera, or General Rivera, or Tonto Tony, or any number of the characters who have always manipulated his imagination, and once or twice as Life Itself, picking up the receiver, slamming it down, and then leaving it off the hook. He sees no one, talks to nobody—with the exception of Will, who doesn't count. The people at work don't count, either. Nor do Meredith's few aborted attempts to lure him into conversation on the stairs, or to trap him into talking in the hallway, hey, Tony, thanks for fixing Will's tire, hey, Tony, why don't you come in for a drink? hear from Sandy lately? When he thinks that she might be lying in wait for him, he takes the death box to the floor above his own and walks down (it is not the descending footfall for which she listens). In retaliation—or as a sign of the indefatigable female spirit, nurturing, sustaining, cleaning, repairing, meddling, and mixing, even as the world burns and the men fling themselves from mountains, flapping their arms as birds move their wings—she has now taken to passing notes to him one or two times a day, either through Will or under the door, I'm going to the supermarket later, do you need anything? Sandy has been trying to get you on the phone, Vega wants to know was it you who sent him that postcard about Jesus watching, do you think I could borrow Sandy's Wailers albums if you're not going to be listening to them?

Tonight, though, he rode around for hours before finally coming home. East Side and West Side, Uptown and Downtown, coasting through the better neighborhoods, racing, hunched with determination, a manic expression on his face, through the worst. Oh, the vast and varied tapestry of the metropolis. Oh, the teeming, steaming city, vivid and vibrant and throbbing with life, with poor and rich, beautiful and ugly, young and old, straight and bent, successful and failed, sober and out-for-the-count, throbbing with death. Oh, the excitement, and oh, the dynamism. The angry smell and the hungry roar. Millions of historically anonymous lives, and every one a story. Every one a potential unmarked grave. Slipping with only a whirr and a clack and the tiniest rattle of the back reflector preparing to fall off, he rode through the seedy, secret streets (what really goes on behind all those windows? behind all those eyes?), rode like Phantom Man, seeing all but never seen, able to laugh and cry in a single sound.

If truth is knowledge, then he must be getting close. His knowledge of the city, at least, could stand up against that of a cabbie or a courier. He can even recognize barrio landmarks: the drunk under the pinball machine on Second Avenue, the junky couple and their dog on the Broadway beat, the man with the parrot midtown, the shopping-bag lady near Wall Street, the skater from Columbus Avenue. He can recognize them even when they're in transit, or other than where they're meant to be.

On the other hand, of course, it is a lot like recognizing the landmarks of hell. Why can't he recognize the pleasant-looking family coming out of McDonald's, the kids still finishing their Cokes, or the lovers kissing right on the corner, in front of everyone, even though the light says WALK? Why can't he recognize a kindly grocer, or the delivery boy with the Walkman, or one of the unsmiling young women emerging from the subway entrances like surly Aphrodites popping up from the sea, shoulder bags swinging, heels clicking, each smug in her knowledge that when she reaches her apartment the phone will be ringing?

All the streets he passed through tonight he has passed through before, but he couldn't say that the kids playing on the barricaded blocks were the kids that were there last week or last winter; that the old ladies sitting in front of the project entrances on their plastic beach chairs, continents away from any beach, were the ones who are there every summer evening, gossiping as the sun goes down; that the girls with their long legs and short shorts sitting on the stoops eating ice cream, laughing and waving and calling whoowee, have ever smiled on him before.

His map of the world is defined not by its high spots and points of historical or cultural interest, but by its dumps and disasters; not by its tallest buildings or most beautiful monuments or clearest lakes or the spot where Magellan waded out of the ocean, but by its razed sanctuaries, bloodied rivers, the scenes of its saddest losses. And just so is his outline of his own history not a progression of milestones and major achievements (gets first tooth, gets first bike, gets first report card, gets first racer, gets first guitar, gets laid, gets first gig, gets first degree, gets second degree, gets married, gets a real job) leading to stability, position, maturity, and power. Instead, it is a mounting list of detours and defeats (loses father, loses country, loses second father, loses third country, gives up racing, gives up music, gives up fighting, gives up), leading to exactly where he is now. Stinking, sweating, hungry, thirsty, lonely, horny, and sneaking into his own apartment with a bicycle over one shoulder and an extremely severe cramp in his left leg.

There are three pieces of paper right inside the door. One from Meredith asking if there is any chance that Will can stay with him on Friday night, unless, that is, he has other plans. Another from Meredith saying that Sandy has been trying to get him on the telephone again and that Meredith herself tried to catch him this morning, to tell him that Sandy was on the phone, but that he must have gone to work very early. One from Vega asking him what he thinks is so funny about a postcard that says JESUS SEES YOU TOO, signed A Friend. What is he trying to incinerate?

He reads them all, still standing in the hall, the bike leaning against him on one side, Zorro panting against the other, sighs three times, moves the bike into its house position, slaps Zorro on the head once or twice and scratches him behind the ears, and staggers into the living room where he collapses on the sofa. He can hear his blood thumping through his veins, his heart rrhumprrhumping away, feel the liquid sluicing down his neck and arms and torso and the backs of his legs. It could be an hallucination due to a temporary state of hypothermia, but he could swear that he can hear the Beach Boys, faint but distinct, singing "Help Me Rhonda." Zorro gives a bewildered, bestial moan, his tail beating against the floor with a steady rhythm like the sound made by the dropping grains of time. For God's sake, Rhonda, help me, too.

"Okay. Okay," he says, not strong enough to look into those begging brown eyes. "Just give me a few minutes. I'm no good to you dead."

It is only when his breathing begins to return to normal and he can close his eyes without seeing road, endless and pot-holed, that he realizes he still holds the notes in his hand. Innocent-looking and ominous. Warrants for his arrest.

He is not avoiding Sandy specifically, though he is also doing nothing to hasten the arrival of the moment when she speaks to him again. It is unlikely that she will have anything to say that he truly wants to hear. Or he to her. What can he say? Hey, Sandy, why don't we give us one more chance to make it real? Hey, Baby, my car's outside, we can take those two lanes anywhere? Hey, honey, I know a guy down in Tampa owes me a favor? Hey, I know a guy in L.A. can pull a few strings? It's not too late too late too late, too late to start again? There's still magic in the nights? I've still got my guitar?

He is avoiding Meredith. Meredith and her secret-police mind, everything you say, do, or can be imagined to be thinking will be written down and eventually held against you. He isn't quite sure yet whether Meredith is out to hang him or to bed him, but he's too old and wary now to take any chances.

Vega he just likes to annoy. Always polite and always offi-cious in manner, always jangling his keys and saying, "Yes. Yes. Yes. Sí. Sí. Sí," his gestures ones of helpless resignation, I only work here, I'm just doing my job. Vega is the guy who sells stolen Army rifles to the Indians, then sells the Indians to the Army and gets a medal and a pension for it. Vega not only takes kickbacks from tenants, but from the landlord as well, if we can jack up the rent you'll get your cut, everybody's helpful friend.

He has stopped counting the scams he knows for certain Vega runs; stopped counting the lies in which he's caught him; stopped worrying about the money he takes from the more timid and gullible, convincing them that he is performing special favors. There aren't enough hours left to his life. And, anyway, he knows damn well who stole his bike.

Tony stuffs the notes under the cushions, drags himself to his feet, and, with Zorro hot on his trail, begins the evening rituals.

The first time the telephone rings he is in the bathroom, wearing his old Mao hat, sitting in the tub, dive-bombing the water with Pata, his plastic duck. It is almost impossible to get rubber ones anymore. Pata doesn't remind him of his carefree childhood (himself small and fat and always smiling, the sound of singing strolling in from every room), nor of those hours of preschool delirium (his mother kneeling by the side of the tub, scrubbing his sun-browned back with a striped cloth, rinsing his hair with water poured from a plastic pitcher, pretending, in laughter, to drown his bright yellow duck). She doesn't remind him of those gone-green days of his life's summer, when the moon was indeed a balloon to pull you up into the mystery of the sky, and the sun was a beckoning angel with warm, wide wings. Pata doesn't remind him of anything, actually. He saw the duck in a store downtown and bought her on impulse. She is good for relieving feelings of aggression. And, also, she keeps him busy when he is trying to ignore, as he is trying now, the soothing voice of Death attempting to lure him into conversation. And then he hears the phone ringing, life demanding its share of his time.

Wham goes Pata, and wham again.

Earlier, coming back from walking Zorro and stopping at López's for some shopping, he saw Death waving to him from the back of a bus, its face disturbingly beautiful, the eyes large and unquestioning, the mouth unsmiling but seductive, the hands waving hi ya Tony, how ya doin' kid?, the arms and shoulders smooth and bare. In this weather, everyone dresses lightly. He glimpsed it only for seconds while he stood beneath the faded awning, perpetually at half-mast, Zorro jumping against his knees, choking on his leash, his own body bent and fingers untying, the kid who does deliveries shouting after him, "Hey, Tony. I'll give ya that book back next week. Okay?" his eyes suddenly looking toward the street at the traffic moving by like a long march of robots, and the stage-set buildings of the city beyond, made aware by some half-dead sense of the face staring into his and the one hand waving through the impersonal night. And when the bus had moved on and the dog was untied and he'd yelled back that there was no hurry about the book, take your time, he was overcome by such a surge of unfocused yearning, by such a sensation of indiscriminate lust, that he was uncertain, for a moment, of whether he'd just arrived or had already been, standing there in his blue, hooded sweatshirt and carpenter's jeans, two cans of dog food, a six-pack of beer, and a loaf of bread in a paper bag tucked under his arm, the beating of his heart the only sound he could hear.

Were he the sort of man to believe in signs or visions, sempiternal destinies or the quicker-than-the-eye hand-signals of fate, he might at this instant be kneeling before a candle-lit altar, just like Grandma Maria, rattling his rosary, or hurrying through the dark forests of the Bronx, looking for a fortune-teller who comes highly recommended.

But he isn't.

Wham goes the duck and wham goes the water. And silent goes the telephone. He hasn't had this much fun since the night last May when he dropped the waterbomb on Liam Clancy, going out for the evening in his only suit. Tony knows, since the polarization of sides in the last tenants' strike (he on one and everyone else on the other), that Liam Clancy is not merely stupid but probably dangerous as well, but Sandy (though she laughed at the time, schoolboy pranks, as long as you are smiling when you do them and shake hands afterwards, are still okay, wanting to sue the New York City Police Department for wrongful assassination is not) is sure that Clancy is connected with the IRA and finds him, therefore, both fascinating and sincere, he's an okay guy, you've got him all wrong, at least he has the courage of his convictions.

He gives Pata a shove that sends her bobbing toward his feet. He knows, of course, that there is no one sitting in the next room with his or her lips close to the wall, whispering sweet nothings in his ear, hey, Tony, watcha gonna do if this is it? Hey, *amigo*, the cell door could swing shut tomorrow, what's it all been for? He knows that, really, but he no longer feels that it pays to be too sure.

And if it's not Death, what is it that he hears?

Life is just a bowl or cherries, don't take it serious, it's too mysterious . . . you something, you something, you worry so, but you can't take it with you when you go go go . . .

His eyes are closed, his body loose, the orange mouth of the duck grins moronically at the faucet. The song is neither on his lips nor in his head, but coming at him through his own time, the voice clear and unselfconsciously melodious, each word ringing like a tiny glass bell, Susan Kalinksi taking her morning shower in his mother's black and silver bathroom while he and his brothers brushed their teeth at the kitchen sink. She, too, has been haunting him for weeks. He can still hear the water hitting against the metal stall.

His mind no longer works on the usual linear, cause-and-effect level, but rolls and roams through the past, picking up memories like trail dust. His body may be walking down corridors, sitting on chairs, sidling toward other bodies and just slightly bending forward or bending away, but his mind trots down its own roads, ten twenty thirty years before. Still thirty, still twenty, still ten and four and eleven and a half. Still in the yellow gingham kitchen with the Mr. Peanut bank on the shelf that stretched from cabinet to cabinet across the window. Still sitting in an overstuffed armchair with a heavy floral cover, maroon piping down the seams, eyes not moving from the six-inch screen. Still lying awake all night listening to the cats wailing like old women in the alley after Nancy Ridell let him kiss her against the lockers at the Halloween Hop.

Lies that never came true, memories and death. All of them with him. All of them after him. All of them diluting his reality to such an extent that nothing seems to matter anymore. Death. A flaking fetus in a jar of formaldehyde, neatly labeled like a jar of pickles, Human Embryo, 10 Weeks—Sandy's child, his child—the lid secure and the bottle placed between Human Embryo 6 Weeks and Human Embryo 16 Weeks on the bottom shelf of the cabinet at the back of some high-school science lab. But, of course, that isn't true, their baby isn't on display. Their baby was vacuumed away like a ball of dust, whoosh, dead before it was ever born, over so quickly you could hardly say it had begun. Death.

Only this morning they found yet another of Parker's clients dead in her one-room apartment, lying on the bed under a lighted sign, Bar, the radio on, the front door locked and chained, lying there for four or five days before anyone missed her, before the super called the cops and they busted down the door, knowing what they'd find, another dead junkie, and the super wondering if there was anything worthwhile he could make off with. It happens all the time.

Parker is writing a poem about it. "At the rate your people are dying," said Tony, "you'll have an anthology before Thanksgiving." Parker didn't smile. He tracked Tony down at lunchtime to read him the first three verses, his eyes red with strain, saying, "It's only rough, you understand. It isn't in its final form yet." " 'Cool Angel'?" repeated Rivera, staring at the light reflected from Parker's gold-rimmed glasses. " 'Cool Angel'?" Encouraged, Parker leaned across the desk toward him, helping himself to a piece of lettuce from the recycled cottage cheese container that held the salad Sandy advises he have for lunch if he doesn't want to get fat like his mother, and which he still eats, unchecked, not out of guilt or sentimentality, but so, when she later says, "I suppose you've been stuffing yourself with carbohydrates while I was away," he can say "No," so there. "I was going to call it 'Cool Blue,' you know," said Parker, his heavy hands slapping shapes into the air, "cool jazz and blue veins and cool blues, you know, that sort of image. But I like 'Cool Angel' better. I think it implies everything that cool blue does, and more," helping himself to a round of carrot. "Don't you?" Crunch. Tony, trying to stab at a cube of soft tomato, breaking the tines of the plastic fork in a spray of Lo-Cal dressing, answered slowly, careful not to look Parker in the eyes, "I don't know, Larry. Don't you think it's a little too self-consciously ironic?" "Ironic?" echoed Parker. "What are you talking about, 'ironic'?" He's never so much as pretended to like Parker—who has only two moods, aggressive and edgy and depressed and sarcastic, and who fuels each with the writing of sincerely felt free verse and oboe lessons—but Parker is not the sort of man who would ever notice. "I don't know, Larry," starting to break off a piece of whole wheat pitta, but thinking better of it, "... cool like dead, angel like dust, you know ..." you know, nobody deserves a death with so little dignity, mourned only by a fifth-rate poem, stiff with guilt, you know. But Larry doesn't know—and maybe he is right, maybe it's better than nothing. "You don't know anything about poetry," snapped Parker, snatching the verses, written on the back of an old memo, economy = efficiency, from the desk top as though even the President of the United States wouldn't get him to reveal it now. "The ambiguity means every-thing. I'm trying for multiple images, Tony. I'm trying to link this one lonely, insignificant death with all of us." "Oh, yeah," mum-bled Tony. "Of course. Multiple images for a multiracial society." Parker stood up then and Tony watched a fragment of lettuce fall from his starched cotton workshirt to the carpet on the floor. "I don't know what's gotten into you lately, Tony, but I think you should know that I'm not the only one round here who has noticed," folding his first draft and putting it into the pocket of his shirt, letting the full import of his words have a chance to drip in. "It's not just me. Ever since you turned down that Boston promotion last winter, several people have commented ..." dropping his voice to the exact level for compassion, "... for quite some time ... your lack of seriousness ... your hostil-ity ... your frequent displays of pettiness ..." your lack of focus and personal ambition, your failure to evaluate clearly the needs and options of our technocratic, urban society, your paranoia, seeing the enemy all around you, your refusal to commit your-self to any long-range goals or short-range solutions, your irre-sponsible individualism, your predictable unpredictability, your lack of enthusiasm and passion on both great and small levels, the fact that you've taken to sleeping with your socks on as though you might have to make a run for it in the night. As he watched him, uninterested in hearing what he had to say, Parker became Sandy, reading his failings aloud from a list she had jotted down while drying her hair. As he listened to him, barely aware of what he was seeing, Parker became Sophie, whacking apart a slab of meat with a silver cleaver, swishwomp swishwomp, saying, her eyes on the pound of flesh, the wooden board, the rust-resistant blade, your father may have had a lot of faults, but sarcasm wasn't one of them, womp womp, making the salt and pepper shakers dance, your father may have been a son-of-a-bitch to live with, but at least he had spirit, raising her eyes to his just for a heartbeat, at least he was always a man of feeling, of passion, even if he didn't think too good. In Sophie's world, a person can have one of two things: a heart, or a head. The heart is often wrong, but the head is almost always treacherous. It was then that it began to sing itself, that other Susan Kalinski number, a memory he'd forgotten he remembered. And while Parker, gliding effortlessly into his role of superior and father figure, clapped a hand on the back of his chair as though embracing him as a friend and told him that if there was anything that was bothering him, anything at all, any problems at home or whatever, he knew, didn't he, that he could always come and talk to Larry Parker about it (after all, that's what he's there for, that's how he makes his living, that's what he's good at, other people's problems) Tony himself began to sing, *Good night, Irene, good night, Irene*, instantly back in that four-room walk-up, drying the dishes while Susan Kalinski washed and sang, *sometimes I live in the city, and sometimes I live in the town, and sometimes I take a great notion, to go down to the river and drown.* And through the sound of her voice over twenty years before, and the sound of his own right then in the small, sunny office with the empty goldfish bowl on the windowsill and the rice sack, A Gift from the People of the United States of America, on the wall, he heard Parker say, "That's exactly what I mean." "What is?" "That is. You're not even listening," turning his well-fed, well-preserved body around and disappearing through the door with a sigh. I'll see you in my dreams.

He can hear someone—it must be Meredith—pounding on the front door, the bell bleating steadily under some determined finger, we know you're in there, Rivera, you've got ten seconds to come on out. If he doesn't breathe, he can actually hear her voice, "Tony Tony Toneeee," you fuckin' well better come out.

He stands up suddenly, rocking the water in the tub, reaching for a towel.

Now the entire floor can probably hear her, "I know you're in there, Tony Rivera. Open this door!"

He grins at himself through the steam on the mirror, the hat askew, holding in his stomach, though the mirror is small.

Several voices have joined Meredith's in the hall, most of them ordering her to shut the hell up.

He pulls the hat down over his eyes and gives the mirror his best Castro-facing-Kennedy smile. Oh give me a break.

Skip is worried about Walt Disney. "That a man can build up something so monumental with his own imagination and his own guts," he is saying, in tones of wonderment, for at least the third time, "... that a man can actually change and influence his society to such an extent—and whatever you may think of him or his work, you have to admit the effect he had on this century, you have to give credit where it is due—and, the minute his back's turned, to have it all corrupted and destroyed ..." He can barely find the words.

"He didn't exactly turn his back," says Maggie, helping herself to more salad. "He died. It's not like turning your back at all."

Skip waves his fork in the air, stabbing at diversions. "You know what I mean." He turns back to his plate, spears a piece of chicken, lifts it to his mouth, and, poking it in, chews as his fork goes back down to scoop up some peas, she watching him all the while as though he is doing something astonishing. "You should try some of the chicken," he says, "it's terrific."

She grinds pepper over her own meal. "I can't eat chicken, you know that."

"But you cook it," he reminds her, pausing in his eating and his talking and his worrying about the destiny of genius to look directly at her with his bright, open gaze, can't fool me.

"But I can't eat it," thinking of all those hormones and those tatty, sinister pens, packed with scrawny fowls, their little heads just sticking through the bars; looking at the roasted meat and seeing little legs and little wings, imagining equally small hearts and lungs, arteries, and veins. She cuts a slice of tomato in half. "It's different."

"That's just what the Nazis said," he teases, dazzling her with a flash of his haven't-had-a-cavity-in-twelve-years teeth, and just a glimpse of his perfect gums.

And she smiles back, her own teeth neither so white nor so flawless, though they have improved noticeably under his care.

"Anyway," he continues, suddenly remembering where he was, "it certainly makes you think."

"Chicken?"

"Geesus," shaking his head good-naturedly. "Not chicken, you dope. Walt Disney." He pours them both more wine.

"Oh. Walt Disney," and is gone for a second, her hand just raising her glass, wondering what it is about which Walt Disney could possibly make you think. That the world will yet be saved by a band of cheerful, warm-hearted, lovable, and efficient animals dressed in caps and jackets and whistling as they work? That there is hope for a planet that can still find a place in its hearts and in its pockets for the delightful, the magical, the sentimental and the unwildly imaginative? Can a mind capable of seeing everything—from water moccasin to nuclear reactor—as basically human be all that bad?

"The fragility of it all," he says, wiping his mouth on a paper napkin, just noticing that she doesn't seem to understand what he's trying to say. "To put everything you are into something and then have it all used for something else ... all changed. Have your name used for something that is the opposite of everything you ever stood for."

Maggie blinks, picking a piece of lettuce from her hair, a sign of even further confusion. When she was little and didn't understand what was being said, she would always answer with "What?" what what what what what, until her mother, fearing she might be deaf in one ear like Mrs. Clark's son, took her to the doctor for tests, hearing perfect. Older now, Maggie merely blinks. "You mean like Christianity?"

"Christianity?" looking like a man who thought he'd bought two pounds of apples but who finds, on returning home, that he has, instead, bought one pound of pears.

"Uh huh. Like Christ and Christianity." She's with him now. "You know."

"No," says Skip, tossing a picked-clean bone on to the serving platter. "Like Walt Disney and the things the Walt Disney studios are coming out with now."

He is fair-skinned, fair-haired, and lightly freckled, large framed and solid, handsome in a way that has always been and will always be uninteresting and boyish. "Oh."

"Remember? I showed you the ad."

"Oh, yeah," that. He'd read it to her while she was mixing the dressing, this ain't no fairy tale.

"It just really makes you think," he says, a private incantation, and sighs so that she knows that he is thinking.

But about what? Who will inherit his drills and his mint-condition record collection? Who will remember his superb capping and the pamphlet he wrote for children, *Timmy Tooth and the Bad Day?*

"Sometimes I just don't know what's happening to the world," he says, beginning to stack the plates, scraping the garbage from one onto the garbage of another, putting the forks and knives and spoons together. "Don't you know what I mean?"

She watches him as, his back to her, he shovels the bones and uneaten scraps into the red pedal-bin, his neat, pearl-buttoned cowboy shirt and his creased jeans, his mind bent in contemplation. He still hasn't totally recovered from the murder of John Lennon.

Oh, yes, she knows.

He turns on the flame under the kettle, takes out a clean filter and fits it into the Melitta he bought her, there's no point in drinking coffee if it's not made right. "It'll be different once we get out of the city," he says, still turned to his task. "You'll see. We'll be able to concentrate on the things that count." She has never asked him what those things might be. He assumes that they agree.

She helps him put the cups on the table; the cups, the spoons, the jug of milk, the bowl of sugar. Unlike Maggie, Skip doesn't like to live out of containers, slap-dash and half-ass is how he describes it, all right for camping trips, all right, maybe, when you're out on a boat, but not all right at home. Already, he has begun to make changes.

She has been trying hard to imagine them out of the dirt and danger of the city, away from the high risks of disease and violence, and safe in a world of sky and grass and spreading trees. Where the things that really count still do. Where a man and a woman can still join hands under God's big sky and build a life for themselves with only the sweat of their brows and the dreams in their hearts. She has been trying. After all, it did her no appreciable harm to have a front lawn and a back garden, a three-speed bike, Girl Scouts, dancing lessons, summer camp, all that air, and all those prospering white faces. It had worked, hadn't it? The good schools and the extracurricular activities. Her parents' life, so predictable and so set, had also worked, from a certain point of view. It was not what she had thought that she would want when she was young and full, as her father used to say, of beans. It was not the life she had imagined when, stretched out on the white popcorn spread of her bed, she had made her girlish plans and fantasized a future full of independence and adventure, art and eccentricity, romance and freedom. A future in which she featured as strong and unyielding, adored but never possessed by fierce, inspired men. A future of promise and multiple meanings. A life that others, less spirited and less imaginative, might fear but would wish that they could emulate. She was going to be an artist, or something like that. A life that others might sing about or write about or whisper about with mouths bent in shock and wonder over cups of instant coffee, glasses of imported wine. She was going to live. A real life, not a cardboard imitation, neatly glued onto a board. Of course, the life she's been having has not been that, either. Of course, she didn't know then what she does know now.

Already, he is planning the life they will lead when they move to the country. He saw the house he has always wanted months ago, but he had no reason to buy it, then. What would he have done, in the middle of somewhere, all on his own, even if it is architecturally unique and has beamed ceilings? At first, he had been thinking of it as a summer house, a place to go on weekends, a little something on the side, but, a piece of luck, it just so happens that there is a practice coming up soon in a nearby town, surely it's a sign. He won't make what he can make in the city, but they won't starve.

Skip is convinced that the blame for the failure of his first marriage (when he doesn't see it as resting entirely with his ex-wife, the status-seeking bitch) lies rather heavily with metropolitan living. The pressures. The anxieties. The constant competition. The corruption and dissolution of traditional American values and life. Whatever happened to good old common sense?

He might well ask.

Next to the tragedy of his not being accepted into any medical school north of the border, the collapse of his marriage has been the worst thing that has ever happened to Skip.

It scared the shit out of him. Those interminable weekend afternoons, time passing not even as slow-motion film but as a series of snapshots, click click click click click click. It confused him, made him feel vulnerable and unsure, and he the boy his kindergarten teacher would have voted Most Likely to Succeed. Those agonizing weekday nights, the solitary meals, the clumsy seductions, the tipsy titillations in expectantly crowded bars, hello, my name's Nelson, a dollar for your thoughts. The repetitious days becoming weeks becoming months, everyone having somewhere to go and someone with whom to go there—everyone but he. For the first time in his life as a social creature—patiently schooled by his parents to get along with everyone but to never let anyone get the better of him—he had reason to doubt his own rightness. Reason to suspect his own superiority. What had he ever done to deserve any of this? For the first time in his life as member of a larger group, he saw his image of himself (nicer and smarter and more deserving and having more on the ball than most everyone else) distort to the point of being grotesque. How could that be he, Nelson Ellis, Jr., slumped in front of the television with a can of beer like some minor character in a soap opera, paralyzed by fear, afraid to make a move in case it might be the wrong one, in case it might attract even more disaster? Was that he, Nelson Ellis, Jr., hunched over the antique desk his parents bought for him when he was accepted at the university of their choice, composing an advertisement for the back pages of the *New York Review of Books*: Quiet, sensitive, caring, intelligent, good-looking professional man, still young, seeking sincere, attractive woman who cares more about love than limousines? He had never, of course, doubted how much he had to lose (not everyone has his advantages, has his brains, has his charm), but it had never before occurred to him that it might be easy to lose it. His obsession with the telephone (would it ring? wouldn't it ring? had it already rung?) took on mythic proportions, grown from a sophisticated instrument of communication into a sadistic cacodemon whose only function in the scheme of things was to torment him, you just missed it, making him wake in the middle of the night, breathless and damp with sweat, was that the phone? He never wanted to live like that, and he certainly never wants to live like that again. He is totally uninterested in discovering to what great depths it might be possible for him to sink.

And so he builds his converted mills in the heavens over Upper New York State. He already has a name for the boat. Blue Skies. Has he never told her how much he loves fishing? Has he never told her how he's always dreamed of having a son to go fishing with him? He took his daughters when they were still his daughters, but the older one thought it was boring and the younger one vomited when she saw the bait. Has he never told her how much he has always enjoyed walking, rambling o'er the woods and fields, how he is able to identify twelve different types of trees and to leave a trail a party of Boy Scouts could easily follow? And Maggie, who (when she was eighteen, or twenty-eight) would have laughed and said, "And I thought Back to Nature was the name of a health-food drink," now smiles and says, "Oh, terrific" every time he lays another log. Hitch your wagon to a Toyota.

She watches Skip precisely pour three-quarters of a cup of coffee for each of them, not spilling one drop.

"So, it's all settled, then," he is saying now. "It'll kill two birds with one stone."

And which two birds would those be?

She has been trying to picture them living happily ever after, but can get no further than the smiles they both are wearing as they stand, holding waists, waving hello and waving good-bye in front of a wagon-wheel garden box on the front lawn. "What will?"

He gives her a smile that suggests that, though exasperating, she is none the less adorable. "Going up to the Grossmans' for the Fourth. That way we can go up and see the house and then go over to the party and come back the next day. It's perfect."

She doesn't say anything in words, but the expression on her lips is oh yeah?

"Don't you think so?"

"I don't know, Skip," she says, surprised to hear her own voice sound so soft and slightly petulant. He is changing a lot more than the way she serves the sugar. "I don't really like parties."

"What do you mean you don't like parties?" his blue eyes puzzled. "Everybody likes parties," saying it in such a way that it sounds as though it must be true.

"I don't."

Then the frown is replaced by a disarming smile, of course, she's teasing. "Don't be silly," moving one hand forward, as though about to pat her on the head. "Of course you do. And anyway, Sandy will be disappointed if we don't show up."

Maggie smiles, her teeth hidden by the tight stretch of her lips.

Maggie's father—whose idea of heaven was to be left alone in his partially finished basement with his magazines and his mystery novels—when asked, usually tearfully, by his wife why they couldn't go somewhere different on their vacation, Gettysburg or Los Angeles, look at the wonderful time Phil and Dotty had in Arizona, always used to say that he didn't have to go to hell to know that he wouldn't like it there. Just so, Maggie didn't have to live with Sandy, two weeks in two rooms, bath and kitchen, to know that she didn't like her. There was no need to put it to the test. Two weeks of having her drawers reorganized and her time-efficiency assessed. Two weeks of enforced compatibility, do you mind? is it all right? oh, I didn't know you were keeping that for something, oh, that's okay, I wasn't really asleep. Two weeks of Sandy bristling through the tiny rooms, one minute slumped in the corner like an orphan in the sun, the next stamping her feet and pounding her fists, I'm not going to take this lying down. She took Sandy in in a moment of compassion (it is not only men who hate to see a woman cry), but that compassion was only a memory by the Saturday morning, Sandy sitting across from her at the table, looking horrified, you mean you've never been on a march? not even in the sixties?

Sandra Grossman has a reputation—dating from about the age of four—for being a person who is always direct. What you see is what you get. She was never one for diplomatic pretense or polite politicking, although she also never forgets her manners. When other little girls would cross their ankles and dimple coyly at the proffered coin from an indulgent uncle or aunt, blushing shyly that they really couldn't take it, Sandra would simply and gracefully accept, her small white hand extended, saying thank you very much, and pocketing the present quickly before anyone's mind could be changed. When the other little girls, sitting on the fence of the schoolyard with their skirts pulled over their knees, giggled and whispered among themselves as the boys noisily played softball, Sandra was the one who jumped down from the fence, talked her way into a turn at bat, and then hit three men home. While the other girls sat on the painted bleachers on one side of the gym while the boys stood at the other, talking in low voices, casually slipping out from time to time for a smoke in the john, and the music played loudly and the chaperones tried to look both friendly and fierce, and the only dancers were the couples who were going steady (and then only when the dance was slow), it was Sandra Grossman who marched fearlessly across the parquet floor and asked David Schwartz to dance. She was the first girl on her block to use a tampon, own a diaphragm, or be expelled from homeroom for refusing to pledge the flag. In high school alone, she led two sit-ins in the cafeteria, one on the science labs, and one silent vigil outside of the library to commemorate the bombing of Hiroshima. She was also a straight-A student, president of the senior class, and reputed to be a good influence on some of the other girls who, unaware of the sociopolitical implications of mass market advertising, the fascistic tendencies of the military–big business complex, the reactionary foundations of the medical monopoly and the subtle, polished politics of sexism and racism, were either always drunk, always stoned, or by and large not there. Teachers described her as having a logical, inquisitive mind, applauding her youthful idealism and sense of purpose. Parents found her reliable and mature, disarmed by her simple level-headedness, no silly tantrums here. Peers found her bossy and, often, not a little daunting, but, because she was impossible to victimize, all right. Everyone always agreed that she probably meant well. It is only people like her mother-in-law who have ever pointed out the many uses put to roads paved by good intentions. Just as it has been only Sophie who has ever suggested that, though there are benefits to be had from having both feet on the ground, the view from that position is not only limited but dependent on the location of the ground in question. Until now, that is.

Maggie would say that though there is a lot that is admirable in Sandy—her energy, her unflagging enthusiasm, her ability to synthesize and analyze information quickly and logically so that she can tell you in a matter of minutes for which candidate you should vote, which toothpaste you should choose, her facility at debate—not everything depends on being able to get the trains to run on time. Who could live with a woman who has devised her own filing system, cross-indexed, for her favorite back issues of at least six different newspapers and magazines? Who could speak for more than two days to a woman who is constantly clipping the dead leaves off your plants, wiping the table clean even while you are eating, I don't know how you can stand these cat hairs everywhere? Who could cohabit with anyone who begins every sentence with the word "I," I think, I feel, I know, I want, I need, I understand his point of view her point of view their point of view, but...?

Apparently, Skip could.

Though Maggie thinks that for a person who seems such an expert on female oppression, repression, and guilt, Sandy exhibits few of the symptoms or consequences herself, Skip has been moved by her plight and her pain (you don't know this guy, Maggie, he's really impossible), finds her sympathetic and vulnerable.

Though Sandy's presence made Maggie tetchy and short-tempered, snappish, and ungracious, it made Skip more gentle and more kindly than he already was, so patient and so sensitive that it was humbling just to be around him, oh, why am I such a bitch?

Maggie studies Skip from behind her raised cup (though it is already empty, he never makes enough), wondering what really goes on in his handsome head. He is off again about the house and how much she'll love it, about the room that will be her workroom, and the room that will be his study, about the good schools and the local craftsmen, it isn't just another town in the sticks, as though there have been no differences between them—as though there aren't a few still hanging around.

Skip likes Sandy. She belongs to that group of people he calls "real folk." It is obvious, he says, that she is a decent, intelligent and warmhearted woman who has suffered mightily at the hands and tongue of a self-centered bastard who was probably never good enough for her to begin with. "Suffered?" asked Maggie. "Sandra?" But he was not aware that it was a question, thought he heard an echo. "She's a really nice person," he said, which she very well may be, "and she's so unhappy," which she most certainly is. Moved by a selfless empathy Maggie could not hope to emulate ("But every time I put something in one place she moves it somewhere else," "But I don't care what she did in college," "But I know that yoga's good for you"), he included her in all their outings. They went out to dinner ("You mean you've never been to a real Vietnamese restaurant? You're in for a surprise"), they went out to the movies ("Oh, I've seen that one. I've seen that one, too. Now there's a Czech film across town . . ."), they went out to the park ("Don't you just love to be outdoors?"), they went out on the town ("I know you're going to love this place. It hasn't been discovered by anyone yet"). They couldn't let her sit in the apartment alone, brooding. Could they? "But what about all her other friends?" whose virtues and tribulations had all been well-documented. "What about all her committees and projects and saving the whale?" "I'm surprised at you, Maggie," said Skip. "I thought you were more understanding." You, another woman, I thought you'd find it easy to be kind. When they made love, quietly and self-consciously, no point in rubbing it in, she could not shake the feeling that, out in the living room, Sandy lay immobile on the couch, keeping score, God, you should hear the racket she makes, I don't know who she's trying to impress.

On the whole, Sandy's occupation of their territory had shown Skip as a sensitive, patient, kind, and endlessly understanding man who would always do what he could for another human being in trouble. And Maggie as a petty, possessive and small-hearted witch who couldn't put herself out for just a couple of days for another woman in distress without making everybody pay for it. It was Skip who offered the shoulder to cry on. Skip who brought in wine and pizza and the Monopoly game he's had since he was ten. Skip who sat up making coffee till one in the morning while Sandy whispered her unhappiness and Maggie cut out sundresses the way the settlers cut out a path to the West. It was Skip who made Sandy laugh, there, that's better, you see? He is more than an excellent dentist, he is a good soul as well. Reasonable with his righteousness, it was Skip who explained to Maggie just how shattered Sandra was, how bewildered and panicky she has been made by the fundamental problems that lie like an iceberg between her and Rivera. "Which either means," said Maggie, neither reasonable nor understanding and certainly not patient, "that she's either just figured out that he's a man and she's a woman, or that she's just figured out what a shallow jackass he really is," or vice versa. "I'd never have believed you could be so mean," said Skip, as disappointed as he was when Watergate broke, watching the bus slowly rumble from the terminal, Sandy at the window waving so long, thank you, thanks. "You really surprised me." And shook his head slowly and sadly, like the old police chief shaking his head at the kid to whom he tried to give an even break. "You really surprised me, too," said Maggie. After all, she'd never been told who else's dentist he was.

"I can't wait for you to see it," he is saying now, and looks so happy that she must relent.

"Me, too." Beneath the table, her naked toes begin to fool around with his hundred-percent cotton socks, and, inadvertently, his ex-athlete's feet.

In fact, Skip was more than happy to see Sandy go. Spending long nights in a midget apartment with two so different women, each of whom thinks she knows you better than the other, each of whom, in some way, holds you responsible for at least a part of her happiness, is no sane man's idea of a good time. Even under the best of conditions (though what, he has wondered, could those possibly be?), it is one of those experiences, like being shot in the stomach at close range, which is better learned from movies than from life. Although, on the whole, he thinks things went pretty well—given all the contingencies that might have gone so wrong—he still jumps when a female voice calls his name, which one is it and what does she want? It was not, he thinks, unlike spending a rainy weekend with his daughters, but you said we'd go to the zoo, but you let her have one after she brushed her teeth, but I don't like Chinese food, he in the middle trying to keep everybody happy, he gripped between them, trying to keep everyone amused. And so if he did, once or twice, give Sandy a secret cuddle or a secretive kiss, stroke a breast while stroking an arm, so what? And so if he did get an extra kick out of having Maggie in the hushed night, knowing that every time he heard a spring groan, Sandy heard it too, so what? Who got hurt? He has danced around the arena with the bull, swirling his cape and playing with his sword, courting danger, even death, his movements immaculate, his bearing proud, and not only has he come out alive, he has come out well, each of the ladies in the stand thinking he acted out of courage and wisdom, each of the ladies thinking, somehow, that he was doing it just for her. None the less, when it was time for Sandy to go he not only helped her pack he insisted on carrying her bags, buying her lunch before her departure, and giving her a paperback to read on the journey. So great was his relief, that he now believes they can all be friends.

"I just wish you'd ... you know ... try to like Sandy a little more," he says sincerely. "I know she can be a little domineering ..." his foot moving beneath hers, slowly slowly, back and forth, "but she means well. She really is pretty upset."

"I know that," says Maggie, sandwiching his toes. "She said it was like going to bed with Prince Charming and waking up next to Dopey."

Skip is disarmed. "Sandy said that?"

"Well, not in so many words. But the meaning was the same," flashing him one of her more alluring smiles.

Skip smiles back. "What did Sandy say?"

"She said it was a rude awakening," and winks.

Over the cups and pitcher and bowl and the white metal top of the table, she grins at him and he grins at her. He loves it when she's playful. It's when he likes her best. It makes him feel as though they share some special secret, some private joke. Though, if he thought about it any further, he might realize that he has no idea what it is.

Against the pale blue of the kitchen wall, her hair fans out like the silhouette of a hill, her eyes are dark as caves. There are times—and this is one of them—when just the sight of her makes him want to wrap his body around her and never let go. Under the circumstances, it is difficult to continue worrying about Sandra, no matter how great her trials.

"How about," he says, his gaze shifting from the warm bow of her mouth to the curved warmth of her breasts, "if I make some more coffee and pour a couple of brandies, and we go into the other room?"

She doesn't ask which other room. "What about the dishes?" knowing how much he hates to leave a mess. It's part of his professional training. She catches his foot between her ankles.

"I'll do them before I go to work," not resisting, passion's willing prisoner.

And is she content that the rest of her life will be composed of many evenings just like this one, warm and familiar, comfortable and reassuring? Content that her remaining life will be spent in a beautiful home that long ago was a hard-working mill, teetering over the edge of a lush and not so primal valley, the river gone, in a tamed wilderness only a car ride from the center of the known world, her shoes on one side of the bed and his on the other, everything between them unexplored and, therefore, unresolved? And that, in time, there will be another child, a new child, different from the first and yet the same, conceived with purpose not bad luck, raised by rules that are tried and true, not instinct and whim?

Oh, yes, she is. She has made a pact with the temperamental, vengeful forces of the universe: let me have this and I will bother you no more.

Does it matter not that, sleeping in his half-embrace—his knees bent behind hers, his arm across her, hands just touching—the dreams that stir her heart are all such small ones? That the peace that soothes the currents of her blood is the same peace that comes when, sickened of the battle, defeated by the carnage and the waste and the futility of even failure, the bloodied warrior lies down among the smoking ruins of the land that was once his hope and home, and waits to simply never wake again?

"But I'm telling you," sighs Meredith into the mouthpiece of the phone, scraping something hard but sticky from the dial with a spoon. "He won't answer the door. I've been banging on it for hours."

"Well, stick a note through," says Sandy, up where the air is cool and clear and reason still persists. "He'll respond to that."

"But I've put notes through. All that happens is he avoids me harder than ever, and two days later I get a postcard in the mail of a rainbow trout or some dead hillbilly." She gives up scraping, moves her face in front of the fan.

Sandy watches Jack and Edith through the sliding glass doors, lugging the lawn furniture into the screen porch for the night because Edith thinks it's going to rain. "And what do they say?"

"How the hell should I know?" asked Meredith. "I don't read Spanish. And I can't get Vega to translate because they're at it worse than ever." The Rivera–Vega matches have kept at least some of the tenants amused and even edified for years, but Sandy turned against them last year when instead of sticking to verbal abuse and practical jokes, Rivera started dragging in the Health Inspector, the Housing Commission, or the cops every time a garbage can was left in the basement or the heat went out, I'm warning you, you bastard, somebody's going to hear about this. "Go talk to the landlord," Sandy would say, reasonably. "The landlord?" Tony would squawk. "You don't think he cares, do you? He's happy to have someone as dishonest as he is picking up all the crumbs he can't reach himself." "I don't know what this sudden obsession of yours with the law is," she would counter, you who have always held it in such contempt, if they can't get you comin' they'll get you goin'. But all he would answer to that was, "A people's war cannot be begun until every hope of legal redress has been exhausted," and though she had been pretty sure he was quoting, she could no longer remember whom, didn't really care. And she the girl who wanted to go to Cuba and harvest sugarcane, but Jack had talked her out of it, don't get involved, they'll forgive Hitler sooner than they'll forgive Castro.

"He hasn't called in the cops again, has he?"

Meredith closes her eyes as the fan blows warm air against her face and throat, imagining her skin being teased by some salty island breeze. "I don't think so. It's just the cards. And every time he sees him or Rice he starts singing some song about not putting a price on his soul."

"Well, thank God for that," says Sandy. Maybe he really is settling down. Maybe he really is finally taking her seriously. Maybe this time when he says he's sorry he will truly mean it; when he says he can change, sincere.

Sandy is already feeling better, feeling more like her old self than she has for months. Though the days before school closed and she was free to head north seemed endless, already the country has begun to work its magic. Then, too, once she was over the shock of Skip's impending marriage, and could cope with it as she knew she should (with genuine gladness for him; he is her friend, she wants him to be happy) (realistically; they were infatuated with one another for a while, but it couldn't last, was one of those things), she immediately began to feel more rational and in control. At least now the issues are clear. It is no longer a question of what am I doing with Tony? with Skip?—but what am I doing with Tony? She can no longer use Skip to obfuscate her real problems. Now she sees that the affair with Skip was an act of desperation. Short of moving to New Zealand, she could have gotten no farther from Tony and his confusion than Skip and his serenity. Where Tony made everything complicated, difficult, and tricky, Skip made everything simple. Skip still has a young man's body, a young man's enthusiasm. He isn't querulous and bitter, putting on weight and putting up objections. He isn't bored and hostile, putting up barriers and putting down everyone else. Now that she has finished with Skip, however, she can be desperate no more, can waste no more time on diversions. She feels ready now to take a deep breath and set about straightening out her life.

"I don't know," Meredith is saying. "All winter I can't wait for the summer. And then when the summer comes I can't wait for it to start getting cool again. By next year I won't even be able to go out in public in a bathing suit anymore."

Jack and Edith come in, bickering about the right way to do up the garden hose.

"I better go now," says Sandy. "Try putting another message under the door. And thank you, Mer. I appreciate all you've done."

"Oh, that's all right. I know you do," says Meredith, who knows she does.

"Was that Tony?" asks Edith, anxious for clues as to what is going on.

"No," says Sandy. "That was Meredith."

"Haven't you gotten through to him yet?"

Has anyone ever? "No," says Sandy, but does not mention the number of times she has tried (the Indian restaurant, the Queens disco, the Jamaican bakery, she shouting at him, "Come on, Tony, stop fooling around"). It is never wise to tell Edith too much.

"How about a drink?" suggests Jack, who isn't interested in what is or is not going on.

"Oh, that's a good idea," says Edith. "What will we drink to?"

Jack winks at Sandy over the bottles of liquor on top of the tea cart.

"It's not a special occasion, Mom. We don't have to make a toast."

"I know that," says Edith. "I just feel like drinking to something for a change—to the summer ... or the roses ... or something like that. "

"Edie," says Jack, handing her the ice bucket to be filled. "Let's not drink to anything. Let's just drink."

THREE

There is beer in the keg, homemade sangría in a plastic garbage pail, and toothpicks with the American flag on one end stuck into chunks of cheese. At exactly ten-thirty, Jack, wearing his Remember Watergate T-shirt, rolled from behind the bar and, by the light of the bugless candles, set off over one hundred dollars' worth of illegal fireworks into the gigantic night. Waterfalls and shooting stars, sunbursts and starbursts and whining rockets, fantastic fountains, and phantasmagoric patterns, wow.

"You will be careful, Jack, won't you?" nagged Edith, smiling so that everyone, especially Jack, would know she was saying it only because someone must.

"I do this every year, Edith," said Jack, cigar in mouth, hands gesturing everyone back. "For Chrissake, I know what I'm doing." His hand touched her knee and she stepped back into the invisible safety zone, appeased. She believed him. She would never think that the mere fact that something hasn't gone wrong before doesn't mean that it won't go wrong now. And they were right. Nothing went wrong. Nothing exploded in anyone's face. Nothing caught on fire. Everyone thought that this year's display was better than last year's, standing on the patio, holding their drinks, while over the trees the sky dripped neon tears, dripped rainbows, threw away amorphous jewels. Stood holding their glasses and their paper plates on the flagstone enclosure which looked as though it had just been the scene of a gunfight (where would all the bodies be when the smoke finally cleared?), Jack saying that next year he would have to get more of those whizzing things, Skip saying that you had to hand it to the Chinese. Several of the guests became nostalgic, recalling their childhood Fourth of July celebrations—the picnics and the parades, the American Legion clambake, the high-school band dragged out of its summer retirement, oh, say, can you see—and the man from across the road, who had had more than a reasonable share of Jack's world famous Bloody Marys, began to recite "The Midnight Ride of Paul Revere," but couldn't get past the first line. Charlie, whose older friends and patients actually call him Doc, made what was for him a pretty profound little speech about the responsibilities and strengths of the democratic system, concluding that, no matter what mistakes may be made from time to time, and there have been some doozeys, it was a pretty good thing, he should say, to live in a country where anybody still could become President. And no one laughed.

"Hey, Doc," called a voice from the fringe of the group. "How long do you think it will be before we have a Puerto Rican President?" Street gangs doping themselves up in the room where Grant once slept, choppers tearing up the White House lawn, cans of Budweiser in the silver ice buckets, brass knuckles and switchblades on Lincoln's desk, boots and elbows on Eleanor Roosevelt's favorite table, dusky-skinned, red-lipped women in tight skirts and stilettos doing it for money in the room where Jack and Jackie once kissed each other good night.

"When they're ready," said Charlie in his diagnostic voice, "the opportunity will be there." And was immediately bundled into the house by Jack, wanting to know the truth about Valium, before Tony had a chance to reply to the reply.

Probably the only intelligent conversation Tony has had all night has been with Will, sitting on his shoulders to watch the fireworks. "Hey, Tony," said Will, "what's that awful smell?" "Gunsmoke." "Hey, Tony," said Will, "when are we gonna have the toasted marshmallows?" "Soon." "Hey, Tony," said Will, "when are we gonna look for the deer?" "Tomorrow, when it's light out and we can see them." "Hey, Tony, can I have some more soda?" "Hey, Will?" said Tony. "Don't you like the fireworks?" And Will had folded his small but pudgy arms on Tony's head. "Yeah," he said, thoughtfully, God watching Adam pitch on to his knees, "it's not so bad."

No one else, it would seem, is particularly interested in talking to him. As though they all know something he doesn't know, that he has already been shelved, returned to the manufacturer as substandard goods, oh, him? he used to be my husband, oh, him? he used to be married to my daughter, she married very young. Even Jack has only baited him a half-dozen times or so in the two days he's been up here, and those halfheartedly, as though he counts for so little now that there isn't any point in wasting a good argument.

And Sandra, whose summons is responsible for him being here in the first place, "I want you to come up so we have some time and some space to talk," doesn't seem to be interested in speaking to him at all. Apart from a quick kiss and hug when she met him, Meredith, and Will at the bus, she has kept at least ten and a half inches between them at all times, arranging for them to have the sleeping bags on the screened porch so that Meredith and Will could have her old room, her mind filled with nothing except the plans for the party, the foul-ups in the plans for the party, Edith's garden and her problems with the rabbits, and Jack's new obsession with the multinational drug companies, first against the wall.

Every time he says that he only endured the journey up so that he could talk to her, that she is the only reason he came, he can get barbecued spareribs back in the city, she says, yes, she wants to talk, too, but they can't talk with everyone running in and out and so much to do.

Last night, after everyone else had gone off to bed, he came into the living room just as she was coming in from the garden, an expression on her face that was at once warlike and dreamy. Her multicolored socks were clumped around her ankles, her ponytails were bobbing. Stopped by the sight of her, he half-expected her to turn and say to him, "Would you want to go for a drink later on?" the way she once did, later leading him through the thick August night to a place she knew, all the while talking and asking, arguing and listening, what do you think? do you think ... what would you do? oh, I think so, too. So strong was the sensation that he could taste again the beer and pretzels on her breath and tongue, feel again the indescribable softness of her skin, as, sitting on the couch in her apartment, drinking coffee and discussing city government, he slid his hands under her pink T-shirt, would you like me to rub your back?

There are men for whom women are the last frontier (and the first as well), but Tony Rivera is not one of them. If he were, it would at least give him something to do. Or, as Sandra said the night she found him working on the lyrics to "Come Back, Richard Nixon, All Is Forgiven," an original composition, instead of on the article he was meant to be writing about the economic and societal roots of mental illness as a contemporary, urban disease, why can't he just fall for some impressionable young girl or become cunt-fixated like all the other men his age? But he is a long way away from those days when sex seemed like an end in itself, himself split into two, the one manipulated by his mind and the other under penis-control, when having an orgasm could be thought to make any difference. A long long way.

And yet, standing, nearly breathless, at one end of the room, gazing at the spot where Sandy vanished into the kitchen without so much as a glance in his direction, he could think of nothing but of having her. Standing where the Navajo rug hides the burn mark in the floor, pole-axed by desire, he was less stunned by the ferocity of his feelings than by their familiarity. When had he felt like this before?

And so he'd followed her into the kitchen where she sat at the table with a pad and pencil in front of her, waiting for the water to boil.

He watched her in such a way that it was not obvious that that was what he was doing (though there was no reason to suppose that she would have noticed or cared), watched the slope of her shoulders and the curve of her breasts, the way her leg was tucked under her so that her heel was touching her ass. She is the most familiar person in the world to him, other than himself, but as he watched her then, noticing, especially, the straightness of her brows and the clearness of her skin, and the way she seems to disappear, right before your eyes, when she is thinking about something, he was aware, so vividly that it came as a surprise, that he would never know her.

"How about a beer?" he asked finally, neither moving toward her nor moving away.

For a moment it seemed as though she hadn't heard him, but then she said, nodding her head, "I'm making tea, thanks."

He came up behind her, his lips just brushed by the wisps of hair too short to be held by the bright blue elastics, and whispered wickedly in her ear, "Sure? Not even half a can?"

It is an old joke between them, and one which she has obviously forgotten. "No thanks."

"How about a glass of wine?" his fingers massaging her firm round shoulders and her long, lean neck. "Feel better?"

"I don't want my neck rubbed, Tony. I'm not in the mood." She had yet to look him in the eyes.

Slowly, as though governed by their own will, his hands moved down her arms, as though they had every right in the world to be there, and up and down and then across the red-and-white of her blouse, to stroke her breasts gently.

"Tony."

He didn't have to look to see her nipples rise. "We could open a bottle of wine. Jack won't care." In the old days, when they were such good friends, she would have been sliding the shirt over her head, letting it drop, with all resistance, to the floor.

But his hands were all that dropped this time. "Not now, Tony. I told you."

"You told me you didn't want to talk."

"My tea," she cried, jumping up so quickly that he fell forward and nearly knocked her down again.

"Okay," he'd said, grabbing the flashlight from on top of the refrigerator, a bottle of wine from the case on the floor, the corkscrew from the pegboard. "Suit yourself," and had gone banging out the door and into the deceptive solitude of the night, tripping and groping, disturbing countless tiny lives. He sat in the bushes, drinking to the dawn, wondering what was wrong with him that he couldn't make her say a simple yes or simple no, what was wrong with them that they would prefer to stay stuck in the mud of their own fears and mistakes than to move a step in any direction. Round about four-thirty, it occurred to him that it was probably quicksand and not mud at all.

Today, pulling into the driveway, returning from the very last trip into town, a trip in which she'd said nothing to him not connected with either food or drink, he asked her how she was feeling, and she said that the pain from the sunburn had finally gone. Later he asked her, cutting the celery, pepper, carrot sticks, and cauliflower buds, if she'd come to any new decisions since she'd been away, and she had shouted for Meredith to bring the willow platter from the dry sink in the living room. And Tony had slammed the vegetable knife onto the chopping block. "For God's sake, I've just asked you a question." "Oh, Tony," said Sandy, looking up from her carrot but not ceasing midslice. "I'm sorry. It's just that there's still so much to do," tossing the strips into a plastic bag. "What was it?" "Oh, nothing," he'd capitu-lated, slivering the celery. "It doesn't matter," looking up at the darkened knotty pine cabinets with their made-to-look-like-wrought-iron handles, seeing Death with a perfect O mouth looking right back, what's ta remember?

What indeed?

And then Meredith came thumping through the door, her hair in braids and a bandanna around her head, her nose smudged from helping with the dusting, is this the one you mean?

Oh, Meredith.

Maybe he should have borrowed someone's old Chevy with white walls, glinting chrome, and pom-poms swinging in the back window, and come up on his own, suddenly appearing in a cloud of dust and a squeal of brakes only inches from Edith's roses. Honking the horn like a man with whom it would be suicide to trifle, whistling with two fingers in his mouth, hey, Sandy, come on out, I'm here and you know why. Maybe he should have brought his guitar.

But that, of course, would have supposed that he wanted to be here, that he had come not because he thought she had something she wanted to say to him, but because he had some-thing he wanted to say to her.

In any event, he didn't come by car, he came by bus. He spent nearly three hours on the bus with Meredith, Will climbing back and forth from his row to theirs, every three and a half minutes finding some new cause for either conversation or complaint, and during every second of those hours all he could think was that at least he'd have been alone if he'd stayed at home. Chatty, even friendly, Meredith nevertheless gave him the impression that he was the fanatical guerrilla and she was the government agent who was bringing him in. Open, even sympathetic, in her way, she effortlessly convinced him that things were probably worse than he had thought. Or not going to be as easy.

"Do you ever get confused?" she asked, passing Will an apple from her Peruvian basket.

Confused? Was she kidding? "What do you mean, 'confused'?"

"Oh, you know," said Meredith, passing him an apple, too. "Do you ever get mixed up between being American and being Puerto Rican?"

And whose psychoanalyst had she been talking to? "Meredith," he answered, making the fruit smile for him. "I'm not Puerto Rican, remember? My father was Argentinian and my mother's black-Italian. How does that make me Puerto Rican?"

"Oh, okay," said Meredith, biting into a banana and conceding gracefully. "You're not exactly Puerto Rican, but you are Hispanic. Right?" All you spics look the same.

"By default," he smiled, only seeming to look her in the eyes. "By default of Sophie."

"What?" And then Meredith, in between telling Will to sit down and cut it out, or to sit up and look out the window in case they passed a cow, explained to him that it wasn't unusual for people of one culture living in another culture to experience feelings of isolation, alienation, and a generally shaky identity.

"And I thought you'd never finished college," said Tony.

"What?"

"Nothing. It was a joke." Causing a meaningful look from Meredith, she knows about his jokes. In fact, it seemed not unlikely that Meredith knew almost everything about him that there is to know. He could hear—behind her strained friendliness and her selfless attempts to understand him and help him to understand himself—the steady, sixty-cycle hum of serious female conversation, intense and personal, honest and edged with scorn. Probably, she hadn't been commissioned officially to act as lay-counselor, objective third-party mediator, but had felt that someone should.

She placed a hand on his knee, yelled at Will to sit down and for-the-love-of-God shut up for five lousy minutes, and went on to tell him of the aloneness and loneliness she herself had experienced during her two years on an Israeli kibbutz. "I used to have such incredible cravings for pizza and my record collection," she smiled, almost shyly. "Silly, really."

"Yeah," said Tony, wondering that they hadn't snatched up Meredith for the Israeli army, woman warrior that she is. "I knew a guy who nearly died in India, but just the thought of never seeing the Yankees play again kept him alive."

"Really?" she asked, looking at him, but seeing something else. "I used to dream of Broadway, you know. Just dream of walking along Broadway. But just when I was going into my building, or going into a bar to meet someone for a drink, I'd wake up." Far far from home, the night filled with rustlings and rumblings, vague threats and vague promises as old as the hills.

And does she think that when he wakes up in the thunderous stillness of early morning that he is surprised to find that he isn't hacking down green bunches of bananas with his deadly machete? isn't walking some soft, white shore, his trousers rolled up past his knees, the water sliding back and forth across his bare brown feet? isn't playing his homemade guitar while the frogs croak and the children laugh and the women call out as they pass along the unpaved road, legs long, hips wide, eyes welcoming?

Hay que dormir con los ojos abiertos, hay que soñar con las manos ...

What does Meredith think?

It is not impossible to tell, but it does change, switching unpredictably at the mercy of some mood. Sometimes she treats him with suspicion and contempt, don't think you can fool me. Sometimes she treats him with friendliness and familiarity, I know exactly how you are in bed, you can't scare me. Sometimes he thinks that she would like to seduce him, could you come over for just a minute, I can't get the fridge to go off Defrost, just to see for herself, just to be able to tell Sandy that things are as irredeemable as she thought, see what a bastard? your best friend.

You can never tell with women.

Or with men.

Still, he has wished, especially lately, that he had a friend like Meredith. Well, something like Meredith. He has had the friends that most men have. Friends with whom to pass the time, or share a joke, or get high. Friends on whom to test your personality and your rap, do they like me? have I passed? And other friends, too. Mrs. Burkowsky is his friend. Mrs. Burkowsky and López and Mr. Weiss who owns the junk store, and Eddie who does López's deliveries, and a couple of the women at work, and one or two other people scattered over the world. But nothing even the shadow of important, nothing that steps back behind the smile. I've never needed anyone to love me, but I want someone to love me now. I've never wanted anyone to know me, but I need someone to know me now. Not even Julio. Not even Sophie.

Hay que dormir con los ojos abiertos, hay que soñar con las manos ...

Jesus Christ. And then Will had decided he was thirsty and Meredith's attention had been mercifully diverted by the necessity of rationing the amount of orange juice that Will was permitted if they were to make it the rest of the way without his having to pee.

I am going to die, to simply disappear, and it is never going to have mattered, I will never even be missed, missed no more than I am noticed.

... sueños de sol soñando sus mundos ...

He has whispered his intimacies to lovers, kissed his dreams onto their lips, traced the outlines of his desires on thigh and cunt and swelling breasts, sought shelter in their strong arms, sleeping to the timing of a heart. To get so close that words don't matter. But the closer he has gotten, the farther away he has finished. So close, so near, and still alone. And now he is most certainly in a place where words don't count, where nothing he says makes anyone hear him.

... hay que soñar en voz alta ...

But Meredith was still speaking. Meredith was saying that she wasn't necessarily suggesting that he pack a bag and go back to Brazil, as she had finally decided that she'd had enough of edgy Israel and gone back home. It was a different situation, really. But he might think of going back, just to see where he was born, just for a vacation. "A vacation in Brooklyn?" he asked, imagining himself disembarking from the D train, wearing an Hawaiian shirt and a Panama hat, sunglasses in one pocket, street map in the other, asking directions from the friendlier natives, colorful in their costumes and quaint in their customs, could you recommend a good hotel where the staff speaks some English? could you point out the way to Prospect Park? and where did you say Joey Gallo used to live? Camera tightly grasped in his hand, money in a belt around his waist, he would wander across the Heights and Flatbush, feet sweating in his comfortable walking shoes, nervous in the poorer neighborhoods, accumulating anecdotes to tell the folks back home. Snapshots of the locals, don't they have amazing faces? look at that little girl, doesn't she look like a doll? and that old man, slouched against the doorframe, doesn't he look as though he's been around forever? You have no idea what it's like down there.

"Brooklyn?" said Meredith, a dandelion suddenly appearing in the perfect daisy chain of her thoughts. "Well, you know what I mean," giving him a second look behind the first slight smile, don't you think you can get away with your tricks on me. And then Will had decided that he had to have a shit, popping up over the back of his seat like some impish marionette, "Hey, Meredith, what do I do if I have to do number two?" "You just hold it," said Meredith, the softness of her voice a threat.

"Have you ever been in analysis?" asked Meredith as the bus passed a table piled with baskets of vegetables, Tomatoes three for one dollar, the children, brown-skinned from their healthy, outdoor lives, waving at the grimy bus, though she must have known the answer well enough.

"Is it the same as having been in Los Angeles?"

He knows that Meredith can laugh (he has heard her often enough, usually from another room or when he is walking up the stairs, and at parties where she stands in dark corners with dark men, her smile as bright and as long as a missile) but she didn't laugh then. "This death thing," she'd continued, as though he'd confessed that analysis was something that had always intrigued him. "It's really pretty simple and straightforward when you think about it ..."

And isn't death always, in the end?

"What death thing?" he'd countered, meeting her inscrutable look with one of his own, wondering if there were any of his secret thoughts or demon dreams that Meredith didn't know and fully understand.

And she had lowered her eyes, lowered her voice, though

why she should have bothered, having entertained the entire bus with graphic glimpses into their lives for most of the ride, was not quite clear. Surely, the people around them, already aware of his estrangement from his wife, Will's bed-wetting, Meredith's varicose veins, always worse in this weather, and the fact that the superintendent of their building only last night threatened his life, loudly and in no uncertain terms, if he didn't get off his case ("Stop complainin' to everybody about me, cocksucker, or you're gonna be one sorry little spic"), could be assumed to be interested in his delusions and paranoid fantasies as well. Surely the elderly gentleman across the aisle, for most of the journey in a trancelike state, periodically fanning himself with his *Daily News*, had twitched with interest at the mention of death. Why should he be deprived of hearing something that might actually concern him? "You know," whispered Meredith, though it was more like a hiss. "Your preoccupation with death."

Making him sound like a doctor. Or a stuntman. Or a racing driver. Or the Joint Chiefs of Staff. Or Meredith herself, always barging in at the most peaceful moments, guess who just died? Last winter alone Meredith had personally known two ODs, three heart attacks, one homicide victim, two fatal car crashes, and one accidental suicide.

"What preoccupation with death?" his voice bouncing against the contented sounds of the bus—breathing, murmurs, the engine's hum—like a twenty-pound weight dropped from twelve hundred feet onto a frozen pond.

But he is not preoccupied with death. Death is preoccupied with him.

"I don't know what you're talking about," he said, imitating perfectly the voice Jack uses when he thinks Edith is being particularly stupid about something, a voice alight with patience and tolerance, at once making it clear that he knows exactly what she is talking about and that if it weren't for his kindness she would have been put away years ago.

But it didn't work for him the way it always works for Jack. "Oh, well," said Meredith, removing from her basket a book she is reading on God and woman, "if you won't listen to your own wife ..." looking up and ahead for just a second, long enough to give the impression that Sandy herself had miraculously materialized next to the driver, eyes wild and shrunken with some desperate grief, hands tearing at her breasts in a supplication of maddened futility, her mouth grimly gripped by a permanent pain, "then why should you listen to me?" If love cannot move you, reason cannot persuade you, history cannot instruct you, and compassion cannot touch you, why should I waste my breath?

The fireworks are over now. Will has had his soda and his marshmallows, has been trotted through the house on Tony's shoulders, past the clumps of partyers in energetic conversations and alcoholic chumminess, past the close-to-kissing couple outside of the upstairs bathroom, she just touching his arm, he leaning over her, not wanting to miss one word, one breath, one significant glance. There is a sign in red magic marker taped to the door of the room where Will and Meredith sleep, the room in which he and Sandy used to sleep: Will Is Sleeping Here, Do Not Disturb. He helped Will get into pajamas that look like a baseball uniform, told him two stories—one about a fish who escapes from the tank of a seafood restaurant in Boston thanks to the quick-thinking of a little girl named Nancy, the other about an Indian who fell asleep in 1735 in Arizona and woke up in 1976 in a motel in Orange, New Jersey, considerably confused— sang him one original composition, "The Day the Angels Went Shopping in Bloomingdale's" (get them out of here, the manager cried, we turn over millions a year, we don't need God on our side), tucked him in, kissed his sticky forehead (what sense did it make to try to get into the bathroom with him, who knew what or even whom they'd find?), switched out the light, and seated himself in the Colonial-style rocker by the window, watching the darkness on the road side of the house.

Where he still sits now. Watching the bats, like phantoms or a trick of passing lights, flicker through the field opposite. Watching the stars, burning overhead, like cosmic campfires, there's always a welcome in heaven. Down the narrow, asphalt road a lone figure walks, moving the night, footsteps soundless, as though he has no need to look, or think, or pause to consider which the way or what the destination. Just like a bat or a star. He presses his head against the glass, blind past three feet, what with the dark, the drink he's been drinking, and the fact that his glasses are still in the kitchen, on the shelf with the coffee mugs, watching himself disappear around a bend, coming from nowhere and returning, dead already as far as the history of the universe is concerned. And sees an instant of himself at five, back on the island with Señor Rivera, lying on his bed, feeling himself floating toward the bright white moon. How can a moment so vivid be so gone? He does not simply remember, but can feel again, from far away, instant after instant of his life—a streak of sunlight, a certain scent, a breeze, the back of his hand, a random thought—each as though it is still happening, somewhere, or never really happened at all. Behind him, not dreaming of anything, Will snores. From somewhere in front of him, Sandy laughs, as though, she too, is somewhere else and better. And instantly he is back on a February night made light and magical and oh so dangerous by heavy snow. Was it 96th Street or 94th? Were they heading east or west? Sandy had gotten exceptionally drunk, and he had carried her home on his back, block after block, her legs around his waist, her head not quite on top of his, their breath meeting, his visibility gone, Sandy directing him down and up the slippery streets, almost the only people stirring, their laughter contagious and echoing, her arms about him, her breasts against his back more intimate even than the most intimate motion of love. And though he must have known it then, it is only now—feeling her weight against him and hearing her gasp, no left, left, you idiot, his own laughter entangled in hers, watching his feet as he pretended to ski down Columbus Avenue, marveling at the reflection of the traffic lights on the snow—that he realizes just how intimate they were. Had been. How much had been taken for granted. Lost in the frontier, their supplies all gone, and all alone, weak and wounded, hunted and hounded as the wolves howled above the Hudson, they had sung "Homeward Bound" in different keys and Sandy, when they rounded their corner, had shouted at the top of her lungs, "Look, there's the white man's city!" at the sleeping street, mufflered in white. "The white man's city! The white man's city!" he'd shouted, so drunk himself that he thought he could run. "Let's rape the white man's women," landing them both on the ground, but still hugging. He can feel the snow. Knows, exactly, how the night stepped back around them. If he were locked in a universe of nights and set, blindfolded, to wander through them, he would recognize that night from all the rest. That was what it was like to be young. Sandy laughs again, only feet from the window but out of sight, a soft and private laugh.

Without thinking about why he is doing one thing and not doing another, Tony moves from the window and crosses the room, sitting on the floor. The screen door slams. He can hear Jack call out above the general noise and the Four Tops singing, "Edith! Edith! Do you know where that Lenny Bruce album is?" The door to the bathroom opens and he hears Meredith say, apparently to someone, "I know there's a great Bob Marley album somewhere in this house and I'm going to find it," and then giggle, in quite an extraordinary manner, as though she is being tickled into orgasm.

He leans his head on his knees and tries to close his mind.

He did go back to the home of his father once, in fact. When he was twenty-one and thought himself a man. A man with a mission. When he was twenty-one and had everything figured out. Home to the dusty pampas and the cosmopolitan bleat of Buenos Aires. Home to meet Sēnor McNair for the first time in all those twenty-one years. He'd thought it was pretty brave of him, and certainly the right thing to do. The only thing. Back to the roots. Find out once and for all who he really was. Find his father. Locate the past so he could begin the future. Look his old man in the eyes so he could finally see himself. He had a degree in psychology, he knew a lot about folk music, he knew what he was doing. He had even imagined all the possible results, all foreseeable scenes. Himself bareheaded at the graveside, Roberto McNair, 1919–1958, his heart a stone, too late. Himself barred from the door, *el señor no está en casa*, thrown into the gutter by an angry army of younger McNaíros, cracking his head as he hit the ground, his duffle bag hitting him in the groin, the women watching from their windows with silent mouths and eyes, the young girls, their skins so flawless, their clothes so perfect, their hair so exquisite, averting their smiles, *yanqui*, why don't you just go home? Himself sitting in his father's study in the death-still depths of morning, their voices, so similar, low and even and gently warm, as regular and as inevitable as the to-ing and fro-ing of the ocean, known at last, *hijo mío*, their eyes, the same eyes really, meeting in the space above the polished mahogany table and the brandy decanter, each of them finally free.

But instead of finding his father, he found himself in an Argentinian jail for two very long months, picked up from a sidewalk café, his coffee only half drunk, arrested for no particular reason (or for no particular reason that was ever explained). After which he felt that he had probably had enough. Maybe God was trying to tell him something.

Sophie thought so, too. Sophie said that he should count himself lucky. Two months in a cell without Bob McNair were a hell of a lot better than two months not in a cell with him. "You had a narrow escape," said Sophie. "You don't know how lucky you were." So that was what it was like to win? Elbows on the table, old tap dripping, heart still beating, further away from everything, himself included, than when he'd begun. And had studied Sophie's face while they ate the three-course meal she'd made to get him healthy again—a few strands of hair escaping from its knot, her eyes so dark and full of secrets, the spoon held in her hand so that nothing was spilled. But could catch no glimpse of what had passed between her and his father. He only knew just which of Sophie's paramours his father was because of something Angela once shouted when he was not supposed to be in the house, you swim three miles with a baby in your belly and I'm the one that's the fool. Sophie would say nothing. "Maybe I would have liked him," he said, quickly dropping his eyes from her face to his soup. "Yeah," said Sophie, watching him like an animal wondering whether or not to make a sudden move. "Maybe you would."

Can it be only his imagination that all the secrets of the world and even those beyond it are guarded by women with distracted manners and no tolerance for petty questions?

Only be his delusion that there is something to be known, but that they won't tell him what it is?

He has always stood in the doorway, distracted by the squeak of their stockings as they crossed their legs, the movements of their bodies and their clothes, their gestures starting beads to clicking and tiny charms to tinkling, their voices saying one thing and their eyes something else. And what do you want? They would turn to him—their conversations, their breaths, the echoes in the room all suspended—*¿qué quieres? ¿qué haces?* Whaddaya want? And Sophie saying, once he was presumed out of hearing, "I just don't know what's wrong with that boy."

So who does?

Maggie is having a worse time than even she would have predicted. She has been sitting in an extremely expensive and uniquely uncomfortable antique chair in a corner by the massive fireplace for over two hours, grimly smiling and grimly sober, refusing to be coaxed into dancing or dragged outside to watch the fireworks, refusing to be tricked into conversations about art or politics or vitamins or hysterectomies, refusing to give her opinion on the punch or the potato salad, Afghanistan, Poland, or Colorado. She has been to parties before. Big parties and little parties, thousand-dollar bashes among the rich and the beautiful in places like Acapulco and BYOs among the creative and the young in places like SoHo. Divorce parties and birthday parties, summer parties on the beach watching the sun smoulder itself out of the sky and winter parties in rustic lodges watching the fire throw ancient shadows on the walls. Parties at which the host disappears before midnight, and parties at which the hostess never appears at all. Sex-and-drugs-and-rock-'n'-roll parties, fundraisers and get-togethers. The ones she remembers most clearly always ended in tears or the arrival of the police. Different but always the same. It is possible, she thinks, that there are things which, if you did them often enough, would make your life seem even longer than attending parties does—assembly-line work, or playing the giant rabbit in a children's show, or New Year's Eve with the Kissingers, everyone wearing paper hats and blowing their cardboard horns, this year was good but next year's going to be even better—but she would hate to have to find out for sure.

She looks into her empty glass, then once around the room. She was given the grand tour by Edith when they arrived, upstairs and downstairs, inside and out, "We brought this back from Europe. It cost a fortune, of course, but we couldn't resist," "Jack found this in this tiny little shop in Maine. They obviously had no idea of the value," "This is the poster Jack did for the March on Washington. It sold very well." And the even-grander tour by Jack, come up and see my oils, watercolors, pen-and-inks, and pastels, suggestive jokes accompanied by a lot of

good-natured laughter by Jack and walls hung with moody paintings of clouds and catatonic-looking women with very small
breasts, Jack stepping back, looking thoughtful with a hand on
his chin, saying, "Now tell me, Maggie, what do you think that's
about?"

What is any of it about?

Sandy, who so badly wanted her to come, greeted her not
like a long-lost sister, "Jack, Edith, I want you to meet Maggie,
the girl I was telling you about," but like a long-lost poor
relation, "We've had to give you and Skip cots in Jack's studio,
but I'm sure you're used to sleeping rough." While Edith and
Jack seemed to have adopted her, dragging her from one room
to the next, what do you think about this and what do you think
about that, I remember one time in Tangiers ... I remember
when we met Andy Warhol ... We went to this party for Philip
Roth one time ... Edith suddenly turning to her over tea, as
though the question had interrupted the steady torrent of her
memories, "Now tell me, dear, what's your ethnic background?"

Skip says that the Grossmans know—or have known—almost
everybody who is anybody in any of the arts and most of the
media, that they are widely traveled and highly regarded, and
that Jack, everyone says, could have been some sort of genius if
(a) his politics hadn't become foolishly obsessive, and (b) his
obsessive politics hadn't gotten him on the wrong side of the
law (though more in theory than in practice), which had the
effect of making him slightly mercenary. Sandy says that Maggie
shouldn't let Jack and his little jokes and affectionate hugs
bother her, he doesn't mean anything by it, it's just the way he
is. "You should meet his brother, Les," said Sandy. "All he ever
talks about are breasts." "I thought I was going to meet your
husband, Tony," said Maggie, wondering where they kept him.
"He's taken Will out to look for Indian trails or something," said
Sandy, obviously glad to get them both out of the way. "They'll
be back later." And then went on to tell her that she also
shouldn't let Edith, who can be a little pushy and abrupt at
times, bother her, she used to be Jack's agent before she discovered her natural talent for selling real estate and it made her
aggressive. But she can't help it and doesn't mean anything by it,
either.

Not only was Maggie not told who Sandra's dentist was, she

was not told, before they left the turnpike, just who Skip's realtor is. Despite all the last-minute demands for her attention, Edith insisted on showing them the house herself, sitting up front next to Skip as they bounced along the country lanes, left at the fork, slow down there's a curve up ahead, combining an impressive cataloguing of all the area's many benefits, living-wise, with an abbreviated history of the community, what farm was owned by what Revolutionary general, what houses were owned by abolitionists or suicidal poets or notorious rock stars, what very famous politician was found in whose field, parked in his Mercedes with a thirteen-year-old who looked much older. It is an area fairly teeming with cultural color and historic interest. And one, it would seem, which has housed very few poor, ordinary, or basically unnoteworthy people; God knows who loaded the general's muskets, or cleaned the poet's log cabin, or repaired the picture window after the rock star threw his girlfriend through it, or towed the politican out of the field in which he had managed to get more than stuck.

Edith says that the house does, in all honesty, need a certain amount of work, but that's what makes it such a steal and exceptional investment. And what about all the fun they'll have, fixing it up, making it theirs? What about that? Good schools, the best cheese store and the best wine shop outside of New York City, yoga classes, Tai Chi classes, batik, pottery, writing and photography workshops, fishing, hunting, and even a certain amount of skiing in the winter, jazz in the town bar on the weekends, and a really exceptional Chinese restaurant only a little further along the main road, out toward the prison. Could you ask for anything more?

Would you want to?

Maggie decides that she is going to have to get drunk if she is going to make it through the rest of the night, that she is going to have to leave the safety of her little corner and get into the spirit of things, one way or another, join the happy throng. Maybe it will improve her mood.

But in the kitchen, where the chilled wine is rumored to be, an unfestive scene is taking place, a woman standing in the middle of the room, her body shaking with peristaltic sobs. It is difficult to tell just what the matter is, but it seems to have something to do with love and a guy named Jeff. "Aw, come on

Lisa," call the young men playing chess on the floor, "sit down and have another drink." But still Lisa weeps and keens, her bright gypsy skirt balled in her restless hands, her eyes the eyes of the living dead, you don't understand you don't understand nobody cares. Maggie edges her way toward the refrigerator, trying to look as though she isn't moving. Somebody should do something. Usually, at a party like this, there is at least one hero present, especially invited for just such an emergency, ready to leap into the center of attention with a coat or arm to fling around the victim, come on, honey, just cry, just let it all out, get some coffee, get some brandy, I hate to have to do this but, wham. If Skip were around (and not sucked into the sweet-hot night hours ago, probably by some reading therapist in satin boxer shorts, flashing her Chiclet teeth, wouldn't you like to see my gums), it would undoubtedly be he. He has risked his life helping blind people across dangerous intersections. He once stopped a mugging, though it was not he, he openly admits, who struck the fatal blow. He believes in helping people. Usually there is some quiet heroine, used to dealing with irrational drunks—men who are kicking the shit out of someone one minute, and crashed on the floor, sobbing about their mothers or their fathers or the bitches who broke their hearts the next, tears in the Michelob, tears in the jacuzzi, and, in the morning, smiles and kisses, what's the matter, are you mad about something? If Maggie were in a different mood it would probably be she. She has always been a sucker. She has always been the one to wind up offering coffee and consolation, still listening, trying not to look sleepy or bored, when the birds begin waking up the world. She's never learned how to say no. But not tonight. Tonight she has no stamina for helping the wounded out of the battlefield, fishing the victims out of the debris. She has already had one unsettling encounter with a woman whose husband was locked in the downstairs toilet with someone named Candy. "Do you think they'll be out soon?" she asked the woman. "Honey," said the woman, the happiest person in the group, laughing fit to be tied, "there's no way she's going to do it, but she'll be in there all night trying." She didn't dare ask what.

From where do they all come?

Is it only the time-honored ritual of the party, in the dark and smoky liquid depths of which it is possible to do anything at all and still be forgiven, still have it forgotten when the sun comes up in the morning and everything goes back to normal? Tomorrow, or the next day, when the hangovers and apologies are done, when that disquieting habit of the mind suddenly to replay fragments of conversations you didn't remember having or flashes of scenes in which you didn't remember participating has been put under control, will they all go back to their jobs as media people, stockbrokers, doctors, teachers, lawyers, and boutique owners; back to their everyday lives? Tomorrow, or the next day, will they go to work as usual, chatting around the coffee machine about the weather or the garbage or the latest world crisis, the rise in insurance rates or how far they run every morning before coming to the office, dressed just like everyone else (no frosted pink hair and rhinestone noserings, no leopard-skin leotards, no wet-look jumpsuit or leather trousers with sixteen buckles on the legs and pockets), smiling and frowning just like everyone else, breaking the seal on their Wrigley's just like everyone else; will there be no clues as to the true nature of their half-mad psyches? These are the people you ride the trains with day after day, talk to on the telephone, chat to in the supermarket, go to for advice and counsel and companionship. Are they normal? What if the man in the bathroom is a nuclear physicist or an economic advisor to the President? What if the other man in the other bathroom—the one she interrupted in mid-zip, mistakenly assuming that because a woman had just come out the room must be empty—is the principal of an elementary school or a psychiatrist? Or a dentist?

She drinks two glasses of wine straight off, leaning against the counter, refills her glass, and, newly determined to have a good time, returns upstairs.

The party seems to have quieted. He can hear flying scraps of conversation, make out certain voices, hear from perhaps no farther than his own imagination the unchecked sensuality of a lover's sigh. Is everyone going home, or, if not going home, coupling in the closets and in the bushes on Edith's award-winning lawn? Are they all about to settle down to an all-night session of dungeons and dragons? Or has Edith, whose idea of fun has yet to catch up with the sex and drugs of post-sixties America, conned them all—too drunk or stoned or overcome with lust to argue—into a game of charades, Jack leading off with *The Communist Manifesto*, and Sandy niftily following his direction with "Women Are the Niggers of the World"? Not until the music begins does he realize that the stereo has been off.

But the record that is playing is neither Lenny Bruce nor Bob Marley. It isn't even the Beatles. It is Merle Haggard, "I'm proud to be an Okie from Muskogee," immediately followed by a communal moan and a male voice saying, right outside the bedroom door, "For Chrissake, who put that garbage on?"

A place where even squares can have a ball . . .

"Turn that crap off!"

"Kenny, shh. This isn't your home."

"What happened to the Four Tops? I'm not listening to this shit."

Before he knows it, he is on his feet and in the hall, watching Kenny's retreating back, a short, slight woman dressed for beach volleyball firmly affixed to one elbow as he marches into the living room shouting, "No one really wants to listen to this redneck slop, do they?"

There are clusters of people everywhere, but no one whom he recognizes. For one maddened moment the hope zings through his heart that he has gotten caught in some cosmic-joke time warp and isn't at Jack's and Edith's Fourth of July fiesta after all. Has turned up at some other party where no one knows him or expects anything—something, nothing—from him. But no, there is Jack on the patio, pouring drinks from an aluminum cocktail shaker, loudly complaining about not being able to find Lenny Bruce. And Edith in the house, swaying, breast to paunch, before a red-faced man in sky-blue, deep in conversation about hibiscus borders or pornography, don't you think that it's really a question of personal choice? And Sandy, leaning against the railing of the patio, made strange by shadows, not laughing now.

And, feet from Jack's elaborate brushed-steel components, lights flashing and pulsating, the slightly staggering Kenny, doing his best to appear both sober and reasonable, saying to a rather feverish-looking woman, "The folks here don't want to listen to this stuff. It's a party, not a goddamn hayride."

"Oh, yeah?" she screams back, stepping forward as though about to grab him by his zodiac medallion. "And who died and left you in charge of the turntable?"

"Honey," coos the blonde, in that voice women use almost exclusively for small children and grown men, "why don't we go get another drink? The record will be over soon," but he brushes her away as he would an insect.

"Well, not the same person who left you in charge, that's for sure," matching her step forward with one of his own, don't you think you can push me around just because you're a girl.

It is clear even to the casual observer, and certainly clear to the blonde, that the moment contains strong elements of potential violence, but the woman doesn't flinch, doesn't falter, holds herself straight and defiantly, the last member of the slaughtered tribe confronting the insatiable, blood-maddened conqueror, there's only one way you can stop me now. "That's right," says Maggie, "so why don't you just get lost?"

If Skip were here, she knows, and not wherever he is, he would already stand between them, one arm stretching across her like a sacred shield, explaining in his pleasant way that she has had too much to drink, doesn't really know what she has been saying or what she has done and definitely won't do again, will you, dear? But then, if Skip were beside her, she wouldn't have put the record on in the first place, would still be kneeling beside him looking for Crosby, Stills, Nash & Young, they really bring back memories. And not headed for a brawl with a man who is likely to be either a plastic surgeon or a divorce lawyer, a man whom, under different circumstances (a dinner, say, arranged by Skip who shared a room with him in college), she would entertain and listen to with warmth and charm and some amount of interest, maybe even laughing at his jokes about Los Angeles. A man who almost certainly will turn out to be a veteran of Kent State or the younger brother of a civil rights worker slain in Mississippi.

The instant arrives when someone will have to make a movement either forward or in retreat. It takes Maggie a full second to realize that that move has been made not by her, or by the purveyor of good taste, or by the anxious girlfriend, but by someone else entirely.

"You found the album, then," he is saying to her. "Thanks a lot," moving in between them as though about to shake her hand. Then, turning quickly, his mouth a slow smile, "You don't mind if we listen to something I want for a while, do you, Kenny?"

"Well, no, of course not," says Ken, though it is clear that he doesn't understand why he shouldn't, is unsure of whether or not he is talking to someone he knows.

"It's just a little joke, you know. For the holiday."

"A joke?" repeats Ken, almost managing a smile. "For the holiday?"

"Oh, a joke," says the blonde, and laughs.

"Yeah," smiles the stranger, "I knew you'd understand," patting him on the shoulder.

Ken's eyes move from one to the other, his hand reaching behind him to hold the hand of his girlfriend—has he smelled a rat? caught on to the trick? But then he says, "Yeah, well, all right. Sorry if I upset anyone. Come on, Barbara, let's go get a drink."

"He didn't mean anything," whispers Barbara, half-turned as she is led away. "He just gets like this when he's drinking."

"Boy," says Maggie, watching them walk away over Tony's shoulder, "I've never met so many people who care about everything and never mean what they say."

"Well," says Tony, turning to face her, "welcome to the Grossmans'."

"It really was a joke."

"I know."

They look at each other, and the rest of the room does not so much cease to exist as cease to matter—the rest of the room, the rest of the world. So that they are standing as they are, arms down, bodies neither touching nor not touching, the light from the Richard Nixon candle flickering across their faces, each about to say something, and everything else is happening somewhere else, as though, in this instant, they alone are real. As though—in another story, at another time—they might fall in love, with only one look. As though there might be some preternatural recognition, in just a single glance. A pure moment in which the universe holds its breath; in which the prophet might recognize the prophecy, the lover the loved, the shaman might decipher the final sign. But it is only a moment. As easily missed as the passage of a fruit fly though an open-air market. As easily ignored as a drunk folded up in a doorway. So slight and speeding by, in fact, that neither of them really notices it at all.

There will be no talk of kismet or of pheromones here. No

talk of fate, or destiny, or secrets on the brink of revelation. Not here, where no timeless secret would want to be revealed, among the chandeliers that used to be carriage wheels and the coffee tables that used to be cobblers' benches. Not here, where the spirit of not so much as one unremembered Seneca tribesman dares to rattle its charms against the electric hum of the hi-tech-age night.

Nonetheless, he notices that she is, though fraught and not his type, oddly striking, like an old photograph whose identity has been lost in the years, like a fragment of Hopi pottery, like a shredding Ming kimono—not so much for what they are (a piece of paper stuck to cardboard, a broken piece of clay, an old robe) as for what they have been. Though in Maggie's case there is no way of knowing, here on the stripped oak floors beneath the stained beams hung with ceramic jugs and pewter mugs, where or what that might be.

Nonetheless, she notices him, wonders why she hasn't noticed him before. "You a friend of the family?" she asks at last, nodding behind her to where Jack's voice can still be heard, talking now about the shortcomings of the antinuclear campaign.

"Not exactly," and he grins. "I'm more or less an honorary member," and more or less on probation.

She looks surprised. "You're not Tony?" She imagined him shorter or darker, fatter or coarser, wilder or more aggressive. If she imagined him at all. Sandy never says "My husband's got shoulders like that," or "Tony's always fussing about his beard," or "Hairy? You think that's hairy?" the way women sometimes do; but only "Insensitive? Don't tell me about insensitive," or "Moody? Do you think that's moody?" or "I wish Tony was as sensible as that," the way women also sometimes do.

"Oh, yeah," he says, "I'm Tony," clearly assuming that she knows the worst. "And who are you?"

"Me?" asks Maggie Kelly, unsure of what to say, she who once sat on a mountain in Peru and bayed her name to the moon, she who was too independent to settle down or take another's name. "Me? I'm going to marry your dentist."

And now he looks surprised, quickly moving his gaze out to the night where last he saw Sandy talking with Skip. "You are?" and doesn't even think to add, "that's nice."

Well.

Maggie sticks her hands in her pockets and smiles nervously, trying to remember the things that Sandy has said and fit them to him, oh, yes, he's just like that, now I see what she means. Had she thought that he'd be pale and gaunt, talking to himself? Had she thought he'd be wearing a striped jacket and a straw hat, cracking jokes and chewing gum, step right up and see the geek? She stares at him, profiled against the movement which surrounds them, and wonders just what she had thought.

He continues to look away from her, thinking about Skip, who three times this evening has come up to him, clapped him on the shoulder, and said, "Well, Tony," as though surprised to find him here, and thinking about Sandy, who makes no jokes for him any more.

And then, because there is nothing more to say, they move, separately but simultaneously, he one way and she the other.

"Thank you," she calls, almost saluting.

He raises his hand, open-palmed. *"De nada."*

One stalwart owl hoots from the tree where Sandy used to have her Tarzan rope. Beneath the fragrant, moonlit sky—or what would have been the fragrant moonlit sky if the smell of barbecued flesh didn't linger and the moon were more than an apostrophe in the recently fired-on night—down the wooden steps and past the artificial pond and the smiling garden gnome, past the silent shrubs and the phantom trees along the flagstone walk, a couple sits on the boulder preserved to maintain the landscape's natural charm, talking in voices so soft they disturb nothing, her arms wrapped about herself, his hands hidden in the pockets of his slacks. It would be difficult to tell, standing at the top of the garden stairs, whether they are together or not, or even if they are real.

In the woods stretching away from the house, the world ticks over, just as it has always done, quietly and surely, inevitably and sanely, God's little perpetual motion machine, all systems go, requiring no outside law or loyalty, no added fuel or faith.

In the house, the last guests drink their last drinks, dance their last dances, kiss and whisper, laugh and cry, while Edith begins to scrape the leftovers into Tupperware bowls and Jack prepares to move the canvas chairs from the patio into the porch, and Tony sits on an ottoman that was once a butcher's block, watching as a man who has survived Auschwitz and ended up in Kankakee selling insurance might look at a collection of photographs from the days before the world turned really bad. All this, too. As though staring at a glass slide, sturdy but fragile, held between Death's clumsy fingers, immovable and aeonian, specimen of human life, North America, twentieth century. What difference would it make if I dropped it now?

What difference indeed?

Upstairs, in Jack's studio, half open to the night with its skylights, half open to other worlds with its paintings propped in corners and hung on all the walls, Maggie rests her arms on one low window ledge and stares out at the huddled trees. From the driveway come the sounds of car doors shutting and engines starting, asomatous voices scooped from their lives calling bye now, thanks a lot, you aren't going to be sick, are you? what the hell did I do with my keys? And imagines the drive home through the lush and homely lanes, the radio on and the night fulfilled, the car pulling into the garage over the same old grease spots, the reaching for the light switch without having to look.

"Hey, Tony," yells Jack, "how about giving me a hand?"

She turns away from the night with all its secrets and back into Jack's room with all of its messages.

Skip says that if they buy the house, when they buy the house, when the windows have been replaced and the floors repaired and the central heating installed, she will be able to have a studio of her own. "You could get into painting again," he says, remembering her old but younger dreams. "There'll be plenty of room. You won't have to worry about money anymore. You can do what you like." And even as he said it she could also hear him saying, "Rinse, please. My wife paints a little, you know. She's really pretty good," pointing to the watercolor hanging on the opposite wall from his diploma, "that's one of hers."

A studio like Jack's, jars of brushes and walls of shapes and colors. And when she is busy, when she just wants to finish a figure before the light is gone, Skip will answer the phone or put the potatoes on the stove, running up the stairs and tapping politely on the door, "Honey, did you want to make the peas tonight?" "Honey, I can't find any butter."

Someone is singing, a prison song, *Delia, Delia, how can it be? you loved all them others, but you never really did love me* . . . Someone is singing in among the thumpings and murmurs and laughter getting lonely of a good time almost over but always ready to be begun, *she's all I got is gone* . . .

In prison, men—and women—will often mutilate themselves, will push themselves toward some more senseless death; will snare a sparrow and paint it yellow, blue, or orange, feed it from their hands and call it something friendly like Billy for the days that it survives, pushing for some sense of life; will poison their bodies, or fight for molecules of power. Will do anything for an hour from the dumb routine of days. Do anything to know that they are still alive, still feeling, still themselves, still real when nothing else is any more.

. . . how can it be? you loved all those rounders, but you never did love me . . . *she's all I got, is gone.*

Maggie sits on Jack's stool, in front of an unfinished canvas, the top of a stone wall and above it a frog-green sky and a single pink cloud, her fingers on the edge of Jack's palette knife, her eyes on the painting, what is he trying to say?

In prison, people make blades out of the filter tips of cigarettes, paint the walls with excrement and blood, chip dates and names into doors. Just so they won't be forgotten. Just so they won't forget.

But things are different, inside a jail.

She picks up a brush and holds it in her hand. She used to do some nice work. Her teachers all said she had promise. As their teachers had all said about them. Her mother always showed her paintings and her drawings to guests, oh, Maggie, show Mrs. Fisher that picture you did of the cat, now this is my friend Miriam's little girl, it looks just like her, do you think I could take Katherine up to your room to show her that picture you did of that woman, you know, the one with no blouse on? Even her father was impressed, now that really looks like something.

She leans forward the way she used to lean forward, her elbow on her knee, her eyes adjusting to the size of the fabric, but it is Jack's image that looks back at her: Jack's wall, Jack's sky, Jack's cloud. As, outside the window with its aluminum frames, the image that looks back at her also belongs to someone else.

◇   ◇   ◇

Sandy has dried her eyes with several of the tissues from the pack that Skip always carries with him, you never know when they'll come in handy. She has dried her eyes, and he has patted her shoulder, feeling better now?

"God," says Sandy, looking up toward the house. "It must be getting late."

Skip pushes a little button on the side of his watch and the time flashes on, 2:15. "I didn't realize the time," says Skip. "Do you think Maggie will wonder where I've been?"

"Just tell her the truth," says Sandy, brushing back her hair, fully recovered now from the effects of Jack's punch and her personal panic. Up until the moment that the bus first nosed its way around the bend, coming up through the avenue of trees and past the supermarket and the liquor store, honking its horn just once, we're here, she had thought she was ready to confront Tony Rivera. She had even written a list in her journal, Major Points, fifteen of them, beginning with Irresponsibility and ending with Never Wants To Go Anywhere. She had had several long if not particularly in-depth talks with Edith, explaining her side of things ("We're not kids anymore, I have a right to expect certain things," and not expect others), and, fair to the end, explaining his side of things, or her explanation of his side of things ("Now that he's finally got a job where he can do something constructive, where he actually has a future and real responsibilities he's suffering a crisis in confidence. All he wants to do is pick fights with people or sue them"), and had come out of them feeling not only that her complaints were justified but that she had put up with more than any other woman would, there's no question of which of them would receive the most letters of support on the *Times* editorial page. Even Jack, who doesn't like to get involved in things like this, I'm a painter, not a family therapist, had made a sympathetic gesture. "If you need any money for anything," he'd said, standing with his shoulder almost touching hers but his eyes on Edith weeding out the flower beds, "all you have to do is ask. I could let you have a buck or two." For a divorce? For a new apartment? For a second honeymoon? Because there was that, too. Aside from everything else, there was a part of her, normally active only late at night, that missed him and wanted to see him again. Until the bus rumbled to a stop, the doors opened, and he stood before her, a knapsack over one shoulder and Will's sailboat under his arm, that look of wariness and weariness in his eyes that had nothing to do with the long bus ride or the heat of the evening. "Don't I know you?" he said, stepping in front of Meredith and shaking her hand. And she began to wonder all over again.

"The truth?" says Skip, though it is not exactly a question.

"Well, why not?" asks Sandy. "Surely she wouldn't mind that you gave a little time to a friend in need, would she?"

"Of course not," says Skip, straightening himself out a little, still trying to figure out how they had so quickly moved from the agonized state of Sandy's emotions ("I just don't know what to do," she sobbed. "I don't know what he wants. Every time he comes near me I just want to scream. I can't go on like this for the rest of my life. Can I?" And though he had no clear idea—not at that moment with the alcohol going to his brain and her head going to his shoulder—of what "like this" might mean, he said, "No. Of course you can't.") to an embrace that was better than friendly by anybody's standards. "We have a very open relationship. We understand each other."

"That's all that matters," says Sandy, feeling frightened and not understood, feeling as though everyone else gets what they want, has happiness practically handed to them on a Wedgwood platter while she is thrown only crumbs. "That's all that counts."

As they come up the stairs, they can hear Jack suggest a nightcap, Edith say that she thinks that's a good idea, and Rivera singing like a hobo in the night.

F O U R

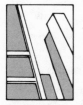

It will go down in the records, for people who are interested in that sort of thing, as the hottest summer since the year they drove the Cheyenne west. Heatstroke, heart attacks, and incidental violence are all epidemic. Tempers are short, water may have to be rationed, and consumers are being cautioned to go easy on the air conditioning, we don't want another black out, do we? Along the coast of New England and the shores of Long Island, where the porpoises still sometimes play, the breeze may be gentle and salty, the sunlight caressing and the ocean stretch into beyond like a crystal carpet of magical properties, but it's not like that down in the city. Down in the city the air is almost visible, the streets stink, and the island itself is like an open prison or a safari park, the inmates all locked by lethargy into their personal positions, so much forgotten they can barely breathe.

Up in the mountains, Sandy sits in her mother's garden, her journal on her lap and a good book beside her, sipping homemade lemonade, and thinking, among other things, about life.

Up in the mountains, Skip squats beneath a happy sun, beside a patient joiner, going over the plans for the kitchen, his cells humming and his heart singing, already feeling like a new man.

In the country, you have time to think and time to be yourself.

In the country, you can realize what life is all about.

In the country, you can see that you are part of nature's grand design, and can think about the thirty or so years you have spent on the planet and the thirty or so years more you can be expected to spend, and hear everything fall into place. Like a leaf falls, or a sun sets, or a river flows determinedly out to sea. Just like that.

So that both Sandy on her redwood chaise longue and Skip on his knees in his shorts and sweatband (more like a tennis pro than a pioneer) would expect the trees, the mountains, the valleys, the rivers, and the winds—if they could talk—to speak of ageless deeds, of simple men but true, whose dreams once fed the earth and raised the sky.

Neither Sandy nor Skip ever thinks much about God, and certainly not favorably. But this morning, when Skip woke early in his sleeping bag on the floor of the living room and saw the sun just burning its way up through the trees, he did think wow and—though the God he has been raised to is a no-frills, no-nonsense old man with a long white beard and a worried expression in his eyes not much given to such things—take it as a sort of sign, you are going in the right direction. And when Sandy lay awake last night, staring up through the window of her room at the dancing stars, she did think ah and—though she has long outgrown the need for myths or superstitions—take it as an affirmation, you deserve and can have all you want, men have walked around on the moon.

Down in the flatlands, however, Maggie sits hunched over her sewing machine in her underwear, the fan on Full, pins in her mouth and a look of panic in her eyes. She might as well be in a sweatshop, really. There is no way she is going to finish the sundresses in time. No way she is going to break even this month. No way she is going to survive this interminable heat. Though she does not, of course, have to be here, could have gone up for a long weekend with Skip. He certainly can't understand why she had to stay behind and work, why she carries on as though her life is not about to change and all her worries with it. Her cells are all splitting and sputtering, and her heart is silent except for the normal sounds that hearts tend to make. She is the old woman still.

Down in the flatlands, Tony lies on the floor of his air-conditioned office, the proposal for the new youth counseling and community center to be integrated into the department and under its control, in its folder, resting on his stomach. He is wondering, musically, why he ever left Ohio, and thinking, among other things, about death, and trying to imagine what the world would be like, will be like, without him. Pretty much the same. If not exactly.

In the city, you have to think all the time and move even faster.

In the city, if you don't figure out what life is all about pretty quickly you probably will not have the chance.

In the city, you can easily see that you are part of mankind's great nondesign, and can think about the thirty or so years you have spent on the planet and the thirty or so years you may yet spend, and hear everything click into place. Like a blade opens, or a bank vault shuts, or a sewer flows resignedly out to sea. Just like that.

So that both Maggie on her old kitchen chair and Tony on his carpet know that if the walls of the city could talk, the tales they would tell would make the fallen angels weep dear tears. That, if the walls could speak, their voice would be a gorgonian wail, the breathless howl of a lover whose beloved lies bleeding life, so red so white so empty in her arms. If they could, what stories would they whisper. If they could.

Thank God they can't.

So he got his ultimatum. Not until the evening after the party, long after Skip and Maggie had driven off in a cloud of dust and a chorus of good-byes like applause, and not long before he and Will and Meredith were due to get back on the bus and drive off in a cloud of carbon monoxide and a chorus of good-byes like a chant. They sat in the living room while everyone else went out to pick real wild flowers to be brought back to the city, and she told him what was going on. He had no doubt that it was an edited version. When asked to clarify certain aspects of her behavior ("Why the hell did you go off like that? Did I come home drunk and throw you around? Did you think I'd try to kill you because you wanted to get away from me for a while? What did I do to make you run?") she relied on the domestic version of the Fifth, I knew you wouldn't understand, losing his questions in the detour. She was straightforward and blindingly reasonable when it came to explaining her needs, desires, fears, and wants, but when it came to listening to his she threw her hands in the air and her voice right after them, "Okay, Tony. Okay. What is it you want? Go ahead, tell me. Is it to be Ché Guevara, Robin Hood, or Willie Nelson?" It was impossible for her to see that the things she wanted did not necessarily bind them to happiness. "What the fuck difference is it going to make if I die a Washington bureaucrat or a Broadway bum?" he yelled, berserk with the frustration of trying to make himself visible to her. "It may not make any difference to your death," she said, calm and right, "but it would make a difference to your life." So that the conversation was little different from the hundreds that had preceded it, ending not with resolution—let's end it now, let's try to understand our limitations and agree to build on our strengths—but with a renewed list of tasks and conditions, complete all items and you win the prize. Wasn't it really no more than he had expected? Was it less? Was it any different from her last ultimatum, given last winter when he wasn't going to take the promotion, when she wouldn't have their child?

"Not this year," Sandy said. She was sitting at the table in the kitchen, working on her article for the high-school guidance counselors' journal: "Education, Can It Work?"

"What do you mean, 'not this year'?" he asked, coming from the counter with a mug of coffee in his hand. "You're pregnant now," just staring.

She didn't lift her eyes from the page she was reading. "You drink too much coffee, you know. It'll kill you."

"Never mind the goddamn coffee," sitting down across from her. "I thought this was all settled."

She had agreed when he'd said that they needn't treat it as a catastrophe. She had agreed when he had said that they had been planning to start a family anyway, in a year or two, it didn't matter much one way or the other if they started a little sooner than they'd anticipated, it wasn't going to wreck the economy. She had stood against him in the entrance to the living room, her arms around him, her ear against his heart, more upset, it seemed to him in retrospect, about the fallibility of her diaphragm than the fertility of her womb. For the first time in a long time she had held on to him as though he alone could steady her, as though he could support her, as though words he might speak could comfort her, could change the unchangeable and bring right the crooked workings of the world. And he had kissed her and cuddled her, he had made his famous instant egg drop soup for her and run down to the corner for a bottle of wine. He had assured her that, though unpremeditated, a baby now was not out of the question, they were together, difficult was not the same as really hard. And, very drunk, he had gotten out his guitar and sung for her the first half of "Forever Young," the only part he can ever remember. Everything, on Thursday night, had been all right.

But by Saturday morning it all had changed.

"It is settled," she said, correcting a spelling mistake. "I made an appointment for Wednesday morning." No need to put off these things.

"Without telling me?"

"You didn't give me a chance to tell you. You started playing your guitar." As though it had been an inappropriate gesture.

"I didn't start playing my guitar till eleven o'clock at night. You could have told me at ten-thirty, or any time yesterday," meeting her cool and level gaze with one of his own.

"It's my body," said Sandra Grossman, wiping out half a sentence with one long red line.

"But it's my baby."

She looked at him then.

"Is this what they call a pregnant moment?" he quipped.

She bent her mouth to talk, but not to smile. "That's part of the reason."

With ceremony and precision, he lifted his mug to his lips and drained off his coffee in one long, deliberate swallow, in a perfect imitation of his father-in-law preparing to reenter a debate on the role of the unions in American politics. "What's part of the reason?"

She moved neither finger nor eyelid, shoulder nor foot, her breath coming from beyond her, so that even her chest seemed not to rise and fall, only her lips moving, her lips and her voice like a recorded announcement, "You're not ready for a child."

"I know we're not ready for a child," he snapped. "We've

been through all that," amazed that she could have forgotten so quickly all that they had thought and felt and said.

And she stared back at him with her new face, the face of a woman who had never sobbed against the beating of his heart, had never laughed within the circle of his arms, had never slipped her secrets into the warm palm of his hand, had never sucked his cock into the wet warmth of her mouth.

"I didn't say *we* weren't ready," she corrected, the red pen nodding between her fingers, ready to turn and scratch a word next to him—unnecessary? hazy? ambiguous? cluttered?—"I said that *you* weren't ready."

He got up to stand near her then, his voice unemotional, his bearing adult, his movements tender. No outrage. No violence. No fists slamming down on tables. "Exactly what are you trying to say?"

"I'm not trying to say anything," she said, her tone implying that he had come in on the middle of the argument. "I'm saying that you are irresponsible and impractical, that you have no interest in the future or even the present, and that you are certainly not ready to accept the responsibilities of parenthood."

If a relationship is a boat full of aunts and uncles, what is a parenthood?

She turned in her chair, the better to look him up and down, posed beside her, his hand on the back as though holding it in place, his face unsmiling but serene, as though expecting a small, nimble man in brown trousers and rolled-up shirt-sleeves to dance out from behind a camera shouting "Hold it!" "You aren't serious about anything anymore."

And, foolhardy to the last, he picked up the loaded ball and tossed it into her court, close to the net. "Name one thing I'm not serious about."

"Life."

"Come on, Sandy, you have to be more specific than that," giving her a smile that once would have dazzled, once would have moved the mountain of her heart.

Then she let him have it. What, exactly, did he think he was doing with his life? Did he think that he could fool around forever? Did he think that he could just make jokes and grumble for another forty years? What the hell did he think he was? The last gaucho in America, riding against the wind, his hat pulled low, his half-shut eyes gazing far away into the horizon? What the hell did he think was going to happen? That he would be able to roll on forever, sniping at everything, mocking everyone, antagonizing everybody, slinking off with his guitar every time the going got rough? They weren't in their twenties, waiting for things to happen, waiting for their turn to come. It had been his turn for a long time, but he was refusing to play. Was he still waiting for his new dawn? For the world to come pounding on his door, aren't you the guy that wrote that song in the sixties, "What Ever Happened to the War on Want?" weren't you the guy who wrote that song in the seventies, "The Impeachment Blues"? gee, they're really great? Did he still think he was twelve years old, his head stuffed with stories worse than lies, thinking he was going to be the one to do what had never been done, to right all the wrongs, win the unknowable prizes, leave his mark on a grateful world? If he wanted to be somebody, exactly whom was it that he wanted to be? How many jobs could he have had or kept or gone for if his attitude had been different, if he weren't always stirring things up, making people edgy and distrustful? Was he still waiting for his goddamn revolution? And who did he think was going to lead it? Him? On his bike? Was he planning on marching on Washington with a handful of vagrants, bums, ex-cons and methadone addicts? Mr. President, we have been dissatisfied with the way things have been run around here for a long time, and we think it's time we took over? What did he have to offer to anyone? What did he have to offer her? Security? Position? Respect? Comfort? Commitment? Did he call what he had commitment? What was he committed to, being knifed in the back by some teenage thug? fighting losing battles for old people who were going to die soon anyway? Even her father, who had always liked him, said he was surprised at the way Tony had turned out, he'd always thought Tony had more on the ball, thought he understood how to work the system better, for someone so political he seems to understand nothing about politics. Even her mother, who had grown to like him, said that he couldn't hide behind a smoke screen of jokes that nobody else really understood anyway for the rest of his life. With his mind and his energy, what couldn't he have done if he hadn't been so busy playing the fool, getting thrown out of meetings, getting barred from committees, giving guitar lessons in his own time to kids who would have been better off trying to memorize their social security numbers than the chords for "Blowin' in the Wind"? Could he remember when they used to go to all the important conferences, concerts, rallies, and demonstrations? When serious journals used to publish his articles? When he used to be invited to speak all over the country and even in Canada and Mexico once in a while, when he was still a bright young thing, a man to be watched? Just watch him now. Why was he throwing his life away? Instead of going to the parties and events that would place him in the scheme of things, with the people who count, with the people who could help him, he went to basketball games and crummy bars with the defeated and the losing. Why was that? Did he think that she didn't want to have a car, or a condominium, or mutual friends in power jobs who were actually contributing to a better world and not just complaining about the lack of it? Did he think that she liked never knowing what she would find when she opened the door to the spare room, some fugitive from justice or pregnant teenage runaway? Did he think that she liked never knowing where he was till two or three in the morning? What the hell was "hanging out" supposed to mean? Did he think that he was still in school? What about her? Huh? What about her? Maybe Meredith was right, and it was better to marry for money than for dreams.

And when she was done, she gave him such a look, flat with the sense of some loss he couldn't understand or hope to know, that he felt, for an instant, that he was already gone, already a part of her past, oh, no, I meant my first husband.

"You don't really believe in anything anymore, you just keep yourself busy," her voice so soft, so still, her anger already so spent.

And between them in that moment—each of them in the same room, in the same apartment, at the exact same moment in time, so close that they could have touched, so near that if either had moved just slightly her warm, even breath would have fogged his gold-rimmed glasses, and his laughter, had there been any, would have rustled the papers on the table—between them in that moment lay the difference of decades, lay nothing but a few inches of air, the white of the ceiling, yellowed with smoke and grease and time, above, and the gray of the floor, scuffed and scraped and dingy, below, his fine, firm hand with its band of gold on one finger and her lean, muscular arm, covered in the sweater he had given her five years before because it reminded him so much of her. A space so small that an insect with a two-minute life span could have crossed it and still had time to throw a party on the other side. But not they.

If he had been a handsome young brave, his knowing dark and awesome, and she the lovely young maiden, her beauty awesome and dark, they could have dived in from their separate sides of those mighty, raging waters, swimming to one another against the furious currents, and the cold depths, cold death of that antediluvian river, their fingers just touching as their bodies succumbed to the treacheries of the world, their love reborn and undying in that final moment of stillness as they sank, eyes forever opened for that one last glimpse of love.

But he was a not-so-young American of mixed ancestry, no longer brave, though handsome still, whose adult heart, beneath his hard but ageing chest, was a perfect muscular pump, breathtakingly simple and unbelievably complex, and she was not a beautiful maiden with thick black braids and promise shining in her eyes, but a mature American woman of clean features, good skin and Jewish descent who wouldn't jump into eternal waters for any man, no matter how brave or beautiful he might be or once have been.

"I just don't know what you want from me anymore," he whispered at last.

"And what do you want from me?" asked Sandy, with no trace of softness and no hint of grace, imagining herself trudging through the city streets, babies strapped to her body in durable canvas carriers, groceries and diapers in a wheeled wicker basket, searching for babysitters, searching for day-care centers, searching for decent schools, scouring the metropolis for one free minute for herself, one spare thought for the future, while her children's father sits in some Chino Criollo café, eating food that isn't good for him, talking to people who worry about who will win the World Series.

"What can I possibly do?"

"You know what you can do," she said. "You can take the administrator's job here, if you won't go to Boston. You can get off the damn streets and all your private little crusades and start doing something real. That's what you can do. You can damn well get your shit together before it's too late."

So he had started doing something real. He had taken the desk job, come off the streets, buckled down and buckled under, started contributing articles to magazines, newspapers, and journals once again, started taking part in mainstream urban life and showing how much he cared.

But things have not gone quite as Sandy planned. He hates the job, hopping around from meetings with bureaucrats to meetings with community leaders, scheming and bullshitting and shuffling papers. He hates Parker and the thought that the most that his future can hold is that he will, in a few years, be Parker, sitting at the head of the table at Monday afternoon sessions, clearing his throat and saying, "I think we have to look at this realistically ..."

He hates his life, fears his death, and now has yet another ultimatum, it's not too late yet. But why isn't it too late yet? Why can't either of them seem to let go? He was going to rescue Sandra Grossman from her knotty pine tower, from her progressive education and her radical chic friends, and show her what life was all about. "Nothing?" she screamed. "Is that all you see in life? Nothing?" She is not, after all, getting any younger herself. She herself has a career that is more than promising; she herself is both fecund and actively maternal, and not only would love to have a family but would make a terrific mother who would never do to her children what her mother did to her, or what his mother did to him. But she will not always be still on her way up, fertile and young enough to have possibilities. She is thirty, after all. She can afford to give him a little more time before invoking the clause in their contract which begins: If either party, at any time, should wish to dissolve the relationship ... But not a lot.

And that was what she dragged him all the way up to the Grossmans' to tell him. Not that she missed him. Not that she didn't miss him. Not that she was sorry she walked out on him like that, or that she wasn't sorry. Not that she remembered, too, the night they first met, at a fund-raiser for migrant farm workers, and the way she let him follow her home on the subway, "I thought you were staying on the Express," "I thought I'd come with you."

"What you want to do," Parker is saying out in the corridor, "is talk to Rivera. He's the expert on street gangs around here. He'll put you in touch with the people you need."

And sometimes I take a great notion, to jump into the river and drown . . .

So Maggie has a home in the country. The home that Skip is rebuilding. Her mother is very happy for her. Meredith is very happy for her. And Maggie, of course, is happy, too. Even as she wipes the sweat out of her eyes with the back of her hand, curses that the bobbin has run out just when she seemed to be making some progress, and knocks the box of pins off the table as she reaches for her beer, she comforts herself with thoughts of how happy she is. Not that the feelings of panic have passed. She still has trouble sleeping, still is troubled by bad dreams, still wakes in the deep of the night with her mind tingling with fears that are not so much nameless as better left unnamed, afraid to think lest each new thought brings twenty more. Meredith has suggested tantric meditation and yogic breathing exercises to overcome and control anxiety, but Maggie prefers to think about the hand-painted blinds she is designing for the bedroom, the covers she will be making for the couch, and whether or not the curtains should complement or match, the mural she will paint in the bathroom and the floor covering for the kitchen. Meredith says that *pranayama* techniques can give you thought and, therefore, life control, and so treat not only the symptoms but the problem, but Maggie has found that by imagining scenes of conjugal happiness in which she is always smiling as she ties up the boat or mows the lawn or rolls up enchilladas or is rolled into the delivery room, Skip trotting beside her, his hand in hers, she can pretty much keep her darker thoughts at bay.

In her time, Maggie has planned meals and trips, jobs, projects, and small drug deals; has planned to move here or move there, join this one or leave that one; has made plans for Christmas or plans for the summer, plans for improving her mind or improving her body, plans for the evening or plans for the weekend. But she has never planned a life before. As though it is Monopoly and not experience that is the great teacher. As though she would have been better off spending her formative years learning how to hustle less adroit players out of lucrative properties, how to build and expand with an eye to her own profit and security and everyone else's total collapse, instead of sitting in the backyard in the old canvas hammock, reading books and listening to the wind. Skip thinks she is a refreshingly quirky and imaginative person, and cute, but even cute people who have a good sense of color and a talent for design can't go rolling along, singing a sing forever. "You can't just let life happen to you," he has patiently explained as though explicating Rule 3. "You have to know what you want to do with it. What you want to get out of it. You have to take control. Life is what you make it. Once you know what you want, then no one can stop you from having it but yourself." Strong thoughts.

Accidents happen; lives are made.

It is no more than she has been telling herself. It is advice she has been taking to heart.

And, all things considered, she has been doing pretty well. Every evening that he is up there—Friday, Saturday, Sunday— overseeing the hammering in of nails and the ripping out of old boards, he calls her to tell her how things are going, how much he misses her, how he is going to ravage her when he gets back to town, and to ask her how she is and what the temperature is in Times Square; and every evening that he calls she has some new project (like pillows that look like shells for the sunroom), or new fantasy of their life together (like picnic suppers by the river that end in them eating each other right there beneath the sleepy sun) to offer in exchange for his attention. And the more she talks about her excitement and their plans, the more she believes in them. Such are the powers of self-persuasion.

Maggie leans back in her chair and stretches, looking around the room at the bare blue walls, inherited from the previous tenant, and the boxes, never unpacked, that stand in one corner, the untouched remains of her previous lives (a box of records, a box of books, clothes and trinkets, beads and bolts of cloth, letters and sketchbooks and notebooks, pictures and postcards, and odds and ends). This is the first real home she has had since the death of her son, and yet she has never fully moved in; has not painted the walls or hung more than a picture or two, has not filled it with her favorite things or bought blinds for the windows or a set of dishes, has not made it the refuge she decided she needed those last months on the road, tired of crying on other people's beaches, tired of living out of a satchel. As though she could get so far and no farther. Get the lock on the door and the light working in the hall, get the bed up and a rug or two down, get a cat and a cat dish and a collar for the cat and a couple of plants—but nothing more.

And still her life comes out of the shadows of night and night's dangerous dreams to grab her.

In the footlocker in the living room, beneath the bedspreads and saris and extra blankets, lie the few things that belonged to Ben which she couldn't quite make herself throw or give away with all the clothes and toys and coloring books that she grimly sorted into Garbage and Salvation Army. They are in the left-hand corner, under a Peruvian poncho, wrapped in old newspaper (Sex Triangle Ends in Violence, Saying It with Flowers, Town Hall Bar Brawl, The Menace of Heroin, the photograph, slightly grainy, of a Nobel Prize winner, Message of Hope) and bound inside a plastic shopping bag, Santa smiling like a jolly old elf, Seasons Greetings. Three handmade Mother's Day cards, two Christmas cards with glued-on silver stars, four monochromatic crayon drawings, and a small, woolly, forlorn-looking dog with a felt bone in his mouth and plastic eyes with moving pupils, Happy Birthday. And two photographs, one taken in front of her mother's house when the roses were in bloom, and one in the trampled snows of Central Park, for God's sake, you weren't meant to really throw the snowball. She hasn't looked at them since the afternoon she wrapped them away, her mother busy in the kitchen, you must eat something, it's not going to help if you make yourself sick, singing along with the radio, *I'm forever blowing bubbles,* oh, listen, Maggie, do you remember how we used to sing that in the car when you were little? Since that indelible afternoon, her eyes so huge and hurting and so incapable of tears; her heart so small and strangled and empty like some broken shell, filled with sand and tiny flies, tangled in seaweed on a beach from which all the bathers had long been gone, their laughter mimicked by the cool gray gulls squawking into the wind. Her mother had made her soup and toasted bread and talked about God and the strange ways in which he works, and how dark it is before the dawn, and how, though it certainly didn't look so at the moment, it might turn out to be all for the best, God didn't do things for no reason. It would not have occurred to Kate that God had had nothing to do with Ben's murder, that it was all down to a Buick and a balding man who was in a hurry and whose reflexes were slow. And so Kate had prayed and wept to herself while she stirred the soup and brewed the tea, lit a candle in the church every morning with a shaking hand, and had silent conversations with God in which she told Him that she knew her grandson's death was a punishment on herself and Maggie (herself for not having succeeded in raising her own child with the right ideas and a sense of Christian morality; Maggie for not having had them), and that she was sure it wasn't too late for the lesson to be learnt. While Maggie stood in the blue bedroom, the walls strewn with painted stars, moons, and magical beasts, a six-years' accumulation of things spread before her, the bag of garbage, fat and misshapen, to the left, disgorging scribbled papers and bits of broken toys—a tiny hand, a miniature felt shoe, a plastic gun with a cracked barrel— her hand upon the corner of a card, all the winds and waters of the world contained within her body, raging for release, some unseen, unasked hand staying her own. Keep something.

The fan whirrs and the cat rubs itself against her, sounding as though it's about to take off. In the back alley, she can hear the super talking about the stabbing last night, and how much water it takes to wash away enough of the blood to make it look decent. Not so long ago she would have leaned out the window and called down, "Hey, Brian. What happened?" but today she is too busy, and soon she will not even be here. Soon, none of this will concern her, not the deaths, nor the lives, nor the custom she will lose if the sundresses aren't finished on time, nor the loneliness that has accompanied her for all these years, in groups, in crowds, in some lover's strong arms. Soon she will be brand new.

On the morning after the Grossmans' party, while Skip was dragging Meredith, Will, and Tony off to see his house, wait'll you see it, just wait'll you see it, and Jack was locked in his studio, there's nothing like a hangover for stimulating creativity, and Edith was locked in her bedroom, there's nothing like a party for taking it out of you, Sandy decided to talk to her at last. She brought her toast and coffee out on to the patio where Maggie was doing last Sunday's crossword. She commented on the party, she commented on the people Maggie hadn't met, she commented on the fine weather, she gave her three tricky answers. And then she said, concentrating on spreading the jam evenly over her toast, "You'll find it pretty quiet up here. After what you're used to," the wild parties, the adventure of travel, the casual sexual encounters of the open road, the drug-taking of the modern gypsy.

"Oh, I don't know," said Maggie, rubbing out three incorrect guesses. "My building's pretty quiet."

And Sandy smiled, with something that looked like it might be understanding. "I meant before. I hear you've gotten around," still smiling even as she bit into her bread, crumbs falling.

Around like a disease or around like a piece of gossip? Maggie watched Sandy's tongue lick crumbs from her lips. "Yeah," she said, wishing, that like Jack, she had a hangover in which she could hide. "Me and Marco Polo."

"Well," said Sandy, who has not spent the last five years organizing the futures of kids who barely have a present for nothing, "I only meant that it must have been pretty exciting, traveling like that." And waved her hand across the blue-gray expanse of flagstone. "Seeing the real world at first hand. You must have some incredible stories."

"No," said Maggie, wondering whether Sandy thought she'd been a tramp or on a fact-finding mission for the UN. "I have some funny stories, and some frightening stories, and some tragic stories, but none of them are incredible."

Sandy's laughter bounced across the patio like a dropped marble. And then she went on to explain, with the directness of a bulldozer, that she, personally, would never feel really comfortable with that sort of life, self-indulgently living off of other people's misery. ("I wasn't working for the CIA or IT&T, you know," interrupted Maggie), not really a tourist and not really a resident, not really harming, maybe, but certainly not helping, and what did you do all day, living like that, just sit in the sun and get stoned?

"I seem to be sitting in the sun getting stoned right now," said Maggie, but Sandy didn't hear. It would make Sandy feel so unproductive, so useless, so meaningless. It would make her feel like an intruder, an opportunist, an interloper.

"I'm sure you're not like that," said Sandy, generously. "You are rather artistic, in a way, aren't you?" no one complains about Gauguin exploiting the natives.

"Oh, I'm sure I can overcome that," said Maggie, watching a bee tiptoe across Sandy's plate. "Jack seems to have managed all right."

But Sandy, having lived so long with the rapacious Rivera, perhaps, was immune to sarcasm and innuendo. "Oh, Jack. Jack's always been so politically motivated, you know. He never does anything for purely personal reasons."

Maggie watched the bee as a thin, tanned hand flicked it to the ground. "Oh, I know."

"He chose to live up here because he found the city so crass. He didn't want to get involved in all the competition and game-playing."

"Oh, of course."

"The isolation and quiet suit him," her cup to her unsmiling lips "But it doesn't suit everyone." Bringing them back to—where?

"Oh, I know," sighed Maggie. "I worry that Skip's not going to have anyone to play squash with on Thursdays," and nowhere to play it.

"Skip will love it up here," decided Sandy, as though his file with all its aptitude tests, attitude tests, and teachers' comments were on her lap and at her fingertips. And then went on to give her analysis of Nelson Ellis, simple family man and concerned dental physician, a man with, really, little experience of the wickedness of the world or the perversities of humankind, a man who wanted no more from life than love and security, who would never dream of having group sex or paying pennies for Indian weaving that he then sold to German tourists for thirty times the price. Skip has no exotic tastes ("Well, he does like tempura," Maggie pointed out), no avaricious delusions, no insatiable ego. He's never craved romantic adventures ("He seems very fond of masquerade parties," commented Maggie), never wished to be other than he is, except, maybe, a real doctor, with life in his hands.

"What I mean," said Sandy, summing up, still showing the skill of the captain of her college debating team, "is Skip's really led a pretty sheltered life. This is the perfect environment for him," her hand panning across the perfection of the environment. "It might seem ... uh ... tame for some tastes. You know, there isn't really a lot happening ... next to the city and places like that. Of course," smiling as brightly as the sun was shining, "it isn't a cultural wasteland or anything. If anything, it's really the best of both worlds. But it's not exactly ... swinging."

Maggie leaned over to pour herself another cup of coffee from the speckled enamel pot on the table near Sandy's elbow. Swinging like a rope or like the sixties? Swinging like a scythe or like singles? Swinging? "No one swings but children anymore."

"Oh, well, but you know what I mean. I mean, I don't think that I could live up here all the time, but someone like Skip can. It was made for him," as some things obviously weren't. "But someone used to the sort of life-style you're used to might find it a little hard to ... adjust." You can take the girl off of the road, but you can't take the road out of the girl.

There was sunshine splattered across the flagstones, sunshine splattered across the garden and the house, sunshine sparkling across the cups and aluminum and their bare arms. Maggie stared at her hand, once blue-white and pink, its patterns indistinct and faint, resting on her thigh, thinking about the style of her life—working, not working, worrying about working, worrying about not working, sleeping and dreaming only then, too serious to be fun, too funny to be serious. "Just what life-style would that be, Sandy?" looking into the Grossman eyes, half-expecting to see the image of herself in short shorts and midriff blouse, cha-chaing across a beach with an entourage of beachboys, brown and grinning.

"Oh, you know," said Sandy, unaccustomed to being cross-questioned unless by the griping Tony. "Footloose and fancy-free."

And Maggie could see herself, though not in Sandy's eyes, as she trudged and hustled around the world, crying for weeks when her envelope of old letters and photographs was stolen from her bag in Greece, phoning Kate collect on Christmas and her birthday, hi, what are you doing? Footloose and fancy-free. Car doors slammed in the driveway, voices sounded over the roof and around the side of the house, breaking the rural silence.

"Hey," screamed Skip, still out of view. "Anybody home?" Maggie stood up.

"We're back here," called Sandy.

And then Maggie turned and, breaking their own silence,

said, "You certainly know a lot about Skip," almost as though she hadn't said it.

The pins have been put back in their box, the bobbin has been rethreaded, the beer can is empty. Brian and his companion have gone from the alley. She gets up and goes to the window, looking down on the collection of things that do or might come in handy, on a half-a-bike propped against one wall, on the new stain in the concrete ground. Footloose and fancy-free, no more.

F I V E

It took Simón Bolívar only thirty-nine years to grow gray, only twelve days for the first socialist republic in Latin America to collapse, only one thousand nine hundred and thirty-six years from the death of Christ for men to walk on the moon, and it only takes Tony Rivera twenty minutes to prepare and eat his main meal of the day, but it takes Larry Parker, M.D. with a Ph.D. in psychology, the better part of an hour to say anything more complicated than hello, and even when it's all over it's as though nothing had happened.

This afternoon, Parker gave him his monthly pep talk on the progress of the department and his progress within the department, the one that begins, "You know, Tony, how highly we regard you and your special skills, and how lucky we know we are to have you on our team," and which forty-seven and a half minutes later ends, "If only you would get in line a little more ... make one or two compromises—that South Bronx project, for example ... You know that when I move on, which may not be all that far in the distance ... strictly between us, there may be something coming up in Washington ..." It depressed him so much that he couldn't stand the alternative prospects of either going home and barricading himself in for the night or not going home and sitting on Broadway with the Captain—his newest acquaintance, who has been waiting for forty years for his spaceship to come back and retrieve him—listening to his stories of a better place. Last night, on his way back from Zorro's last walk of the night, he finally stopped in front of Richard, stretched out on the pavement with his back against a wall, highlighted in lamplight, and asked him what he was reading, but Richard only turned his great dark head toward him and his round, untroubled eyes on him, and said nothing, his silence as eloquent as any words. So, if he isn't Death, he's probably God. This morning he had another exchange with Vega, this time about whether it was dog piss or human piss on the first-floor landing behind the radiator, ending with Vega trying to sell him tickets for some subterranean lottery, it's for a good cause.

And so, he got on his bike, refusing to go for a drink and a game of Space Invaders with the others after work, and started riding, remembering so vividly the Forest Hills to North Hampton Marathon his club held the summer he was seventeen that he could feel the sun beaming down on his sweating back, and only now, coasting along Columbus Avenue, having passed this way once before, turned around, and come back, does he realize where he's going. Anyway, Sophie would be furious if she knew he was so near but had only come so far.

The day, of course, had ended with an argument, just as it had begun. In between was a memo from Parker about the grant they'd been counting on which had only half come through. Like all departmental bad news that it is Parker's responsibility to break, the memo had been unsigned, but the more astute of the staff had known immediately from whom it was; the "We're sure that we can count on all team members to do their utmost to cut down on waste and needless extravagance" could only have come from a poet's typewriter. Aside from the questions it had raised as to the exact nature of necessary extravagance, the memo had set the tone and tenor of yet another day. Bullshit, end to end. The downtrodden in and out all morning, lying and scheming and hustling without hope, meeting his own cheerless pretense of being able to help, of being the cavalry on its way, with the wall-eyed look of the last Indian, staring dumbly at the empty whisky bottle at his feet. The apprentice and master ball-busters out and in all afternoon, lying and scheming and congratulating themselves on their selfless work and sterling intentions, meeting his facetious pretense of being the cavalry thundering across the acrid plains with the smirks of seasoned journalists and politicians, this will pull them in. And woven through them all, the students, medical students and sociology students, psychology students and health education students, trainee social workers and trainee administrators, all of them more interested in how much they're going to make when they graduate, or with what stunning maneuver or innovation they will make their reputations and be asked to advise the President on inner cities, than in actually learning anything. By the time Parker lured him into his hole to discuss, he said, the Old Age Home project for the seniors, he had almost no strength left with which to argue.

Even as he watched the sunlight melt over the parking lot outside of Parker's window, and heard Parker's voice slide from its normal tone of friendly insincerity to its official tone of formal insincerity, even as Parker tilted his adjustable executive's chair slightly back and drummed his fingertips, clean and health-club brown, manicured and ringed on one hand with a wedding band and on the other with a college ring, Tony had known not only exactly what the argument would be, but how it would start, how it would develop, and how it would end. Sometimes they argue about political or moral intent or principles; sometimes they argue about personal style, administrative organization, department priorities, or the differences between organizing a center for high-school dropouts from the ghetto and a project for graduate students from the better neighborhoods; sometimes they argue about methodology or teaching techniques; sometimes they argue about Karl Marx or China or the Bronx or about whether or not the advent of the computer age signifies man's salvation or his end. Today they argued about which programs were expendable and which weren't, Parker favoring those that would look the best in his annual report over those that might mean the most on the street. Both of them knew that it wasn't the private rest homes versus the Lower East Side People's Storefront Health Center about which they were really arguing.

"I was having another look at the figures," said Parker, demonstrating the oratorical flair that has had him on the public speaking circuit for a decade. And Tony had felt his heart drop like a man shot at close range with a buffalo gun. Whop. And thought to himself, this must, indeed, be hell, he and Parker forever doomed to tango together through each repetitious year, their teeth in each other's shoulders, continually treading on one another's toes, the music pumped in through a box on the wall, and jowl-to-jowl as they glide across the conference-room table to apathetic applause and discreet tittering. So much for youthful dreams of glory and immortality. So much for his young-man's hopes of significance and revolution. There will be no distinctions, no citations, no footnote in the encyclopedia for him. No hero's grave with a single red rose laid against the simple headstone awaits his corpse. No blazing, bloody moment when the enemy's bullet rips through his heart and his own last shot brings a demon wail as a body jerks and falls. No dank and putrid cell where he lies beyond his own tortured body, count-ing his own breaths, hearing the whispers of his own blood, his dying like a candle in the endless endless night. No comrade, slick with sweat and mud and blood, to shoot him with his own gun as the fascist troops thunder up the stairs. Nothing like that. No one will so much as name a bowling trophy after him. With his life, he will die of a heart attack in the back of some badly heated classroom of some rinky-dink community college while Parker shows his slides of China and the half-dozen students forced to attend sleep gently with their eyes wide open.

"I know how you feel about the Chinatown project, but if you'll just look at these numbers with me, I think you'll agree that by closing it down, just temporarily, till we see what the next budget brings or we can drum up a little extra support from somewhere else, we'd be better off deploying our resources uptown for the old folks' homes. We can use about three times the number of students, and not just special students from the locality, but students from all over. Don't you think?"

"Not much," he'd smiled back. "Not anymore."

But still Parker went on, despite the fact that it had all been said before, would all be said again, and would always finish the same way. He turned on him his I-am-a-fair-man face, can't you understand my problems, and dug his hands into the pockets of his polyester slacks. Giving Rivera his cue to tilt his chair back slightly, cut his eyes down to the size for calculation, cross his legs, and say, with only the threat of a smile, "Just what are you trying to say, Larry? That you think there's more money in making busy work for a bunch of ambitious middle-class kids from the suburbs than in keeping open a neighborhood project that has actually worked and done some good? Is that what you're saying, Larry?"

Saddest of all, though, is the fact that none of it matters. Larry keeps him around as a king would keep a fool, to keep him on his toes and nimble, to criticize him in private so that he is prepared when anyone criticizes him in public. Larry keeps him around because he is good at his job, but not so good that he poses any threat, not so good that anyone is likely to overlook his outbursts, his run-ins and what Parker calls his "pathological disregard for systems, protocol and rules." Larry also keeps him around because, when he was out on the streets, he used to be even better at his job, largely built the foundation on which the department's reputation rests, had such a high profile that there was no way he could be totally ignored. He might have been dangerous then, certainly troublesome enough to deserve a safe promotion, but now he is not even really annoying, can be easily shuffled over to Social Services ("Well, you know, the cutbacks have affected us all") if he really starts giving them a hard time.

"No," shouted Parker, slamming his fist against the air, "that is not what I am saying. What I'm saying is that the biggest wheel gets the most grease. You may think that we're running a charity here, but we're not. I'm running a business. I can look the other way when you fiddle a little extra for that one or a little something for this one. I can forgive you constantly interfering in things that don't concern you—I never said anything about that number you pulled about Martin's mother, did I?—but you've got to understand that to keep the ball rolling we need money, and money we don't get for teaching half a dozen kids to take blood pressure. You act like I'm the enemy. For God's sake, Tony, I'm on your side."

Probably he is wrong, and he won't die of a failed heart while sitting on a plastic chair, his fingers digging into his styrofoam cup, the liquid dribbling across his paled hand while Parker drones on about community action. And if he does, probably Sandy is right, and it is better than being knifed by some crazy junky.

Probably.

He draws up outside of Sophie's building, dark and undistinguished, where she has lived now for five years, something of a record, the only person he knows who would move from a good block to a bad one because she likes the people better.

He wheels the bike into the foyer, gives the bell that says Rivera, S. the three short rings of old, and waits to hear his mother's voice crackle over the intercom. In the past, everyone in the building would have known who he was, would have waved to him from their windows or slapped his hand as they passed him by the door, hey there, Tony, how're ya doin'? But now he is met only with looks of suspicion, is he a salesman or a cop?

"Yeah?" Sophie's voice comes blasting through the tiny speaker. "What is it?"

"It's me," he shouts back, and then, because it is hard to tell what that meant to her, adds, "Tony. It's me, Tony."

She is standing in the open door as he comes panting up the stairs with the bike over his shoulder, he isn't going to leave it on its own in this neighborhood. "I've got people coming," says Sophie as he staggers on to the landing.

"I just thought I'd stop by since I had to come this way anyhow," and leans forward to give her his kiss on the cheek, *hola*, mom.

"Oh, yeah?" says Sophie, looking him up and down without seeming to do so. "And chain that bike up by the stairs. I don't want it messin' up my floor. I've got guests."

Obediently, he chains the bike and follows her into the kitchen where there is already a bottle of whisky and two glasses on the table. Sophie's displays of maternal affection and understanding aren't everyone's, but they do exist. "So," she says, plunking a pitcher of water on to the table as well. "What's wrong?" and immediately turns back to what she was doing before he came in, calling over her shoulder that he should pour out the drinks.

"There's nothing wrong. I just suddenly realized how long it's been since I've seen you, that's all."

"Oh, yeah?"

"Oh, yeah. I was in the area, so I thought I'd come and see my old white-haired mama and find out how she's doing."

"She could be dead and buried by now. I haven't seen you

since you borrowed that car to take me over to Jersey last May and the cops picked us up right outside the tunnel."

He lifts his glass and swings it toward her, *"Salud,"* and drinks half of it down in almost one swallow. "It's not my fault if the men of the New York Police Department are only human and a little overzealous and capable of making silly mistakes." They let them go, in the end, didn't they?

"Oh, no," says Sophie, taking her glass from the table and toasting him back. "I'm sure it's not. I just thought that maybe they had arrested you for something after all. Since I hadn't heard."

"No," he says. "No. Everything's fine. I've just been very busy lately, that's all."

"Oh, sure," says Sophie. "That must be why you're never home. I've been calling you for weeks but I never get no answer."

He drinks down the second half even faster than the first. "There's been trouble with the line."

"Oh, yeah," says Sophie. "And that probably explains why every time I do get through someone hangs up."

And he gazes back, also unsmiling, more like she than he's ever known. "The phoneman says it's something at the switch. It's because of the heat."

What dreams the young Sophie might have had as she held her first son in her arms those many years ago when she herself was little more than a girl are not apparent in the look she gives him now, appraising and not without concern. He was, when very young, a fat and happy child, always moving, always laughing, always talking, yapyapyap morning noon and night. Now he is thin and withdrawn, his jokes and glinting smiles the tricks of a good illusionist, look over there, over there?, no over there. But all she says is, "And how's Sandra?" offering him another drink.

"She's fine. She's up at her parents', escaping the heat."

"Oh?" says Sophie. "Do they live in a supermarket now?" and heaves herself out of her chair, glass in hand, and back to the counter. Standing with her back to him, she slices vegetables with a stainless-steel blade, flinging them by the handful into an oversized wooden bowl, pausing in her rhythmic thwack thwack thwack only to take another drink. She has never been like other mothers, Sophie, but he doesn't know if this is something he has always held against her or not.

In the way of mothers and sons, they discuss his brothers, his cousin the priest, the people Sophie knows who have been injured or fired in the past two weeks, Mrs. Burkowsky's legs which gave out completely in front of the building the other day so that he and López had to carry her up to her apartment without actually seeming to do so, Sophie's back, never the same since the attempted mugging, how Zorro isn't eating with the weather, and the electric coffee grinder he bought yesterday on impulse. Then he says, straining to sound matter-of-fact, "What ever happened to Susan Kalinski?"

Thwack, thwack, thwack, whoosh, not missing half a beat. "Who?"

He waits until she is in mid-whoosh and repeats, "Susan Kalinski." Then adds, as she picks up the knife again, no sign of having heard him slowing her movement, "You know. The one who lived with us for a couple of months of 76th Street. The one with the kids."

She rests the blade on the chopping board and turns to face him, her dark eyes thoughtful, her red lips ready for either a smile or a scowl. He hardly ever notices that she is still easily beautiful, but he notices now.

"You know, the one whose husband tried to beat you up on the stairs," and Sophie had pulled out her surgical knife, borrowed from the hospital, seven stitches, Sophie saying later that there was no sense in scaring someone if you didn't really mean it.

"Susan Kalinski?" she echoes, her eyes now boring back into the past, searching out the correct memories, the forgotten words and images that will bring the Susan Kalinski of the black toreador pants and pink angora sweater and Hit Parade repertoire out of the tiny yellow kitchen of over twenty years ago and into the large white kitchen with its hanging pots and hanging plants of today. "Susan Kalinski?" making the name sound unnatural in her mouth. And then, as though the repetition of the words has, in fact, reactivated the pattern of thought so long unused, "Jesus Christ. You don't mean Susan Kalinski?" She gazes at him with something that might possibly be mistaken for maternal admiration, but which is simply wonderment. "Susan Kalinski? I haven't heard from her in years." Without looking, she reaches one heavy, braceleted arm behind her, picks up her drink, brings it forward, and swallows it down. "Susan Kalinski," she says once more. "Jesus."

"Oh," says Tony, wondering, as ever, what it is she sees when she looks at him like that. "I just thought you might have run into her. Or something."

"Or something?" parrots Sophie. "Or what?"

"Well, nothing, really," and looks to the corner where the giant spider plant shoots its offspring into the space above the washing machine. "I just thought that you might have kept up with her, that's all." Lately, she always makes him feel defensive. It is one of the few things she has in common with his wife.

Sophie sighs and for the first time he notices the apron she is wearing, wrapped around her butterfly tunic.

"Is that a map of Puerto Rico you're wearing?" happy enough to change the subject.

But Sophie isn't so easily diverted. She gives him the same look she used to give him when she knew that he was high but couldn't prove it, and turns back to her work. "Susan Kalinski," she says between thwacks. "She probably married some other bastard and had three more kids."

Sophie never was a woman to waste any sentiment.

"Yeah," laughs Tony. "She probably did. I was just thinking about her the other day, that's all."

"Thinking about her?" she says. "What made you think about her after all these years?"

He can guess the expression on her face, her brows just slightly drawn together, her eyes broody, and her mind clicking, trying to figure out what's really going on. She was never a woman to take much for granted, either.

"Nothing special. I just remembered her, that's all." And adds, as she dumps one last handful of cabbage into the bowl and finally faces him again, wiping her hands across her stomach from San Juan to Caguas, "I wouldn't mind having an apron like that myself."

"You don't 'just remember' somebody after almost twenty-five years," says Sophie.

"Yes you do."

There is a stiletto-sharp moment of silence, silver and gleaming, in which he pours out another round, replaces the bottle carefully in the center of the table, and lifts his glass to his lips;

in which she watches his movements, his lean arm and his always-watching eyes, and then she says, "You mean *you* do."

With just a little effort, he can unfocus his eyes so that he seems to be looking at her with real attention, but can't actually make out her features. "Oh, for God's sake, Sophie, give it a rest, will you? Everyone has memories."

She doesn't say that she thinks his memories are all either highly colored, highly warped, or highly insignificant. She doesn't say (as Sandy has) that he uses the past to mask, excuse, and justify the fact that he has given up on the present. She doesn't say (as she often has) that gone is gone and the sooner you forget about what was, the better off you are. "Everyone has a brain, too," says Sophie.

And then looks up at the old kitchen clock, shaped like a teapot, which has followed her progress from one neighborhood to another for close to three decades, as though she had forgotten there was even such a thing as time, and her eldest son says, "I'm sorry I mentioned it." Which is certainly true.

Sophie begins to untie the apron from around her ample waist, surprised to find herself staring at a middle-aged man in a blue-and-white checked cowboy shirt and faded jeans whose hair is gray and thinning, whose shoes are unpolished, and whose Adam's apple protrudes in a fleshless neck, a middle-aged man whose eyes look tired and whose features are mimicked by the lines that surround them, a man you would pass on the street and never notice unless you happened to catch the flash of his orange socks, just another man. Surprised that he is her own child, making her feel so old, and something in the moment brings back the voices of the long-dead days and the feelings of long-gone moments, and she sees him, unexpectedly, momentarily, as he was in his teens, cocky and flamboyant, not wild like the others with their small-time scams and hustles and close calls with the law, but unsettled. "That kid," her sister used to say, shaking her head over the coffee cups, "that kid just don't fit." "Don't fit what?" Sophie would snap back. And Angela at-least-I-was-married-to-the-father-of-my-children Calavetta, who always gave the impression of knowing more than she would ever tell, would say in her simple, sisterly way, "Don't fit nothing."

So clear is the image that, if for only a heartbeat, it seems more real than the room they are in or the people they have become. But then it goes, too. "I don't know," pulling the loop of cotton over her head. "One minute with you everything's all logic and reason and the dialectics of materialism and the lessons of history, and the next minute you're carrying on like you're in some musical comedy and you can't figure out why everybody else don't start singing. One minute you can't talk about somebody being beaten up by her husband without turning it into a political debate, and the next you're making a big deal about some woman you haven't seen since you were fourteen and who you wouldn't recognize anyway." She folds the apron over the back of a chair. "It wasn't like she was a close friend or anything. She just needed a place to stay for a while and I helped her out. I don't know how it came to be one of the most important events of your childhood."

Nor does he.

"So Sandra's all right then?" she asks at last, a sure sign that his time is nearly up.

"Terrific. She's getting a really good rest, she's lost a couple of pounds, and she's taking up jogging." He drains off the last six drops of liquid. "I was thinking I might start running myself."

"Oh yeah? Where to?"

It is a symptom of his relationship with his mother that he has never fully understood her sense of humor, or, indeed, even if she actually has one. To hell. I want to beat the rush. "Edith gave me a track suit." Which is true: a red one with white stripes and a large plastic zipper up the front of the jacket, a mended patch in the knee, and permanent sweat stains under the arms that she picked up at some rummage sale for a worthy charity. You could hardly consider it a gift, though Sandy does.

"That figures," smiles Sophie. "She told me at the wedding how they always raised Sandra to be concerned about the plight of the poor."

As he prepares to leave, waiting for her to wrap up some bones she's been saving for Zorro, she tells him that she is going up to the Bronx for a while, to look after Angela.

"Don't tell me she's getting obscene phone calls again."

"No," says Sophie, giving him the package in a bright yellow plastic bag. "It's not the kids this time. It's God. She's had a little heart attack."

He sticks the parcel under his arm. "And you didn't tell me?" My own dear aunt and you didn't let me know?

"How could I tell you?" asks Sophie. "When you've got so much trouble with your phone?"

At the door, she gives him two quick, sticky kisses, one on each cheek.

"Really," he says as they disengage, "where'd you get the apron? I'd like to get one for Mrs. Grossman. *Arroz con pollo*'s her specialty."

"I got it from an admirer," says Sophie, almost looking as though she might wink. Then adds, just as she starts to shut the door, "You're not the only one allowed to have private jokes."

It is raining as he comes out of the building, large, determined drops racing like mad to be the first to evaporate against the heartless city streets. He wishes he'd never gotten up this morning; wishes he'd never come to see his mother; wishes he'd never remembered Susan Kalinski and the sound of the shower she took every morning and her voice above the domesticated downpour, *Good night, Irene, good night, Irene,* before she began the dumb routine of one more day, of washing and dressing and feeding the kids and drawing circles in pencil around likely-looking apartments and possible jobs, *Life is just a bowl of cherries, don't take it serious, it's too mysterious.* He wheels the bike off the curb and through a mound of chicken bones, looking both ways before pushing off the way he came. Everything left unsaid unasked or unanswered. Not knowing why he came in the first place; not even knowing whom Sophie was expecting or why she hadn't asked him to stay, he is, after all, her son. But Sophie has never been the sort of mother who likes to involve herself in her children's lives, take me along, too, or vice versa. "I'm your mother," Sophie has always maintained, "not your guardian angel."

Halfway home, he wobbles to a stop at a light and sees a woman who reminds him of Sandy as she might have been, might yet be, in a green trench coat and a paisley scarf, her arm linked with the arm of a man whom he could never have been, will never be, in a white summer suit and Panama hat, half trot, half slide across the intersection, laughing as only lovers do, and behind them Death in an orange windbreaker with its hands in its pockets, head tipped down, singing to itself, barely audible, *me and the wife settled down . . .*

The couple doesn't notice him, but Death does, nodding as it passes the front of the bike. And for the very first time, Rivera nods back.

Meredith is doing Maggie's cards. Last winter when she did them the future they foretold was murky and ambiguous, could have turned out well or ended badly, could have included poverty and ceaseless loneliness or sudden success and buckets of love. But now it is summer, the evening hot and the sky close enough to blue to pass, and the future they foretell, though not definite, of course, though not the absolute but the potential, implies large measures of self-fulfillment and happiness, domestic bliss, and a secure mortgage.

Meredith would staunchly and sincerely claim that she never reads into her readings what she knows, or hopes, or thinks she knows, but that is not precisely true. Last winter, the things that Meredith knew about Maggie were her name, her age, what she looked like, how she made a living, how long she'd been back in the city, and that she always drank her coffee black. Her past was boarded up and her present empty. They met through the friend of a friend of a friend who knew that Maggie needed a partner and Meredith needed something to do. "Oh, God," Maggie would say, pulling off her boots as she flopped onto the couch, "if something doesn't happen soon, I'll die of boredom before the spring." "Oh, God," Maggie would say as they went over the books and drank giant mugs of herbal tea, "if I had any money I'd blow it all on boys and booze." "Jesus," Maggie would say as they trudged through the Village, boxes in their arms, dressed as though ready for a dogsled race across the Yukon, "I still keep forgetting what winter is like." And Meredith, quick off the mark, would nudge, "Were you living in the South?" And Maggie, even quicker, would block, "I always seemed to be in the south of something." But now, though she knows no more about Maggie's past or what she really wants or hopes to find than she did last winter or the summer before, Meredith does know the shape of things to come. Like the first one to move out of the old neighborhood, like the first on the block to get a scholarship to Harvard or a fantastic job in San Francisco, like the first to move out of the tenements and into some suburban paradise, Maggie carries with her the brunt of everyone elses' dreams. Or at least of Meredith's. She is proof that tides can turn and things still happen, that it isn't too late, after all. When they first met, Maggie had been back in the country for nearly a year, had no real friends, no lover, no money, and no real prospects. And only months ago, Maggie sat across from her, the cards on their square of silk between them, saying that what she was looking forward to was the Third World War. Because then, Maggie said, when civilization had been obliterated and there was only nothing left, all the lonely, bewildered, and largely ignored and unhappy women of the world would be ready. After decades of sensual and emotional deprivation, after year upon year of heartbreak and frustration, humiliation, rejection, and denial, they alone would be prepared to climb out into the mocking, mutilated landscape and simply survive. Without hope or help or clean sheets or anyone to get them an aspirin for their radiation headaches. Unused to having anyone to rely on, unaccustomed to being looked after or thought about for more than a long weekend, they alone would be able to look up at the bleeding sky and say, "So what?" "Big deal." Now, however, Maggie sits across from her in the same old chair, drinking iced tea instead of coffee, talking about terracotta tiles and mermaid murals, saying, "Well, Skip thinks that we should use the entire downstairs as a kitchen–family room," "Well, Skip says that the heat wave is going to break at the weekend," "Well, Skip says that we'd be better off concentrating on the clothes for down here and the novelties for up there," and wondering whether or not Mrs. Ellis, supermom, will insist that they have the wedding in her apartment with its good view, doorman always on duty, and rambling rooms.

"Right," says Meredith, dealing: a column of one, a column of three, a column of one and a column of four; the Eight of Swords, the Seven of Cups, the Hanged Man, the Magician, the Seven of Coins, the Eight of Cups, the Eight of Barons, the Chariot, Death. The Magician and the Chariot are both reversed. "Let's see what we've got here."

As once she might have gazed up at the secretive sky, or searched within a lover's longing eyes, Maggie now peers at the soiled and dog-eared cards, wanting to know what they have to say. "Shit," she says. "That doesn't look good."

"Oh, no," Meredith immediately shakes her head, her earrings jangling, easily as capable of misinterpreting the future as of misinterpreting the past. "Oh, no. You always overreact to Death, but it's really very positive."

"Uh huh."

"It means that the last obstacle in your realizing your true self is going to be removed."

Sounds like death to her. "It does?"

"Yes. Definitely. See," her stubby finger moving from card to card, "here's the Eight of Swords. Now what she says to me is that you've had a rough time in the past. Maybe you've been very alone, or have had a hard time keeping things together. You know?"

"Um," says Maggie, though what she knows is that Meredith—who often has to choose between the telephone bill and a bottle of bourbon, who often has to choose between one night of mediocre sex and poor companionship with a man who has mirrored tiles in his bathroom and black loafers and white socks on his feet and another night drinking herself to sleep with the liquor bought with the money that should have gone to pay for the phone—thinks that all women, with the exceptions, perhaps, of her own mother and the Queen of England, have had a rough time and mostly alone.

"So you've kind of been trapped in this and it's really hard to get out. But here you've got Death, see? And that says to me that you're about to break your old patterns. You see?"

"Uh huh," says Maggie, though what she sees is herself the Eight of Swords, about to grasp a rope dangled down to her in her dungeon of adversity, and painstakingly grasping the wrong one. "What about the Hanged Man, then?"

"Oh, the Hanged Man," and Meredith readjusts herself on her chair, her psychic cells plugged in like electric razors. "Now that is interesting. See, Death could mean a kind of destruction, right? But the Hanged Man, you see, the Hanged Man says that you can adapt to the change."

And, yes, she knows she can adapt to the change.

"Meredith," says Maggie, sounding more like herself than when she was talking about Skip's new interest in wildlife and his determination to build his own bird feeder, "what do you mean, 'Death is a kind of destruction'? How many kinds of destruction are there?"

"Well," and Meredith clears her throat, "a lot. What I meant was that it isn't physical destruction, you know. Nobody's going to die or anything." It is difficult to tell from the expression on Meredith's face, so intense and so sincere, if she knows that spirits die, as well. "What it says to me is that your circumstances are going to change radically, and that maybe you're going to have to give up some things you've been clinging to that you don't even know about. But that once that's done, your way is clear." She looks up, smiling.

"And the Magician? What does it mean that he's upside down?"

"Oh," says Meredith, as though noticing it for the first time. "The Magician reversed. Now that is interesting. See, I would think that that means that if you don't take hold now, that if you show any weakness or hesitation, you'll stay trapped. See, upright the Magician is strength and triumph. Or he's a teacher, he's part of the Way. But upside down, he means weakness and failure. Instead of pointing the Way, he's blocking it." Meredith takes a paper napkin from the holder on the table and wipes her sweating face. "You see?"

Maggie says, "Yes, I guess so," knowing that Meredith is only trying to tell her what she has been telling Meredith, that marrying Skip will change her life and change her luck. But when she looks at the cards she cannot see what Meredith sees. Meredith can look at the figures and identify lovers, parents, feuding friends, and callous bosses, can look at the numbers and detect clues, have the baby, don't take the job, move to Santa Fe. For Meredith the major arcana is like a family album, isn't that your uncle with the four wives? isn't that you and your sister at the beach? was that when you had pneumonia? For Meredith the minor arcana is like the words of inspiration and advice on a gift calendar: Today's a good day to start something new, As no man is born an artist, so no man is born an angler, Have the courage to face a difficulty lest it kick you harder than you bargained for. Maggie sees another game.

"God," says Meredith, reaching for another napkin, "it sure is hot in here. I wish I could afford an air conditioner."

Maggie has slept on beaches as old as all imagined time, has sat with witches in the changing darkness of a mountain night, has crossed continents with no companion but herself, has lived in lands where the past is stronger than the present, and in lands where tomorrow can only be the same as today. And she has seen magicians and fools, lovers and hanged men, kings and queens, and priests and death and its destruction. When she looks at the cards, she sees her own dreams.

She leans back in her chair and yawns. "I'll have to get going soon. Skip will be phoning," and both of them automatically glance toward the clock.

"Do you want me to finish the cards? My date's not coming over till ten. His family's on Fire Island and they usually call around nine."

Maggie shakes her head and unsticks her body from the back of the chair. "No. I think I've got the general picture," looking again to make certain that she has. And, yes, of course Meredith is right, there they are, not ancient symbols and a ritual code tricky to translate or make concrete, but the common difficulties and solutions, triumphs and defeats, easy enough to recognize when they appear on the street or in a friend or in your heart.

Meredith gets up and stands half-turned for a second, wondering what she was about to do. "I did my cards last night, but it was so hot and I was so depressed and Will kept waking up with nightmares and all I could get out of them was that I should never have married Bobby and that my mother was right, I should have finished college and taught first grade like she did." The cards have been telling Meredith these or similar things for the past three years, or since the evening her husband moved across town with the stereo and a physiotherapist from Milwaukee. She opens the refrigerator door, covered with magnetized plastic letters in red blue yellow orange and green that seem to spell out something but which, in fact, do not, and comes back with the pitcher of iced tea in her hand. "You want some more?"

"Just half. I've got about four more hours to do on those sweatshirts tonight, so I can let you have them to be finished off tomorrow."

"Maggie," says Meredith, carefully selecting her words, "you're not really going to keep slogging like this once you're married, are you? I mean, if you're worried about me I can always go back to typing cookbooks or something."

"I told you," Maggie cuts in, her consonants snapping as

though Meredith might be going deaf, "we're not contracting, we're expanding. I don't know why you keep going on about it."

"I keep going on about it," says Meredith, her earrings swinging, "because if I were you I wouldn't do it. It's going to be harder than ever to keep things together. I'd just sit back and take it easy." She looks at Maggie sipping her tea, but Maggie is watching the lemon bob in her glass. "I mean, what's the point?"

The point?

Though she could never discipline herself enough to be a painter, though she could never love anyone enough to be a wife, though she could never manage the selfless devotion cited by Kate as a prerequisite for being a good mother, though she could never seem to maintain enough interest in anything—not even money or feeling good—long enough to make it a way of life, she has always had her work. She has always had herself to fall back on.

"Things are just beginning to work," Maggie answers, now studying the little yellow truck beside the sugar bowl. "I'm not going to stop now."

Meredith studies Maggie's face with the intensity with which she previously studied the cards.

There are people who have no inhibitions about getting up on network television and discussing their personal histories and domestic problems, the nitty-gritty details of their lives, loves, and nervous breakdowns, with a melodious-voiced interviewer who is on everybody's side, tell us about you and your husband's sexual difficulties and please look into camera one, tell us, have you ever had a homosexual experience, and what would you say was the primary cause of your drug addiction? There are people who don't mind baring their battle-scarred bosoms to whomever isn't too busy stirring the chili or checking the balance on the speakers to listen. People who wind up crying in the kitchen or the bathroom at parties. Men who sit in your living room until dawn, staring at their hands for minutes on end, drinking your whiskey by the tumbler and ending every new disclosure of their unhappiness or inadequacy with either, "I really better go now," or "I hope I'm not keeping you up," or "You must find this pretty boring." Women who just stopped by to say hello and who stay through the supper they have no appetite to eat, cataloguing all the times that life has let them down, but did I ever tell you what happened then? To some extent, Meredith is a person like that; but Maggie is not. Maggie knows all about Meredith's unhappy childhood in Queens and her kind and generous father and neurotic, destructive mother; all about Meredith's unhappy marriage to Robert the Bastard; all about the lonely struggle she's had since, a woman alone with a child in a world run by men for couples. But Meredith's knowledge of Maggie is largely incomplete and greatly assumed or imagined.

So that Meredith knows that she is not going to be told any more and must come to her own conclusions.

"No . . . no, I suppose you're right."

"I know I'm right," winks Maggie, who also knows that Skip, though he applauds her ingenuity and determination, and is delighted by her creativity and talent, who's a clever girl?, gives her work less importance than fitting braces and only marginally more than canning your own tomatoes. Just as she knows that Skip regards anything done for less than thirty thousand dollars per year as a hobby, but will permit her most anything if it keeps her amused. "Come on, Will," she shouts down the hallway to where the television fills the room with happy voices. "It's time to go. We've got to feed the cat."

Meredith is instantly on her feet, fetching Will's undersized orange knapsack from the floor beside her chair. "Everything he needs is in here: his toothbrush, his lamb, clean underwear, clothes for the morning, and his favorite storybook, but don't let him con you into reading him more than one."

"Don't worry, we'll be fine."

"I really appreciate this," says Meredith, as Will comes charging into the room in a pair of madras shorts and Snoopy sunglasses, screaming, "Let's go! Let's go!"

"You just have a good time."

"Oh, I will," says Meredith, though deep in her heart she is sure that she won't.

Coming down the stoop, they see Tony Rivera across the street, sharing a doorway with a giant man who looks as though he could be John the Baptist.

"Who the hell is that?" asks Maggie.

Will breaks off from his frantic waving and calling yahoo. "That's Tony. He fixes my bike."

"No, not him. The other man."

"Oh," and he shrugs his small shoulders and looks surprised. "I don't know. Meredith won't let me talk to bums."

They had been sitting side by side, not noticing the downing day, each eating an apple and staring at nothing in particular, but suddenly Tony sprints across the road, Zorro in his arms and the fruit still in his mouth.

"Hey, Tony," cries Will, immediately wrapping himself around one leg. "I thought you wasn't going to say good-bye."

Tony lets Zorro drop and takes the apple from his mouth. "Of course I'm going to say good-bye. Good-bye." And, leaning over conspiratorially, "Where are you going?"

"I'm going to Maggie's," now kneeling beside Zorro who is quietly licking the chocolate from his face. "See?" pointing to the bag in Maggie's hand. "I've got all my stuff with me."

"Even the hamster?"

"Nooo, not Jerome. He wouldn't be able to breathe in there would he? I'm only going overnight." Already experienced in dealing with women, he takes a quick look at Maggie to judge her mood. "Meredith's having company."

All the mothers are having company tonight. "Well," says Tony, who has not yet acknowledged Maggie standing not all that far from him, silent but not invisible, "since you're going such a long way, why don't I walk up to the corner with you and we can get you something to eat on the trip."

Maggie begins to say, "Oh, that's all right," but her words are obliterated by Will's whoops of delight, "Hey, Tony, I've got a better idea. You and Zorro could walk us to the bus."

Maggie starts to say, "Now, Will. I'm sure that Tony and Zorro . . . ," but her diplomacy is demolished as Tony says, "Okay, you've got a deal. I might even let you ride on my shoulders. Seeing as it's so late." Then, as though there'd been no need to before, he turns to her and says, "I was wondering if I could ask you a favor?"

"You want me to carry the dog." She must have seen him smile before, but it is only now that she actually notices. He has a very nice smile.

"No. Meredith says that you sometimes go up to the wilderness for weekend retreats. I was wondering if you'd take something up to Sandy for me."

She says nothing, maybe waiting for him to explain whether it is a bomb or a Hank Williams tape, she probably knows all about him, too.

"Just a couple of things she needs. They're not heavy or anything."

"Oh," says Maggie, almost sounding disappointed, "oh, sure."

"I don't want to make any problems for you."

"Oh, no. It's fine. I never take that much myself, so it doesn't matter."

He unwraps Zorro's leash from around his waist. "I hear you'll be moving up to the new frontier soon yourself."

"Oh, yes," she almost grins. "I've just got one more mule to buy and I'm ready to roll."

And then, for no good reason, and although Will is tugging on his arm, and though he wasn't expecting to, he turns his attention up the street, his hand to his forehead as he scans what has been built to replace the horizon, and says, she assumes to her, "I'd rather live beside a freeway, myself."

"Well," says Maggie, turning in the opposite direction where the cars zip by. "That's all right then, because you almost do."

"Hey, Tony," shouts Will. "Let's get going."

"Okay, *amigo*," and bends down to hoist the small boy on his shoulders, surprised to see that Maggie has already taken hold of the dog. "Just one more thing," and turns to face the street. "Hey, Richard," he calls, while Will stares ahead with interest and Maggie wonders what's going to happen next. Suddenly, all she wants to do is get home. "Hey, Richard. We're going to walk up to the bus," and watches in an amazement equal to Maggie's as Richard slowly comes to his feet, makes a perfect basket into the trash can in front of him with his core, and comes gracefully across the road as though strolling through the parting seas.

"Is he coming, too?" ask Will and Maggie as one.

"It looks like it," says Tony, wondering if this is a good sign or a bad omen.

They have had a good night, she and Will. He is pleasant and good-natured, he is nice to the cat and he likes to help carry things to the table. Although he has difficulty in following the plots of his very best shows, his stories are interesting and his comments always illuminating. "What I don't like about this kind of movie," says Will, "is that everybody's either yelling or crying." They had bologna boats for a snack, played two rounds of War, and when Skip called she let him answer the phone, hi. "I didn't know you liked children," said Skip, clearly impressed. "There's a lot about me you don't know," making him laugh. "I know that I love you," he continued, his voice at once soft and serious. "I know that you're beautiful and intelligent and sexy and sane and understanding. And I know that I'm going to spend the rest of my life getting to know everything about you, where you went to high school, and who your first boyfriend was, what your favorite things were when you were a kid, what your favorite foods are, and where you spent your summer vacations . . . Everything."

Perhaps, for the questions he asks, the answers he gets are sufficient.

They sit together on the bed, her deadlines forgotten, Will bathed and wrapped in a beach towel, his hair wet and standing up, leaning into the circle of her arm, a bowl of potato chips between them and a horror movie on the "Late Show." "You don't have to be scared, Maggie," says Will. "I'm here."

"Oh, I know that," she assures him, removing a heel from her knee.

When the commercial comes on, he says, "Richard was pretty nice, don't you think so, Maggie?"

"Yeah," says Maggie. "He's all right. He's very tall."

Will is the only person she knows who can eat potato chips and talk at the same time. "He sure is. When I was on his shoulders I could reach higher than anybody," his smile reaching farther still. "It's a good thing Meredith didn't see me."

"Um," says Maggie, wondering how much to say. "It sure is."

He doesn't remind her of her son at all. Where Will is fair and pudgey, looking, when he scowls, like a young gorilla, Ben was thin and dark, looking, her mother said, just like her father when he was a boy, the spitting image. Will is tough but cautious, whereas Ben was quiet but fearless. Will likes trucks and astronauts, but Ben liked animals and Indians. Will likes to dip his French fries into the catsup, but Ben liked to pour the catsup over his French fries.

The differences are pretty endless.

Why has she never told Skip about Ben?

"If you want to close your eyes," says Will, "I'll tell you when to open them again."

"It's okay, Batman. I make my eyes go wonky when I don't want to see."

Does she think that Skip would turn her from his door, out into the snow you whore? you mother of a dead bastard? you brazen Jezebel? Does she think that his knowing would change the way he sees her, no longer the bright and carefree seductress who came up to him at Meredith's Christmas party, a glass of red wine in her hand, saying, "Remember me? The classic case of a physical injury causing toothache?" No longer the lovable if aging sprite who'd never before had a reason for settling down? Or that Skip, who sometimes gives the impression of having learned his English from T-shirts, would sap her with his sympathy, his, geesuz, that's awful, I know what you must have been through, I know how you must feel? Would he use the knowledge to misunderstand her, I don't think she's ever really gotten over the tragedy, of course, you would say that; to misjudge her; to maneuver her?

It could be any of these reasons; it could be all of them; it might be none.

"Hey, Maggie," coos Will in his I'm-just-a-little-kid voice. "Hey, Maggie, we forgot the lemonade."

"Who's 'we,' little white boy?"

In the blue-gray light of the vampire's dungeon, he smiles the smile he usually smiles only behind his mother's back. "You."

Like the silver rose bowl in the bottom of the refugee's satchel, like the withered woman who watches each season's recruits parade through the town as forty years before she watched the departure of her only lover, like the one letter saved, the only photograph kept, perhaps it is simply all that she has left. All that is her own, kept to herself for so long that to reveal it now would be, somehow, to trivialize both his life and her pain. To misrepresent both the circumstances of his birth and the circumstances of his death.

The vampire is getting ready to suck all the heroine's life juices through the deep, full lips of his lover's smile when Will says, "Maggie, if you're too scared we can turn this off."

"Well, if you're sure you wouldn't mind. I am pretty tired."

But when the set is off and the room is dark and silent with the sounds that buildings make, the gushing water, the sighing pipes, the slamming doors, he sleeps with his left leg up to his chin and his right flung straight behind him and his hand across her hip, and she lies close to the edge, her dreaming disturbed by thoughts and other dreams.

Far from the room where Will and Maggie sleep, far from the street where Tony and Richard keep largely silent watch on the progress of the night, Zorro dozing between their feet, the moon wheels slowly across the spangled sky and nocturnal hunters go scramble crackle crunch across the darkened ground. Safely tucked into their old, oak bed, Jack and Edith sit, each propped up by pillows, she reading a detective novel set in London, where all the best murders seem to happen, and he reading a novel about Buddy Bolden.

"Didn't Tony used to sing a song about Buddy Bolden?" asks Jack, scowling behind his glasses as he tries to remember the tune. It is the eighth time that Tony Rivera's name has been mentioned tonight, but neither of them has been counting.

"He used to sing a song about everything," says Edith, her eyes not straying from the page.

Jack sighs. Tonight Skip came to dinner, and though he has gotten used to having him around lately, and will have to get used to having him around more, now that Skip is giving up his usual vacation of sailing along the Eastern seaboard in favor of getting the house in shape, tonight Skip's presence seemed to underline Tony's absence, and all the questions that Jack has studiously avoided asking since Sandy's arrival are buzzing around in his mind like the notes of the song he can no longer remember.

"I don't understand," says Jack, peering sideways at Edith. "If Skip's up here for a whole month, why isn't what's her name coming with him?"

Sometimes, as now, Edith's lips move as she reads. Which makes him think that she has answered him before he can actually hear her speak. "I don't know."

"She doesn't have a job or anything, does she?"

"I think so."

"You think so what?"

Edith's lips move, Edith's voice speaks. "I think she has some job."

"Oh." He flattens the book on his lap and turns to look at her openly, but she reads on, practiced at behaving as though he isn't there. "Edith," he says after a few minutes.

"What?"

He wishes that she would look at him, that she would give him some help. A man of many words on an endless selection of topics, he nonetheless has always had difficulty in discussing the more basic issues of his life. He predicted the murder of Lumumba, he predicted the fall of Allende, he bet Edith ten dollars that Nixon would resign, and he never once said that he thought the American people would never make a movie star their President, but he has never been really sure what was going on in his own home, in the hearts and heads of his wife and child. So that instead of saying, "You don't think there's still something ... you don't think there's something going on between Sandy and Skip?" which is what he wants to say, he says "You don't think this thing between Tony and Sandy is serious, do you?"

"Of course not," says Edith, turning a page. "It'll all blow over soon."

"Oh, good," says Jack, who for all his ranting on about the imperatives of history and the inevitable cycle of social change likes his own little world kept pretty much the same. "That's good." He picks up his book and stares at the text, suddenly remembering a fragment of refrain, *I thought I heard Buddy Bolden say, just before they came to take him away* ... "That's good. I know Tony's a little strange, well, a little difficult ..."

Edith, who finds almost everyone either strange or difficult, continues to move her lips, but says nothing.

"But I've become quite fond of him—over the years."

Edith mouths the words "... but if the events of the evening were ...," but all she says is "Um."

"I just thought that things seemed to be taking a little longer this time than usual," says Jack who, up until tonight, has actually given the matter very little thought, is not even very sure of what he means, has always, in family disputes, especially when they involve him, opted for a stance of reasoned neutrality.

"It's summer," says Edith, as though that simple fact is

explanation enough, and, finally admitting defeat, closes her book. "What's the matter, Jack? Can't you sleep?"

"Of course I can sleep," humphs Jack, annoyed, as usual, by Edith's inability to follow a conversation logically. "I don't want to sleep yet. I'm reading this book."

Sandy is driving Skip home. Skip, imbued with an almost childish enthusiasm for the start of his vacation and high as a satellite on his new happiness, has had too much to drink. Sandy said that she didn't think it would be an auspicious beginning to Skip's new life if he began it in traction in the local hospital, though Edith pointed out that the hospital is new and extremely up-to-date and already gaining a reputation in matters of the heart. And Skip said, "No, no, no, I'm fine, really," then tripped over that deceptive single step leading into the living room. Jack walked over and took the keys from his hand. "I'll drop your car off in the morning and you can give me a lift back."

Sandy, her eyes responsibly fixed on the ghostly stretch of road before her, half-listens to what he is saying, half-thinks about something else. Skip is in a really good mood. If before he had any doubts about what he is doing—suddenly being swept off his feet at his age, suddenly deciding to just start all over again, new wife, new home, new practice, new children—he certainly has none tonight. And for that, he feels, he has Sandy to thank. She was there last autumn when he really needed a friend, when he was so close to cracking that his mother was beginning to mention her bridge friend Helen's son, Ted the top psychiatrist, even diplomats' wives go to him. She was there, offering him sex and companionship, conversation and cunnilingus, sympathy, affection, understanding, and enthusiastic love-making on a regular basis, and she is here now, his friend still, maybe the best friend he has ever had, happy to see him happy, concerned enough about him to drive him home. He wants to show her how much he appreciates her, he wants to let her know that though they are no longer lovers there is still love between them, more now even than before, that he wants her to be happy, too.

"So how's Tony?" he says unexpectedly. "You hear from him lately?"

This is the eighth time this evening that Sandy has heard the name Tony Rivera mentioned, and she has been counting. "I talked to him this morning," she says, taking the turn just a little too fast, and not adding that it was she who called him.

"Oh, that's nice," croons Skip, "that's nice," slamming his feet straight out in front of him and holding on to the dash. "So things are working out all right?"

"Oh, yeah," says Sandy, narrowly missing a terrified rabbit, "things are working out." She will soon be receiving two pairs of jeans, one sweater, one Joni Mitchell album and two blue sneakers that she doesn't really need, all because the conversation to which she thought her call would lead never occurred and she felt she had to say something. It has never before happened that Tony has failed to take the initiative, or at least to make some tentative gesture of reconcilement or compromise. It is hard for her to tell whether this new attitude is the result of a mature respect for her or complete disinterest.

"I'm glad to hear that," says Skip, as indeed he is. "I'd hate to think that anything I'd done might ... might ... Jesus Christ! Is that a cow? Sandy!" swiveling so quickly that he makes himself dizzier, "I think that was a cow."

"It wasn't a cow," says Sandy, not so much stopping in his driveway as landing.

The lights aren't working because the electrician is in the middle of something complex and dangerous. She helps him to the house, or he helps her, and together they grope their way to the Ellis encampment, a sleeping bag and an army cot, a Coleman lamp and a Sterno stove, a pile of magazines and manuals on home improvement, my wife, myself, my three children, and my Springer Spaniel converted the old attic into a family room, with a bar and a laundry center, in only two weeks. Since it is too much trouble to make even instant coffee, he insists that they have a nightcap, though just a little one, because he knows she has to drive back. They chat a little about this and that—the chaos the electricians have left, the havoc the builders have wreaked, how nice it was of Edith to say that he can use their bathroom as his own until the difficulties with the plumbing have been solved—and then, with the single-mindedness of the drunk, the senile, or the child, he returns to the always interesting subject of happiness. She deserves all she can get. Though theirs was never what you could call a serious affair, he has always had the greatest respect and admiration for her. Respect, admiration, and gratitude. For her strength, for her character, for her kindness and generosity. Making her sound like the loser in an election. After all she's been through—with Tony, with him, with her problems at work, with that problem last winter—it seems that there is nothing he wants more, next to his happiness, than hers. If there is anything he can do, he will do it. If there is anything that she wants, he will get it. If she needs anyone to stand by her, he will stand. He pours them both another drink, not spilling a drop, not even in the exaggerated shadows of the lantern. They sit side by side on the cot (where else can they sit?), he staring at his feet, she smiling, if tightly, at the glass in her hand. He is glad that they can still be friends, that nothing will ever change that.

"So am I," says Sandy, though she is feeling far from glad. She had been so surprised to actually get Tony on the phone this morning that she had talked for nearly fifteen minutes, getting responses from him that sounded as though they were being read from cue cards, before she had finally asked him if he'd been doing any thinking. "Oh, yeah," he said. "I've been thinking." "And what have you been thinking about?" "I've been thinking about Susan Kalinski." "Susan Kalinski? Who is Susan Kalinski?" It hadn't really upset her that he'd been thinking about another woman, at least that wasn't abnormal. "She used to be a friend of my mother's." "Oh. A friend of your mother's. And what were you thinking about her?" "I was wondering if she was dead."

She is hearing Tony say "I was wondering if she was dead," as though it were the only thing he could be wondering about, as though it were the only thing in his entire life that was of any importance, as though it were something that mattered, when Skip says, "You know, I've never ... ah ... I've never ... um ... I've never said anything to Maggie about us."

"Of course not," says Sandy. "Why should you?"

"Oh, no, what I meant was ... well, just that I've never said anything to her." He hunches over his glass, lonely with his guilt. "I mean, it really doesn't concern her, does it?"

She reaches out to touch his large, steady hand. "Of course it doesn't," running her fingers though his. "And it doesn't concern Tony, either. I told you that from the start."

And Skip sighs, ahh. Sighs ahh, and turns to pull her closer to him before he even knows what he has done.

S I X

Over the delicately languorous weeks of the summer, Edith has sold two houses and rented two more for winter retreats, has dealt with the geraniums and waged war on the rabbits, and Jack has finished two paintings, three book jackets, and decided to become active again in the antinuclear movement. As they have sat on the porch at the end of an evening, sipping their cocktails and watching the lightning bugs blink on and off in the garden, they have remarked to one another on several occasions on what a fine woman and daughter-to-be-proud-of Sandy has turned out to be. "Remember when we were so worried about her?" Jack laughed, shaking his head that he could have been so foolish. Edith remembered. "It was him I was worried about," said Edith. "Him and his big mouth and his wild ideas. She was completely under his spell." And Jack had knocked the ash from his cigar and choked, "My God, do you remember the wedding?" And who could forget it? "Remember that getup Señora Rivera had on and that guy she had with her? The two of them babbling away in Beginner's Swahili through the entire ceremony." Edith smeared the tears from her eyes. "And the priest," she gasped. "I never really believed that that man was a priest. I've known several priests in my time—remember Helen Montalbano's son?—but none of them were like him. Even if he did come from Colombia, that's no excuse." "He was all right for a priest," said Jack, who has never cared for them either singly or in a group. "He must have done some amateur boxing when he was younger." "And the rest of his family . . ." wailed Edith, at a rare loss for the words to describe them. "And your sister's face when the tall one was trying to sell her a car . . ." The Rivera contingent huddled together like cattle in a blizzard, drunkenly shouting to one another in their multilingual way. The Grossman entourage homogenously winding in and out among the furniture, the men telling old but bluish jokes and the women obliquely guessing whether or not the bride might be pregnant. While the bridal couple danced in the moody light of dozens of candles, barely moving, drunk on more than champagne, their bodies magnetized with lust, Edith and Sophie stood shoulder-to-shoulder in front of the gifts' table, Edith's neat navy suit contrasting smartly with the intricately veined dashiki that Sophie wore, both of them unnaturally quiet and restrained, Tony's brother, Frankie, the one from the Coast, passing from Grossman to Grossman, trying to sell each in turn a beauty of an automobile, a real steal. Though Jack did have what he now remembers as a fairly invigorating conversation about Stalin's betrayal with Julio, who was bisexual and interested in Buddhism at the time. "The young one wasn't too bad," said Jack. "He had some terrific grass." "I can remember thinking, when they were exchanging the rings," reminisced Edith, brushing a gnat away from her drink. "I can remember saying to myself, 'Why would a girl who's known nothing but love and security—who has so much to offer the world— marry such an unsuitable man?' It wasn't as though she had to rebel against our authority. Was it?" Though a conversation they have had many times, over the years, it is one of which they never tire.

But now, of course, things are looking different. Once they feared that Antonio Rivera, though he was a nice enough young man, a little immature, maybe, but not a Republican, a banker, a criminal, or a pump jockey, would prevent Sandra Grossman from realizing her full potential and enjoying the life they had always had in mind for her (it is not, after all, only nations that have manifest destinies). Although, as Jack kept pointing out, it could have been worse, it could also have been better. Now they can see that their fears were unfounded, that they were only being nervous and overprotective parents of an only child. She may have been a little headstrong, a little in love with hardship, poverty, and the spirit of revolution, and heavily infatuated with a man who'd had his nose broken in a street fight, who'd only stayed in college to avoid the draft, and who would have been content—if love had not redeemed him—to scrape along from day to day and band to band and gig to gig for the rest of his life—but she wasn't silly. The values, virtues, and ideals they had instilled in her as soon as she was able to distinguish their voices from everyone elses' had not been shifted. The attitudes, hopes, and ambitions they had encouraged in her as soon as she was able to figure out that there was a direct correlation between their moods and her behavior had not been undermined. Not only has Tony Rivera not succeeded in pulling her down into the hole he has been digging for himself for the last forty years, but she has managed to keep him out of it as well. There have been several times when she has come close to dropping him—or he has come close to squirming away—but always Sandra has triumphed in the end. "She's going to go far," said Jack. "Mark my words. She has the strength of character and the determination of . . ." and, because he almost said "Lenin," sucked an ice cube out of his drink and then spat it back, ". . . Helen Keller."

And so the weeks, so sensuous and so undemanding, have moved along like a slow loris for Sandy, too. Sometimes she sits in the garden and reads, or analyzes herself and others in her journal, sometimes she goes over to what she has teasingly dubbed "Skip's Folly" to give him a hand, or, more often, watch him work stripped to his Bermudas with a paper bag over his still-crisp, still-curly hair. Sometimes she runs errands for Jack or Edith, sometimes she helps out in the local charity shop whose profits all go to support radical health workers in Africa. She has written two letters in response to articles she has read—one to the Editor of the local weekly, and one to the Editor of the *New York Times*—has joined a workshop in herbal medicine and one in yoga for relaxation, has befriended the woman who runs the halfway house for emotionally unstable teenage girls one town over (and they think that city kids have problems) and has come up with what she feels is a major innovation in the current jobs-training schemes run by the Board of Education. She eats well, sleeps well, spends her time well, and is enjoying all the things for which the country is meant to be enjoyed—the blue blue sky, the green green grass, just a little on the yellow side because of the substandard rainfall, the ripening fields and untoiling wild flowers, and, of course, the clean clean air, so much like the breath of God, though Sandra doesn't quite see it like that. She is also enjoying the lack of pressures and demands, and the freedom it has given her to reflect upon man, nature, and this thing we know as life. Here, in what used to be God's country, in what used to be Algonquin country, she has had the possibility of being neither Ms. Grossman nor Mrs. Rivera; of being, simply, a thirty-year-old female Caucasian of average intelligence, superior education, and strong opinions, raised in one of the testicles of the twentieth century; of feeling herself not as the things she has become but as the thing she is, a solitary creature among many, wandering purposelessly in a universe only the simplest tricks of which can be seen, but are still unlikely to be understood. It was never an extremely large possibility—civilization being what it is, and people being how they are—but no matter how finite or militantly mobile, it was there, and it was real.

She is missing Tony.

She is missing Tony, the way Zorro always sits on her feet, the spinach salad served at her favorite bar, the park, her friends, her students, her groups, her armchair, her bathroom with its hard, hot shower, and her kitchen with its well-organized work space and extensive selection of utensils and herbs. The past several weeks have given her ample opportunity to remember all the things about Jack and Edith that drove her crazy when she lived at home. In direct proportion to the amount of time they have spent together, the number of conversations Edith begins with sentences like "I always do it the way your grandmother showed me ...," "Is that how you make the dressing?", "I thought you would have put the heavy things away first ...," and "I've never seen anyone do it like that before ..." has increased at a rate that can only be described as prodigious. And, also in direct proportion to the amount of time they have spent together, the number of conversations Jack begins with sentences like "For God's sake, Edith ...," "Shut up, Edith, you don't know what you're talking about ...," "Why do you find it so difficult to cook a potato ...," "Fifty dollars? Fifty dollars for *that*?" and, "All right, who moved the book I was reading?" has increased at a rate that can only be described as competitive. Though she likes them both and always has, though she enjoys her hikes with Jack, the two of them singing "I Dreamed I Saw Joe Hill Last Night" as they break through the underbrush, though she enjoys her scrabble games with Edith, each of them playing so tight a game that the ignorant alien visitor might think the object was to cover a square area in the center of the board, she is nonetheless tired of Jack's corny jokes and tetchy sarcasm and black moods when to enter his studio is to risk assault by hurling brush or tube, and Edith's constant not really criticizing but correcting and perfecting and reminding. She may have forgotten what it was like to be fourteen, but they haven't forgotten what it was like for her to be fourteen. She feels lonely, lonely like a newcomer or a foreign observer or the only person at the party who doesn't have a lover or a spouse, and in this new mood thinks more about the things that she and Tony share than the things they don't, more about the things she likes about him than the things she loathes.

And there is one thing more.

The desire that burned in her so fiercely and so relentlessly all last autumn, and which then glowed steadily on through the gray and grimy winter, distorting the world with its glare and heat and obscuring smoke, fueled by her own unhappiness, is now just a small, outdoor fire of affection, kept under control. Is now just warm and cozy and friendly, so much so, in effect, that it is now a task requiring some imagination to understand what all the fuss was about. Where last September she lay awake in the ghostly predawn light, even the sound of her husband's breathing annoying her, now she wouldn't mind at all waking in the night to find him sprawled and snoring beside her, his mouth open and one ankle laid against one of her own. Where last autumn she watched Tony like a lioness studying the zebra herd for the weakest and most vulnerable, weighing every movement made and word spoken and finding them all wanting—the way he laughs, the way he eats spaghetti, the way he always fiddles with his hair, the way he pretends to not understand what is being discussed, purposely confusing and querying just for the sake of argument, the way he makes love—now she watches

Skip in much the same way, noticing his most tedious habits and irritating mannerisms and ticking them all off against him. Though Skip was never, of course, a serious contender for her truest affections, she no longer sees his impending marriage as either her betrayal or her loss. Though Skip is handsome and considerate, easy to get along with and reassuringly sensible, an enthusiastic lover and a sympathetic friend, she now sees clearly that it was only emotional exhaustion, it was never likely that she would fall in love with a man with a hundred-watt smile and a deep lack of concern about every aspect of the earth's future except its teeth. Skip would say that it was just one of those things. If he hasn't said it already.

And so, as the summer rolls along and Sandy grows more restless, becomes more short-tempered with her parents and more bored with Skip, remembers more of the things that make her life, it seems likely that there will be another ultimatum in the offing. Sooner or later.

The summer has made its sluggish progress in the city, too.

Sophie has packed her old kit bag and gone off to the wilds of the North Bronx to look after her sister who is recovering from a second stroke, leaving her own apartment in the hands of one of the younger nurses with marital problems who needed a place to stay for a while. She has also had a small but untypical success at work this summer, testifying against the defendant, a whiz-kid doctor from Harvard, in a malpractice suit, and not only has not been threatened with dismissal, but has been treated as something of a heroine with principles by at least a majority of the staff. Meredith has had her heart badly bruised by a lawyer who never expected her to pay her own way, and Will has grown nearly an inch and learned to sing "Blue Tail Fly" (though not flawlessly) while accompanied by Tony on the guitar. Maggie has cut off all her hair. ("Jesus Christ," Tony said, recognizing her only because she was coming down the stairs with Will. "What'd you do? Sleep with a Nazi?" "Everybody else says it's very becoming. Meredith says I look more mature. Skip thinks it makes me look like a new woman." And he'd given her one of his sudden grins. "There was nothing wrong with the old one.") Mrs. Burkowsky's eldest son has called and said that it wouldn't be a good idea for her to come out for a week this summer after all, things have been hard, his wife needs a break. A man was stabbed to death in the laundry room, leaving a dark trail winding through the basement that looked, at first, like oil. López, as is usual at this time of year, is talking about going back to Puerto Rico, maybe next year for sure. In what is assumed to be either a bid for sympathy or proof that he isn't so bad as some people think, Vega has been going around saying that he knew the woman who, with her three small children, was thrown from a tenement window by a jealous boyfriend, and has begun a profitable sideline in the installation of window gates, though where they come from in the first place is anybody's guess. And Tony has had a letter from his wife, hand-delivered by the shorn and subdued Maggie Kelly, ten worryingly legible pages of thoughtful, well-reasoned, and fair-minded analysis of the meaning and difficulties of life in general, and of their lives, especially his, in particular. Sandra would probably never kill herself, if only because she would be asleep before she got through the suicide note. The letter, though friendly, even positive, sounded so much like a political speech loaded with those demon words "freedom," "liberty," and "democracy" (as likely to mean their opposites or nothing at all), that it has left him not relieved—everything will soon be back to normal—but anxious— everything will soon be exactly as it was. She may think that she has given him one choice, but he knows that she has given him two: to make a decision, or to let her make it.

And Richard has had a dream.

It has taken him six nights to tell it. Six nights so hot and humid that the streets themselves seemed to be sweating, the two of them wandering from one doorway to another, Zorro trotting gamely ahead, from bench to stoop to fender, Richard speaking sporadically in his voice as soft as the footfall of an ant, "I just know, man, that's all. I just know." At the end of the six nights, Tony is certain of only three things: he doesn't know what the dream was about; it terrifies him in a totally new way; and he doesn't want to be in it.

Richard's dream begins around 551 B.C., during the Eastern Chou Dynasty, and ends, apparently, somewhere in the year 3000 in a place that sounds a lot like America in the early 1800s. Tony doesn't actually seem to be in it, but almost everyone else that Richard has ever known (and a great many he couldn't possibly have known, are). Gautama Buddha himself makes at least one appearance a century, usually shaking his head sadly, "He didn't do anything, man, he just looked straight through them and shook his head," and Jesus of Nazareth turns up at several interesting locations, including eighteenth-century London and the Louisiana Territory, "And he just raised his eyes to the sky, man, you know what I mean, he just raised his eyes to the sky." Aside from that, the dream, told in fragments, is a catalog of horror and atrocity—bloody wars and premeditated cruelties, children bloated with starvation and grotesque with disease, men and women stripped of their humanity, humiliated, tortured, and destroyed by human deeds as indifferent as those of the universe but far from benign—through which Richard's mother wanders aimlessly, dressed in white, her arms filled with flowers or severed limbs, and Richard's father runs and runs and runs, hounded from one epoch to another, sometimes seen disappearing through a door or hanging from a tree. "I don't know what it means," said Richard, resting his elbows on his knees and staring at the hubcaps of the Land Rover at the curb with eyes that are rarely seen to blink. "All I know is I'm always having it. Over and over. But I don't know what it means. What do you think it means?" Meredith, who is into dreams, and Sandy, who is into analysis, and Skip, who when he still thought he was going to become a medical doctor considered the possibility of a career in psychiatry because of his interest in behaviorism, would all have had answers—or at least questions—but Tony had none. "I don't know. How does it make you feel?" "Exactly like you think," said Richard, always ambiguous when asked a direct question. "All I know is that when I'm dreaming all I can think of is waking up. And when I wake up it's like I'm still dreaming," and shrugged his massive shoulders, never quite smiling but coming uneasily close.

Now López thinks that Richard is probably a psychopathic killer. "I've seen these guys," said López, ringing up the beer and the dog food, the bread and the cheese. "They get really quiet afterward, like they're listenin' to angels or somethin', real philosophical and above it all, you know what I mean?" Like the eight people they massacred in Pinefield, Wyoming, were part of some great scheme.

And now, at this moment, Rivera sits on the roof smoking a

joint and drinking a bottle of beer, thinking about Richard, whom the drunks all stop to talk to in the smallest hours, though he never talks back, and the Captain, who has disappeared from his usual island bench and will probably never turn up again, another *olvidado* forgotten, and the Grossmans, who, at this very moment, are very likely to be going around the block for the fifth time in search of a parking space, hurrying to meet him for dinner. Sandy said that Jack was coming into the city anyway, she and Edith thought they would come as well and they could all have a meal in that place downtown, the one with the great jukebox, just like they used to.

He couldn't think of how to say "no."

He couldn't think of any reasons why he wouldn't want to see them, wouldn't want to eat and drink and talk with them, especially Sandy, whom he knows he misses.

Though he could think of a pretty good one now.

The other thing that has happened is that he and Vega have had a fight.

López and Eddie were just setting up the crates in front of the store when he and Vega came limping home from the police station this morning, walking together but separately, hands in pockets, shoulders hunched against a wind that blew no trash along the pavement, flapped no awnings, hiked no skirts, Vega mumbling every block or so, "Man, you are one crazy son-of-a-bitch." López spotted them first. "Where the hell have you two been?" "Man," announced Vega as soon as they were within screaming range, "this here is one crazy son-of-a-bitch," pointing his finger to his head, screwy. Vega looked as though he were wearing eye makeup, had a bruise on his cheek and a cut, small and dried, on one corner of his mouth. The other guy had blood on his shirt and his lips were swollen, his eyes wide and stiff from being open for over twenty-four hours. "Me and Vega," he said, trying to smile with just his ears as Eddie and López came out of the shadows to meet them, "go jogging every morning, see. Only this morning we were mugged over by the river by a bunch of football players wanting to get in a little early practice." Even as he thought of it, he could see them, tall and broad of shoulder, grotesquely well-built and well-fed, their colors good, their eyes as bright as aluminum foil caught by the sun, their muscles bulging for release from their T-shirts, hey, you guys, where the hell do you think you're going? "Oh, yeah?" said López, wincing in the morning light. "This lunatic," interrupted Vega, immediately into his humble lackey routine, don't beat me, massa, I'm only a poor old slave, "this lunatic tried to kill me last night."

He didn't, of course, try to murder Vega. Which is not to say that had he tried he would have succeeded. He only wanted to hurt him. All he was after was one whimper of pain, one glint of sincere terror in those eyes that never show anything but your own reflection staring back. That's all. He just wanted to feel how good it would feel to punch that bastard in the face, to feel the fatal power of a gunman who only has to bend back a finger, who only has to be feeling that way for a second, to make a life forever stop, so much for all of your everything—the power of a god. But instead of the clean, cool, honorable deed he had imagined—his knuckles whamming against a cheekbone, Vega nearly weeping with remorse, saying something in Spanish, saying I'm sorry, I'm sorry, how's the old lady?, saying *Madre de díos lo siento,* saying you win man, I know when I'm beat—it had turned out to be a messy brawl, ending with the two of them crashing into the laundry room, scattering sheets and shirts and ladies' lingerie, a slim black stocking caught on Vega's arm as he landed the punch that sent Rivera sprawling against the washing machines, the woman from the second floor keening in a corner, her fingers still gripped around the sundress she'd been taking from the dryer when they bounced through her plastic basket, the young architect from the fifth hovering behind them, his hand reaching out and jabbing back from first one wild warrior and then the other, why don't you guys just sit down and we can talk. It was he who phoned the cops.

The first thing he'd done after Mrs. Gittelson, the building's early warning system, told him about Mrs. Burkowsky's accident, "She just came down those stairs like a sack of potatoes ... you know how that light's always out on that landing," was to go over to the hospital to see how she was, but though she was alive, thank God, they wouldn't let him see her, no visitors at this time of night. The second thing he did was to decide that even imprisonment was too good for Vega, it was time for blood and tears. And Vega had wanted to know if it was his fault that the old lady decided to go wandering through the city at all hours just because she'd run out of milk? Was it his fault that the light was out in the hall again? Was it his fault that an electric light bulb does not last forever? Was it his fault that there are cheapskates in the world who will steal the bulbs from hallways just to save a few cents? Was it his fault that Mrs. Burkowsky doesn't have enough sense not to use the stairs when it's too dark for her to see properly, and her with her bad legs? Is it his fault she's old and can't walk right? "Ain't I always telling her she should move some place where she won't have no stairs to climb?" shouted Vega. It was then that, instead of saying with the exaggerated coolness of true menace, "You are the most contemptible piece of scum I have ever personally known. I'm going to drain the blood from your body drop by drop and use it to poison the rats," he screamed back, "You lousy bastard. I'm going to take every goddamn light bulb in this building and stuff them up your ass," hitting Vega so quickly and so hard that he caught them both off balance. "What's all this about?" joked the friendly cop. "Some nice little piece of ass?" Tony spat some blood and what might have been piece of a tooth from his mouth. "Why? You runnin' the book?" "We don't need no wise-asses," said the other cop, snapping on the cuffs.

It is peaceful, up on the roof. Across the walls and door run the legends of lovers and heroes now gone, Pete&Julie4ever, Hector Lives, 99% is shit, Come back, Maria, you're still the only one, CCC make the world go round, Angel, I love you, Some day we'll look back on this and it will all seem funny. Across the horizon the skyline is dematerializing in the twilight and the smog, a magical kingdom visible only once every hundred years, and only then to a special few. And on what was once a river trail, traffic is snarled, and motorists, advised to use alternate routes, wipe the sweat from their brows and grip their steering wheels as though reining back spirited stallions.

Tony Rivera, his sneakers dusted, his jeans clean, and his shirt newly ironed, sits on an old orange crate, trying to assure himself that the swelling in his lip has gone down. In the fluid, diaphanous shapes in the distance he sees no golden city or sylvan shore, no blue-green, fecund land of hope and possible glory beckoning him on and on, but all the city summer nights like this, doors slamming and sirens wailing, the subway rumbling and the Bronx burning, when there used to be so much to do, so much that had to be done, when he couldn't wait to get going, "Ah, come on, Sophie, I'll do it later, I've got to get downtown in fifteen minutes," "Ah, come on, Sandy, they can wait a half an hour, we can tell them there was trouble with the trains."

Sandra's letter, which still lies opened on his desk, its pages marked by three folds, is structured like the outlines they were taught to do in English for their term papers. Only it is not, of course, about Mexican mythology. It is about The Meaning of Life: (1) What Life Seems To Be About In Your Teens; (2) What Life Seems To Be About In Your Twenties; (3) What Life Seems To Be About In Your Thirties; (4) What Life Seems To Be About In Your Forties; (5) What Life Is Really About. Though it tends to ramble and confuse points, it stresses planning and commitment, flexibility and determination, says that he must understand that everybody feels as he does at some time in their lives, that all he is suffering is a crisis in confidence, that nothing has changed (the world has not changed, and she has not changed) —except maybe him. He can come back, and all will be forgiven, again. She says that everything else will follow naturally, automatically, once they establish where they are going.

But he knows where he is going. He is going to die.

He stares out across the rooftops of Manhattan, or some of the rooftops of Manhattan, thinking about change. He can remember when Sandy was a vegetarian, when she wouldn't take so much as an aspirin, when she wanted to be a Legal Aid lawyer, when she wanted to adopt Third World orphans, when she wanted to have a son and a daughter of her own, named after martyrs in the Spanish Civil War, when she thought that Jack and Edith were reactionary and bourgeois, I appreciate all that they've done for me but I will never be like them, when she laughed at people concerned about the gathering of credentials— degrees, titles, garden apartments, country bungalows, vacations in Europe, wine cellars, write-ups in significant newspapers and magazines, friends who'd made names for themselves—when she thought there was as much dignity in digging ditches as in transplanting kidneys, when she would never want anyone but him. And yes, she is right, she has not changed, is still the girl she was, dropped from the night like a star, to be put in his pocket, held forever ready to illuminate the way. She has not changed. Has he?

On the roof of the building opposite, three young boys lean over the edge dropping waterbombs. He remembers something Sophie said to him that night last winter when he got so drunk he had to sleep on her sofa. "How do you know that it's yours?" "Jesus Christ," he shouted back. "You're some terrific mother, Sophie, you know that?" But did not add, "Of course it's mine," or "Sandy would tell me if she wasn't sure," or "I don't ever want to hear any crap like that again." "It isn't going to be anybody's," he said instead, looking her right in her prying mother's eyes. Because he had known, of course, just as he had known that Sandy was seeing someone; he has always been able to tell. It is not romantic love that has held them together. It didn't matter. But then he had been thinking of the child, of the fact of the child, the life of the child, and now he is thinking about Sandra, and wondering if it does matter after all. "I didn't stab you," said Sophie. "It was only a question."

He is twenty minutes late, so that by the time he does arrive Jack is already mellow and the eyes of the women are markedly small.

"What the hell happened to you?" they all ask as one.

But he is ready. "One of the guys on the methadone maintenance program got a little wrought."

"I thought it was meant to be safer, working in the building," says Edith, but the others pretend that she hasn't spoken.

All three of them ask him, in rote, what he's been up to, what he's been doing, how things are going. Sandra asks after Zorro and Edith asks after the plants, has he been giving them plenty of water in this heat? In return for his brief answers— "Not a lot," "Just the usual," "Okay," "Fine," and "Yes"—they regale him with stories of their aestival activities and exploits. Jack has sold two paintings through the local gallery, Edith won first prize in the county flower show with her roses and Sandy has just been told that Wolff is definitely going to Chicago and she is tipped for his demanding and influential job.

"I wrote a new song," says Tony, gulping down his second drink as he sees Jack motion for the waiter.

"Oh, really?" says Jack. "And what's it about?"

"Oh, really?" says Edith. "I didn't know you were still doing that."

Sandy says nothing, but scrapes the flesh from an artichoke leaf with her teeth and a look on her face that suggests that she thinks she knows to whom the song is dedicated.

"Artificial insemination," says Tony, and nods to the waiter who is looking at him quizzically, handing him his empty glass.

"Oh," says Edith. "Does it have something to do with work?" Causing him to wonder what it is she thinks he does.

"Oh," says Jack, in a voice that sounds dubious. "I take it this is a satire." Causing him to wonder what else Jack thinks it might be.

"Wouldn't you like to have some wine?" asks Sandra, with exquisite sweetness. "Instead of another of those?"

He drowns the toast in his onion soup, holding it under to the count of ten with the bowl of his spoon. "Yes. It's to help raise money to set up a sperm bank for the medical school. The plan is to collect the sperm from every level of the community. Not professionals and men of outstanding achievement, but everybody else. Especially those at the very bottom—assembly-line workers, pimps, street hustlers, winos and ex-boxers, guys who work in mailrooms, gas station attendants and the guys who rob them. And to use that sperm to inseminate women in every part of the country. No, of course it's not a satire. Don't you think it would make an interesting study?" Can they imagine what a difference it would make to Marylou or Fenton, Jr., raised in the suburbs of Atlanta or Minneapolis, to know that their real father was not a scientist or a naval officer or the man who refined the neutron bomb, but a junkie from Pelham Parkway, a bankrupt candy store owner in Brooklyn, a clerk in the civil service? That through their veins courses not only the blood of people who have striven and fought and toiled and cheated or been lucky to see their dreams fulfilled and the land of their dreams both righteous and secure, but of the poor slobs who never stood a chance? Can't they see what a breakthrough for humankind this would be, systemized outbreeding, limitless possibilities for one and all? And just think of all the sociobiologists it would keep busy.

"You can't stop progress," says Jack.

And who would want to?

"It depends on what you call progress."

"It may not be wholly good, but it isn't wholly bad, either," says Jack, who has been doing some thinking of his own about the future of the planet and is planning a picture book, done in black and white with only one full page of color, about the holocaust yet to come. "Our only hope lies in science and reason." Doesn't he agree?

"Of course," says Sandy.

Edith nods.

The walls of the restaurant are covered with what were once the walls of a barn in Pennsylvania, the windows are lined with plants that are tended by a company in Brooklyn, so perfect and so bright of leaf that they look as though they can't be real. Edith picks through her salad as though looking for slugs, Sandy wipes the grease from her mouth with a chequered napkin. Jack looks twice at the waitress sliding by the table with a loaded tray, at the roundness of her breasts and the roundness of her ass and the fullness of her smile, and Tony, tired of waiting for his drink, pours himself some wine. God for him has always been a Catholic. A gray-haired priest with a quick temper and a distinct disinterest in excuses, who whacks the world the way Father Burns used to whack a softball over the metal fence of the schoolyard and out into traffic. God for him has always been the providence of others, his grandmother with her little altar in the corner of the room, candles and the Virgin Mary and a sweetly suffering, boyish Christ, cards of all the saints propped in a line against the wall, talismans, beads, and bunches of dried herbs intricately arranged in a pattern that was never to be touched. When it stormed or was dry, when there was no money for the rent or the cops were at the door, she took to her room with a swish of skirts and the rattle of bracelets, down on her knees in the flickering dark. "Where's grandma?" one of the boys would say, and Sophie, with a mouth like a cowboy, would answer, "She's praying." His loss of faith—which was less a loss than the realization of its absence—was quiet and complete, logical and irrefutable. If he was right, then Jack is right. If Jack is right, there probably is no hope at all.

"What about art?"

The waiter, who, like the walls, tables, candleholders, and glasses, is probably really something else, reappears with another bottle of wine and another whisky, removing the used plates as though he's doing them a favor.

"Art?" repeats Jack, and hoots. "Art who? You do art for yourself and for no other reason. It has nothing to do with saving the world."

What about proletarian painting, muckraking novels and protest songs, asks Sandy, the only child in her high school in its entire history to read the Lanny Budd novels from end to end as part of what Jack termed her "real" education. Edith says that she has always found "Blowin' in the Wind" very moving. Rhetoric and propaganda says Jack, but none the less looks rather cheered by the arrival of their dinners.

"This looks terrific," says Sandy as the wooden platters and wooden bowls are laid before them.

"This doesn't look like medium," says Edith, sniffing at her steak.

"It's medium, see?" and the waiter points to the blue plastic flag poking up from the meat.

"And tell me, Tony," says Jack, lavishly pouring more wine. "Just what to you think is mankind's most significant creation or achievement?"

Listening to the conversation of the couple behind him about skiing and how each of them was recognized as a natural the minute his and her feet hit the practice slope, he thinks that Jack has said "mutation or bereavement," and so can only blink. "What?"

"What do you think is our most significant creation or achievement?" waving his knife and hitting the bottle with a ting. "In any sphere. Just off the top of your head, one single thing." Jack up to his old parlor tricks, there's nothing like a good debate to flex the brain.

"Oh, for God's sake, Jack," snaps Edith. "Don't start."

"No, come on, Tony. This will be interesting." Though it has never been interesting before.

"Dad," says Sandy. "I haven't seen Tony for weeks. I don't want to talk about which is better, penicillin or the wheel."

Jack waves her aside with a piece of homebaked-looking bread. "For God's sake, I'm only making conversation. Come on, Tony, which is it?"

"Orange juice," and lifts his glass to his lips so that Jack can't tell if he's smiling or not. Or if he's wincing in pain.

"Orange juice?" For reasons of his own, Jack was backing the printing press this time around; had been thinking along the lines of combustible steam engines, technocratic medicine, Christianity, Marxism, and the atomic bomb. "Orange juice?" he says again, then looks around the table at his only wife and only daughter, to see if they have ever before heard those words.

Neither of them are looking at him. Edith is still squinting at her steak, clearly about to send it back, and Sandy is looking at Tony as though he has just suggested to Jack that they swap wives.

"You know, you're right," Tony says, looking around. "This place does have an amazing atmosphere."

"Was that a joke?" asks Jack, his fork poised over his fried potatoes.

"Was what a joke?"

"Orange juice. Was that a joke?"

"Of course not, Jack. I'm completely serious." Slowly, he cuts himself a mouthful of meat which it is almost impossible for him to eat. "In fact," laying his knife on the edge of his plate, "in its concentrated form you could almost say that orange juice is man's gift to God."

"This isn't medium," says Edith, a woman who, over the years and bullying, has developed amazing powers of concentration. "It's oozing blood," and holds the flesh apart between knife and fork so that everyone can see it bleeding.

"So it's not a joke?"

Sandy waves one finger at the waiter.

"I've never been more serious in my life."

"Then would you mind telling me just how you decided that? I may not have your education, but I always thought that the orange was a product of nature."

"I ordered medium," says Edith, holding her platter aloft. "This isn't medium."

Dutifully, the waiter, who could write a book about his experiences, peers at the lump of meat. "You're right," he winks. "It's steak."

"Technically," says Tony, through a wedge of fried onion and pain. "Technically. But it's man who turned the orange into a billion-dollar industry, so it counts."

"It doesn't count," stabbing another slice of potato. "It's not what I meant at all, and you know it." Then, catching the eye of the waiter who is reluctant to leave, says suddenly, "You going to change that meat, or what?"

"You're full of shit, Jack, of course it counts. Where would the orange be today if we refused to have anything to do with it?" or anything else, for that matter?

Sandy reaches across him for the salt, brushing her elbow against his wrist. "You're being ridiculous," she says, without seeming to move her lips.

But now he is hitting his stride. "If we have to take the blame for poverty, fascism, and sophisticated forms of torture, I think we should be allowed the orange as a point in our favor."

This time she reaches across him for the pepper, nearly knocking his fork into his teeth. The pain is breathtaking. "Why don't you just shut up, Rivera? You know you shouldn't mix your drinks."

Can he see her? Does he hear her? Is he aware of any of them—Jack sipping his wine like a vampire sipping blood, Sandy holding her fork like a weapon, Edith scouting through her asparagus for insects? Can he feel himself dancing away from them down the misty, rainbowed shore of his own imagination, while they stand against the boardwalk railing, hands waving, mouths moving, their words being blown away by the cool, incessant wind? Can he tell by the look in Sandy's eyes that she no longer considers him a wise fool?

"If you're looking for something that is purely beneficial, that, even in the wrong hands, can do nothing but good, then it's orange juice you seek." He doesn't look to check reactions, barely pauses for air. "Fresh, frozen, canned, or in waxed containers, the orange offers both health and hope, refreshment and salvation in one easy, convenient, biodegradable package." And smiles at Jack who is slapping catsup on to his chops the way another man might chisel marble.

"What about apples?" asks Edith. Unlike her daughter and her husband, Edith has rarely tried to take anything seriously.

"Apples? Oh, no, Edith. Apples are another bowl of gefilte fish entirely," you old tease, you.

"Can you pass the catsup, please, Dad?"

Edith looks over her shoulder with a practiced eye. "I wonder what happened to my steak."

Chewing meditatively, Jack levels his gaze at the man who, in the eyes of the law, at least, is like a son. "You know, Tony, sometimes I don't have the slightest idea what you're talking about," giving him the open, honest look for which he is sometimes famous. "Why do you think that is?"

Tony shrugs, looking not at Jack but at the couple behind him, getting ready to leave. "I don't know," he says at last, voice hooded, eyes on the woman, whose body was never intended for the intimacies of modern urban dining, as she whams Jack in the back of the head with what looks like a school bag. "Maybe it's my accent."

Seeing the waiter approaching, Edith turns back to the table, content. "But you don't have an accent ..." she begins. And then, misinterpreting the expressions on the faces of her husband and her child, amends it to, "Well, not much."

And so it goes. Not so much a night out, Sandy says later as they stand at the stoop, as an evening in the reception room of hell. But not the great, sadistic inferno, hell, with its downward spiral of punishment and grief, its profoundly endless and spectacularly imaginative system for giving out what is deserved. Not a poet's hell, or an artist's hell, or a shaman's hell, and certainly not the hell of a lesser or greater god—not even the hell of the average person, five-thirty in August on the Long Island Expressway, forever locked in Creedmoor on Thorazine, trapped in a subway with a stoned and drunken street gang out for a night of fun and harmless homicide, sitting between a banker from Detroit and a Connecticut debutante as the jumbo jet hurls itself into the ocean. Tony Rivera's hell. The smallest of them all.

"If you like orange juice so much," she says, standing as far away as Sri Lanka with their bodies close to touching, "then you should try drinking it some time."

Had he started a fight, leaping like Douglas Fairbanks over pine table tops and fat red candles, the women shrieking and sighing, the men standing against the tables, arms like walls? Had he tried to lead the room in a heartfelt rendition of "We Shall Overcome," no eye dry, no soul untouched, even the arriving armed police and the undercover agent who had been there all the time, eating his fried clams, looking just like everybody else, stilled for an instant in their pursuit of law and order? Had he refused to pay the bill, you'll get no fucking tribute from me? Had he exposed himself, running madly through the rooms and along the six-foot bar, scattering ice cubes like jewels, I at least have nothing to hide? What had he done? "What did I do?"

"Nothing," she says, sounding disappointed. "As usual. Absolutely nothing. You can't even insult people openly."

Edith leans from the window of the car, calling, "Sandra, Sandra, we have to get going."

"You go out of your way to humiliate me."

He is about to say that that isn't true, but thinks better of it.

"And what happened to your face?"

"I told you, there was a punch-up at work." Suddenly, he doesn't want to let her go. "You should stay here tonight. He's not safe to drive with." He can feel her almost weakening, his hand on her wrist, her head just turning over her shoulder to see for herself Jack drunk at the wheel, and then, as luck would have it, who comes out of the front door but Vega, immediately beginning to limp.

"Mrs. Rivera," shouts Vega. "Mrs. Rivera. Nice to have you back," coming to a pained halt at the bottom of the steps. "Did he tell you how he tried to kill me?"

And she stands there staring at the two of them, an indecisive expression on her face, as though it might still turn out to be a joke, to be a dream.

"Did he tell you? Look at this," pointing to his eye, "and this," pulling down his bottom lip. "I'm going to need a false tooth. Do you know how much that's going to cost?"

"Oh well, you're talking to the right person now," says Rivera. "She's got a very good friend who's a dentist," regretting the words even before they are out of his mouth.

Jack gives two rapid barks on the horn.

"Oh, Sandra," calls Edith. "Your father wants to know what's causing the delay. Are you coming?"

"Yes," shouts Sandy, her eyes on Tony like dissection pins, "I'm coming."

"Look, Sandy," letting her arm fall away from him. "I can explain."

"Sure," says Vega. "He can explain. Just don't leave out the part where you attack me for nothing. Just don't leave out the part about busting up the laundry room."

"Can you?" she says, God pushing aside a couple of clouds to peer at Cain. "Well maybe you'd like to start with exactly what it was started all of this. Is this all part of your hate-Vega campaign? Or is this your idea of an enthusiastic reunion?"

He can just make out Edith, leaning over the back of her seat, squinting at them through the window of the car.

"I thought we had a new agreement," says Sandy. "I thought things were going to be different."

"They are different," he points out. "I don't usually get into fights."

At the corner, the gray station wagon stops for the light and Sandy turns to watch Rivera climb the stone steps and vanish behind the old glass door. Instead, she sees him put his hands in his pockets and cross the road, going over to where a bum sits in a doorway; sitting there himself.

"I don't think we should go back there again," says Edith. "The service was really appalling."

No one can feel truly safe when her or his mother is around. Where no god or devil, law or army, threat or principle can influence or impede, all it takes is a mother with her lips set in that certain way and her bones sighing to bring everything to a spectacular halt. Men who think nothing of rigging elections, slaughtering innocents by the thousands, or destroying finely balanced cultures with useless goods and dangerous delusions grow as anxious as adolescents at the thought of spending an evening in their mother's living room, did you wipe your feet? put your glass on the coaster, eat that before you drop it all over the rug. Women who take no shit from nobody, whom no sweet words can woo nor pleadings move, who can't be fooled by wide-eyed promises or tight-lipped threats, who cannot be bullied and cannot be bought, who would never consider eating something they hadn't ordered, sitting through a movie they didn't like, or staying among a group of people they couldn't stand just to spare someone else's feelings, fall apart like dead flowers at the mere sight of mother reaching to the top shelf for a dish that everyone knows is going to be dirty. A mother can turn the most reasonble, good-humored, and delightful person into a raving lunatic just by the repetition of a few familiar words—You never did have any common sense, It's just like the time you threw that tantrum and poor Mr. Porter had his heart attack, I never understood what you saw in him. A mother can turn the most cunning killer, pragmatic politician, or ambitious businessman into a small and not especially bright or interesting child, simply through the way she purses her lips when he says he's never really cared for spinach. A beautiful house with jacuzzi and three-car garage, your name and picture in *Newsweek,* your life story made into a film, three appearances on Johnny Carson, clumps of letters after your name—what can these things mean to a woman who knew all that was ever necessary to know about you before you were even born?

Maggie's mother, Kathleen Margaret Macauley Kelly, is at this very moment shoving herself, her overnight bag, her black patent leather purse and two plastic shopping bags into the back of a yellow cab outside of Penn Station, and saying to the driver, to whom she has just recited her daughter's address, "That's a bad neighborhood, isn't it?"

Maggie sits in the wicker chair with the cat on her lap, staring in the direction of the front door as though expecting bullets to be fired through it at any minute.

Kate Kelly—having extracted a solemn vow that there are no cockroaches in the apartment—is coming for a visit. And, in honor of the occasion, the mother of Nelson Ellis has invited them to dinner. Tonight. Skip has come down specially, though he hates to break off work just when results are beginning to be seen. He is looking forward to meeting Maggie's mother, and his mother, he says, is also looking forward to meeting her, though that is probably a lie. Of all the things in man's universe, the only ones which have ever received Mrs. Ellis's full approval or enthusiasm are bridge, Bloomingdale's, and being right. People, on an individual basis, have never really appealed to Sarah. Like a doctor who knows that the one thing threatening his professional fulfillment of his job is an interfering patient, Sarah gives the impression of knowing that the world would be a much better place if she were running things and there were no one else in it.

Down around Columbus Circle, Kate Kelly is advising Dom Quiñones on the best remedies for his heavy cold. "Garlic," she says, shouting through the little holes in the partition. "Garlic and rose hip tea. But you should also try some elderflower or comfrey." She calls them miracle drugs. Her advice is that he forget about cold capsules and antibiotics, aspirin and medicated hot lemon drinks, and stick to the things that God purposely put on the earth so that we would be able to take care of ourselves. These things are all very simple, really, says she for whom these things really are. And Dom, for whom things are never simple, who no sooner thinks of fifteen reasons for doing one thing than he thinks of fifteen reasons for doing something else, says, "Yeah, but if I've already started with the drugs, then it's stupid to mess it all up by switching to something else." What he wants, he explains, though not in so many words, is not so much a cure as relief. If he doesn't make some money this week his girlfriend will probably leave him. "Oh," says Kate, "stress. What you need is to eat plenty of spinach. Or brewer's yeast." "Uhk," says Dom, largely to himself, but she hears him even above the squealing brakes. "You can sprinkle it on popcorn." She clings to the door strap as they bounce over potholes. "Or put it in a milkshake. It'll do you a world of good."

Hanging and bopping and clutching her purse to her stomach like a warrior's shield, dressed in her summer pumps and bagging stockings and the water-repellant coat she wears through every day of the summer (in case she goes somewhere that's air-conditioned), her hair colored a shade of red that looks best in dark rooms, and in her heart a belief in Jesus that some might find unjustified, Kate Kelly doesn't look dangerous. She looks like a little old lady in her seventies, a little boring, perhaps, even bothersome, but, basically, rather sweet.

But to Maggie she is no less dangerous than if she had a sawed-off shotgun or a hand grenade in her bag instead of a book of daily prayers and a rosary. To Maggie she is no less threatening than if she were a CIA agent masquerading as her mother for the last thirty-odd years, watching all her movements, tapping in on even her most private thoughts, and not an ordinary woman, old now, whose only great longing in life— always to be unfilled—was to fall purely, perfectly in love with a man who was a little like Clark Gable and a little like Spencer Tracy and a lot like the men in her favorite novels.

But like the gangster's ex-lover and the dictator's ex-best friend, Kate Kelly knows too much.

"You don't know my girlfriend," says Dom. "If I miss just one night this week, she'll be back at her mother's with my tape recorder and the slow cooker before you can say bronchitis."

Further uptown, in an apartment that has a view of the river that would have, at one time, been worth having, Sarah Ellis checks the coq au vin, everybody, she says, eats chicken, the woman isn't a vegetarian, is she?, and tells Skip where the ice bucket is, for the second time. He drags the old step chair out from its corner next to the broom cupboard, and climbs up to the cabinet over the sink. "I'm sure you and Maggie's mother are going to like each other a lot," he says, smiling his this-will-be-painless smile.

"Not the silver one," taking off her glasses, steamed from the oven, and wiping them on her flowered apron. "The one that looks like wood and brass."

Since she doesn't, in truth, care for Maggie very much, it is relatively unlikely that she will like the mother any more than the child. After all, if Maggie is flighty, opportunistic, unstable, and slightly gauche, as Sarah believes, then what is Kate but the mother of a woman who is not good enough to marry Sarah's son?

"What was it you said Maggie's father did before he died?" asks Sarah, reaching for the bucket which is neither dusty nor gummy but just-like-new clean. She chooses her housekeepers carefully.

It doesn't occur to Skip to say "lived." "I think he was a bartender, or something like that," says Skip, having no idea himself what something like that might be.

"A bartender?" repeats Sarah. Skip's first wife's father was a gynecologist.

"Or maybe that was her uncle," returning the chair to its place. "Maybe her uncle was a bartender and her father worked in Bohack's."

"In Bohack's?" echoes Sarah, who isn't sure what Bohack's is.

"Yeah, I'm sure that's right," says Skip, helping himself to one of the canapés Sarah has arranged on a large white platter, to go with the before-dinner drinks. "Her uncle was a bartender and her father managed the meat department."

"The meat department?" says Sarah, removing the platter from his reach. "Well, that's all right, then. She's bound to like the chicken."

Though not the sort of person you would automatically or even easily associate with epic verse, Kathleen Kelly does show a certain Homeric tendency to describe all her friends by their epithets—Mrs. Dellacalce, the pacemaker's wife, Mary, mother of Julia who married the Jewish widower with three grown sons, Felicity, abandoned alcoholic and jeep-driver, three-strokes-and-arthritis Mrs. Kunzer. Over the chicken, which she ate only out of politeness, she never did go in for fancy cooking, she told a long and astonishingly complex story about the feud she has been having with her neighbor, Ellen the hard worker and fanatical housekeeper, which involved not only Ellen's husband, Bob of the few words and Celtic temper, and Ellen's son, Richie who does the lawn, but several people who have been dead for at least six years each, Maggie's father, may God have mercy on him, and Maggie herself when she was in her teens. The Ellises, mother and son, unfamiliar with people who view the present as intimately linked and dependent on the past, with people who see life's intricate pattern as one of eternally overlapping or finely connected circles, who can bring in characters from stories that took place thirty years ago to explain a story that happened yesterday without a wink or a blink, have, as a result, found their considerable social skills put to the test and found wanting. Every time Kate has turned to Sarah and said either, "Don't you think so?" or "Haven't you found that's true?" Sarah has responded by trying to change the subject as quickly as possible to things like skyrocketing prices, the rising crime rate, or her granddaughters, Elise, who is fourteen and a female version of her father, and Samantha, who is twelve and, it must be assumed, not like the Ellis family at all. And every time Sarah mentions children, Maggie holds her breath. Only minutes before Kate arrived at her door, Dom behind her, carrying her bags and sneezing, Maggie tossed a coin and it came up heads, don't say anything to her. Experience has proven that the quickest way to get Kate Kelly to tell someone something is to ask her not to tell them. And, miraculously enough, it has worked. So far. Maggie thinks that this is a matter of luck, but it isn't. It is because Kate sees the world as divided into two groups: friends and strangers. Friends are people she likes immediately, like Dom, who was such a nice young man and even offered to help her upstairs with her things; and strangers are people she knows she will never like, like Sarah, who treats everyone not in her own circle as though they are foreigners and must, therefore, be servants. You do not discuss things like dead grandchildren with strangers.

Now they sit around the table, the fat just beginning to congeal over the remains of the chicken and a couple of tiny onions left behind, the slender white candles, dripless, still burning brightly, a piece of escarole clinging grimly to the floral centerpiece, like people longing to pay their bill and leave. Sarah, just noticing Maggie's plate, bare of bones, comments that it is unusual to find two people together who don't like coq au vin. Skip says that if they have their coffee in the living room, he will show them the before and during pictures he has been taking of the house. Sarah says that would be nice. Maggie says, "Oh, Skip." Kate says that she has brought some pictures, too, and, catching the look her daughter gives her, adds defensively, "What's the matter? There's none of you in the bathtub." Maggie suggests that she and Kate should first do the dishes. Sarah says that that isn't necessary, her cleaning lady comes on Saturday mornings as well, why don't they all just relax and get to know one another? Skip says that the best idea would be if he and Maggie did the dishes and left the mothers to get to know one another. Maggie says that Sarah really must give Kate a quick tour of the apartment, she's done such wonderful things with it. Kate says that, since John died, may he rest in peace, she has gotten interested in handicrafts, even though she has arthritis bad in both her hands, and if Sarah will just let her see what color scheme is in the bathroom, she would love to crochet a toilet-seat cover and matching mat for her. "I crochet the flowers and leaves separately," she explains, "and then sew them on at the end." Sarah says that it is obvious where Maggie gets her talent.

"And your husband," Sarah says to Kate as they stroll together over the champagne-colored carpet of the dining room and on to the polished parquet splendor of the hall, "was a bartender Skip told me?"

"No," says Kate, who has only seen homes like this in magazines and movies. "My brother was the bartender. John, God bless him, was a butcher." And sits herself, girdled and squeezed into the good dark suit that has never before been worn to anything that wasn't a funeral, demurely if nervously on the edge of the couch. "It killed him."

"Killed him?"

"Too much red meat," nods Kate. "And hormones. They pump everything full of hormones these days. You can't be too careful."

Sarah says that she agrees.

In the kitchen, Skip kisses Maggie while the coffee perks in its electric, ceramic pot. If the room in which Sarah and Kate exchange views on mass-market production looks like an advertisement for living-room furniture, which it does, then the room in which Skip and Maggie nudge and stroke and nuzzle looks like an advertisement for the complete modern kitchen—as though the apartment has not been put together year by year, accumulated through living, but won as a set in an afternoon game show, get the next three questions right and you win the mahogany dining-room ensemble, including portable bar, and a complete range of glassware.

Skip thinks that Maggie's mother is absolutely wonderful. "She's marvelous," he says, not unlike the way his own mother describes her Nicaraguan seamstress, her Puerto Rican cleaning lady, and the staff of the hotel at which she vacations in the Bahamas every February. "Does she really knit toilet-seat covers?"

"No. She crochets them," and Christmas candles, throw pillow covers, lovable animals, and afghans. What she can do with old beads, shells, an aluminum pie pan, and plastic is only this side of unbelievable.

"She's just like the mother in a movie," he smiles, rubbing his chin against her forehead. So is Sarah, but from quite a different film. "I bet when you were a kid she always read you a story before you went to sleep," and brought your supper in on a tray when you were ill, and sat up half the night typing your English term paper, and saved for months out of the housekeeping to buy you the coat you wanted with the wooden buttons and the pile lining for Christmas. Though Skip has always been proud and fond of Sarah, who still looks young enough to be mistaken for his older sister, she has never been quite the mom of his imagination, the mom of apple pie and floral housedresses, a little frumpy and a little old-fashioned, wise in the ways of broken arms and broken hearts but not in the ways of the world. As the percolator plop plop plops and Maggie leans her head against his shoulder, it is almost as though he can see Kate standing in the doorway of the house that is more like a bungalow, holding the aluminum screen door with its weathered K, the cat meowing between her slippered feet, calling, "Maggie! Maggie! Supper's ready!" out into the street where the children noisily play. And from there, it is no great feat for a man of his imagination, for him, to picture Maggie herself (though not, perhaps, in a cheap print dress and an apron that says *Don't Kiss the Cook*), standing in the sturdy doorway of their house on a summer evening that has yet to come, calling to the child who has also yet to come, "Hey! Soup's on!" He is not, himself, particularly interested in crocheted toilet-seat covers, or artificial flowers made out of styrofoam egg cartons, but he is interested in the other things that Kate's comfortably rounded body, the breasts not grown to be teased or twisted, fondled or kissed, but leaned upon and cried on to, suggests. Safety and Stability. Loyalty and Succor. If she is not the sort of woman to abandon an ailing child for a bridge tournament in Chicago, can Maggie be? If she is not the sort of woman to abandon a good husband for a stockbroker with his own private plane, is Maggie? Oh, no, she couldn't be. She obviously has not led the sort of life that he considers normal—she was never sent away to camp, she never belonged to a sorority, she seems never to have had a real job, she has never been married, she has never owned a car, she once confessed, in an intimate moment, to it never having occurred to her that she might one day own a home, he doesn't always understand her sense of humor—but he is more than satisfied with Maggie the way she is—or the way he sees her, restless by circumstance more than intent. None the less, it is reassuring to know that through her veins runs the blood of good old, solid, earthy Kate, who used to cry when times were hard for the cheap meats of this world, throwing the apron over her head as she dished out the honey-glazed Spam or the tuna fish casserole, and the dear, departed John, who every day went to work and every night came home again. It is good to know that at last he has found a woman who thinks as he thinks, dreams as he dreams, sees as he sees. He has, in his short time, disappointed himself, who would have preferred to be a plastic surgeon or a consulting physician for the space program; disappointed Sarah, who would have preferred to be the mother of John Kennedy or John Glenn; disappointed his first wife, who would have preferred to be married to John Kennedy or John Glenn, and so is relieved to have at last found someone whom he can't disappoint.

And in that, at least, he is almost right.

"The coffee's ready," says Maggie, for the third time, her voice slightly muffled by the solidity of his chest and the smooth regularity of his hundred percent rayon shirt, her neck aching slightly from its intimate position against his breast and the difficulties this presents to breathing.

He rejoins the moment when she pulls away from him. "What?"

"The coffee's ready."

"Oh, right," grins Skip. "The coffee."

And Maggie removes the plug.

"This was taken the summer we had a bungalow in the mountains," says Kate, passing along a black and white photograph of herself and her two daughters, all three of them wearing Bermuda shorts and holiday smiles. "Maggie was twelve then."

"How nice," says Sarah.

"Look at that haircut," says Skip.

"John always said that there was nothing like mountain air for making children grow. We always made a lot of good friends on vacation. Do you know that I still get Christmas cards from people we met then? Do you remember the Madells, Maggie? He's dead now, God bless him, but she still sends me a card every Christmas. What was her daughter's name? The one with the braces? She married an engineer and moved to Houston."

"At one time," says Sarah, "we were sending out over two hundred and fifty Christmas cards a year. When Nelson passed on, though, I decided to send cards only to relatives and close friends. It just gets to be too much after a while. Don't you agree?"

"The son, poor thing, was killed in Vietnam. Such a shame. I didn't know, of course, so I sent her a card as usual and she wrote me this very lovely letter back. I think his name was Sherman. He was always collecting dead animals and burying them outside the house."

"Nelson, of course, had hundreds of friends. And then there were all his business acquaintances. They all had to be remembered." Sarah sighs. For the ever-popular Nelson? For the thousands of cards with their printed legends, Mr. and Mrs. Nelson Ellis, Sr., Nelson and Sarah Ellis, the Ellises, addressed and sometimes signed, sent, and then thrown away? For the thirty or so December 25ths with their roasted turkeys or roasted geese, the white artificial Christmas tree with its silver balls and twinkling blue lights that now resides in Jersey City with the daughter of the last housekeeper? "Now I only keep in touch with people who are close," says Sarah, her well-defined and mirthless smile a clear indication of the stiffness of the criteria for belonging to that group.

"Mrs. Gray's son was killed in Vietnam, too. She never really got over the shock. Her husband used to find her in the garden in the middle of the night, looking for his grave. What was his name, Maggie? You remember him, don't you? The one who always walked around with a transistor radio glued to his ear. Was it Mark or Martin?" and shuffles through the snapshots on her lap, looking, perhaps, for one that isn't there.

Maggie doesn't look up from pouring the coffee into the bone china cups. "Patrick."

"He was a very decent boy." She stares for a moment at a photograph of their old dog, Fred, sitting on the front porch with a sailor hat on his head, then puts it at the bottom of the pile. "Your father always liked him. Now these," passing three slightly orange color prints to Sarah, "were taken at my older daughter's wedding. That's Julie between John and her father-in-law. And that's me and Vic's mother. My friend Mrs. Soskel made the cake special," and looks up at each in turn, as though revealing all. "Her father was a baker in Dresden. Before the war."

"Which war?" asks Maggie, but Sarah is already talking about the picture of herself in her wedding dress and twelve-foot veil that appeared in the *New York Times,* Sarah Elizabeth Scudder weds Nelson Skidmore Ellis, Radcliffe Beauty Marries Congressman's Son. "We both came from very old families, you know," sipping at her coffee as though she knows it must be bitter. "Nelson's mother's family is one of the oldest in America."

Maggie speaks into her coffee. "You mean they're Indians?"

Kate pours milk into her cup from an exquisite china pitcher that is neither cracked nor chipped nor even visibly aged. "The girls are third generation on my side." She takes one sip, smiles, then leans forward to add more sugar. "Of course, John always wanted to go back to Ireland. You know, to see where his family came from." The spoon makes a sound that almost sparkles as she lays it on her saucer. "His sister used to go every year for a month in August, come what may. She wound up dying there, poor soul. Do you remember, Maggie? It was that summer you were in Greece and you sent me that very nice scarf with the birds on it. It would have broken John's heart if he'd been alive to see it."

"One of those dreadful bombs?" asks Sarah, though it is not really a question, though she can clearly visualize the smoking debris and bits of bodies, Kate Kelly's husband's sister's arm, the fingers frozen in a grip, still clutching at the old sod. "Almost the same thing happened to Nelson's partner's wife," and so engrossed does she become in the tale of Evelyn Danzig, who moved down to Miami after her husband died to escape the crime and brutality and encroaching poor and was fatally stabbed before three months were up by a surprised burglar, that she does not hear Kate say, "No, a bus," and then go on to tell about her friend's brother-in-law who walked away from not one but two airplane crashes and then was killed in a motorcycle accident, just going into town to get a paper and a battery for the radio.

When Skip comes back from driving the Kellys home, Sarah, in a seashell-pink nightgown and matching robe, is taking a glass of port in the living room while she reads the one chapter of a good book that she reads every night before going to bed. "Well?" he says, sitting down in the opposite armchair and helping himself to a glass of wine. "What do you think?"

"I think," says Sarah, fixing the word she was reading with one impeccably manicured nail even as her eyes rise from the page, "that we'd better not have the reception here."

◇　◇　◇

There is nothing wrong with Kathleen Kelly. There never has been. Oh, she was never what anyone—least of all those who have known her best—would call especially smart, or especially wise, or breathtakingly perceptive, and now she is a little more forgetful, a little more obstreperous, a little more opinionated than she was before when she had more things to do and less time in which to do them, than she was before when she wouldn't make a move before asking someone else—husband child sister friend—in which direction, but she is still incorruptibly nice.

"Use any towel you want, Mom," calls Maggie from the kitchen where she is brewing a pot of Kate's own sleepy-time tea. "It doesn't matter."

Nice from the time of Maggie's memories of candies in the candy dish and teardrops in the stew. She never bitched or complained like some of the other mothers, ripping phones out of hands and dumping wardrobes on the lawn, you don't leave this house till I say so, you don't see your friends till your homework's done. She may have been a little overwrought from time to time, a little sensitive and prone to weeping in the face of domestic disasters (when confronted with exploding boilers or exploding husbands and children, exploding pressure cookers or exploding dreams), but she was always Mom, ready with a shoulder or a handkerchief, an aspirin or a resolute "We'll see about that."

The bathroom door, which always sticks, can be heard to grunt open, and Kate calls above the sound of the running taps, "How about this blue one? Is this the guest towel?"

Oh Jesus.

Maggie puts the tea cozy that looks like a goldfish (left over from last Christmas's novelties) over the old brown pot, counts silently to three, and yells back, hardly sounding exasperated, "Yeah, Mom. That's fine."

"And where did you say the washcloths are?"

"There aren't any washcloths. You'll have to use that sponge on the side of the tub."

There is a moment of human silence in which the cat comes to complain at Maggie's feet, hey what about me, and Kate has time to squeeze her old woman's body through the small bathroom window, tiptoe on her fluffy pink slippers along the narrow ledge, grab hold of the fire escape ladder and leap into a world of guest towels and washcloths and toilet-bowl cleaners that look rather like daisies, driven by despair, or time to turn around and identify the sponge sitting between the red plastic fish and the multicolored family of tiny swans, and then she says, "Oh. You mean that brown thing?"

And Maggie says, yes, that brown thing, but Kate had better hurry or the tea will be cold.

Really nice, this little old lady from the suburbs, fifteen years a widow, fifteen years of classes in handicrafts, fifteen years of sending back postcards from her organized jaunts to dude ranches, gambling casinos and Playboy clubs, fifteen years of intensified maternal lobbying and guerrilla activity for what she's believed her children should want.

And what should they want? Security, stability, love, companionship, good times like the times that she and John had when she felt so happy it almost always made her cry?

And what has her younger daughter wanted instead?

Kate stretches and sighs, holding her head in its plastic shower cap well above the foaming, scented waters of the bath. She has had a big day. Her legs hurt, her back aches, and her head throbs just a little from the unaccustomed wine she had with dinner. If she were an astronaut, she couldn't have traveled farther than she has today, waking up in her own blue bedroom, crammed with the furniture and paraphernalia of another life, and winding up in Sarah Ellis's living room, afraid to touch anything in case it should break. When she describes the evening to her friends she will talk about the china and the material of the curtains, the paintings on the walls and the carpets on the floors, the pedigree of her daughter's future mother-in-law, one of *the* Scudders, the professional credentials of her daughter's future husband, his hands have touched the teeth of two prominent newscasters, one famous talk-show host and the sister of a notorious actor, and the comforts and measurements of her daughter's future home. When talking about the Ellises she will recite facts, just as when talking about herself or her daughters or her husband she has always restricted herself to weights and heights and problems buying shoes, to promotions, graduations, troubles with the plumbing. "We had this French chicken," she will say. "You know, with wine and mushrooms and that sort of thing." Too rich for her and her gallbladder. "She has a beautiful apartment," she will say. "And a clock almost just like the one my grandmother brought over from London." Which was never seen to work. "His wife treated him very badly," she will say. "But he's still devoted to his daughters." And has always longed for a son. Those are the things she will say later, but now, splashing lazily, accidentally, in the shallow waters of the old chipped tub, those are not the things she is thinking. She is thinking of herself when she was younger; of Maggie when she was younger; of the world when it was young. She is thinking of a yellow dress and a white shirt with thin blue stripes, of Maggie with a baby in her arms, of the picture of her daughters that stands on the bureau in her bedroom, next to a picture of John. She is thinking of Skip, who of all Maggie's lovers whom she has met is surely the most presentable, the most secure, the most polite, the closest to the son-in-law of her dreams, and wondering why she doesn't like him more than she does. She is thinking of Sarah Ellis and wondering if Maggie will call her Mother.

Maggie, as she lays the chocolate chip cookies that Kate brought on a plate, is wondering, too. She is wondering what it is that she has always wanted out of life. She used to know what she didn't want, now knows what she should want, but the thing itself—it seems to her in this moment (so familiar and so fine that she is a girl again, safe at home)—eludes her still. What has she wanted with her degree in art and her single parenthood? her fantasies of discovering the meaning of life in a tube of paints or a foreign room? Even as a child, when chuckling uncles and clucking aunts broke away from their adult talk to ask her what she wanted to be when she grew up, she never knew what to say. How was she supposed to know? Once she had answered "Alive," and been rewarded with a watery laugh from her father and a slightly off-key "Alive? Of course you'll be alive" from her mother, who then sent her into the kitchen for more ice. Even as a teenager, when the older children of friends and family had grown up and gone off to seek their fortunes in the world, and the reports came back about their separate but equally glorious progresses in the forms of snapshots, newspaper clippings, and verbal narratives passed along from mother to mother, and Kate would say things like, "Wouldn't you like to be in advertising?" "Wouldn't you like to live on Riverside Drive?" "Wouldn't you like a wedding like that?" "Wouldn't that be a good college for you to go to?" Maggie could never believe that the question was a serious one. How should she know? None of the worryings over grades or boyfriends, dresses or girlfriends, extracurricular activities or good schools ever seemed to have much to do with her. "You only got a B," Kate would say. "But I thought English was one of your best subjects. I was always so good at composition." "Nobody asked you to the dance?" Kate would frown, a woman who, when young, had always been asked to dances, the ever-popular Kate. 'Are you sure no one asked you? Do you want me to have a word with Mrs. Shopa? I'm sure her son doesn't already have a date." "You can't go out like that. Are you going out like that? What will people think?" her features stiffening with worry over what all the people who always could have thought only the best about her might think about her child.

Like a doll whose body could bend in a multitude of positions, whose legs and arms moved even at ankles and wrists, whose eyes opened and shut, whose hair could be cut, curled, let loose, or pinned up, she was dressed and undressed according to the dictates of mother and fashion, and hauled back and forth in her father's old Pontiac, Kate behind the screen door, waving goodbye, have a good time, waving hello, did you have a good time? "I could have been a competition dancer," Kate would say, fox-trotting her up and down the living room, practicing for the ballroom dancing class, leading her into every piece of furniture and furnishing. "I was always considered a good dresser," Kate would say, following her into the changing room, whipping aside the cheap nylon curtain, oh, you're not really trying on that shade of green? with your coloring? "When I worked in the Empire State Building," Kate would say, circling all the spelling mistakes in Maggie's English paper, "even Louis Bauer, who had a degree from Harvard, even he used to call me the Walking Dictionary." "I weighed ninety-eight pounds when I got married," tugging at the legs of the Jamaican shorts that fit her younger daughter like bathing trunks. "I had an eighteen-inch waist. I was always dainty."

And so—though neither particularly sociable nor especially good at school—Maggie accepted the invitations and took the exams. And so—with no real and less imagined interest—she joined first the Brownies and then the Girl Scouts, the Catholic Youth, meeting on Wednesday evenings in the bingo hall to grapple with the century's crucial moral issues of virginity and contraception, the school orchestra, desperate enough for members to have no true standards of proficiency. And so—hopelessly and joylessly—she took lessons in dancing, lessons on the violin and the piano, lessons in swimming and tennis, and dutifully went on Friday nights to the monthly hop in the school gym, there to sit beneath the spotlights at the end of the bleachers with the other girls who were too ugly or too drippy ever to stir the shoot-green lust in some young groin, rigid with terror at the alternative possibilities of someone asking her to dance and no one asking.

By the time she asked herself for what it all was, and for whom, she only was certain of what she didn't want to be. She didn't want to be like Kate, frenzying through the hours of one day into the hours of the next like a mouse in a wheel. She didn't want to be like John, slouching through the days of one week into the days of the next like an old plough horse. She didn't want to be like her sister, or her friends at school, or the people she saw all around her with their lives all sewn up, unable to imagine what they might be missing, that there might be something to miss.

But what else could she do?

A girl like she—raised by a subtly complex code of behavior and expectations, always be polite and never break our hearts—couldn't stick her toothbrush into her back pocket and hitchhike to L.A. A girl like she—raised in a complicated but subtle atmosphere of fear and retribution, you might not get a decent job, you might get killed or worse—couldn't run away with her best friend and paddle down the Mississippi on a raft. Couldn't join the army and see the world, ride the rodeo circuit looking for that one special horse, or wash dishes in some all-night diner in Columbus while writing the definitive play of our times in the afternoons. It didn't even help to be able to play the guitar, particularly.

A boy who fled the life he'd been born to lead might end up in jail or with his limbs twisted around a smoldering motorcycle, whispering the name of his true love as the death-spurt of blood popped from his mouth. A boy might end up freezing to death in the Wyoming winter, his only companion a dog named Blue baying over his cold corpse, the unopened last letter from the only woman he ever really loved tucked away in his bedroll with his mother's wedding ring and the picture of his father before he was killed in the war. He might end up a sad-eyed gangster with a love of children and dogs, who every Sunday goes back to the old neighborhood to have dinner with mom. Or a reluctant hero, shunning fortune and fame, forced by his own proud dream to move on to some place where no one has ever heard his name. A boy could expose himself at his graduation, leave the boss's daughter standing at the altar in silk and tulle, her relatives standing behind her with their mouths and eyes shaped like "o"s, looking like a family of pigs on a Sunday outing, or rob every small bank between Eureka, Nevada, and El Dorado, Arkansas, a mauve handkerchief left behind, his trademark, and become a figure of romantic alienation. But not a girl. Not a girl like Maggie, neither especially pretty nor exceptionally bright, neither particularly talented nor outstandingly bold, neither unswervingly determined nor sufficiently desperate.

And so she had gone along, from month to month and year to year, from what Kate described as one crazy phase to another, waiting for something to happen; waiting for everything to fall into place, click plop. And in a way, of course, everything had done just that. Things had happened; and in happening had caused other happenings, had made patterns in the space of the universe like snail trails along the beach at low tide. And in the happenings and makings had caused a momentum which for so long had seemed like intent. You see, you see, I'm not like you, I'm me.

And now?

Kate comes shuffling and snuffling into the kitchen, where the tea and cookies are arranged on the table with milk and sugar, spoons, and paper napkins.

"It's the city air," she says, picking up a napkin and blowing her nose. "It's my allergies," and plops into a chair like a very heavy cushion.

How many men has she loved? How many homes has she had? How many zipsplash moments of pure intoxication, my God, I'm alive, alive and really kicking? How many disasters? disappointments? How much despair, wounded and not even dead?

"Well," says Kate, snapping a cookie in two and studying the lines of the sugar bowl.

"Well."

Maggie pours the tea, Kate staring at the flow of liquid as though counting the escaping leaves.

"They certainly have a beautiful home," helping herself to milk. "I was afraid to touch anything."

"Was your bath all right?"

"She seems like a very intelligent woman. She went to Vassar, you know."

On the short ride home, Kate had talked what she herself would describe as a blue streak, on and on on some supersonic breath about her menopausal neighbor, her neighbor's blood-hungry dog and malicious children, what Broadway had looked like in 1933, the meal she'd had the last time she was in Atlantic City, the warmth of Sarah's bathroom, all in toast and marmalade. Now, it seems, she has nothing to say.

"So," says Maggie.

"It was very nice," says Kate. "I used some of your talcum powder."

"So," says Maggie, sipping her tea and wishing she'd fixed herself a drink. "What do you think of Skip?"

But Kate has been Maggie's mother for too long not to be shy of possible loaded questions; not to remember how many times she has blithely answered the simplest queries about colors or film stars, painters or politics, only to have her own words flung back in her face like spit in the wind, Jesus Christ, you don't understand anything. She hesitates to answer for the near-certainty of saying something wrong. If she says she likes Skip, will Maggie immediately shout with a satisfied snarl, "Aha! He's a drug dealer, he's a child molester, he's a necrophile"? If she says she likes him, will Maggie in the same instant hurl her teacup across the table, its contents sliding like tears down the wall, whydoyoualwayshavetoruineverythingforme? If she says she doesn't like him, will Maggie sneer triumphantly, nothing you can do can stop me from having he whom I love? If she says she doesn't like Skip, will Maggie laugh, I never expected you to understand? If she says she does like the nice young dentist, will he immediately be dumped?

Kate passes Maggie the plate of cookies, saying that she should try one, they're the kind she always loved.

Maggie takes the smallest, saying that she hasn't had them

in years, she can still remember when she and Vicki Besterman used to have them with gingerale-and-chocolate-syrup tea.

"I pray every night for you," Kate says as the smiles die. "I'm happy to see you happy. It's all I've ever wanted." And, yes, she has prayed every night, every night from the night of conception on. Prayed and prayed, bowed with her pleas, fueled by a futility she could never recognize. John always told her to leave the kids alone. Either they'll be all right, he'd say, unconcerned about their achievements, whereabouts, or future plans, or they won't be all right. What did she think she could do about it? You bring them into the world, you feed them and you give them a home, he'd repeat time after time, what more do you think you can do? And she would say, her lower lip trembling, that he didn't understand what it meant to be a mother. Nor did he. John could easily have left his daughters for a month or for a year or for ten years, seeing them infrequently, talking to them on the telephone now and then, occasionally sending a letter or a card, Happy Birthday, Sweetheart, Love, Dad, without guilt or remorse or fear, but Kate could barely make an overnight visit to her sister in Queens without turning and tossing all night in the back room with the picture of Jesus with the Little Children over the single bed, worrying about what was happening back at home without her. And what might or might not take place if something happened to her and she never got back home. You've got your own life, and they've got theirs, he'd say, willing to leave them on their own for a night or even a weekend, never mind the possibilities of fire, burglary, murder, rape, wild parties or older men. And so he did. But they were Kate's life.

And, yes, she is happy. Or at least relieved. A person cannot really think of herself as a failed or forsaken mother with two daughters married to respectable, well-behaved men with good incomes, educations, and backgrounds.

"I know," says Maggie, feeling less happy than she must be, but can think of nothing to say after that. It seems strange, sitting here, noticing how old Kate has become (unlike the mother she has always carried with her in her memory, the mother of the fashionable clothes and sticky red lips, the mother of the Evening in Paris cologne and seamed stockings that came three pairs in a box, who was always photographed smiling maniacally in front of summer cabins or summer trees, or grinning tipsily in rooms papered, carpeted, and upholstered in conflicting floral patterns), that the years should have sneaked by so, that they are not still in the kitchen of the past, arguing about whether or not Maggie is going to art school in California, with so little behind them.

What mother was it, then, who has been hotly pursuing her through the thirty-eight years of her life? The one of her remembrances, so strong and bright and so determined; or this one here, in her pink flowered bathrobe, three pink plastic curlers in her hair and cookie crumbs in her tea? Whose letters dogged her footsteps around the world, first from one college or apartment to another and then from poste restante to poste restante, the pastel envelopes with their borders of flowers, butterflies, or adorable children turning up on grimy, worn counters from Goa to Bogotá, whose tales of drunkenness and cruelty, whose catalogs of domestic disasters and triumphs and local births and deaths tracked her down across swamp and desert, mountain, forest, lake, and sea, not the boy who used to look after the lawn who went to Adelphi, the one who shot his father ... Reverend Miller, you know, who so admired that bag you made me, dropped dead in the candy store next to the movies on Friday ... they'd tried for six years and then as soon as they adopt this beautiful little refugee boy, she gets pregnant ... and then the man came to fix the color on the TV, thank God ... she was so frightened that he was going to come home drunk again that she brought the kids around in the middle of the night and I gave the littlest that old stuffed dog of yours, you remember, the green one with the odd ear, and she slept with him in her arms, just like an angel? To whom was it that she wrote her vague and uninformative replies about the temperature and the rainfall, the nice couple she met on the train or the friend she made in Sydney airport, the cows or sheep, goats or llamas sauntering through the village streets?

"You know I've always wanted only what was best for you," says Kate now, and though she is tempted (perhaps from habit, perhaps for other reasons) to add, you are happy, aren't you?, it is what you want?, manages to look as though she is satisfied that that is what Maggie now has.

If Kate has changed, has she?

If Kate has changed, and she has changed, why do things

seem oddly the same—as though she has fallen through the looking glass of her own imagination; as though winning Kate's approval and not winning Kate's approval have always been identical, damned if you don't and damned if you do.

And if this is what Kate has wanted all along (and it was she who said, all those used-up years ago, when it was Ben's birth that was the problem and not his death, that Maggie should marry and settle down, the love would come, children weren't conceived for no reason, children needed fathers), then why does each of them feel minutely but distinctly disappointed, as though Kate had always expected more of Maggie in reality, and Maggie even more of Kate?

"Yes, I know," says Maggie, who almost does, at this instant; who can almost see, in the dull light of the kitchen dingy with the stains and accidents of others' lives, all the things that Kate has always wanted for her, all the things she herself never had. "These cookies are really terrific."

"It's all in the creaming," Kate says modestly, but not without some pride. Intimidated for nearly seventy years by anyone wearing a suit, owning a better house than she, or possessing a college degree, she nonetheless has her sphere of authority. "Of course, with my arthritis, I can't do it so well anymore." She brushes some crumbs from the front of her robe. "My friend Ruth, you know, the one whose daughter went to that place in India with the guru, you remember I told you about that?" pausing for Maggie's nod, "and then she got so ill and Ruth had to go all the way out there to bring her back ... you wouldn't believe half the stories she has about it," Kate's head shaking, mouth pursing, and eyes widening in a silence more descriptive than any mere words, "you wouldn't believe what goes on, what was the name of that place ... the one that sounded like it was in California ..."

"Poona," says Maggie, trying valiantly to remember the letter or the conversation in which Ruth and her runaway daughter appeared.

Kate dabs at her tea-wet lips with a napkin, as her mother taught her ladies always do. "And she trained to be a nurse, too. Ruth has always been so active in the church ... it's hard to understand ... I think she really always wanted to be a nun. Your father always said she was one of those fanatics. If there hadn't been all this trouble with Suzanne, she would have gone into a convent when Harry died. I'm sure of it ..." And both stare at the table where one of them has spilled some sugar, and at their separate images of Ruth the near-nun dragging Suzanne the near-nurse through the all-too-human streets, the specter of Harry, bald but wearing his tartan golf cap, bobbing above them, thank God I died, Suzanne, or this would have killed me. "Ruth says I should use the electric mixer—she always does, no matter what—but I just don't feel it would be the same."

"The same as what?" Once, before this time, this conversation would have made Maggie moan and curse, slam down her cup with a crack and a rattle and say good night, but now she only thinks that it is remarkable, if you think about it, that Kate can talk about cookies, God, religion, death, electric mixers, cult frenzy, kidnapping and emotional anguish all in very close to one breath.

"The same as creaming by hand."

The lights are off inside the apartment, the night has settled down. Maggie lies beside Kate, lullabyed to doziness by the rain falling against the window like butterflies, or, maybe, moths. She is almost dreaming when Kate whispers, "Maggie? Maggie, are you still awake?" In the dream, it sounds as though Kate is crying. "What?" Back to back, neither of them moves or turns or lifts herself up on one elbow. "Did I ever tell you why I married your father?" "Um." Now John drifts into the dream, fat and grinning as he almost always was, and hurries out again. "I married him because he was the closest I could get to love," says Kate. And, having said that, pulls the sheet more snugly around her, closes her eyes, and is soon asleep.

In the darkness, so much like any other darkness, in the night that is only one night out of thousands, Maggie lies awake, listening to her mother breathe and her own heart go brhump brhump brhump in the silence of the universe.

SEVEN

López wants to know how come it is Richard talks to Tony and to no one else. "He talks to you." "Oh, sure," said López, wiping his forehead with one of the napkins he keeps in a pile by the counter for the kids with their ice creams and ices. "He says his name, he says 'Good day to you, sir,' and he says 'Thank you.' Sometimes. I got a sister in Jersey has a dog says more than that."

"That guy a friend of yours?" Vega asked the other day, jerking a thumb at Richard across the street, staring in the direction of a river as though his ship were coming in. "He's an undercover narc," looking Vega straight in his shifty, restless eyes. "If you look under his robe you'll see he's wearing white socks."

Even Mrs. Burkowsky, who, still unable to get around or even up, had Tony move her enormous old mahogany bed, piece by piece, into the living room so she can look out of the window, is curious. "I saw you talking to that colored fellow," she said last night, exhausted in the ripped and faded armchair after their nightly slow crawl around the rooms, the doctor says the exercise will do you good. But he was shaking out the sheet as though it might lift him up through the ceiling and out into the wide-open sky. "You don't have to shake it like that," said Mrs. Burkowsky. "I just want it aired. It doesn't have bugs," forgetting the rest of what she had started to say.

Sophie would say (or would probably say) that the great question is not why Richard talks to Tony, but why Tony talks to Richard, seeing as he has so little interest in talking to anyone else. Sophie, however, is imprisoned in the Bronx, being driven slowly mad by her sister's incessant complaints and demands—it would have been nice if we could have a little chicken for supper, do you remember when Mama was ill how I never left her, even for an afternoon? they're all the same, these kids, the minute they're able to go off on their own they go and never give you another thought—and long and whining reminiscences of a past that substantially never was. Though she calls him once or twice a week and tells how she is ("Crazy. Absolutely crazy. If her heart doesn't kill her, I probably will."), she has given up trying to find out about him ("Don't tell me. You're fine, and Sandy's fine, and the dog's fine, and nothing's happening.").

Mostly, of course, he and Richard don't talk at all. Like the old men on their benches—occasionally exchanging stories of the lives they used to have, the friends they used to know—like long-settled couples in their living rooms—occasionally exchanging comments on the clothing of the newscaster or the love life of the talk-show host—they mostly sit in companionable silence, neither asking questions nor expecting explanations.

Richard has never taken any especial notice of Tony's arrival in his world; has never, unlike everyone else, ever questioned his motives or his meaning; has shown no curiosity about his comings or goings or the reasons why. Perhaps, to him, having Tony beside him, passing an apple or passing the time of night, is much the same as being alone. Perhaps, to Tony, strolling one foot at a time next to Richard as they make their way from one cramped street to another with all the time in the world and all the world before them like a mirage of miracles, it is exactly the same as being alone.

Perhaps.

But when Richard does speak, it is like listening to your own voice in a dream. When Richard does speak, it is like listening to the ghost of Christmases yet to come, describing all the things you knew but didn't want to know, pointing out with total calm and no constraint the obvious results of the world's behavior, which you never really wanted to see in the first place, which you tried so hard to avoid. Or so it seems to Rivera.

Homeless, statusless, and adrift in time with no directions and no bonds, unknown and uninterested, if the thirty-six tzaddikim did exist, if the universe really had room for wisemen or prophets, if it were possibly deserving of divine vigilance and supervision, then it would not be impossible that Richard counted among them. Or so thinks Tony. The only times that he is worried about neither living nor dying are when he is with Richard, watching the world churn on without them and there is nothing about which to care. "Look at that," Richard will say, nodding toward the children running through the hydrant, nodding toward the women in their skimpy summer tops and shorts or softly swirling skirts as they sashay down the avenue with so much to do, so much to think about, so much waiting for them, nodding toward the men flagging down cabs, looking at their watches, their briefcases polished and locked, nodding toward the guy lying with his head in a puddle of urine in the phone booth, the cops standing around him like buzzards, hardly blinking. "Look at that," and then will turn away himself—never adding "ain't that shit" or "isn't that great," "I wouldn't mind getting to know her better" or "I bet she's great in the sack," "what a load of bullshit" or "wouldn't it be nice"—to look at something else. Sometimes, triggered by a sound or scent or distant shape, he will talk of moments or events, but it is never clear whether he is recounting memories or dreams, or simply repeating stories learned from some previous time. Richard never remembers, not like other people do, never longs for and never misses, never wants. "If you could have anything you wanted," Tony asked him, "what would it be?" And Richard had slowly lowered the container of orange juice from which he'd been drinking, placing it on the pavement between his legs as though made of the finest hand-blown glass, staring straight ahead and through the passing people and the buildings that for so many many years have watched them pass, as though conjuring the image of his greatest desire from somewhere beyond the flesh and stone and glass and kaleidoscoping noise and color. "I wouldn't mind having a little gin right now," said Richard.

So simple is it for some.

Does Richard have a home or a past? a future or even a present? Does he have no friends, relations, or lovers who remember him still as once he might have been? no employer, social worker, counselor, or psychiatrist who even now might think of him as he or she sits in the backyard, keeping an eye on the fire and sipping a summertime drink, I wonder whatever happened to that crazy guy with the dreadlocks? Didn't he have the same fantasies and fears and misconceptions as all the other little boys, sniggering in the back of the classroom if anyone mentioned the words "bra" or "reproduction," jerking off in his bed at night, longing for the women in the magazine hidden under the mattress, their nipples hard, their cunts exposed by their own knowing fingers, wouldn't you like to have me, too? Didn't he cry and worry, laugh and yell, hang on to his mother's hand as they made their pilgrimage to store and bank and church and friend? Didn't he want to have money and nice clothes and fast cars? Didn't he want, ever, to be someone? make something of his life? find someone to love? change the world? Doesn't he bleed and cry and fuck and shit and dodge the fears that come in the ebony heart of the night, searching for some kind of God? Isn't he human?

Yes, he does bleed. He turned up at López's one morning for his breakfast roll and coffee ("What the hell," says López. "It don't cost much and it keeps the troublemakers away. They're all scared shitless of him."), his forehead cut open and still bloody, his hands looking as though they'd been punching through walls, or something. "What happened to you?" grinned López. "Get into a fight?" But Richard, with the demeanor of a king just offered a slug of Gypsy Rose by a friendly bum, replied that he didn't fight unless he had to, took his roll and styrofoam cup of weak coffee, and drifted back into the street. "See what I mean?" López shrugged at Tony, buying tea for Mrs. Burkowsky. "He ain't even grateful."

But he doesn't cry and he doesn't laugh. And to Tony he is like no one else. If he is mad (which he certainly must be), it is a different madness. No sad stories and no sad lies. No apologies, no excuses, no reasons. No raging silences, just look at what you've done. No impossible dreams, improbable schemes or tape-loop memories, didyaknow, didievertellyou, iremember thisonetime. He has known people strung out on many things—drugs, alcohol, violence, sex, poverty, weakness, fear, strung out on their own insanity or the world's, but Richard is strung out on none of those things. He simply isn't there. He told Miriam in the office about him. "He sounds like that guy who used to live in the basement of Occupational Health," she said, able to talk and type at the same time. "You remember. He thought he was John the Baptist. Every time there was a lecture or seminar he'd go up to the speaker, look him up and down, then stare him right in the eyes and say, "No, you're not him." Don't you remember? He was around for months." "Yeah, yeah," said Rivera, "I remember him." The subway was stopped for an hour and a half the morning he fell onto the tracks in front of a Downtown Express, Parker poetically distraught but obviously relieved to be spared the trouble and notoriety of having to have him expelled from hospital property by the police. "He's not like him at all."

But there was no sign of Richard this morning. Tony and Zorro have come to the park on their own, Tony wearing his new wraparound sunglasses, so that he is, for most practical purposes, blind, and Zorro sporting a brand new turquoise bandanna and a Ban-the-Bomb button. It is a hot, bright day, and the park is so busy it fairly bops. Couples nuzzle on the grass, tough-looking young men with tattoos and knife scars beat out tunes on makeshift drums and old guitars, winos rustle through the trash, and children whoop and holler from the playground. On the benches, sitting with their legs crossed, the mothers watch out for kidnappers and killers while they glance through magazines and talk to one another about husbands, children, or the political situation in Nicaragua, and the couples who meet here every weekend as if by chance, hold hands and pretend to be interested in the boys doing tricks on their skates.

Three times he has thrown a stick across the path and into the next dull patch of lawn, and three times Zorro has happily bounded after it, tail wagging, and three times returned with a different stick, a trick that requires a certain amount of ingenuity. Now, each exhausted, they lie together on the grass, Tony propped up by his elbows, and Zorro propped up by Tony's feet.

What, he wonders, do the others make of him? Do they nudge each other and whisper, hey, get a load of that guy over there with the mutt, do you think he's a cop? a dope peddler? an actor? a history teacher? an unemployed physicist? a failed lawyer? Do any of the men look at him with envy? Any of the women gaze at him with incipient lust? Do any of them think, hey, that guy really looks like he's got his act together? Or do they not even really notice him, absorbing not only his image but his essence by some sort of spiritual osmosis, Jesus, another one? Does he excite any curiosity, stir any anger, trigger any fear? Make anyone wonder? Wonder, as he wonders, his eyes moving from one to the other, from the old men to the young women, from the shrieking, self-absorbed children to the sullen, wary kids, what do they do? what do they think? what do they feel? what do they know? How do they get from one day to the next?

Nearby, a girl laughs. Just like Susan Kalinski used to laugh. Just like he used to laugh. But the girl is not like he, and not like Susan Kalinski, either. She is young and rather pretty in an uninteresting way, and there is no suggestion about her of ever having been alone or afraid, or that she knows that the worst is still to come. If of anyone, she reminds him of Sandy, confident and pleased to be exactly who she is, just the way she sits and laughs and touches her hair when her companion talks, a clear indication to any passing demon or god, you better not mess with me, I've got a contract.

If he went up to her now and asked her, in his old persona, the Puerto Rican janitor, escuse me, mees, ees thees the Broncks?, what would she say? If he went up to her now and said to her, in another of his old personas, the Latin Lover, hey, mami, *ven acá*, hey, sweetie, let's go look at a tomb together, what would she do? Call the police? Scream for a hero? Patiently explain that they're in Manhattan, rolling her eyes at her friend when she thought he wasn't looking, Jesus Christ, what a jerk, he thinks this is the Bronx?

"You know," said Parker last Friday night, having lured him into the local bar for a friendly drink, one heavy hand on his shoulder as they left the safety of the street. "You know, Sheila and I have a very happy marriage. Better than most." Parker likes Fred's Place because it reminds him of his humble origins, the décor nonexistent, Frank Sinatra on the jukebox, the regulars all rough men who have never been ready for anything in their lives, except, perhaps, death. It is part of the charm of the place that no matter how often the colonists from the hospital go there no one will ever so much as nod in recognition. Tony got a black eye and a broken wrist in Fred's last winter, defending the drunker-than-usual Parker after he propositioned the wrong woman, Parker sitting in Emergency with him saying over and over, "I'm really sorry, Tony. How was I supposed to know she was with someone? You saw the way she was looking at me."

Parker bought him a beer. "You know," he continued, "Sheila's a remarkable woman. I've been very very lucky." Which is certainly true. In a more primitive and realistic society, where you actually had to be fit for something to survive, Larry would have been left out on a ledge in a blizzard years ago.

"Yeah," said Tony, sniffing at his glass. He has seen cockroaches as big as tanks in Fred's. "Yeah. Sheila's very nice."

"Not that it's always been easy," Parker droned on. "Every couple has their little ups and downs," and smiled his knowing, man-of-the-world smile, you know what women are like. "It hasn't always been easy."

"Oh, no. No, I'm sure it hasn't." And though the remarkable qualities of Sheila Parker have persistently evaded him, he couldn't suppress a tiny bleep of sympathy for her, wed for at least a quarter of a century to the people's poet of Scarsdale, the poor old cow.

"Sometimes a man needs ..." gazing into his beer as though into the heart of the universe. "Sometimes a man needs something more."

Instantly, he decided not to understand. "More? You mean the impossible dream? The unreachable goal? The unwinnable fight?"

And Parker blinked and decided, as he usually decides, to ignore what he wasn't quite sure he understood. "Do you understand what I'm talking about, Tony?" his hands out before him in a gesture of sincerity, his hands out before him, stretched like a bridge over the chasm of confusion and subjectivity separating self from self. "More."

Tony sipped his beer, one small swallow at a time, his eyes firmly fixed on the sign behind Parker's head, YOU DON'T HAVE TO BE CRAZY TO WORK HERE BUT IT HELPS. "You mean love and work."

"Love and work?" repeated Parker, as though Tony had only just learned the language, was still having problems with vocabulary and pronunciation.

"Yeah. Freud said that personal happiness depended on love and work."

"Freud?" repeated Parker, for once, it seemed, uninterested in what Freud had to say, he who has been in analysis for most of his adult life with no sign of boredom, disenchantment, or progress; he who would recommend it for a kid who'd spent her first six years locked in a closet, only brought out on weekends to be beaten.

"Freud. You know, the Austrian dude with the beard."

"What I mean," said Parker, carefully selecting his words, as only a man with his command of the language could, "is more."

But more what? More wives like Sheila with her credit-card heart and her charitable interest in young male athletes from deprived homes? More ranch-style houses in expensive suburbs with two-car garages and real fireplaces? More grants, more degrees, more invitations to Washington to address Congressional Committees on the problems of the inner cities? More poor sons-of-bitches, trapped or dying, to inspire his howling verse? "I don't know what you're getting at," said Tony, with the sinking feeling that he must. With all the mysterious and complex creations of the universe, Larry Parker is most certainly not one of them.

"You know what I mean, Tony," Parker urged in the hushed tones of conspiracy. "Sometimes people get in ruts. They need something a little different," his hands outlining the shape of his stein. "Just to get the juices flowing."

"Uh huh."

"Sometimes a man needs a little extra excitement," his eyes shifting restlessly around the dark and smoky room where daylight traditionally stops at the door. "A little romance."

At the bar, one of the regular whores laughed, slapping her hands on the counter. "Oh, Harry, you really are a card." Romance?

"You know."

Of all the people in Fred's at that moment, only he and Parker didn't look as though they had probably lost their jobs, their families, or their last friends that afternoon—although, maybe it was only Parker. "No," said Tony. "I don't know. Are you suggesting that I need a hobby?"

And Larry smiled, which, probably because of the lousy light, made him look like a pumpkin, all cut out and ready for a candle. "Something like that." He took a deep breath and finished his beer. "A man doesn't have to be a womanizer to take an interest now and then. There's nothing wrong with grazing in a new field every now and then." Grazing in a new field? Jesus. "As happy as Sheila and I have always been, there have been times when I've ... I've ..." looking up at the strips of flypaper hanging from the ceiling like totems. Strayed? Wandered? Fooled around? Sought refuge in the arms of some forbidden lover? Quenched the burning yearning of his passionate soul in the clear cool streams of some young bright love? "I've had other relationships. Nothing that would ever interfere with my marriage, you understand."

"Oh, sure. I understand."

"But nothing trivial, either."

"Oh, of course not."

"It's just that sometimes a man needs a little more than the love and companionship of a wife."

And who knew that better than Tony, whose hand was in plaster for a month because Parker wanted to start up a meaningful relationship with a woman done up like a female impersonator whose boyfriend had no sense of humor? "Is there someone you want me to introduce you to?" asked Rivera, resigning himself to another round.

"Oh, for God's sake, Tony," snapped Parker, forgetting his soulful tones. "Why do you have to make everything so hard?"

"I'm not making everything hard, Larry," he protested, picking up his empty glass and preparing to trudge to the bar. "I don't understand what you're trying to say."

He could hear Parker sigh even as the jukebox went on, Patti Page singing "Mockingbird Hill." Time has obviously decided to stop and stay in Fred's.

As it turned out, what Parker was trying to say was that Tony, perhaps, just maybe, it was a possibility, needed a little variety to spice up his life. Parker knows that Tony didn't want to come off the streets, and even though he, personally, wouldn't want to lose him, and even though he, personally, can understand why Tony turned down that out-of-town promotion, he does wonder if Tony isn't getting himself stuck in a little middle-age morass. Parker wasn't talking about love, of course. Well, thank God for that. Not love like between a husband and wife. He was talking about excitement, about fun. He was talking to him like a friend. "Don't talk to me like a friend," begged Tony. "Talk to me like a stranger," or an enemy. Parker thought he was joking.

"I know the kind of man you are," said Parker, his eyes slightly misted, though whether it was from the stale air or the stale sincerity was difficult to tell. "I've seen it all before. I've watched you. Don't think I haven't." Oh, he didn't think that. "You're a solitary guy, Tony. You're very close." But close to what? "Ever since that unfortunate accident last summer," said Parker, his hand-knitted tie dangling into his beer.

"And what accident was that?" asked Rivera, suddenly painfully sober again.

"You know," said Parker. "The incident with the Martin kid," looking for all the world as though he himself believed what he was saying.

"That wasn't an accident, Larry. And it wasn't an incident, either. There were five bullets in that kid. That makes it a murder." They had been walking down the street one minute, he and Martin, talking about nothing, talking about how hot it was, talking about stopping somewhere for a beer, and the next minute there had been two guns pointed at them, just hold it right there, and Martin, mistaking the cops for someone else, was reaching for his knife and Tony was hitting the pavement, holding on. It was over in seconds.

"They thought he had a gun."

"They should have asked him first."

"The kid had a record a mile long, Tony. He had some very heavy connections."

But he was with me. "He never murdered anyone in broad daylight on a public street, though, did he?"

But that, said Parker, was not the point. The point was that since the whateveryouwantedtocallit, and since Tony came into the office, still refusing to answer the door when opportunity, or anyone else for that matter, knocked, Larry Parker has been watching him become more and more withdrawn and hostile, and more antagonistic and counterproductive. "We can't all be the enemy," said Parker, but Tony had simply watched his mouth moving, not so sure.

"Are you offering to pimp for me? Is that what you're saying?" he'd asked at last, if only to stop Larry from saying any more.

"Jesus H. Christ," groaned Parker, running his fingers through what is left of his hair. "All I wanted to know was how things are. All I meant was that maybe you could use a little extra interest in your life."

In movies, Tony knew, men often have conversations like this one, but it had never occurred to him that it happened in real life. If, that was, you could call this real life.

Love, my God, he's had enough of love—can no longer even imagine what it could mean, might be. And enough of sex, too. Though Parker, of course, was in actuality pushing neither. Like the host of a daytime children's show, he was pushing activities for a rainy day. Depressed? Bored? Confused? Restless? Is your job not enough? Is your family not sufficient? Pick a good cause and get yourself on talk shows. Pick a good hobby and impress your peers with the breadth and depth of your sophistication and manual dexterity. Try jogging, or weight lifting, or sky diving. Look at how much everyone admires gazelles and they don't think very much. Look at how much everyone admires football players and what do they contribute to the workings of the universe? Still feeling that something's missing? Still feeling your own aging like a cold, dank breath at the back of your wrinkling neck? Still afraid of dying without having felt that you have lived? Still afraid of being dead, the world spinning on without you, with not so much as a bump or a sigh, with not so much as an obituary in the *Times* or a mention in *The Encyclopedia Britannica*? Screw around. Call it love or call it virility, a man cannot be condemned for either his reckless heart or his teeming hormones. What matter thickening waists, hardening arteries, or thinning hair; what matter foolishness, tediousness, or anonymity; what matter a sense of personal failure, a sense of self-loathing, or a sense of immutable futility so long as you can still get it up and find some one or two or twenty who are still interested in taking you in? I fuck, therefore I must be.

Must be what?

Last winter, Tony was in love for exactly six weeks, give or take an hour or two, with a schizophrenic dancer named Judith who had an answer for everything whether she'd been asked a question or not. A permanent temporary high. Zip bang whizz varoom. Wham bing pow. He felt all the things people always say they feel, that he had never really felt before. He felt like a superman, he felt like a kid, he felt like nothing else mattered at all. He felt so alive he was another color in the rainbow, another star in the sky, a living, breathing part of God. And then one day he'd looked at her and she'd looked at him and it had been obvious that neither of them really liked the other very much. He had seen in her only what he had wanted to see, making excuses for all the things he didn't want to know or understand. He had—still has—no idea of what she'd seen in him, who she thought he might be, what she thought he might be able to give her. It was frantic lovemaking one minute, and Judith who? Tony what? the next. Sophie, who knew without being told, who gave advice without it having been solicited, made him eat two bowls of pork and pumpkin stew and said that the things a man will devour when he is starving cannot be considered the same as he will consume when he is not. Whatever the hell that was supposed to mean. All he knows is that it had never happened to him before, and it is never going to happen again. He knows that Sandy, from time to time, has had a lover, but he has always assumed it was merely a symptom of her greater ability to make friends, to live her life right out in the open, fearlessly, a woman who is in touch with herself is free to touch others. Let Parker go around slapping cologne all over his jowls and polishing his leather sports jacket, let Parker and all the other Parkers of this world toss feverishly in their beds at night, careful not to disturb the wife, composing poems and songs of love to the secretaries, students, and wives-of-colleagues who have stirred the banked embers of their soot-coated hearts with their long tanned limbs and stewardess smiles. Let them crawl through the corridors, rings of sleeplessness around their anxious eyes and a tremble in their hands, unseeing, unhearing, and unheeding of the fretful bustle of the world around them, their minds on more important things (the smoothness of a thigh, the secrets in a smile, the way she laughs at the jokes and stories of which everyone else has long grown tired as though they were something bright and private and new, the difficulties of being in two places at once). Let Parker have his weekend trysts in secluded, romantic spots like Brooklyn Heights or the Lower East Side, bottles of sparkling wine and containers of Indian take-out, and call them love. Life is too short for all those games. Or so thinks Tony. Too short for the stuffing of mushrooms, the peeling of grapes and the self-induced hallucinations of terror. And daily shorter still.

Zorro sees something interesting down the path and bounds away, Tony leans up on one elbow to call, "Hey! Zorro! Get back here!" in his most authoritative voice. He has gotten into fights over Zorro before; once had to be rescued from a track-suited madwoman with a Weimeraner by two young cops with school-boy grins, yeah, buddy, we see it all the time.

But it is not a handsome young spaniel after which the intrepid Zorro runs. It is not a man-eating German Shepherd on a stainless-steel chain from which he will have to be protected, or a pedigreed Chihuahua which will have to be protected from him, get your mutt away from my dog. It is a woman and a child. He lifts the plastic glasses and squints, and can just about make out Will, jumping up and down like something on a string. Oh, God, now his cover's been blown.

He lies back down, pulling the shades once more over his eyes. He won't speak to Meredith—nobody can make him. If she does insist on intruding into his solitude, swishing the dull dry grass with her gypsy skirt, linking her bare plump arms around her knees, trying to pump his soul with her ceaseless chatter, he will speak to her only in Spanish. What could she do? Yell back with her edgy, nasal vowels, "You fuckin' bastard, no wonder your wife can't stand the sight of you anymore," "You lousy son-of-a-bitch, why don't you just die and save everybody all your aggravation?"

"Ooh, Maggie, look!" Will squeals. "Look! It's Zorro!"

"What's he all dressed up for?" asks Maggie as Zorro rushes up, obviously glad to see them, his tail wagging away like a beserk windshield-wiper, his tiny body hurling itself against them in frenzied joy.

"He's not dressed up for nothing," says Will, ducking the more exuberant licks.

"Yeah," says Maggie. "That's what I mean. What's he dressed up for?"

"Oh, Maggie," moans Will, his patience as small as he is. "He always wears a scarf when he goes to the park."

"Oh, right," says Maggie, I should have known.

Maggie, too, has been thinking this morning of love. Ever since Kate's visit, which left behind it a pink shower cap, a half-dozen chocolate chip cookies, a jar of instant coffee, and a notable amount of unrest, she has been thinking of little else. What was her mother trying to pull? Bubbling on about happiness and the practicality of slipcovers with young children one minute, and popping up in bed like a reluctant corpse the next, making disquieting revelations about the nature of life. What was her mother trying to tell her—that she is right to compromise or wrong? She hadn't really thought, before, that she was so much copping out as wising up. And even if she had, on nights as lonely as they've ever been, thought of herself as giving up (but what?), it was easy enough to ignore it in the general din of others' approval, at last you've got what everyone really wants.

This morning, though, with Meredith off on a weekend of passion in the arms of a divorced toy salesman who looks like a loan shark but is said to have a terrific sense of humor, and Skip far away in the piney wood hills, whamming his hammer and swinging his axe and singing "Country Roads" right out loud, and Will hot and bored and hard to please, love—or its illusion— seems to be the only thing about which she is capable of thinking. Even though it seems likely that the thoughts themselves will eventually reduce her to tears, right out in public, as she and Will shuffle home, hand-in-hand, he screaming into the stream of Sunday shoppers with their cartons of juice and bags of rolls and Sunday papers and pungent wedges of cheese, "Hey, Maggie, what are you crying for?"

Maggie Kelly has never been in love, not even for roughly six weeks. She has loved, yes; she has loved and she has lusted, she has fantasized both ecstasy and destiny within the blind circle of a hot and rhythmic embrace, but has always found herself lonely again, lonely and alone. And now no longer understands the philosophies, the songs, the rhymes and words of love which others use to vivify, embellish, and make real their routine lives. Finds it difficult to remember (as time has passed and the magic and the beloved one with it) whether what she felt was close to love or farther than the Ring Nebula. Difficult to separate the infatuations and the pheromones, the comfortable partnerships and frantic emotions from what might have been something more.

That old black magic.

And so she has let Will lead her through the weekend-empty streets, where the ghosts of crowds still surge and wail, nodding, yessing, and oh-no-ing, stopping when confronted by a small but thunderous face to say, "Of course I'm listening. You were talking about the boy at school whose father's a mass murderer." "You see!" screamed Will, his eyebrows an unbroken line. "See! I was not. I was talking about Stevie Greaves whose father let him bring in a hand-grenade from the war. He was a hero." And so she has let Will lead her here, here where the young girls parade their bodies and the young men parade their smiles, here where the single mothers and single fathers make their weekly pilgrimages, it's so close to McDonald's, and the couples have eyes for no one but each other, parading their love.

She has been in a state that might be mistaken for love for days and weeks and months and even years, but of all those loves is there one that she remembers with more than a sigh? More than sadness or regrets? More than thoughts about the wasting of time? Ben's father? Any one of his predecessors? Any one of his successors? Any one whose memory now makes her think not what a jerk she was, but how lucky forever, even if it had only been for just a little while?

Perhaps she's never had a heart. Perhaps she has been sealed within herself, a cocoon that never opens to free the life within, doomed to see no more than could be seen, to feel no more than could be felt, to know no more than could be known, those walls made of herself and by herself and for no one else.

The pop tops pop, the music moves the pavement and the trees, and Maggie sighs.

What has it meant, that thing that passed for love? One day you can't imagine living without him, and the next day you wish he'd drop dead. One day you would trudge across the frozen tundra with your baby in your arms for only a word, a look, a brief embrace, and the next you wouldn't cross the street in a sedan chair with an armed escort to receive his heart on a silver tray, so who's crying now. One minute you want to hear his views on everything and anything, can hear see and imagine nothing without wondering what he would think, and the next you would rather spend the rest of your life in a convent in Colombia than to have to hear him tell you one more time about the things they used to do for fun when he was a kid.

Yes, she has cried and raged and rolled herself into a small, tight ball, holding the hurt in the center, how could it have happened, how could it be? She has been left and badly treated, forsaken and pushed around, found him in the sweeter embrace of a dear friend, and simply found him gone, I'll be in touch some time. She has her scars, like everyone else, but she's not dead yet. Is she? Has anyone, in all the strange days of the world, has anyone ever died of a broken heart? From loneliness, boredom, and guilt. From broken heads in lovers' quarrels, from jealousy and mad revenge. But not from damaged hearts. Dogs sometimes do, and dolphins now and then, but the species of man is made of sterner stuff.

Or so says Maggie Kelly, who can just remember thinking, one, two, maybe five or six times, well, this, then, must be love. Who has once twice maybe three times said "I love you," looking into his eyes and thinking she saw something of herself.

If all that is true, though, why should she worry? If all that is true, why does she stare at the faces and magnetized bodies of every couple they pass as though trying to locate something that she's lost? If all that is true, then she has already made the wisest choice.

"Hey, Maggie," says Will, his fat little hand hooked into Zorro's bandanna, looking as though he's about to go for a ride. "Hey, Maggie. Look! There's Tony." He is more excited than he was when they met the dog. It is only now that she realizes that of all the men Will knows, of all the men who troop through Meredith's life, in one door and out the other, hopping him on to a knee for a few minutes before good-nights are said, winning him over with candies and tiny plastic cars in irridescent colors that whirr across the kitchen floor, of all the men who stop long enough to read him a story or help him string a kite, to ask him what he thinks of the Yankees or what his favorite television show is, there is not one of whom he has been really fond. Meredith thinks he's got a thing about men, and why wouldn't he, with his father? But Will likes Tony. When he was so ill last winter, it was Tony who had to come over every evening to get him to take his medicine and sit with him till he'd fallen asleep, who spent hours every Saturday losing to Will at War, checkers, and Junior Scrabble. When Will fell through Meredith's glass bedtray last autumn, it was Tony who had to pick the splinters of glass from his hands (Meredith doesn't really care for blood), who rode him to the hospital in a cab with a groaning horn and a handkerchief flapping out the window and stood beside him while the doctor put in the stiches, talking about what a coward Zorro was when he got that splinter in his foot (Mededith has never cared for hospitals). And Tony calls him *amigo* and fixes his bike. Tony calls him *compadre* and makes him laugh. Tony doesn't have to say that he likes to have Will around.

"Where?"

But, maybe, the feelings she has known have been as far from love as Christianity from Christ. Maybe, the men who have wanted her to lie with them or live with them, who have doggedly pursued her or persistently wooed her or angrily claimed she had failed them, were not really offering love, either.

What does Skip with his eager kisses and endless blueprints offer? When he whispers, oh, honey, I love you, what is it that he means?

"Over there. See those red sneakers just poking up? That's him."

Stretched out on the unenthusiastically green grass, he looks as though he's dead, the animal owners, child owners, and sunseekers around him sitting far enough away in case he starts to stink.

"Are you sure?"

But, maybe, if the feelings she has known have not been love, then love is not a thing to be known. Maybe everyone, like Kate, has got to settle. Maybe it is easier to love a thing, selflessly and truly (a god, a cause, an ideal, a thought, a memory, a dream) than it is to love someone. "At least if you'd become a nun," Kate once said, "I'd know you cared about something."

"Of course I'm sure," and zooms on ahead with the dog.

He can hear the footsteps pounding toward him, the thudding of Will's basketball sneakers and the rittittat of Zorro's claws, and right behind them the clunkslapclunk of Meredith's Dr. Scholl's. He doesn't have to look. He can hear the puffing and the panting, the grunting and the yelp, and behind them the nasal whine of Meredith, imagine meeting you here. He'll pretend to be asleep. She may think he's passed out drunk or drugged and leave him alone, rushing home to get to the telephone, wait'll you hear what the son-of-a-bitch did this time.

Really, what could she do if all he will say is *"No entiendo. ¡Hablas en español!"*?

Will hits his knees in a running tackle. Zorro licks his nose.

"And what are you dressed up for?" asks a voice directly above his head.

It isn't Meredith at all.

"I'm trying to elude my many adoring fans." He sits up, pulling the glasses from his face so he can be sure that it is she.

"Oh, yeah," she says, plopping down on the ground beside him. "Well, it looks like you've succeeded." She wipes the sweat from her forehead with the rolled-up sleeve of her shirt. "My God, it's hot. This kid doesn't understand about heat and the old."

"Hey, Tony," shrieks Will, standing now and tugging at the shoulders of his shirt. "Hey, Tony. We found Zorro."

"I think I might have to give you a reward for that," sneaking in a quick hug. "Why don't you go and get us some ice cream? I want chocolate," and reaches into his pocket for change.

"I'll go," says Maggie, already half on her feet.

Automatically, he reaches out to stop her. "Don't be silly. It's only over there. He can go. What do you want?" Why can't he remember her name?

She looks down at his hand. "Over where?"

"Over there."

Not near the curb at all.

"Oh," she says, and waits until he's let her go to fall back down. "Over there. I'll have an orange ice." But watches nonetheless as Will, holding the coins in a tight, grimy fist, races over to the ice cream man and his cart, Zorro at his heels.

"And a vanilla cup for Zorro!" Tony yells after him.

It is not as though they have nothing to say. They have, after all, spoken before. Almost frequently. Right after the fight with Vega, she even asked him what happened to his face. "Who hit you?" "You'll be happy to know," he'd said, "that the other guy looks a hell of a lot better." She'd squeezed past him, her arms filled with brightly colored sweatshirts in a cardboard box. "He'd have to." Now, of course, they could talk about the weather or the sun-dancing crowd. He could ask her where Meredith is, or how the house is coming along, he's heard great things. "Oh," she would say, "have you heard from Sandy recently?" "Oh, sure," he would say, "she writes me almost every day," Dear Tony, Last night I had a dream ... Dear Tony, Yesterday I was talking with Jack about relationships ... Dear Tony, I was remembering the first time we needed a separation ... She might ask him if he comes here often, what's a nice guy like you doing in a park like this? She could tell him about the morning she's had, how the fan broke and the milk was sour and Will couldn't remember where he'd left his shoes. He could ask her what her name is.

But neither of them says anything.

"What he doesn't understand," a voice to their right is saying, "is that I'm not him. I'm me."

Out of the corner of his eye he can see Maggie smirk.

In any event, he's remembered her name. It is Maggie, Maggie Meredith's friend, and suddenly understands, in the way that you sometimes do, that it was she with whom Sandy stayed when she was hiding out from him. How does he know that? Why? And then remembers that Sandy dislikes Maggie, finds her a failing in Skip. "I don't know what he sees in her," Sandy had said as they picked through Edith's underbrush, looking for cigarette butts and discarded cups and napkins. "If life were a candy bar, she'd eat the wrapper." Something in that moment comes back to him now—a tone, a movement, a look in her eyes—something that he'd barely noticed at the time, and causes him to turn to Maggie now, wondering if she already knows what he's only just guessed. And finds himself studying her—one of the most historically, sociologically, psychologically, politically, and philosophically uninteresting people ever to skitter across the earth, if Sandy is to be believed—but he still can't understand why she would want to marry his dentist.

Each of them stares over to where Will squints shyly into the sun, trying to remember what he's meant to be buying, Zorro waiting patiently beside him for something to drop.

And, in any event, exchanging pleasantries on the stairs and chatting at a bus stop do not count as real conversation. She knows he knows that she is Meredith's friend, and must have figured out that she is Sandy's silent, secret ally, another spy, accepting his ice cream and patting his dog, asking him about his houseplants and whether or not his office is air-conditioned just to get him to drop his guard. She wouldn't talk to her if she were him, so why should he?

"Wait a minute, Will, I'll help you," he calls suddenly, in midstep, one hand outstretched to grab a falling pop.

She takes the pop he hands her with a small "Thanks."

Lately it is Skip who is always asking her about Tony. Has she seen him? How's he looking? Does he ever speak to her? Is it true that he's hanging out with the bums? She hasn't noticed any strange people coming out of the apartment, has she? "Are you working for the CIA or something?" she asked, pulling the pins from her mouth. "Just curious," he said, in that voice he has which suggests that to question his motives is to admit to having several dark ones of your own. "Sandy's very upset by what's been happening, you know," dismayed by her lack of sisterly sympathy and the hardness of her heart, I never expected this of you. "But nothing's been happening," she argued. "She wants to get away from him, and then she can't leave the poor bastard alone." "I think you're simplifying things," Skip continued, as though he knew things she didn't know and could never understand if she did. "Meredith seems to think he's falling apart." "Oh, for God's sake. Meredith says that about everyone. It's the only thing that cheers her up." "She's never said that about me," said Skip, not intending for it to sound like a question. She eats her popsicle quickly, trying to beat the sun, wondering if there is any point in trying to get Will to get more in his mouth than on his body, wondering, for the first time really wondering, why Skip should be so concerned about Tony, so anxious for Sandy, is it only kindness and sympathetic affection?, and, glancing toward him, wondering what Tony Rivera has done to deserve so much critical attention.

Only after he's licked his stick clean does he look at her directly, wiping more sweat from above her lips, and say, "How come you're not up in God's country with everyone else?" Peace, serenity and twenty degrees cooler in the shade.

Maggie shrugs and answers as a reflex, "Oh, I had too much to do down here. I usually go up for the weekends, but things got sort of on top of me." Melting orange ice dribbles down her chin. "Business."

"Oh," he nods.

But she can question as a reflex as well. "Why are you still here?"

He is about to answer that he couldn't get enough time off work to make it worth his while, that he doesn't like to leave the apartment alone for more than a day or two at a time, that the cops have orders to shoot him on sight if he moves one foot north of Pelham Parkway—but, instead, he says, "Who are you shitting?"

She is surprised to realize that she is less surprised by his response than relieved. "Well," she says, stabbing her stick into the ground next to his. "It has occurred to me that if you really wanted to be up in the woods, watching the shrubs grow, you would be. No matter what anybody said." And stops breathing for a second, trying to figure out what made her say that. It is the first simply honest statement she has made in months—maybe years.

Will begins to wail. "He's eating my ice cream. Tony. He's eating my pop."

"For Christ's sake, Zorro," Tony screams, leaping to his knees and hauling Zorro back by his bandanna. "You've had your own. Don't make a pig of yourself." He sits back down, the dog imprisoned by his legs and his eyes filled with hurt. "It's okay, Will. Just eat it fast."

It's a point that no one else has thought to make, certainly not Sandy herself, who was not brought into this world to believe that anyone else shouldn't or wouldn't do as she says. He takes his time in answering. "You think I should have gotten into my Chevy, driven up there at ninety miles an hour, and dragged her back?"

"No," says Maggie, letting Zorro lick the syrup from her fingers. "I just wondered why you didn't."

He straightens the scarf on Zorro's neck, assiduously repinning the badge so that it isn't lost in the folds. He could explain that Sandy is not a child to be dominated, that she has a right to make demands and have them accepted, that she has a right to say what she feels and wants and have it respected. It is what he believes. He could say that his role as husband is not to coerce and enforce compromise, that if Sandra Grossman says she doesn't want to see him, then she doesn't want to see him, he can surely take a hint. "I don't know," he says finally. "I just don't feel like fighting anymore," and immediately thinks of Richard, shuffling along like the survivor of a holocaust. He touches his head where the hair is not as blue-black and shining as once it was. "I'm getting old."

"Okay, Tony," cries Will. "I'm finished now."

He opens his legs, but Zorro just sits there. "Go on," he urges. "Go on, go play with Will," giving the dog a shove. "The way I see it," he says, now sitting Indian-style, "if she was going to leave me for good, she'd have done it by now. And if she isn't, she'll come back when she's ready. I don't think," he continues, watching to make sure that Will doesn't go out of sight, "that it has very much to do with me."

In the seconds of silence between them, she watches an ant cross the great width of her foot; he squints into the distance, watching nothing.

"Really?"

"More or less."

A young man in cutoffs dances by with a stereo under his arm; Will immediately begins to move, Zorro lies down. Maggie wipes her hands on her jeans and rests back on her arms. "And who's your friend? The one you're always sitting with in the gutter?"

"We don't sit in the gutter. We sit in doorways."

"God," sighs Maggie. "I'd trade Will's sneakers for a can of beer."

"You met him. He's just someone I know."

"What if I run over to the deli and get a couple of beers?"

He smiles at Will who is waving madly that Zorro's brought a stick back. "I've got a six-pack at home. We could stop on the way and get Will some juice or something."

Maggie brushes the ghost of hair from her eyes. "You mean you're not into Thunderbird yet?"

"Only when I'm outside."

"Come on, Will!" she calls. "We're heading back."

"Ooooooh. We're just having fun."

"Come on," calls Tony. "We're all going home together. You and Zorro can play hide-and-seek."

She swings her bag over her shoulder, dusting the grass from her ass with one long, slender hand.

He picks up the sticks and wrappers and the empty cup to

throw into the trash can on the corner, and fastens the leash onto Zorro's collar.

"Actually," says Maggie as they cross the street, Will swinging between them, Zorro pulling them all ahead, "he reminds me of a guy I knew in Guatemala."

He veers to one side of the traffic light and Zorro veers to the other. "Who does?"

"God, Will," says Maggie. "Your hands are covered in goo." They shuffle sideways around the pole. "Your friend. I don't know why. They don't look alike."

They all stop while Tony untangles the leash from between his ankles. "What friend?"

Simultaneously, they each let go of Will's hand, and he scoots ahead. "The guy you don't sit with in the gutter."

More or less at this very moment, Meredith, who is feeling slightly guilty and has been calling Maggie for reassurance that she needn't, puts the receiver back in its cradle and resnuggles herself into the arms of Stan, whose entire bedroom, except for door and floor, is covered in cork. "They must have gone out," she whispers.

And more or less at this very moment, Sandy is helping Skip to a wedge of Edith's renowned Spanish omelette, and describing in detail the dream she had last night in which she singlehandedly brought about the truce that ended the ten-day siege of a Harlem high school, while Jack pours himself coffee and asks if Skip's ever thought of decorating his waiting room with original works of art, and Edith butters a bagel and wonders aloud if this might not be a good day for an antiques hunt.

And also at almost this very moment, Sophie, who is sitting in her sister's small backyard, reading a mystery while Angie dozes in the sun, her body protected by a thin cotton blanket, her head shaded by an old straw hat anchored under her chin by a piece of orange chiffon, looks out across the few shy rose bushes and the half-baked square of lawn, remembering an incident that happened over twenty years ago that made her laugh at the time and now makes her smile.

"Are you keeping an eye on that chicken?" asks Angela, waking and speaking almost simultaneously. "You know I can't eat it if it's all dried out."

"Oh, really?" says Sophie, uncharacteristically placid. "I didn't know that."

Nature does, of course, have its moments: sudden showers, unexpected storms and squalls, winds whipping up the sea where only moments before it seemed asleep with calm, slumbering mountains, perfect for climbing or picnicking or taking in the view, turning in an instant into raging monsters of destruction and death. And sometimes, in the clearest and bluest and most cloudless of skies, a shower of frogs will unexpectedly fall. But though occasionally surprising, and even abrupt, the general behavior of nature is logical and predictable, or at least understandable, follows laws and principles where cause and effect are easily related. But not so man. In all the universe, it is only man—and, maybe, God—who works in ways less mysterious than purely baffling; whose surface signs of words and actions not only often bear no connection to one another, but no connection to what is actually happening in those regions no eye can see and no ear hear.

As an example of the peculiar sort of behavior one can expect from the human being, Tony has been telling Maggie the story of his friend, Joe. Joe was happily married for fourteen years, and happily the father of Seth for thirteen. Then, one unexceptional Wednesday evening ("Why Wednesday?" asks Rivera, passing her two cans of beer from the fridge. "Why not wait until Friday? Or Sunday? Or Thanksgiving?"), Joe came home from work to find a note from his wife, Ellen honey, explaining that she could no longer continue living a lie. Had he worn down her love with his sloppiness and forgetfulness? Had he doused her passion with his refusal to take a vacation in Trinidad or buy a microwave open? Had he buried her yearning in the rubble of everyday living, where's my blue shirt, you know I hate liver, you really are a stupid bitch? No. Since the day of their wedding, Ellen had been having an affair of undeniable passion with George, Joe's college chum and Best Man. George, it seemed, was not only Ellen's true love but the true father of her son as well. George was sick and tired of sneaking around and being called Uncle by his own son and being referred to in public as good old George by the mistress of his heart. "Can you believe it?" asks Tony, snapping a pretzel in two. Maggie says she can.

◇   ◇   ◇

It is not just the pressures of propinquity, the problems of proximity, which make Sandra look at them like that. Anyone can get on anyone else's nerves. There are days when Jack barricades himself in his studio, slamming through the house with his arms filled with bread and cheese, salami and olives, a bottle of mineral water and a bottle of wine, shouting so that even passing motorists might hear, "And when I say I don't want to be disturbed, I mean for nothing. I don't care if there are Martians in the kitchen. Don't knock on that door!" But by the evening he is always all right again, has forgiven Edith her pedestrian mind, the way she exaggerates all her stories, or the remark she made about his stubbornness; has forgotten his tantrum over Sandy's tidying of his room and the throwing out of his favorite brushes, or his hatred of her ability to remember accurately every word he has ever spoken, out of context, and use them to defeat him in new arguments. There are days when Edith zooms through the rooms like a domestic robot, pro-grammed to polish, dust, scrub, or move anything that is stand-ing still, walloping the wash into the machine as though it has done her some personal harm, stomping out to the garden with her canvas gloves and her spade and fork and murder in her eyes, woe to the weed who threatens her lilies or the human who disturbs her as she wrenches the screaming roots from the soil. But by the next morning she is bustling and beaming again and there is coffee in the pot and cold juice in the pitcher, and she is wanting to know how everyone slept and whether or not anyone wants to drive into town with her. Even Skip has had his days when his buoyancy is slightly forced, his pleasantness strained, his wide and easy smile just that little bit thinner and somewhat hard, when he cannot be coaxed into a walk with Edith or a game of Go with Jack but buries himself in the local paper, apparently obsessed with learning the results of the weekly bridge tournament.

Sandra, however, is beginning to make them all feel lonely. Even when, for example, on a day like today, she appears in the morning in a guise they prefer—happy, peppy Sandy Grossman, cheerleader with a conscience—setting them all off into parox-ysms of normality, the knowledge hovers that it cannot possibly last, that what once was real has now become its own imitation. They are not unlike a group of tourists, lost in a rented car in the badlands of Yugoslavia, tired, hungry, and running out of fuel, each one worn down to the bone of her or his weakness, the nerves running to their personal fears swollen and exposed, racing along with the map on the knees of the navigator, still chatting about the scenery, the food, the wine, the architecture, and the people, between arguments over who misunderstood the directions, who chose that last lousy hotel, who has to go to the toilet the most, pretending they each still know both where they are going and why.

It is Skip, uninitiated into the politics of Grossman family life, who is getting the brunt. Dropping by on a slowly dimming evening to suggest a game or a movie or a visit to one of the local bars, where real truck drivers hang out and there is a pool table and Willie Nelson on the jukebox, he is more likely to receive a silent stare from Sandy, as though, having just axed her parents to bloody pieces before her big brown eyes, he is now inviting her to dance, than the "Oh, that sounds great" of yore.

The hot, bright afternoon is just beginning to shrink. In the houses, cabins, apartments, tents, and mobile homes of eastern America, people are beginning to shift restlessly, relieved that yet another sluggish, superfluous Sunday has nearly passed and they can start thinking about getting back into the routines of the week. In the front, sixth-floor apartment of No. 45, Maggie and Tony are beginning to talk about dead and unborn children and feelings of homelessness, while Will and Zorro watch television in the bedroom, exhausted with contentment. In the Grossmans' back garden, Skip and Sandy are beginning to tire of helping Edith with the weeding, while Edith herself, though still clipping at the hedges rhythmically, is also showing signs of slowing down.

"Right," calls Jack, suddenly appearing at the edge of the patio with a tray in his hands. "Time for a drink."

"Thank God," says Sandy, who has lost most of the enthusiasm with which she began, oh, I'd love to do a little gardening. "I've lost all feeling in both legs." How, she wonders, already removing the canvas gloves her mother insisted she wear, can Edith spend so much of her time crawling around on the ground, doing a job that always has to be done again if nature is not to have its unorderly way (or, as Tony has often put it, bossing around a bunch of plants)?

Skip straightens up with a happy groan. "You know," he says, "I think I could really get into this."

And Sandy sighs. There are few things more boring than a man who is always good-natured. Just for a second, she feels a rush of nostalgia for the old days with Tony, before he stopped trying to communicate entirely, before his jokes and outbursts ceased being self-expression and became self-protection, when he would have pulled out half the flowers just to see the expression on Edith's face when he said, "Oh, Jesus, Edith. I thought those were the weeds." And then she sighs again. She is not a girl anymore, after all.

"Oh," cries Edith from the balcony. "That looks lovely. I knew Skip must have a green thumb." Then turns to Jack and says, "Well, they seem to be quite happy."

"Um," says Jack, and hands her her drink.

They have never really discussed Skip. They have never believed in overt interference in their daughter's life. Though they have always thought themselves quite liberal, even radical, in reality it has its degree, like anything else—and that degree stops short at discussing their child's love life. And, anyway, they like Skip. Over the months, and over the summer, they have come to look on him if not as the son they never had, then as the boyhood friend of the son they never had. He is polite and generous, he is responsible and considerate, he doesn't borrow things he doesn't intend returning, he doesn't get drunk and puke up in the driveway or beat them at Scrabble, he is sociable, helpful, a good listener, and he never wins an argument. And he likes them. He has nothing but respect and admiration for Jack (doesn't he wish he could paint or do something creative like that?), and nothing but esteem and affection for Edith (doesn't he wish that his own mother had as much get-up-and-go?). There are many of Sandy's friends and acquaintances who have made, or make, them feel old, tiresome, and even foolish, but Skip is not one of them. Neither is Tony, for that matter, but that is not because Tony treats them as though he thinks they are intelligent, experienced, and sensible elders from whom he could learn a lot.

"It's nice they're such good friends," says Edith—which

could be a hopeful statement, a cryptic remark, or a whistle in the dark—as she watches them make their way up the garden path, smiling and shaking the dirt from their forks.

"Um," says Jack, and leans his elbows on the redwood railing, waving two fingers as Skip and Sandy disappear into the garden shed to put the tools away.Two or three nights ago, after a particularly vicious game of Diplomacy in which Sandy treated Skip pretty much the way that the American government treated Allende, he asked Sandy if she had it in for Skip, or something, and she told him to go to hell. "Thank God she'll be going home soon," he sighs.

Skip has been telling Sandy what a good day this has been and how much he has enjoyed himself, how much fun he's had. Now, in the cool, gray space of the shed, out of the Grossmans' field of vision, he brushes a smudge of dirt from her face and gives her a friendly kiss on the ear. "We're still friends then?"

"Of course we're still friends." But her back is to him as she puts the gloves into their drawer, and it is difficult to tell whether it looks friendly or not. "I've just been feeling restless lately. I don't mean to take it out on you."

Because it has been such a good day—one in which she has neither criticized him, yelled at him, nor accused him of being stupid—he has the confidence to go on. "I just thought that maybe ..."

"Maybe what?" and turns so quickly that he jumps.

"Well, you know. Helping me get the house ready for Maggie and all ... that you might be feeling ... you know ... a little ..." resentful? jealous? rejected? dumped? betrayed? used?

"A little what?"

He takes one of her hands in his and stares down at it as though inspecting for fingernail dirt. "A little low."

"I hope you don't think I've been acting like a spurned mistress," she says, smiling but snatching back her hand. "I hope we understand one another better than that."

"Of course we do," he says, and moves forward to give her a little hug. "I just want you to know that I'm going to miss you when you go home."

Home?

And where would that be?

◇   ◇   ◇

Tony has just finished telling Maggie that he has never felt as though he had a home ("Every time we'd get settled somewhere she'd have a fight with someone and we'd be packing our bags again. And even when we did stay in one place, Sophie had it so filled with immigrants you would have thought the apartment was Ellis Island."), that after years of listening to everybody else's analyses of their analysis he was fairly certain that this was not because he has such a colorful if vague ancestry, but because he mistakenly landed on the planet earth when it is quite obvious that he was meant to have surfaced somewhere else ("Sometimes, when I'm reading the newspaper, or I'm at a party, or I'm just sitting on a bench in the middle of Broadway, just watching everybody, I get this feeling that there must be something everybody else must know that I will never understand, and it has nothing to do with once wanting to change my name to O'Rivera."). "I know all of the sociological, psychological, anthropological, and biological reasons," he sums up, "but they don't make me feel any differently."

Maggie takes the papers and the plastic bag from the space between them and begins to roll a joint. "When I first started traveling," she says softly, very slowly, "I thought that your home was something inside you. That if you left all your possessions—and things like that—behind, you would always be able to make a new home somewhere totally different."

He lights the match. Oh, the great community of man.

"And then, after a year or two, I realized that there were some things I always had with me—and every few months or so I would add something to them ... a bracelet, or a drawing, or a postcard ... anything ... Little things. But they had sort of become my home. I caught someone trying to steal one of my bags on a bus in Mexico once, and I went completely mad. Like he was trying to kill me or something. So then I thought that home must be the things you keep around you."

Automatically, he looks around the room. Which things would he not want to lose: the old El station lampshade? the photograph of Sophie before she met his father? the wobbly table they found in the garbage that took him an entire winter to strip and revarnish, and the plaster head of Joseph Stalin, winking, that sits on top of it that he made the postgraduate summer he was supposed to be setting up a constructive, and noticeable, neighborhood project for a bunch of kids who were so passively aggressive they could have bombed Hanoi without planes? Señor Rivera's guitar? the rock he bought for five dollars from Gene because Gene swore it had come from the moon and Tony couldn't bear to let him down? the silver ring on his right forefinger, the only McNair heirloom Sophie ever kept? the single souvenir he brought back from Argentina? his old Panama hat? his priceless collection of brochures—*How to Speak Spanish to Your Servants, The United States Air Force Helicopter Museum, The Famous Wax Museum of Florida, Brother Zeke Will Pray for You Too and Talk to Jesus on Your Behalf*—gathered on his travels around the country in the cause of community action?

She takes a toke, watches the smoke swirl, spritelike, between them. "And then I came back here. And I realized it was something else entirely."

His mind is filled with so many images and thoughts that he feels he must be thinking of nothing. "And what's that?" he asks at last.

Maggie turns to look out of the window as though she might be able to see the magical descent of the evening sun. "I don't exactly know."

Sandra doesn't exactly know, either. She is sipping her drink and smiling encouragingly as Skip explains the gardening hint he heard on the radio which involves the use of beer in the control of slugs, but it as an extraterrestrial who has taken over the body of a Sacramento housewife would sit down to a Margarita party by the side of a backyard pool, watching what the real humans are doing, thinking of a distant planet with seven blue moons and lots of rocks under which to hide. A ghost in her parents' home, a visitor at Skip's, and a memory in Tony's, as her summer of self-assessment and reckoning slumps toward its close, Sandy is feeling both fearful and confused. Not the sort of person truly to appreciate panic and all of its subtleties and ramifications, not the sort of person suddenly to wake at four in the morning, overwhelmed by the falseness and futility of life's actitivies, electrocuted by her own aloneness, not (like Maggie) the sort of person who gains comfort only from the thought that the natural result of human behavior is the apocalypse, she is nonetheless definitely worried.

If she thought that her summer would clarify some things (her feelings for Tony, her feelings for herself, her feelings for Skip), give her the perspective and the leisure in which to sort out herself (what she really wanted to do, where she really wanted to be, who she really wanted to become), then, for the first time since she took control of her life at about nine and a half, she was wrong. She has miscalculated; has somehow misjudged. She has guessed herself badly. Herself or someone else.

If she thought that the summer would shake up Rivera, would clear the air like a sudden storm, she has now, as the days shrink imperceptibly and the concerns of man and nature subtly shift from celebration to hibernation, to face the fact that it doesn't seem to have shaken him up at all. Oh, sure, at first he was disturbed and distressed, eager to plead his cause, furious to make his demands and reconcile, as ready as ever he has been to swear that he would change, could change. He followed her around that Fourth of July weekend like an ambassador seeking an audience with the powerful ruler whose alliance alone would spell success, just talk to me and I know we'll agree, just listen to me and I know you'll understand.

"You know," Skip is saying, having just been told by Edith that she will personally oversee the arrangement and planting of his front garden. "I really think I'm going to love it up here. I feel like I've come home at last."

Jack pours himself another drink, holding the glass before him at lip level, following the movement of the liquid from pitcher to tumbler with the concentration of a bingo player waiting for the next number.

"You know," says Edith, "that's what everybody says."

Home is the dentist, home from the drill.

Sandy comes close to smiling, but then realizes that no one spoke.

Of course, she hadn't listened. As is usual when there is a point to be made, she had refused to understand. As has always been customary in major confrontations between them, she had stuck to her guns. So that now, it would seem, he has decided to throw in his lot with the barbarians. This time, it would seem, he has decided that if she says she doesn't want him with her he will go on without her. Despite the fact that everyone has always agreed with her that it is Tony who is dependent, who relies on her support and stability, who expects her to be beneath him with a net of tolerance, self-reliance, practicality, and lust, she has a flash of self-pity which almost makes her cry. How could he suddenly change his mind? How could he behave one way for so many years and then zapwowpow justlikethat show signs of a different nature? Dr. Jekyll and Señor Rivera. Why isn't he acting as he's supposed to act, the way he always has?

"I'll bet there's something you don't know, Skip," says Jack suddenly, and apparently apropos of nothing. "I'll bet you don't know that there's a very large Buddhist community up here."

Skip blinks. "No, I didn't know that," says Skip, clearly grateful for the information. "Now that really is something."

Edith asks Jack if he thinks she could have another drink.

On the other hand, of course, it has occurred to Sandy that the fight with Vega was not because of Mrs. Burkowsky, or Vega, or even Tony himself, but because of her. Because he was so anxious about seeing her again. She has given this quite a good deal of thought, bringing all of her sophisticated methods of objective analysis to bear, and would have to admit that it is difficult to argue with her conclusions. He couldn't wait to see her, but was terrified that she didn't really want to see him. He'd been imagining having her with him again—making in-jokes over dinner, putting his arm around her as they strolled to the car, Jack and Edith too far ahead to overhear their whispers, inviting them back to the apartment for coffee, just come into the bedroom for a minute, Sandy, I want you to see what I've done—and then was so worried that the reality would not live up to the fantasy that he had to sabotage it himself. So great was his fear that she would not stay with him the night, she has convinced herself, that he made it impossible for her to stay.

Jack waves a yellow jacket away from his glass with one hand. "Have you ever noticed," he says to Skip, "the large number of single, middle-class women over thirty who are attracted to Buddhist monks?"

Skip shakes his head. "Really?"

"Well-known fact," says Jack. "I've done some research of my own on it over the years. The statistics would amaze you. Monks and convicts. I'm surprised no one's ever written a book about it."

But even though he probably misses her subconsciously, it

is difficult, even for Sandy, to ignore the fact that, consciously, he still seems not to miss her at all. When she calls him he is rarely there. When she writes to him—whether short, breezy letters filled with chitchat and anecdotes about Jack and Edith that he is sure to find amusing, or short but thoughtful letters about the seriousness of life and their commitment to one another—he doesn't respond (unless you consider the occasional cryptic postcard a response). "Do you think maybe he isn't getting his mail?" she asked Meredith. And Meredith, back in the land where no birds sing, no breeze refreshes, and no one exists to whom she could write a letter from what still remains of her heart and soul, had banged her bottle of cola against the receiver and moaned, "How the hell do I know? Do you want Will to ask him? He won't talk to me."

And does Sandy miss Tony?

Who can tell?

She certainly thinks that she does, that she must. At this moment. But Sandy is a person who thinks that it is possible to know what goes on between other people, to understand not merely their words and actions but the feelings that lie buried beneath the rubble in their hearts. With that attitude, it is unlikely to occur to her that we are each and to ourselves one of the greatest mysteries in the entire universe. With that attitude, it is equally unlikely to occur to her that she may just be missing the familiar—Sandra Grossman Rivera with her books and her plants and her many belongings and her many friends and her scores of activities—might just be missing the feeling of sameness and uniqueness which comes from having a personal world that daily vindicates and confirms your existence.

"You know what I feel like?" asks Edith suddenly, interrupting Jack's monologue on the psychosocial reasons for groupyism.

Jack rattles the ice cubes in his glass ominously, Skip looks confused, and Sandy tries not to think of what she herself feels like.

Edith seems not to notice their disinterest. "I feel like going out for supper."

E I G H T

There has been an unexpected cold spell in the mountains and several days of steady rain, morning, noon, and night, flooding on the roads and mud in the unpaved driveways, water seeping through the windows and dripping through the cracks. Half-converted vintage mills can be tricky to heat, and lonely and inhospitable when you are all by yourself and sleeping in a nylon bag on an army cot, your watch and change on the old stool that holds a reading lamp and a library book in which your place is neatly marked by an unpaid bill for lumber. There is, undeniably, companionship, entertainment, and even heat over at the Grossmans', but Skip is weary of the Grossmans and their competitive board games, Edith totaling up the scores like a priestess reading some poor sheep's intestines, Jack when he is bored and losing suddenly whamming the pieces into the air, shouting "Hurricane!" Sandy sitting on the sofa reading some book with a title he can't understand, periodically looking up and smiling tolerantly, oh that's nice. He is beginning to wonder just what he is doing, all on his lonesome, straining his muscles and bruising his flesh, only to have Edith or Sandy stop by and say, sweetly and appraisingly, "You know, there's a man in town who's very good at that sort of thing," or to have Jack lope in around lunchtime with a bottle under his arm, saying, "Oh very nice. Very nice. I wish you'd had a word with me, though, before you started this. I could have given you a pointer or two." He is beginning to forget that it will not always be like this, he the stranger with his roots wrapped around his ankles, waiting for transplantation, he the outsider trotted along to cocktail parties and barbecues. "This is Skip Ellis, the best dentist we've ever known. He'll be moving up here soon," he smiling competence and confidence, your wives and children are safe with me.

Because of all these things—and maybe one or two more—about an hour after the toilet backed up he decided that he would surprise Maggie with a visit, bring her the new polaroids of the kitchen and the patio before they were two inches under water, and the electricians' assurances that there will be heat and light before the first snows. Bring her himself, all brown and hard and horny and hungry for some uncritical affection.

But Maggie isn't at home.

That's the trouble with surprises, he thinks as he heads down to Meredith's to see if Maggie is there, an impulsively bought bottle of champagne under one arm, you can never be sure just who the recipient will be.

Meredith isn't at home, either. He rings and bangs and tries to see in through the peephole but receives only silence in return. He is about to consider the possibility of visiting his mother when he notices the Rivera front door. Why not? After all, he and Tony may have both too much in common and too little ever to be considered friends, but they are acquainted. He has put his finger in Tony's mouth and asked what he thought of the mayoral election. Tony has given him advice, which turned out to be sound, on stereo equipment and the best sort of alarm system for his car. They once shared a joke, but though he can remember the two of them laughing, Tony sitting up in the chair and pulling the paper bib from around his neck and he swinging back the tray, he cannot remember what it was about. They are each without his woman.

Tony opens the door on the chain, Zorro's nose poking through the crack, his manner wary. "Yes?"

"Hi. Tony? It's me. Skip."

"Skip what?" asks Rivera, but shuts and unbolts the door, and opens it again, even as Skip is saying, "Ellis. Skip Ellis."

Tony has a length of flex draped across his shoulders and a metal lampshade in one hand, a screwdriver in the other.

"Hi," Skip says once more. "I was looking for Meredith. Well, actually, I was looking for Maggie." He has opened the door just so far, but no further. "But they're not around." Skip pauses for a second for Tony to say, oh, come on in, and when he doesn't continues, "So I thought I'd just stop by and say hello, you know." And, inspired, lies, "Sandy said to say hello if I saw you." And, even more inspired, additionally lies, "I brought some wine. I thought you might feel like a drink."

"Oh?" says Tony, really?, but steps back on to Zorro's paw and opens the door just that little more. "Come on in."

The three of them trot down the dark hallway, Tony and Zorro leading, Skip banging into the bike, walking into the coats that hang from pegs on the wall, wondering why the hell no lights are on, and into the kitchen where several candles stuck in jars and lids and a candle holder that looks like a fish all glow, romantically, perhaps, or perhaps eerily.

Skip places the bottle on the table and unwraps it. "You blow a fuse or something?"

Tony hands him two glasses from the dish drainer. "My God," he says, "is that champagne? What are you trying to do, seduce me?"

Skip smiles feebly in the feeble light, wishing that he'd either bought a bottle of gin or gone straight to his mother's.

Tony steps on to a chair and on to the table. "I'm trying to hook up a new fixture," he explains, and stretches to reach the hole in the ceiling, the lamp dangling. "How's that?"

"How's what?" asks Skip, trying to open the champagne as though it is just another bottle of plonk, adjust to the lack of light, and come to terms with the fact that he is, for the first time, in Sandy's home. It is not, somehow, as he had imagined— but what had he imagined? A cave? A garret? An underground cell? A miniature reproduction of the Grossman testament to taste, style, quality, and the best of all ethnic worlds? Flute music on the stereo, political posters on the walls, *la historia me absolverá*, cushions on the floor, and a photograph of Karl Marx's grave taped to the door of the refrigerator?

"How's the length?" grunts Rivera. "I don't want it to look like an interrogation room."

Every time Skip moves he trips over something. Can it be the darkness alone that makes the room seem so small, so small and so threatening? Can it be the alien light, so bright and at once so dull and full of shadows, that makes him feel that he has entered not merely a strange apartment but a stranger world? He spills champagne all over the hodgepodge of tools, screws, and the page of instructions that came with the shade, and knocks over a candle in his haste to make everything all right again. He would like to be able to wander around, to look through the living room, check out the bathroom, peek into the bedroom, as he would in anyone's home, not so much from curiosity about the ways that people live as from an interest in whether or not they are doing it better, have more to show for it than he. He wishes, also, that Sandy were here, offering him coffee, offering him a snack, offering to show him her high-school yearbook or her favorite print, hung on the wall in a plain glass frame. He wishes, already, that he'd never come. "It looks okay to me," says Skip. Though, really, how could he know?

"Are you sure?"

"Well," says Skip, stepping back on something soft and thick and trying not to start. "It could be over a little to the right."

Protected by the inexplicit light, Tony closes his eyes and silently sighs. It is only a matter of seconds before his body either locks or collapses, before he shifts his weight just a little too much in one direction and down the table. "Yeah. Sure. But what about the length?"

"How low did you want it?"

"Not so low that it heats the salad." Although he knows, in his heart, that Skip is a good, a dedicated dentist, and probably even a reasonable human being, as human beings go, he has never found it easy to like him. And is finding it more difficult now. He has no recollection of them ever having shared a joke.

"Then I think it's all right."

"Great. Now if you'd just come around here and grab hold of the shade ..."

Altogether, it takes fifty-two minutes to get the light in place, Skip mumbling conflicting directions every six and a half seconds or so, Tony on his toes, wiring blindly, tools gripped in his teeth, Skip going oh and um and ah, Zorro moaning softly like some prophetic beast. The first time they turn on the power, the light won't go off. The second time, the fuse does blow.

"I give up," says Tony, practically falling down. "It'll have to wait till I can see what I'm doing."

"Are you sure you hooked up the wires right?" asks the ever-helpful Skip, who has had more than his share of the wine, and cocks his head to one side. "You know," he says thoughtfully, slowly, "maybe it is a little low."

From one point of view, it is sometimes difficult to believe in God. What supreme power, capable of constructing something as intricate as a fruit fly, or a sunrise, or a heart, able to design and balance all the forces of the universe and the systems of life upon the planet, to combine beauty and function in the small and in the large, make a tree or a crying infant, create a pansy or a glowing fish, would then go on to create a species dedicated to unsystematically destroying it all not through some great demonic design but in the futile search for power, in the useless attempt to control and understand that of which it is only one small small part? Or so has Tony Rivera always reasoned. If he could make a duck or a polar bear, a rain drop, a grain of sand, or a sunset over the Gulf of Mexico, he wouldn't then fuck it all up with the addition of swarms of little men with big mouths, big ambitions, and tiny, immoral hearts who use words of hope to increase the world's despair. On the other hand, however, on a night such as this, when you find yourself navigating the less well-lit, the not-so-bright-and-busy streets with a man who views life as he would an X ray of the oral cavity, left right center, lower upper, it is difficult to believe that it could be all that accidental. Some enormous intelligence—unseen, unacknowledged, and not all that kindly or benign—must be working like mad to make things turn out the way that they do. Or so he has been thinking for the past hour or so.

Zorro keeps wrapping the leash around his ankles, jerking first in one direction and then lurching in another, braking suddenly from behind as he pursues his incessant study of the smells of the gutter. Skip, for reasons of his own which Tony is too tired and too depressed to try to guess, has been talking nonstop about the idealism of his youth: how he marched on Washington, how he worked one summer in a factory in California, how he burnt his draft card in 1965 ("And they didn't arrest you?" grinned Rivera, sensing a familiar aroma. "Well, actually,"

Skip grinned back, "it was my old draft card. Before I got deferred."), how he'd always intended to join the Peace Corps ("Oh, really?" grinned Tony. "And sterilize the world?" And Skip again grinned back. "What?"), how he wept when Martin Luther King was shot, how he wept when Bobby Kennedy was shot, how depressed he was when the Equal Rights Amendment was defeated ("Wow," beamed Rivera. "You must have taken to your bed over My Lai," Skip looking slightly puzzled and having no reply.). There seems no way of shutting him up. After the lights went out and the champagne was gone, Skip suggested that they go out together and get something to eat, maybe go for a drink, it's been a long time since he's been in a real bar, Tony must know a place or two. Tony, who has himself never been to an unreal bar and would like to see what one is like, what the people are like and what they say, how they behave when they are too drunk to stand or count their change, smiled grimly. His only hope is to get Skip so drunk that he passes out, or to take him somewhere where the possibility of his getting his almost luminescent teeth knocked out by the real fist of some real shit-drunk brawler is high.

"Well," says Tony as they step through the door, "this is the End of the Line." Dark and denlike as it is, there is enough shape in the shadows to be able to see that this is probably true.

It is only just possible to make out the sounds of distinctive voices, to hear what you yourself are saying. And, like watching a piece of meat moving with maggots, just possible to see that the dimness sways with many separate movements. There are at least three people sitting at the bar who may be dead.

"Wow," yells Skip. "What's the name of this place?"

This is the third bar in which they've been, but the others, though real enough, or depressing enough at any rate, were quiet and empty as well. They made Skip, who believes in group activity and who treats solitude as though it were a social disease, uneasy.

"The End of the Line," please God that it is.

"Is that because it's the last bar before the water?" shouts Skip, causing the woman beside him, against whose back his arm is pressed, to quickly spin around, giggling slightly hysterically.

"What water?" Perhaps it is time to start being someone else, Randy Rivera, that smooth Latino lover, or Ponco the outlaw, cynical and silent, a knife in his boot, a question in his eyes, this place ain't big enough for you and me.

"Aren't we near the water?" asks Skip as Tony orders the drinks.

"Honey," screams the woman, thumping him on the shoulder so that he nearly loses his balance, "we're on an island. We're always near the water, ain't we?"

Everybody within earshot thinks this is pretty funny. The barman, who is a friend of Julio's and who used to be a dancer, winks at Tony. "That your brother-in-law or something?"

"Or something," whispers Tony, wishing he hadn't brought Skip here, here where everyone knows him.

"Where's your friend, then? Richard. Where's he?"

Shrugs amid the fumbling for change. Where indeed? Richard hasn't been around for days. It is his absence—so unexpected and so enormous—that has had Rivera cleaning the floors and putting in new fixtures. Even López's Eddie, who delivers for blocks in all directions and knows about a million people who never move from the streets, has seen no sign of him, heard no rumor. He's either dead or in Boston.

"I haven't seen him since last week with you," says Nicky, pondering as he pumps out a beer. "What was that? Sunday? He usually comes in on Wednesdays. I always save him some of the barbecued ribs."

Tony lays the money in a pool of water. In all the times that he has moved around, or been moved around, in all the times that he has been abandoned, forgotten, or left behind—whether for a day, a week, some months, or forever—he has never really missed anyone (except maybe, when he was young, Sophie; and often he thinks of Señor Rivera). But he misses Richard now.

"I wound up eating them myself," says Nicky, with a philosophical shrug of his shoulders. "He didn't miss much."

Sometimes Tony and Richard come in here very late at night, or very early in the morning, and sit in the corner by the window, its curtains closed, and Richard will slowly drink his spritzer and eat his dry-roasted peanuts, one at a time, looking around with his usual self-possessed passivity, I may be in the world but I am not of it, his lack of response a comment of its own. When the chairs are upside down on the tables and Nicky, or the other barman, Dan, who used to pitch in some minor league team, is sweeping up, humming along with the jukebox ("Heart of Glass" if it's Nicky, "San Antone Rose" if it's Dan), Richard will talk, about the lost tribes of history (about which he seems to know a great deal), or the great victims of history (about which he seems to know even more), or music (though he can never remember more than three songs in an evening). Often he says nothing.

Being here with Skip is not the same—but what place would be?

Skip does have a need to talk. Silence makes him uncomfortable. Strangers make him insecure. The president of his high-school class, the most popular boy of his year, he learned early the value of always grasping the initiative, always entering with your mouth going, of convincing all newcomers that they have nothing to fear from you, you're just like them. Were he a little smarter, or a little shrewder, he might have made an excellent politician, the first dentist in the White House.

Tonight, Skip is trying to make Tony like him. He has already had too much to drink and is trying to make Tony see what a regular guy, sensible but sensitive, he really is. He knows for a fact that Tony doesn't like him (that is, he knows that Sandra has told him that Tony despises men like him, blond and handsome, successful and balanced, men who not only have come to terms with the world in which they live but who enjoy the terms to which they've come. "It's part of his disease," she has explained. "The minute he sees anybody who's nice or happy or just normal, he immediately thinks that they're either stupid or lying. The only thing he trusts is doom.") and he is going to change Tony's mind. He is going to prove to him that even though he, Skip, has never known hunger, poverty, nonoption hopelessness, moral or physical degradation, terminal deprivation, or nonromantic alienation he is still human. Skip wants to prove to him that even though Tony has this thing about the middle class (because of his mother) they are really on the same side.

And what side would that be?

At the moment it is the far side of the End, sitting on a bench attached to the wall, their drinks on their knees. There are several people—bent over the pinball machine, bent over their glasses at cramped tables, bent over each other in intimate conversation—whom Tony knows quite well, but, as is the way here, they don't jostle their ways through the crowd to say, "Hey, how about a drink?", "Hey, man, how are you? Long time no see," "Wow, I was just thinking about you," only move a head or an eye or a finger in recognition.

"Gee," says Skip (or something that sounds a lot like "gee"), "it sure is crowded in here," and looks around him smiling, as though there is nothing in life that he likes better than being squeezed against filthy walls and sweaty strangers, drinking a screwdriver from a glass that still bears the phantom imprint of some woman's red red lips.

"Friday night," says Tony, but Skip thinks that he said "Bound to be a fight," and looks around with renewed interest.

Although Skip has, naturally, often had dinner in the restaurant of Joey Gallo's last supper, imagining the bullets splashing through the glass, blood on the linguini and in the wine, imagining the sounds of warfare in place of the chatter and friendly laugher and the waiter recommending the fried clams, he has never before seen anywhere that so un-self-consciously promised personal and indiscriminate violence. In Skip's opinion, there is almost no one here who couldn't be a criminal of one sort or another, who wouldn't get you anything you wanted, hot video equipment, hot women, drugs or guns or sweet young boys, who might not follow you as you weaved your way back into the street, just give me your wallet, man, and there won't be no trouble. Oh, he has hung out in the hangouts of the famous and the notorious, where expensive call girls drink gimlets and the directors of multinational drug companies send back the béarnaise sauce while discussing the latest Broadway musical with affordable politicians. Even his own well-loved and much-respected father, Nelson Sr., might, in the thinking of some, be called a crook, has been blamed for more than one untimely death (although they were, of course, all suicides). But he has seen nothing like this. This is different. The pushers in here are not the aging hippies he knows who provide the pot and cocaine for your wilder parties and who used to be *avant-garde* film makers in Third World countries, who used to run porn magazines or do the sound on hard-core sex movies, who still talk about the time they drove across country, naked, hanging moons on the interstate. The hookers in here are not the well-dressed girls with good teeth and clean hair whose companionship he has sometimes bought in unfamiliar cities, strangers' cities, where everyone else has some place to go and someone with whom to go there, girls who look like secretaries, models, or, possibly, art students, whom you could introduce to your aunt or the head of your school of dentistry (should you run into either of them) as your cousin or an old girlfriend from college. The thieves and hustlers here are not just guys with a little sideline in illegal prescriptions or essentially legal tax-dodge schemes, whom you meet at parties every now and then, who always say not bad, not bad at all when you ask them how things are going, who always have a new wife or an old wife in a new coat and coordinated jewelry. And the drunks here are not the drunks that he has known, the college boys barfing out of the window as the car takes a corner on two wheels, hey, Joey, keep your goddamn eyes on the road, the guys you find passed out in the bathtub after everyone else has gone home, the women who begin to flirt after the second glass of wine and begin to undress during the brandy, whew, it certainly is warm in here. The people here are for real. Skip finds it all pretty exciting.

"So," says Skip, other people's noise not enough for him. "I hear you used to be a musician."

Used to be? Tony stares at the label of his beer. He drinks nothing that is not a bottle in the End, not since they carried Charlie Rappaport out on a stretcher, victim of a fellow customer's practical joke. "Yeah," he nods, "but I can still ride a bike."

"I used to fool around with the guitar, too," grins Skip.

And Tony can imagine him with his lean arms, hard and sinewy from so much drilling, wrapped around the female shape of some red-faced guitar, his mouth, his cock, forcing apart the strings, fooling around.

"We had a band in college, you know. There were four of us. Jimmy Montoya, Tom Smythe, Bobby Gordon, and me." Skip and the Light Fantastiks? Every time Skip takes another sip of his drink, he seems relieved to discover that it tastes like gin and orange and not heroin. "Boy," he says, oblivious to the fact that Tony is the only person who hasn't looked at him since they came in, "I haven't been in a place like this for at least twenty years."

He looks at Skip now, wondering what cosmic catastrophe,

what youthful madness unleashed by a bout of drinking in the frat house, could ever have occurred to bring Skip in his madras shirt and loafers into a dump like this, did his mother know where he was? "Oh, really?"

Skip gazes at the red plastic stirrer in his drink as though it might speak or at least let loose a clue. "Yeah. We used to play one of the bars outside of town once and a while." He makes a gesture which would probably suggest openness and sincerity, were he a statesman not-explaining an especially tricky bit of foreign policy, but which, in this light, in this unquiet room, seems only hopeless and forlorn, a gesture like a sigh. "They used to have poetry readings and that sort of thing there on Sundays. You know."

Tony looks around. The only poetry here is written on the walls of the toilets and of the darker niches, Maria I will love you forever, Doreen sucks cock, When Jesus comes back he's gonna be mad.

He looks around, but he doesn't so much as smile. "Yeah, I know," he says. "Sounds pretty bohemian." Even staring straight at the sweet transvestites in the opposite corner, who are smoking a joint, he can easily picture the bar of Skip's youth: the waitress in her turtleneck sweater and short black skirt, a ring on a chain around her neck and a meet-you-in-the-parking-lot look in her eyes, the bartender, who once spent a summer in France picking grapes, and who once nearly met Jack Kerouac at a party on Long Island, willing to slip your date triples for only a nod and a small tip. Even listening to the couple behind him compare their separate experiences in Bellevue, he can hear the eager voices of Skip's past, "I mean, what does she think I am, a child? I'd die before I'd treat any kid of mine the way she treats me," "What women of my mother's generation can't understand is that you don't keep a man by tying him down," "Of course it's impossible. Have you ever tried to stick your finger in a moving bottle? Here ... look ... I'll hold the bottle and you just try to slide your finger in it," "God? How can anyone believe in God when we're almost ready to walk on the moon?" He looks over at Skip to see if he can see and hear them, too.

"Crazy," says Skip, shaking his head and grinning his lopsided, boyish grin.

Who's crazy?

"What kind of music did you play?" Though he could fly sooner than not guess correctly. The other advantage of bottled beer is that it is rare for anyone to go to the trouble of watering it down, so you can pretty well judge how many it will take to get you good and drunk. At the rate things are going, he will need another twenty.

"Oh, you know. Sort of folksy rock."

"Um," says Rivera. "There was a lot of it going around at the time."

"And you?"

"Oh. A little of this and a little of that. I used to bring the house down with my rendition of 'I'm Goin' Down the Road.'"

Skip says that he doesn't know that one, and Tony volunteers to go for two more drinks.

"You want me to get rid of that guy for you?" asks Nicky, able to hit a piece of ice off the back of his hand and into a glass without even looking. He winks, but it is unlikely that he is joking. He decided to become a dancer after seeing *West Side Story*. "I said to myself, 'Nicky,'" says Nicky, "'If it works that good in the movies then it's bound to work even better in the street.'"

"Thanks, Nick, but not this time. I'm just minding him for a friend."

"Oh, sure," says Nick. "I just thought he might be a cop," and turns his head to where Skip is sitting, hunched over his knees, suddenly pretending not to be there. "He looks like a cop."

"He's a dentist."

"A dentist?" elegantly raising one dark eyebrow. "Well, what do ya know. Yeah, I guess you're right. He doesn't look stupid enough to be a cop."

"Oh, he's stupid enough," says Tony, opening his own bottle of beer. "He's just been educated for finer things."

"So what's he doin' here?"

And they turn once more toward Skip, sitting among the regulars like the First Lady posing among a few chosen victims for National Birth Defects Week.

"You got me," says Tony. "Either he's my guardian angel come to save me or he gets lonely easily."

Skip looks casually around him, trying to appear at ease,

hoping to see Tony elbowing his way back to him, but Tony is still talking to the bartender, his back to the room.

Nicky is telling Tony that he got a postcard from Julio on his way to India through Tibet only this morning, "Now this is what I call high," and that he doesn't sound like he's going to be coming back home in any hurry, and that Nicky's girlfriend left him again last night, this time for good, she says, but that he isn't going to worry because as soon as she realizes what she's missing she'll be back with the toaster oven under her arm.

"That's what you said the last time," says Tony, who has seen Nicky through more than one broken heart, including the worst one after his ankle was splintered by a wild bullet during a robbery in the store in which he was buying a bottle of wine and his financée gave him back his ring and his personal possessions because she couldn't stand the thought of spending the rest of her life with a cripple, maybe he no longer had one to worry about, but she still had her career to consider. "What gets me," Nicky said at the time, "is that she waited till we were in this fuckin' Italian restaurant to tell me. I kept thinkin', it must be a joke."

"Naw," he says now, wiping a hand on his apron. "This time it's different. You'll see. Suzie really loves me. It's her mother doesn't like me very much."

Tony makes a face at Nick, but his thoughts are on Skip. What a relief it would be if Skip were not a mild-mannered dentist at all, but an angelic imposter, out to get his wings by saving one poor lost soul. A minor savior come to show the hopeless Rivera how valuable his life really is, how much he is loved and respected and needed, how different things would be if he had never appeared on the planet, no matter how humble or insignificant his place. Once and for all, Tony might be convinced that it is not necessary to be a doctor or a lawyer to save lives, not necessary to be a writer or a revolutionary to change hearts, that even though he has done no more than pitch dumbly from one year one thing one dream to another, razing his bridges behind him, the life of each man is important and interconnected with the rest. There ain't no islands as far as heaven is concerned.

"Yeah," Nicky is saying, "I have to sleep on the kitchen floor last night. I was afraid she might call and I wouldn't hear it." His eyes scan the room for any signs of trouble, his arms on the old, worn bar. "She'll call tonight for sure."

At the end of the evening, as they stumbled home together, the specter Skip intoxicated by the earthy vodka, Tony grimly drunk on his twenty-one beers, they would walk through different streets, to a different destination, passing all the people he would never have known, and he would see for himself what his life has meant, is meaning. "No, no," Skip would say, over and over, swinging around the lamp poles, lurching drunkenly into the road. "Don't you understand? They don't know you. You were never born. They're not the same people at all." And what would he see? Sandy climbing into a Volkswagen Rabbit with her husband, a Trotskyite sociology professor who has written the definitive history of contraception in Western civilization, and her 2.2 culturally sophisticated, well-motivated children, debating among themselves the merits of one manufacture of computer over another? Sophie shuffling through the locked-out blocks, rags around her feet and a bottle of tawny port in her arms, ranting to an indifferent populace and even more indifferent God, childless and twisted because she had never had Tony and so had never gone across the hall to use the phone to call the doctor on the afternoon that Carlos Rivera was there for dinner? López, his dreams of going home long dead and gone, the bodega failing, he an old man in a stained sweater and bottle-bottom glasses, his wife dead from worry, his children gone to open motels in California, ripped off by the local shoppers, blackmailed by the local gang, winding up shooting some teenage robber in the stomach, all because he never found anyone with whom to swap bad jokes? Mrs. Burkowsky shuffled away to sit in front of a television in some old-folks home outside of Philadelphia, her apartment now a brothel run by Vega who patrols his domain dressed in a three-piece linen suit, his grin shot through with gold, his wife and children all sold into slavery in Chicago, all because there was no one around to keep an eye on him? Parker asked to head an impartial committee to investigate alleged CIA terrorism in Nicaragua, coming back with a special commendation from the President and a poem about the nobility of the poor, all because there was no one around to keep him in line?

"How long did you say she's been gone?" He is suddenly aware of Skip's head seeming to float above the rest as he wonders what happened to his drink and his new friend. He does look like a cop.

Not only can Nicky slap an ice cube into a glass from a foot away but he can open a bottle with his teeth as well. "Well, she's been gone a few days now, you know, a day or two. But I haven't been around all the time. She'll call for sure tonight."

When Tony does get back to their bench, Skip doesn't ask him what took him so long, or where he's been, the way anyone else would. He doesn't say that it took Tony long enough, what was he doing, blowing the glasses himself, or make a joke about beginning to get worried that he'd been abandoned or set up. "You know," he says, still managing a smile, "this place must really be getting to me. I just thought I saw a ghost peering through the window."

"Oh yeah?" says Tony, passing him his drink. "A ghost?" But he turns to look anyway.

Like a mythical kingdom, too good to exist below cloud level, floating by on a friendly miracle, the towers of the city stand illuminated against the flat, gray night. No stars twinkle down on the restless metropolis, only a moon that seems but a pale reflection of itself looks on. This is not the country of God, where the night kneels down to kiss the earth, where all the lives and dreams beyond the living scoot about in unseen, unseeable busyness as they carry the planet to another dawn. This is man's land, and it is nearly midnight in Manhattan, when people start getting serious.

Maggie is sitting in a striped cloth chair on a penthouse roof, holding on to a glass of wine and listening to the sounds that the night here doesn't make. The sounds it does make—the hummings and ringings, the clinkings and whirrings, the blur-rings of words—go on around her, largely ignored. Maggie is feeling serious, too. Now is certainly no time to be cute.

Dragged along for her own good by the ever-solicitous Meredith, who hates going to parties by herself, Maggie has been huddled out here for nearly three hours—though it could be ten or twenty or four hundred and sixty-six—becoming quietly, if not unaggressively, drunk. Several cheerful people have approached her (Don't you just love the city at night? Aren't you kind of lonely out here all on your own? Haven't you always wanted to dance under the moonlight? This party's pretty boring, wouldn't you rather go somewhere else?), but to each she has said, simply, no. Every so often Meredith materializes at the sliding glass doors, each time her eyes a little brighter and her voice a little louder, her face a trifle more flushed and her makeup a trifle more indefinite than the last. Why don't you come inside and dance? Why don't you come inside and meet this guy who just came back from China? Have you eaten anything? The tacos are really great. There are some people playing backgammon in one of the bedrooms. I thought you liked backgammon. But Maggie likes very little tonight. "I'm all right, Meredith," she says each time. "You enjoy yourself," and smiles as though such a thing in such a place might actually be possible.

Though Maggie's body is here, occupying both time and space, weighing down the canvas of the chair, lurking in the shadows like a fugitive without a gun or a prayer, capable of breathing, of feeling, of talking, of consuming, even capable of moving and of reacting (should something happen deserving a reaction), her irreconcilable thoughts are elsewhere. Where? Oh, here and there. Gone to other summers and other illusions. Gone to different nights and different realities. Just gone.

Like an old woman sitting for the last time on her front porch, her vision blurred as sweating and shouting men haul the possessions of a lifetime out the old screen door and down the rough, worn steps, Maggie sighs. You don't necessarily have to have a gun at your head or a hand at your throat or poison flowing to your heart to see your life go flip-flopping by, right before your eyes. You don't necessarily have to see death all around you, piously clasping its hands and smiling like the Mona Lisa, winking every time you make a plan, giggling every time you make a decision, to see moments of yourself zip by in front of you in one fixed pattern, all the moments when the ends were open and possibilities waited. All the moments that led you to where you are.

From nowhere—from a window at the side, from the barbered shrubs that grace one wall, from a secret panel in the sky—a couple comes dancing by, cheek to ear, almost walking. "What do you think it is gets most people up in the morning and into another day?" she asks, her voice a nudge, pulling her head back just enough so that their gazes touch. It could be that he smiles. "Mortgages," he says, seriously. Then laughs. "Mortgages and college loans." "Really? You don't think it's some god-concept?" "Jesus Christ! God?" and his laughter is as warm as a baby bunny. "My dear girl, religion is important in establishing the society's moral-ethical code. But God doesn't make the world go around." Well, not anymore. Not this world. And what does? "Money does. Money and status. It's the same for nations as for people. Power."

They turn the corner and disappear again.

Her moments have led her here.

Maggie Kelly has never had any dreams of changing the world. No fantasies of freeing the enslaved, feeding the hungry, blowing up the burdens of the oppressed, or of just blowing up the oppressors; no pale but vibrating visions of a better time and better place where all women and men might stand with equal dignity, their stomaches full, their fears acknowledged and shared, their limits determined by their own hearts and minds, beneath a glorious and unendangered sun. Neither prophet not poet, leader nor revolutionary, scientist nor artist, she has always been just a girl from the suburbs who thought that life should offer more than the people she knew most intimately had ever had. Did this thought come from John with his packages of prime cuts, his biographies of doomed adventurers and his big dream of owning his own liquor store? Did it come from Kate with her wildly hennaed hair, her stacks of useful magazines (How To Feed Your Family in the Dog Days and Still Stay Cool, A Summer Romance Perfect for the Beach), and her private dreams of endless love? And more what? More joy? More truth? More beauty? More shit? More passion? More honesty? More hypoc-risy? More lies? More things?

More.

Like the Ghost of Summers Past, without moving from the brightly colored chair (so much like the ones they used to lug to the beach with the red-and-white thermos, the old blankets, and the flimsy beach umbrella that her mother got with stamps), Maggie can move above the city, over the Eastern seaboard, far and away from this wracked, this wretched, this indescribably magnificent planet, and watch herself in other guises, sitting in rooms and standing on lines, walking through streets and fields and shopping malls. Far behind her, the Stones sing "Let's Spend the Night Together," but it is only her heart that she hears.

Meredith's face glows in the doorway. "Maggie," she says. "Maggie." Maggie looks around, surprised that everything is still here. "Maggie ..." and it is obvious from the smile on her face and the inflection of her voice just what she is about to say. "Maggie, I'm going to go now. Will you be all right?" It is not, in fact, a question. Will is spending a week at the shore with his grandmother, and Meredith, high on her sense of liberation, wants nothing more than to saw off the remnants of her chains and boogie on down the road to where the love and the good times wait. "Of course I'll be all right," says Maggie, suddenly wishing that Meredith would stay with her in the darkness and talk as women sometimes do, in amorphous voices discon-nected from the hoopla of their lives, separate from the actuality of their days. "Great," grins Meredith, almost moving backward. "I'll see you, then. I'll call you tomorrow." Wishing that Meredith were a friend from a younger time, with plans and secrets still to be exchanged, with so much to say and do and the universe so open and so new. With so much felt and known and ready to be told. Maggie has, in her way, sought that place where people are revealed in all their loneliness and pain and weakness, but, like justice, it seems not to exist—or only from time to time. She has, in her way, tried to force her own single life upon the fabric of the world, and, instead, has found herself just another piece of the pattern, her mouth filled with trivia and her heart almost stopped. She would like now to say to Meredith, "Why are you going off with some bimbo who will probably make love like an animal that's just discovered it's got hands?" or for Meredith to say, "I know I'm an asshole, but what else can I do? How can I stay so alone?" "Okay, then," says Meredith. "I'll see you." "Yeah," says Maggie. "Have a good time." A good time.

What's that?

Through the doors, she watches Meredith beneath the hall-way light, twirling an embroidered shawl across her shoulders and kissing several jolly looking people good-bye, bye-bye, the glasses in their hands twinkling like amulets, the smiles on their faces as fixed as the light from a satellite, a man beside her with one hand on the doorknob and one on her elbow, eager to be kissed. And Meredith, like the gypsy dancer about to swish and jangle from the firelight into the bewitched lushness of the night with the lover chosen for her by the forces of the cosmos, laughs—as though she is not going to Great Neck but to ecstasy.

Only when the door shuts behind them does Maggie haul herself from her chair and stumble over the aluminum doorframe and into the heart of the party.

A good time seems to be what everyone else is having.

Deep in conversation, deep in hallucinations, embraces, or drink, they look not so much like party guests as actors in an ad for carpets or platinum, Spanish sherry or cheap perfume. Comfortable on cushions and on couches, comforted by the indirect lighting, the pretty good food and the not so bad wine, they could be an advertisement for twentieth-century life itself, see how well it works.

The man are not all handsome and the women are not all intelligent or bright. Their clothes are not the finest, their jokes are not the funniest, their analyses of the political situation, the lives of their friends, and the motives of themselves are not always the correct ones. Their facts are not always facts, their fantasies are not always theirs. Not all of them are kind, or generous, or understanding, or compassionate. Not all of them have led, lead, their lives with open minds and open hearts, striving for some fragment of wisdom, some external, irrational truth. Few, if any, are any less boring, petty, mean-spiritied or small in heart, frightened, insecure, selfish, suspicious, or defensive than anyone else, than Maggie herself as she moves woodenly but with determination across the room, wondering where she is going and why.

Poised behind a couple discussing the ornaments on the bookshelves—handmade tools and roughly hewn lanterns and pots, he explaining that his brother brought them back as souvenirs from his time in the Peace Corps, they're really pretty old, grave stuff, mostly, she unable to understand why his brother hadn't kept them, they're so lovely, really—Maggie brings her empty glass to her lips and pretends to drink. This is just the sort of party that Skip would love.

He is saying that though you could probably call this stuff loot, well, heh heh, some people do call it just that, he is saying that in the long run you have to admit that it is a lot better off being cared for and protected by someone who knows what he is doing than buried in some old hole in the ground with a bunch of long-dead Indians, of no use to anyone, and she says that she has to admit he has a point, she used to collect arrowheads out on Long Island when she was a kid but thinks that her mother probably threw them away, what do you want with a bunch of old rocks? "See what I mean?" he shrugs.

Skip maintains that her unconventionality, what he likes to call her bohemianism, what he likes to call her "feminine individualism" (pleased at his own joke, though no one else ever seems to understand what it is), is not a symptom of imagination or creativity (though, obviously, there are some things to be said for creativity) but of fear and insecurity. You loathe what you most want and cannot have. "You do?" asked Maggie, and he had patted her shoulder just as though she'd just had new dentures fitted, fully aware that she had gone to art school and not to a real college. Sure. When he was an undergraduate, he knew a lot of guys—well, he knew a couple of guys, guys on football scholarships and ghetto grants, that sort of thing—who were always going on about the establishment and the revolution and all that bullshit, but when you got right down to it they were just sore because they didn't have what everybody else had. Everybody? Oh, for God's sake, Maggie, she knew what he meant. And that's why he thinks she has never settled down, never held a job for more than nine months, never had a husband or a child, traveled across the planet like a hobo for all those years, never knowing where she would be or with whom from one day to the next, preferred to take her chances selling her work on a piecemeal basis rather than get a steady, well-paid job as a designer? And that's why he thinks she has never settled down, never held a job for more than nine months, never had a husband or a child, traveled across the planet like a hobo for all those years, never knowing where she would be or with whom from one day to the next, preferred to take her chances selling her work on a piecemeal basis rather than get a steady, well-paid job as a designer.

Really?

Well, not completely, of course. Life is never as clear-cut as the theories of classroom psychology. But even she would have to admit that there is some truth in what he says. Wouldn't she?

Hasn't she always been just a little envious of the things she has renounced the most loudly? A little jealous of the people she has denounced the most vehemently? A little afraid of not getting the things she most loathed? Don't you see, Skip says, all your life you've been running away from yourself. Running and running, not to, but from. Running and running from a normal life, from the stability and security, from the simplicity and fulfillment that can be anyone's, that can be hers. Fear of failing. He has even experienced it himself—how he put down doctors when he realized he would never be one, calling them pseudoscientists and charlatans, deluded mechanics and pompous simpletons; how he railed against women and marriage and even love when his own deserted him, calling them deceitful, fraudulent and lies, swearing he would never let himself be used like that, hurt like that again, bitches all of them, let the ex-Mrs. Ellis come to him with her teeth in her hands and he wouldn't so much as recommend a good dental surgeon—but that was before. Before he realized that dentists have more time for sailing than doctors and are rarely accused of manslaughter? Before he realized that Marianne was never good enough for him anyway? Before he was asked to speak at the dentists' convention, his own words in print, everyone congratulating him on his important contribution to practical science? Before he discovered that there are hidden hordes of women in this world willing to feed you and fuck you, buy you shirts and pick up that book downtown that you never found time to pick up yourself, asking little more in return than a little time, a compliment of two (about their cooking, or their understanding of American foreign policy since 1945, or their sense of style, or the original way in which they decorated their kitchens), a healthy erection when they slip into the bedroom in a garter belt, black stockings, and four-inch, red high heels? Before he accepted the fact that he had never really wanted two daughters with naturally curly hair, freckles, and an aptitude for the violin and ballet dancing, respectively, looking and acting just like their mother and their mother's mother, that what he had always really wanted was a son just like he, just like he might have been? Before he met Maggie and discovered what true love and happiness could be.

Oh.

The man is saying that it's really something, if you think

about it, all these old and simple things that were once actually used by people, just like that lamp over there and the bowls filled with potato chips, corn chips, guacamole, and Californian onion dip, and the woman is saying that she likes to visit the Museum of Natural History at least once a year, the Egyptian exhibit has always fascinated her.

But hasn't Maggie, in fact, believed what Skip has said to be true? Hasn't she run and run—ready to go anywhere, try anything, be anyone, as long as it wasn't the same, was new, as long as it was something most people would never do, some place most people would never see? Hasn't she, just. No matter what the risks or difficulties, no matter what the loneliness or hardship, no matter whose life might vanish forever just because she was trying to make a point?

Then, of course, she hadn't thought that it was running. Then she had thought that it was dreaming. Sleeping, with her eyes wide and her heart open; dreaming with her body, images and worlds and memories all streaming from her own hands. Then she had thought that she was immutably rooted in the universe, endlessly, timelessly connected to the heart of all the worlds, her dreams the dreams of a river or a sun, so ordinary, so special, so sublime. So ordinary, so special and so sublime that to squander just one day, to let pass just one year like a cloud, you in the house with your feet up and the radio on, was to do something that could only be described as sin.

"You know," Skip once said. "I really used to believe that all men are created equal. You know, that everyone is pretty much the same." Because he was raised to believe in the American system (which he certainly does), in democracy, in the principles of the Constitution, no matter what special privileges his parents might have had (and might have bequeathed to him), no one ever called them snobs. "But they're not. Some people really don't care about making anything of their lives, no matter what opportunities are open to them. Some people just go from day to day, never making any plans, never having any goals. And then, wham, it's all over. And what have they got to show for it?" moving his hand in the empty air where hovered no boat, no house, no son at Harvard Medical School. "Nothing, that's what," six feet under the ground in an overpriced box, a few flowers scattered over the first handful of dirt, the grave diggers leaning on their shovels, taking a break until the mourners are ready to go, and not even a deep freeze back home to keep your memory alive or at least plugged in. "At the end of the day, they've got nothing." Nothing to show, and no one to whom to show it.

"You know," Tony had said to her, "I used to believe that everyone is better than everybody else." Because sometimes he felt so, oh, alive, he guessed, alive or something, like knowing you were the third star in the handle of the Big Dipper, just pulsing away, just there, a song. Because he thought that every-one must feel like that at one time or another, must be able to feel like that, so incredibly aware of life, of their own aliveness. "But the way I feel now, it seems more like everyone's just as bad as everybody else," his hands not moving from the table where they rested, his eyes not moving to look at her from whatever it was that he saw. "None of us are what we could be."

The man is saying that what he really thinks is wrong with the world today is a crisis of values, doesn't she agree? And she is saying does he mean like stocks and bonds and things like that? And he, thinking she must be making a joke, laughs, heh hah, he knows, almost instinctively you could say, that she feels as he does, that we, that many of us, though not all of us, by any stretch of the imagination, have turned our backs on the very qualities and ideals that most strongly reflect and protect our humanity (though he doesn't go on to eleborate just which those might be). "I know just what you mean," the woman sighs, and they look at each other with intensity and significance for an instant, thinking of different things.

Brave in her drunkenness and aggressive in her boredom, Maggie has an overwhelming desire to tap each of them on the shoulder, his blue and cotton, hers bare and brown, excuse me, but I was just wondering what it is that you think gives life meaning, what it is that you think makes a person crawl on from one day to the next, even when there is less than no reason, even when there is no point at all. Tap, tap, his shoulder hard and muscular (naturally, he runs and plays a little tennis, when he has the time) tap, tap, her shoulder dry and smooth (of course, she would never sit in the sun and bake for hours, a lamp is the only way). "Excuse me, but do you think that if the government suddenly decided that no one could ever get a mortgage again that the country would be stricken with an epidemic of suicide?"

"What?" asks the woman.

"You what?" says the man.

"Oh, nothing," says Maggie, childish again. "I'm a little drunk."

"Me, too." He smiles, raising his glass. "What else are parties for?"

And though she hasn't thought of him for several days, and though she hasn't seen him since the day in the park, except once, going out of the building as he was coming in—oh hi, hi, how are you? oh, okay, *bien,* this weather sure is something, yeah, it sure is, I'll see you, yeah, see you around—she thinks of Tony Rivera now. Of the busted guitar hanging on the wall in the hallway, This Machine Has Killed, of the picture of him that hangs over the cupboard in the kitchen, in a bar somewhere playing with some band; of the way he laughs at his own jokes; of the way he laughed at hers. She thinks of Tony and she wants to see him now. Just to ask him what he thinks about mortgages.

Since she doesn't know the hostess, the host, or anyone else for that matter, there is no one to whom she must say good-bye, I've had a great time, that bean dip is something else, no, I really can't stay, I've got to be up early in the morning, wow, what the hell did you put in that punch? No one to kiss or tell a lie, no one to hug or tell the truth. Since no one has really noticed her presence, no one is likely to notice her absence. And isn't that always the way, she thinks, or almost always, or really? And, well trained by her mother and by her years of depending on the hospitality of strangers, she takes her glass to the kitchen, which is dark but for a few candles, and filled, it seems, with college teachers and mature law students, and places it carefully in the sink. Who's had too much to drink?

But even though she is not so drunk—not so drunk that she can't see, or can't walk, or might have to throw up in a garbage can—she goes two blocks in the opposite direction from the subway, and when she does find the station and get on the right train everyone in the car looks desperate to her. Desperate or beyond despair. Are they characters in some powerfully meaningful play? But, no, the passengers bounce and rock in the silence of the subway's reverberating din, outlined by the writing on the walls, so soundless and immobile, their expressions so expressionless and their bodies positioned so as to suggest nothing, that they could only be real, not manikins, not actors, not visitors from an uglier planet. Maggie tries to read a computer dating ad, and swallows a hiccup. The lights dim and the local stations flash by like flip cartoons. If they were symbols, and not people, thinks Maggie, they would represent Futility, Fear, Hypocrisy, Self-delusion, Ignorance, and Madness, all bound for no glory at the end of the line. And she, what would she represent? Grief? Regret? She closes her eyes and tries to will herself sober. More sober. Or something else?

No light shines from the front windows of the Grossman–Rivera apartment. No figure moves within, no face stands at the window, watching the street. It doesn't mean that he isn't home—he could be in there, reading by candlelight, picking his guitar in the dark, lying on the floor with the dog at his feet, practicing for death, sitting in a closet, barely breathing, there ain't nobody here—but she is pretty sure that it does. Still, she hasn't come all this way to give up now. Still, she hasn't gotten this stoned to be defeated by his absence.

It is late and the street is as close to sleep as it ever comes. The shops are caged, the dog walkers are all locked away, no bopping revelers or hurrying pedestrians with urgent destinations disturb the untranquil quiet of this night. The air trembles with the hum of millions of air-conditioning units, but the only sound Maggie hears are her own footsteps and distant sirens; her own blood moving and an earthly wail—a cat? an infant? a woman being injured? She stares at the bells as though unsure of which one to ring, unsure of whether or not she should. What the hell is she doing here, alone in the hours that always hold surprises, always hold such treacheries behind their incandescent smiles? Is she crazy or something? She hardly knows the man. Has she finally and truly lost her mind? It's not as though she needs another friend. She already has friends; strong, stable, sane friends, with their feet on the ground and their eyes raised upward, toward their soaring futures. She could find a place for the night in almost every country on the globe; could find someone to talk to even in Wyoming. She could turn around right this minute, go home, and phone any one of a dozen people, all of whom would be more than delighted to give her their opinions on long-term loans, God, or artificial sweeteners.

She could swing around right at this moment, take a cab back home, and phone any one of a half-dozen people who would tell her that they love her (her mother, Skip, the guy she left in São Paulo, to name but three), and at least one of them would mean it seriously. But who else does she know who knows three entire songs about Sacco and Vanzetti by heart? She rings the bell. She rings the bell again. But there is, of course, no one home. She doesn't ring Meredith's bell—just in case.

Across the street, next to the chained-up grocery where a fat ginger cat sleeps in the window next to a Budweiser sign, is the doorway where Tony and Richard often sit and pretend to watch the sun go down. What would anyone else tell her that they haven't told her before?

Unheedful of the dangers awaiting a lone woman on a city street in the still-dark morning, Maggie thumps back down the stoop, crosses the road, and sits down on the stone of the step, her elbows on her knees and her chin on her hands.

And she is sitting on the porch at home, her left knee grazed and her socks around her ankles, a comic on her lap and an apple in her hand, watching her father mow the lawn while, in the bedroom, her mother reads out loud from the Bible to stop herself from crying. And she is sitting on the front seat of someone's car, her legs out the open door, a can of beer held to her mouth, a hand not hers encircling one breast, watching the fireflies twinkle against the trees, while in the back seat Steve and Louise take off Louise's bra. She is sitting in an airport terminal, a canvas satchel between her feet, one hand on her stomach, one hand holding a letter she has read before, her eyes on the family moving like a tugboat through the lobby, a child on his shoulders, a child in her arms, a child behind, hurry up, hurry up, it's not far now. She is sitting beneath the portico of a church in some other country—Italy, maybe, or, maybe, Spain— waiting for the rain to stop, waiting for the bus to come, watching an old woman like a crow climb the steps as though making a rosary, one step one step one step more, and the streets filled with hurry, one step, one step again, thinking about mustard seeds.

And she is sitting in a doorway along a city street in the middle of the night, dressed for a party but all on her own, watching the cars flash by the intersection like shooting stars, watching the last lights go off in the buildings across the way, and thinking of how the sun goes down over the Gulf of Mexico, just as though someone had dropped it.

Maggie and the cat sit together on the living-room floor, looking like furniture, or, perhaps, laundry, looking like one more shape in the colorless, undetailed shapes of the room. In the bedroom, Skip sleeps the sleep of the very drunk, the sheet wound in a heap at his feet, his lips moving in his intoxicated dreams. It is not quite dawn.

Her hand across her knee, Maggie is thinking about her son, whose face she can see so clearly and so vividly, whose hand she can feel in her own so surely, that he should be real. Its tail curled around its feet, the cat is thinking about nothing in particular, though soon it will begin thinking about food. Skip, his hands on the pillow as though on a ledge, is thinking (if memories and dreams are thoughts) of the time his parents went abroad for a year and left him behind, in a good school with a priceless reputation, with boys of his own caliber and teachers he should hope to emulate, left him alone. It's not quite dawn.

And soon things will go back to normal. Soon there will have been no uneasy changeling night, no unquiet thoughts, no memories gnawing away like worms at buried things. Soon—but it is still not quite dawn.

There are places in this world where time has not passed but piled up. Where magic and mystery are commonplace still, as ordinary as a blue sky or a green tree or a red wound or a silver plane. There are still places where the miraculous is as everyday as death or laughing, birth or tears. Where time has not erased but incorporated; where, beyond, behind its own exterior, the earth lies waiting to speak, to sing its strange songs, to surprise and befriend you. Places where it is as easy to know the unimaginable as it is to breathe—easier even, than squeezing a trigger or telling a lie. There are few, if any, places like this left in America, and none in New York City. When you see a miracle performed around here, you are seeing a trick. In this town, when you see a ghost or an angel zip through the streets, peer in at the window on a stormy night, or hover above your bed at four in the morning, eyes wide with warning, you are either seeing a burglar or your own conscience. This is one of those places where time perpetually obliterates and plows under, where everything is such that it can be explained (several times), can be analyzed, can be understood and worked out, where even God's best parlor tricks are no match for the mind of modern man. There's no scaring the natives around here with volcanoes or eclipses of the sun. No sense in sending in the spectral missionaries to whisper their messages against the whining wind. When people drop to their knees in this metropolis, it's with their ears waiting for the promise and the check already in their hands.

Nonetheless, there were some seconds this morning, just as they turned the corner and came into view—high on one end, low in the middle, and not so high on the other end; void of particularness and immense in image—when it was possible to believe that the three pedestrians of the apocalypse approached.

Pride, Frailty, and Liberality?

Maggie got to her feet for a better look, or to get herself ready to run. Was the block haunted after all? And then she heard a voice singing, *I'm goin' to German, I'll be back some old time . . .*

Groucho, Harpo, and Chico?

But there was, nonetheless, just as they appeared at the end of the buildings—slow-moving and lumpish, bowed but determined—a moment in which it was possible to think that they might be pilgrims drawing near, feet bare and calloused, their way clear before them, their bodies sore but their hearts content, ready to sit and pray or tell a tale or play the flute, ready to speak of all the wonders they had seen and sought, of all the squalor and all the joy.

Kings? Priests? Shepherds? Outlaws?

Though there was really little mistaking them (Richard with his air of benediction, Tony with his air of resignation, some poor drunk being towed home between them), they were so not what she was expecting that she had difficulty in recognizing them or what was happening.

The foolish, the lame, and the blind.

When Tony first saw Maggie, he nearly dropped the not-quite-unconscious Skip. Had he been capable of speech, he would immediately have begun shouting, "It's not my fault," so much did he mistake her for an avenging angel, or Sandy come to surprise him, to catch him out, you see what I mean?

He had no idea of what was happening, felt as though he'd been sleepwalking and had woken up wandering around on a street that wasn't even his. Was it just that sort of night? He remembered sitting in the corner of the End, listening to Skip who, fighting back the tears, was going on about deciding to become a dentist because he would be able to reserve restaurant tables and theater tickets as Dr. Ellis (how would anyone *know* he wasn't a brain surgeon at Columbia?), and how it has always been women who have seduced him (and the next thing he knew she was undressed, and the next thing he knew after that, he was). He remembered the woman sitting next to him leaning over and saying, "You know, I don't think your friend looks too good," and remembered Skip saying, "You know what I mean, don't you, Tony? A man's just not safe. Sometimes things just happen that aren't my fault," and then the next thing he was sure of they were on the street again and Richard was beside them like an illusion of the night. Without a word, Richard fell into step, knowing where they were going without having to be told, knowing (or so it seemed to the beer-bleary Rivera) why. All the long way home, Skip, whom he largely ignored, seemed to be trying to apologize for something, kept saying over and over, a locker-room chant, "You know, you're really a nice guy, Tony. I really like you," and Richard, whose attention he continually tried to attract, sailed silently along like a man on a mission. All the difficult journey, they swayed and staggered and stopped, Tony paranoid, ready to drag them all into the road at the sound of a footstep behind them, Richard removed, and Skip drunker than he'd ever before been in his life, delving into his memory for all the things for which he was sorry and all the things that hadn't been his fault. And then, like a voice from the clouds, Richard suddenly said, "My mother's dead. Did you know that?" and laughed. "My mother's dead," Skip's hand tightened on the robed shoulder, "Really? I'm sorry. I'm really sorry. I didn't know that." And then, only yards from home and safety, they turned the corner like a bus on two wheels, and there she was. And it seemed to him that everything was at once familiar and strange, expected but out of place, unexpected but as it should be—that death, that something like death, was confronting him at last, time's up, stop fuckin' around. Why was this happening to him? Why was it happening to him now? As though God herself had chosen to put in an appearance, you can't go this way no more; God herself just waiting for him, not as judge but as memory, not as omen but as reminder, you have no one with whom to reckon but yourself, how long do you think this can last? Everything stopped, becoming no more than pictures of itself—a lamp pole, a parking meter, a car with an American flag sticker on the windshield, a building, a crushed milk carton, a shadow, four people standing in the starless night as though anything might happen, as though the world and its universe were bottomless and without time, as though all possibilities existed, undamaged by the history of man, unmutilated by his trompings and his trampings, his slashings and bumpings in his manic pursuit of himself. As though all the things that no one remembers might yet be unforgotten. And only they were real.

Then Zorro barked and went racing up to Maggie, his tail moving his body, he, at least, sure of what was what, knocking his head against the sandals in her hand. Everything began again, all back in its proper place. They were just four people and one small dog, up too late and still at large and much the worse for wear. There would be no revelations, no mysteries unraveled, no instant of epiphany, though it did seem quite likely that there would be a fight.

"Hey, I'm sorry," finally finding his voice. "Really. He didn't tell me he was supposed to be meeting you here," even as she was saying, "I've been waiting for you."

Had he heard her?

"Maggie!" cried Skip, trying to grin. "Maggie, I've been looking for you."

Hadn't he?

Richard let go, stepping away into the shadows as though on cue, Tony just managing to keep himself and Skip on their feet. Maggie grabbed Skip's unheld arm.

"Sorry about that," said Skip as they steadied him between them. "There's something wrong with my legs." And then, as though it were someone else who had just spoken, asked, "What's wrong with my legs?"

"I think," said Tony, "that you'd better get him home."

"Home?" repeated Maggie, afraid that her voice might echo in the night. "Upstate?"

"No, home. Don't you have a home?" Did she think he expected her to drag Skip aboard a Greyhound in the dead-end of the night, traveling along the highway like interstate exiles, two dollars and a Hershey bar between them, let's get off at the next town, our luck's just bound to change?

Oh, home. "No," she said. "I spend my nights in doorways."

And he grinned.

He must have heard.

"I'll get a cab. If we move him against this car, you'll be able to hold him up."

He got the cab, he helped them into it, he stood, patiently, half in and half out, while Skip hung on to his hand, jerking it up and down, "I'm really happy we got to know each other, I'm really sorry. I'm really glad we had this talk," he gave the driver the address, *ésta bien, ésta bien,* listen, man, he's not gonna be sick, he leaned in through the window to say so-long, see you around, *te veo,* he stood in the gutter with Zorro, and waved at the shrinking cab.

She had the cabbie drive once around the block, but neither of the figures sitting in the shadows, legs folded, arms crossed on top, gave any sign. "I missed you," mumbled Skip, his head slumped against her shoulder. "I was lonely and I missed you." She didn't say, "I missed you, too."

Every time she tried to wake him on the journey uptown, come on, Skip, we're nearly there, he would say again (not unlike the baby doll she once had that would wail ma-ma ma-ma every time you flung it on its back), "I was lonely. I missed you." But when the cab finally stopped, he brushed her aside. "I'm all right, Maggie. I'm fine. Don't worry. I can get out by myself," and he pulled on the handle and spilled into the street.

"You want some help with him?" asked the driver, as though it were a question he had asked a million times before.

"No, it's okay. He's almost standing."

Like injured soldiers, separated from their unit, they limped into the building, into the elevator, into the hallway, and into her apartment.

"What's that song you were singing about Germany?" asked Skip. "Whose mother died? Did your mother die? Jesus Christ," stumbling them into a wall, "is my mother dead?"

She steered him into the bedroom and onto the bed. She pulled off his shoes. "Come here, honey," he coaxed, trying to get his arms to reach her. "I've missed you. Give me a kiss." She pulled off his socks. "Why won't anyone kiss me anymore?" he asked the walls and the ceiling and the woman unzipping his trousers. "Why doesn't anybody love me?" No one in any of the surrounding apartments began to sing or laugh or play the piano, no door slammed shut, no siren moaned; the world made no attempt to make its presence known. No one said, oh, don't be silly, I love you, or your mother loves you, or hundreds of late adolescents with straight teeth love you, probably even your own children love you. "All I want is to be loved," Skip pleaded, an arm across his sky-blue eyes, imploring a faceless audience demanding in its silence. "What's wrong with that? What's wrong with wanting to be loved?" She tugged at the cuffs of his pants and change jingle-jangled on to the floor. "Why doesn't anybody ever really care about me?"

She stood back with his clothing in her arms and helplessness trapped in her heart. "Here," she said, in a voice he had never heard before, and would not remember having heard. "Here. Pull the sheet up. You should get some sleep." He lay like a paralytic while she tucked it up around him.

"No one's ever really loved me. No one."

As though it should be impossible that a person could possess good looks and money, health and personality, a good education, a good credit rating, and good intentions and still not be loved. Impossible that the blessed should not also be protected. As though only the old, the ugly, the poor, the weak, the deficient, the unwanted, the maimed, the ill, and the hopeless should suffer loneliness, live without dignity in an indifferent world. "You get some sleep," she said, kissing his cheek, "you'll feel better in the morning."

"My kids," he called out suddenly, making a move to move. "I have to talk to my kids. I don't want them to forget me."

She held him still with her fingertips until his urgency had passed and his head rested once more on the pillow, his hand around her waist. "You can't call them now, Skip. They'll be sleeping. You can call them in the morning."

"My kids," he repeated, but this time they were less an image (two little girls sitting shoulder-to-shoulder against a paper sky, their hair in identical braids, their ears pierced by identical gold studs, their smiles identical except that one is missing a tooth, as they appear in the photograph he carries in his wallet) than an idea (two little girls who owe their lives to him, who owe him something). "You're right. I'll call them in the morning."

He was asleep before she turned off the light and shut the door behind her.

There was too much around, though, for her to close her eyes. Too much night and too much fear, too much silence and too much talking, too many ideas and moments with nothing to contain them.

She could hear Skip snore.

And here she has sat, thinking about a lifetime of things, and thinking about the dentist asleep in the bedroom, still wearing his The American Dental Association Recommends Three Times a Day T-shirt. Here she has sat, never so fond of him before—not in any moment of intimacy, no look no word no kiss—and never liking him less. Because of his weakness? Because of his need? Because of the sorrow he feels for himself? Because he wastes his tears? Or just because?

She has sat with the cat, thinking about Nelson Ellis, Jr., and about those other men she has known—men whose bodies she has undressed, whose anger she has soothed, whose tears have fallen upon her skin. None of them were much like Skip. They were wilder, or bolder, or brighter, or angrier, or funnier, more serious or more imaginative, or, often, more cruel. They were not like Skip. Not much. Before, the dreaming always ended; with Skip it simply never began.

But if they could not stir her heart for long, could not sustain its hunger, how could he? Why should he? Why should anyone?

Why, even, should a tiny child be expected to do so much?

It is nearly dawn.

Maggie stretches backward, arching her spine, disturbing the cat who decides to relocate.

She gets up slowly, and goes to make some coffee. As she scoops the grounds into the aluminum basket, for the first time she wonders who else it is who has failed to find Skip lovable.

◇　◇　◇

Out in the streets, Tony Rivera, who has sat through the night watching his home as though someone (Sandy? himself?) was likely to look from a window, turn on a light, appear in the entrance, stretches, too. He and Richard have exchanged one sentence all morning: "Where've you been?" "I've been around." That's all. Where've you been? I've been around. What else can anyone say, ever? What details matter (I had a meal, I had a fight, I discovered a cure for arthritis, I wrote a beautiful poem, I signed an important treaty, I won a crucial battle, I cooked a great meal, I made a lot of money, I spent a lot of money, I saved ten hectares of land in Amazonia from being razed to the ground, I fucked myself senseless, I wrote a letter to the President, I marched for peace, I prayed for justice, I took the kids to the movies, I murdered a son-of-a-bitch the world is well rid of, I wrote a brilliant novel, I composed a song that will still be played fifty years from now, I watched television, I went to Honolulu)? Where've you been? I've been around.

As the night was casually edged from the sky, he thought of the things he had thought about Richard. Thought or imagined. Like an infant, or a new lover, or a new friend. Richard is ripe for fantasies. He could be anyone, could have been from anywhere. Unlike Tony, who can only be himself. In his remoteness, in his aloofness (in his madness?), Richard could indeed be a shaman, could indeed be a prophet, could, indeed, be death, already gone. But earlier this morning, falling back into the anonymity of the city, relieved to be relieved of all responsibility, it suddenly occurred to him that in his imaginings of Richard, so big, so black, so free of speech, in the lives he has constructed for him (orphan, bastard, beloved but misunderstood son, city poor, country poor, scion of the only black lawyer in town), in the stories he has told himself about him (twisted into a cell by poverty and prejudice, shuttered in insanity by the smallness of human imagination, driven into mysticism by the despair of a stupid world), he could, in fact, have been imagining himself.

Oh, how promising must man have been—must he still be. How promising, with his courage and his leaping intelligence. How hope-giving, with his questing beauty and his staggering capacity for love. Wowee, God must have whooped, rolling the planets and scattering the stars, I've invented the human being. The human. From which comes the adjective humane (kind-hearted, compassionate, merciful), from which comes the noun humanist (one who seeks to promote human welfare), the adjective humanitarian (concerned with human welfare and the reduction of suffering), and, in its way, the adjective inhuman (brutal, lacking normal human qualities of kindness, pity, etc.), as well. From whom comes hatred, sadism, ruthlessness; from whom comes jealousy, greed, and slaughter; from whom comes cruelty, degradation, and fear. The cure and the curse, all in one handy, biodegradable package.

Could God sue man for breach of promise?

Tony stands up and bends at the knees. He could sit here forever, and, like Richard, content with his own thoughts, simply watch the world slog by, hovering between realities like a levitating saint. Right now, he could trot across the street and up the steps, rummage in the linen closet for an old sheet, wrap it around his once fine body, and come back to take his place on the street, finally committed to something that will never let him down, that can never disappoint him, and which he can never disappoint: the pursuit of nothing, the acceptance of uncomplicated survival. Is that oh so different from the pursuits and commitments of everyone else with their tears and recriminations, their obsessions and their plans? Is it any different, drifting through the streets like a dust mote on the breath of time, aggressively rootless and without direction, than striding through the world, carting along your appliances and your opinions, your rightness and your computerized washing machines? If a man who has everything he could want, everything he has ever wanted or been taught to want, can weep because he still wants more, and a woman can change her heart and change her mind because she can't imagine what more could be, and if a woman can sell herself for less, for no better reason than to keep out of the cold, then who is the worse for the wearing? Richard, calmed by his private voice? Or who?

Zorro stretches at his feet as though taking a bow.

If a man can abandon his dreams because he thinks that they have abandoned him, because he has never found the way to live up to them, if a man fears his own heart, then what choice is there? What difference between going and stopping? running and sleeping? living and dying?

"We're going up now," says Tony, the first voice of the

dawn. And adds, though probably Richard isn't even listening, though probably even if he were listening he wouldn't care, "I've got to feed the dog."

Past the corner a jogger runs; behind them a radio begins to play, it's another hot, humid day in Manhattan.

If you don't change the world, must the world change you?

Richard's head rises, quite unlike the sun. "Yeah, sure," he says. "You take care of yourself, man." And lets Zorro lick his hand.

NINE

The summer has almost come to its end. All along the Eastern shore, urban tribes, brown from the sun, frisky from the air, and lean from countless games of beach volleyball and vigorous dips in the ocean, are beginning their autumnal migrations home for the winter. Inland, too, at river, lake, and mountain, the lush hills echo with the sounds of retreat as they wave good-bye to their summer encampments and hello, we're back to their cities of stone, rested, healthier, and with a working knowledge of tent pitching, boat rowing, trout fishing, outhouses, washing by hand, and being back with nature. For the last time, the sand is spilled from the sneakers and shaken from the bathing suits, the lanterns are lighted and the marshmallows toasted. For the last time, couples stroll along the coast at sunset, the children running ahead with splashes and cries of excitement, looking for just one more perfect horseshoe crab shell or a round white stone. The gulls wail and the ducks quack and the raccoons lay siege to the garbage cans that will soon be empty and put in a shed till the spring. On porches and boardwalks, mothers stand with their arms folded, the evening breeze teasing at their hair, the evening sun dipping into the deep blue water, thinking about the things still to be done to get the kids ready for school, and gazing at a world that soon will be deserted, soon be just beautiful and quiet and ignored once again, a potato chip bag among the seaweed, a plastic soldier poking through the sand the only signs that once this beach was a picnickers' paradise; a fly caught in the bushes at the top of the falls, a rubber sandal hanging from a tree the only signs that not so long ago this land was a vacationers' playground. And in the enormous night, voices drift by on the static, heavy air of summer's close, This has really been a wonderful vacation, I wish the summer would never stop, I promise I'll write, We have to come back next year. Soon, everything will be as it was, as it really is. No more moonlight madness. No more sunlight insanity. No more intuitions of magic as the stars burn or the owls call or the porpoises dance through the Sound like mermaids. No more wild dreams of love or freedom or perfect solitude. All those hot kisses on all those hot nights, all those private promises made far from anything, will soon be as forgotten as the cellophane bag, the little green commando, the imitation aphid, and the sandal. The real world—where fish come in tanks or in plastic, where you can't hear the heartbeat of the world over the electronic hum, over the sound of man's voice, so much louder than God's, where the wonders of a digital watch that plays "The Streets of Laredo" at twelve noon are more important than the wonders of the Galapagon tree-finch—is returning.

Probably with a vengeance.

Everywhere, the August nights are ripe for nostalgia. Whether it is the ocean, the earth, the barbecued spareribs, or the traffic backed up in the tunnel that you smell, the aroma is there. Whether it is the ahh-whish of the tide, the crackle rush and silence of nocturnal animals going about their business, the snap-fizz of cans and bottles being opened, or the urgent scream of sirens that you hear, the mood is everywhere. Whether it is the waves like bursting stars, a lone tree in the field like a petrified fountain, a woman behind a screen door with her back to the light, or a gang of kids on the street (the boys leaning against an old parked Buick, passing a joint, the girls strutting in place, smiling among themselves) that you see, the feeling is present.

Jack, Edith, Sandra, and Skip, sipping their drinks in the garden, feel it. Meredith, Maggie, and Will, having a picnic supper in the park feel it. Even Tony, getting an unwanted lift home from Parker, who has a new friend in Brooklyn, a really remarkable woman who put herself through graduate school by stripping, feels it.

Tony likes it when the streets are full. As they've come barreling through the Bronx, Parker (probably thanks to the variety of women he has wooed) taking every shortcut in three boroughs (he can always become a poet-cabbie should his attempts at being a poet-administrator fail), Tony has almost been able to turn him off completely, giving his attention to the street. He cannot hear it (Parker won't let him open the window because of the air conditioning, won't let him turn off the George Benson tape because it helps him to relax), but he can imagine that he is hearing it: the chatter and the laughter, the traffic and the sudden blasts of music or intimacy, the girl crossing at the intersection, her fist shaking at a man in a convertible, stupid mothafucker, the women shouting from fire escapes and open windows, the white nylon curtains flapping around them like wings. Parker talks incessantly, as though the sound of his voice gives at least him some comfort. Parker is constantly pointing out things of no interest—Hey, now that's a nice car, Do you know, I grew up around here, just a couple of blocks over, Those buildings used to be really something, can you believe it?—but still Tony can recognize every sound and every scent, every movement and every look. This is the only time of year when New York seems more a network of communities than an outdoor shopping mall; when there is more to be seen than people going to or coming from, hurrying in one door and out another; when you can tell what a neighborhood is like not because the liquor stores are caged or have a sign on the door NO THUNDERBIRD NO GYPSY ROSE but because the life is visible, intruding on the wonder-filled streets.

"Look at them," challenges Parker, nervous about having his windshield wiped ("Oh, for Christsake," said Tony. "It's only the bums give you a hard time. The kids aren't going to bother you if you don't want to pay. They're businessmen, not desperados." "Oh, yeah?" snapped Parker. "Is that what you think? That just shows you how often you drive in a car in this city."), "you'd think they'd have something better to do."

They bounce by two boys dancing on a corner to music

from a radio, a smiling girl bopping behind them, her hands clapping in time, everyone around them swaying and ready to sing.

"Like what?" asks Tony. "Going to see a Broadway play or stealing cars?"

"You're a romantic, Tony," says Larry, who has said this before. "You refuse to see the truth even when it's spread out before you," and spreads his hand, moving it from the steering wheel to just below Tony's chin. And spreads his hand, to indicate the avenue in front of them, the clumps of people with no restaurant or party or concert or weekend retreat to which to go, the grimy-looking shops, the vandalized walls, the old marquee WRE TLING! LIV EVERY RIDAY!, here and there a hole where a building used to be. "Wrestling! Jesus! That used to be a fine old movie house."

Tony will never see what Larry sees. "And what's the difference between going to a movie every weekend to see the Indians get beat to shit by the cowboys and going to watch a match you know is fixed?"

"You don't understand what I'm trying to say," moans Parker, who has also said this before.

"I understand what you're saying, Larry," refusing to turn his eyes into the car. "You're saying that instead of hanging out on the street, they should all be inside watching educational television or learning to play chess."

"There you go again as usual," shouts Larry. "Twisting my words."

"Oh, Larry," says Tony, "I'm sorry. What did you mean? That they should all be home reading *You Can't Go Home Again* or *King Lear*? Or that they should all be downtown at that little French restaurant you discovered with the fantastic snails? Or did you mean ..."

"What I meant," roars Parker, accidentally blowing the horn, "is that they aren't doing anything constructive with their time. What I meant is that they have no drive or motivation. When they get a little money they just squander it. Look at them," his hand banging against the glass, pointing out to the street that is no longer vibrating with life but crawling with society's vermin looking for easy money and cheap thrills; pointing out to the street that is no longer vital and comforting but sleazy and contemptible, home of whores and hustlers, pimps and junkies, home of the ignorant, the stupid, and the lost and losing, home of people who would rather watch a soap opera or a boxing match than *Die Fledermaus*, or a sensitive dramatization of *The Raj Quartet*, people who think that Beethoven's Fifth is a whisky. "The great unwashed!" He sighs, as only a man who has tried—tried to understand, tried to help, tried to wash—can sigh. "People like you," says Parker, his voice level and controlled once more, the voice he uses for public debate, "think you can change things with your sentimental intentions." Stopped at an intersection, a basketball thuds onto the hood and soars off across the road, but only Tony watches to see where it lands. "People like you think that there's no difference between a janitor with a tenth-grade education and the president of the Chase Manhattan Bank."

"Oh, no," says Tony, with conviction if not volume, "I think there's a difference," you couldn't turn your back on the president of Chase Manhattan.

But Larry, intent on cutting a cab, doesn't hear him. "People like you," he is saying in what has become a lament, "think that there's something immoral in wanting to get ahead, in wanting the best that life can offer." They glide out from between the warehouses and along the green and busy park. "I know your sort. I know you secretly despise me." Secretly? "I know you've got everyone laughing at me behind my back. People like you are suspicious of everyone else's success. People like you can only relate to failure. Failure you love. Give you some slob with twelve kids who beats his wife and drinks any money he ever gets his hands on and you're happy. But give you some poor jerk who's worked his butt off for thirty years to be someone, to give his children a decent start in life, and you can't wait to see him fall flat on his face."

Either his wife's finally left him, one of his daughters has married an immigrant mechanic, or he didn't get the job in Washington. Tony looks over at Larry, whose face is red and mottled, who is perspiring despite the automatically controlled temperature of the car, just above freezing, whose hands now grip the wheel so that the knuckles bleed white. If he gets any angrier, he'll have a coronary and neither of them will have anything more to worry about. He didn't get the job.

"There!" yells Parker, making Tony jump and look wildly in all directions (for looters? for a bunch of kids gangbanging some Connecticut matron, in town for the day? for a couple being quietly led into a police car, their children huddled around the social worker with the papers in her hands?), until he sees where Parker's jaw points, over there by the benches where some boys are playing drums not badly. "There. You see what I mean? I suppose you think that's culture." And tries to laugh caustically.

Tony stares at the cars, the trees, the buildings that flash behind Larry's head as they barrel on. "Pull over."

"You see?"

"Pull over, Larry. I'm getting out."

"What do you mean you're getting out?" looking over, puzzled but smiling, now what's wrong?

"If I have to jump from this car, I'll tell them with my dying breath that you pushed me."

"Oh, for Christsake," says Parker. "There you go again." But the car begins to slow. "What are you sore about now?"

"I'm not sore," grins Rivera, who certainly doesn't look sore, who up until about an hour ago had been coping quite well, practicing, who still looks very much as though they have been having a pleasant drive and a friendly chat. "I just want to visit my mother. I thought I told you."

Parker eyes him suspiciously as they bump to a halt. "I thought your mother lived further uptown," he says to Tony's back as he climbs from the car.

Beyond the green slopes of the park on which children play and couples stroll, the shore of New Jersey glints gold and pink beneath the falling sun. Beyond the lush slopes of the park by the river where people search for money and trinkets lost in the grass, and office workers, released for the evening, laze, the interior of Manhattan begins to shine like a rainbow beneath the darkening sky. Once, he was going to do some planting here. Once, before he'd considered that there were no points to be made, he was going to do some secret sowing here, one moonless night in the early spring, dressed all in black, he was going to come here with a bag of seeds (corn and carrot, tomato and hemp, pumpkin and lettuce), scatter them in the least trampled corners, the spots hard to reach by bike or passion or ball-bearing skate, and then he was going to wait with the patience of the obsessed, wait for summer and the growing, wait to see their faces when the crops started coming up. He would come on Sundays with Zorro and casually stroll, sniffing at the ruralesque air, saying, "Come on, boy!" and "No, no, Zorro. Over here," the way the other dog-walkers do. And he would smile affectionately on the scruffy boys, I can remember when I was that age, and the teasing young women, young girls, with their easy sensuality, I can remember when they were my age. Just another weekend walker, just another sunshine stalker, just another poor son-of-a-bitch stuck in the city for the summer, eating a snow cone and hoping to run into someone who wouldn't mind a short conversation on the eccentricities of the species canine. And he would watch. Watch for the heads to turn, the gazes to lock, the foreheads to wrinkle, the looks of curiosity to sneak into the eyes. Watch for the faces to register something—surprise? interest? amusement? wonder?

But the face looking at him now belongs to Larry Parker, and its mouth is saying, "I thought maybe we'd have time to stop somewhere for a drink. I mean, if you aren't doing anything. Just a quick one. I have to be in Brooklyn twenty minutes ago. Just one."

Yes, he is his mother's son: son of Sophie with her war-wounded dripping their hurts and dragging their bewildered helplessness over the floral carpet and the black-and-white linoleum. Son of Sophie, who has spent a significant portion of her life sitting at the old formica table in the kitchen, pouring drinks of coffee and whisky and beer and tea, listening, beneath the audible counting of minutes by the teapot clock, to the sad stories of people she hardly knew, who would never know her really or really care to; listening to the fragile details of lives that were separated from hers by more than years of circumstance, never stifling a yawn or suggesting that she might have something else to do, something else about which to think. So that, even now, he is tempted to say, "Oh, okay, Larry. Just one quick one," knowing that it will mean hours listening to Parker explaining why he didn't get the job, why he should have gotten the job, why he wanted the job, why he didn't want the job, whose fault it was that he didn't get the job, whose fault it obviously wasn't. Even knowing all of that. Is it only pity?

But there is a woman and a small child standing on the other side of the road, bodies tense and heads swiveling, judging the right moment to hurl themsleves into the homebound commuters, and there is something in the way they are holding hands, something in the way the child looks at its mother, something in the way she glances down at her child, that is stronger even than Parker's angry hurt, stronger, even, than his own. "I'll tell you what, Larry," says Tony. "I'll make you a bet that those kids back there with the drums know something you don't know."

"Huh?" squinting at the Rivera smile. "What are you talking about now?"

"I'll bet you five bucks those kids with the drums could answer a question pertaining to the culture of our times, and you couldn't." Light ricochets off his glasses. "It's sort of a quiz. Like an IQ test."

The steering wheel is lodged in Larry's hip. "What?"

"Five bucks," taking out his wallet and extracting one green note, waving it close to Parker's face.

"This isn't going to be some question like who's the featherweight champion of Puerto Rico or where the biggest shooting gallery in Manhattan is?"

"This is strictly a general aptitude question. Five bucks."

"Okay. Okay," never one to decline a challenge. He heaves himself into a sitting position, and from the jacket of his wrinkle-resistant suit removes his wallet, and from it a five-dollar bill. "This better be kosher."

Tony looks up for a second, over the roof of the car, to watch them run to safety, she swinging the child on to the curb with a laugh. "It's kosher," bringing his head down so that he is staring into those sensitive blue eyes. "For five dollars, Dr. Lawrence Parker of Scarsdale, steadfast worker in the cause of suffering humanity, who is buried in Grant's tomb?"

Larry looks as though someone's just laughed at one of his poems. "Stop fucking around, Tony. What's the question?"

"Who's buried in Grant's tomb?" Even without a moustache, a cigar, or a toy duck, he can wiggle his eyebrows. "This is the throw-away question, Larry. Who's buried in Grant's tomb?"

Parker blinks, just as he did when he was short and skinny and called "Hey, kid." "Who's buried in Grant's tomb?" He knows it's a trick, but what can it be?

The bill flaps back and forth. "Yeah, Larry. Who's buried in Grant's tomb?"

Parker takes a deep breath and thrusts forward both of his chins. "Grant. Grant's buried in Grant's tomb."

Whish goes the money from his hand. Whish goes the smile from his lips.

"Wrong!" crows Tony, jumping back like a punching bag. "The answer to the question "Who is buried in Grant's tomb?" is: your mama!" and he slams shut the door and salutes; stuffs the money in his pocket and darts across the street.

Sophie sits on the Sormanis' brick porch, a glass of iced tea balanced on one thigh, watching the man across the street as he washes his car, an operation that entails a great deal of equipment and an even greater deal of shouting into the sleepy air, where's that cloth, where's that drink, I thought Joey was gonna help me. Her feet hurt and she is dying for a bath, but, only minutes from home, they at last met someone Angela knows, Carla Sormani, sweeping her path, and now here they are on her porch, having a nice cold drink and talking (at least Carla and Angela are talking) about children.

So far they have established that boys are harder to raise than girls, that all children—with the exception of Carla's Susan and Angela's Robert—are disappointments, causing more trouble than they are ever worth, costing more in tears and sleep and worry and self-denial than they ever repay. When they are little and helpless and look to you for approval every time they make a move, you never have a minute for yourself, not one single minute in which to think about nothing but you; when they are grown and settled and think that you are too old to understand anything, too old or too stupid, you could drop dead in your chair waiting for the phone to ring, knowing they won't find your body before Christmas, did Sophie remember poor Mrs. Ricco? So far they have proven that the best, most selfless mother can have the most selfish, insensitive children, that the sweetest, kindest woman ever to change a diaper or walk four miles in the pouring rain to get exactly the right pair of sneakers can be the mother of a self-centered, self-indulgent slob who always forgets her birthday.

"Take my sister, Marie," says Carla, though it is clear from her tone that she wouldn't.

"Oh, Marie," says Angela. "It's a shame, that's what it is. A shame."

Carla's voice is thin with emotion. "Two years," she hisses, making Sophie turn her head. "Two years! And for what? Two years of grief and crying and blaming yourself, and for what? You should see her house now, Angie. You should see it. Remember what a good housekeeper she used to be? Remember her bathroom?"

Yes, Angie remembers, you could eat off her floors, you could invite a queen to sleep on her sheets.

And now? Now nothing. Now there are always dishes in the sink and dust over the doorsills. Now she shuffles around all day in an old housedress and will never make her famous lasagne again. She'll be lucky if her husband doesn't leave her. "And for what?" asks Carla once more. "My husband tried to tell her. 'Marie,' he said. 'Marie, that boy was no good. He was always crazy. Always.'" In the pause Carla takes for breath, Angie throws one sharp little glance at her own sister. "Of course, he couldn't tell her everything. Not in her condition. But he used to find him down in the basement with those hoodlum friends of his, smoking ..." lowering her voice, "those marijuana cigarettes. 'That Tommy,' he'd say to me. 'That Tommy's going to end up bad.'" And bad he did end, hopped up on pills and liquor, driving his little red Volkswagen through a highway divider and into an oncoming diesel truck, killing himself and injuring the other driver, all because his wife loved someone else. "Nineteen," says Carla. "Nineteen. If that's not crazy, what is?"

What, indeed?

Sophie shifts a little in her folding chair as the man across the way picks up his buckets and cloths and gadgets and trudges into his garage, calling, "Joey! Joey! Come on and give me a hand." Between her feet is her old straw purse, and in her old straw purse is something to remind her of each of her own sons: a silk scarf, decorated with one perfect, hand-painted rose, from Julio; a hand-tooled man's leather wallet that has the word Mexico worked into the design from Gene; a gold pillbox, in which she keeps stamps, from Frankie; a postcard with a picture of Richard Nixon in an Indian headdress on one side and the message "The natives seem friendly" scrawled on the other from Tony, which arrived in this morning's mail.

"You know what he said to me once?" Carla is saying, widening her eyes and lowering her voice to a shocked whisper. "He told me to 'shut up, you carzy f---in' bitch.'" There is a moment of silence in which Carla looks at Angie and Angie looks at Carla, beat that. "Can you imagine? To me. He said that to me. Right in his mother's kitchen."

"Crazy," says Angela, who has been told pretty much the same thing, on more than one occasion, in more than one kitchen, by her eldest nephew, whom she brought into her home and treated like a son, the little bastard. "Crazy," and she moves her eyes and mouth in an expression of exasperation and disgust, but says no more.

It is Sophie's move.

This morning, when the postcard arrived, and Angela, having read it twice and scanned the picture for several seconds with her X-ray eyes, handed it to her with the same look on her face she was wearing the time Sophie came back from Argentina, pregnant and in tears, oh, no, you wouldn't listen to me; the same look she was wearing when Sophie came back from the blue of the Caribbean, surrounded by small children and blood in her eyes, of course, you wouldn't pay any attention to any advice I gave you, there was yet another skirmish in the war which has simmered between them since the day they both could talk. "What's that supposed to mean?" "It's not supposed to mean nothing," said Sophie, sticking it into the purse that lay open on the table. "It's just his way of saying hello." "Oh, yeah?" said Angela, the only person who, just by the way she folds her arms across her bony chest, can make her sister want to hit her. "Most people I know, when they want to say hello, just say it." "Most people you know," said Sophie, freed from diplomacy by Angela's last visit to the doctor and her own packed bag in the bedroom, "don't have the brains to say anything else." On one of the occasions when Tony told Angela an abbreviated version of what he thought of her, you crazy old bitch, why don't you stop minding everybody else's business, Sophie's only response had been to say to Angela's impassioned indignation, "Well, you are a crazy old bitch. You don't think I brought my children up to lie, do you?" So that, now, it is Sophie's turn, Sophie's turn to come plopping down on the side of the maternal angels, and all she has to say is, he was probably on drugs, or it's disgusting the way some of these kids behave, or if one of my boys said that to my sister I'd belt him in the mouth, I don't care how big he is. Sophie takes another sip of the iced tea that tastes nothing like the whisky she would prefer to be drinking, and turns her head away from the other women, down the block to where Carla's husband leans his back against a black car, his arms folded over his no-longer-rock-hard stomach, chatting to a man with a pair of hedge clippers in his hands. Of her own four sons, Frankie spent five years in Sing Sing on a narcotics charge, Gene runs through jobs, towns, and women as though he's working to a quota, and Julio has a tendency to change his sex and his religion without much warning, but it is only Tony who has ever caused her any real concern. Is it because he is the eldest, her first born, doomed to be different? Or is it because he is so much like each of his so-different fathers, the pale but passionate McNair and the dark but furious Rivera? Or because he is so much like she?

The conversation beside her has strayed to the way the young girls are dressing this summer, flaunting themselves all over the streets, and the recent article Angela read about drugs and prostitution in city schools. There is nothing, it seems, that would surprise either her or Carla anymore.

"I blame television," says Carla, who does.

Angela blames what she calls rock-in-roll. "It's all the same," she says. "It's all sex and drugs," spitting the words from her mouth so that it is clear that she, personally, knows nothing about either.

Sophie knows that if she weren't sitting here now, with her hand stiff from holding the green plastic glass and her bottom numb from pressing against the nylon webbing of her chair and the gnats banging against her skin, Angela would now be talking about her. Angela would be saying, "Tommy? You think Tommy Delilo was something? Have you ever met any of my sister's sons?" the junkie, the bum, the queer, and the madman. And Sophie also knows that, in the final convolutions of Angela's analysis, three of them would be vindicated, wild in their youths but all right now, not so bad, really. For Frankie was never really a junkie, Gene was never really a bum, and Julio is really very artistic. For Frankie has a nice little business and a pretty young wife and delightful twin sons, and Gene has been everywhere, seen everything, brought back souvenirs from all over the place, remembers everybody at Christmas, and is solemnly Catholic, and Julio is, after all, some sort of a monk, which must mean something. Their crimes are all familiar and circumstantial, their sins are all acceptable, they may be eccentric but they are all three still normal enough, or normal enough for this day and age. Three of them would win Angela's grudging acceptance—but one of them would not.

Sophie can picture him now as he was before, can almost see him, short and fat and frowning, shuffling up the block in his blue jeans and his green baseball cap, a comic book stuck in his back pocket and a bottle of coke in his hand, whistling some song to himself and thinking about ... Thinking about what? The Yankees' doubleheader? Becoming a lonesome cowboy? Naked women? What Father O'Gormon would tell Angie when he found out who let the frogs loose? Up this same street she can see him come, always alone, his eyes moving warily from side to side as he walks but his mind clicking away on other things, his body tense as though waiting, just waiting, for an insult or a rock to be hurled in his direction. And he is the same now as he was then—unlike his brothers and unlike his fathers and unlike herself—unable to settle or smoothly compromise, doomed to discontent. And so is it true that Sophie knew then what she only seems to realize all these years later in the shade of the Sormanis' two-family house, with the dying light so full of ghosts and the air so full of the sounds of other people's lives, knows that Angela, as wrong as she has always been, was right: he doesn't fit. Not then; not now. More powerful than a gypsy curse or the contemptuous gift of a bad fairy, more lethal than a dose of thalidomide in the third month of preganancy or a heavy fall on a still-soft skull is Tony's affliction. First fruit of her wild womb and restless heart, he was formed, was born, simply incomplete. Incomplete, with his arms filled with brightly colored eggs and no basket in which to put them. Incomplete, with his head full of ideas and no safe place in which to let them loose. Incomplete, with a name and an ancestry and a family and an address, but no home. Better to be born without an arm, or a leg, thinks Sophie, her eyes still on a child no longer there. Better to be born without a thought in your head or a light in your soul.

"Isn't that true?" asks Angie, in a voice to shatter Plexiglas.

Sophie swings her head quickly, as though unaware that she wasn't alone. "Isn't that true?"

"Isn't it true that my Robert was always very sensitive, even as a little boy?" Robert is an advertising copywriter, famous for such lines as "You can only do without it if you've never had it." "He was never like the others. He was always so serious."

If Tony were here right now, he would catch Sophie's eyes as he said, "Oh, yeah, Robert's serious all right." But he is not here, he is somewhere else, somewhere that his mother is trying to imagine, somewhere that she almost feels—for an instant—she can understand. So she says it for him. "Oh, yeah," says Sophie, heaving her purse on to her lap, it's time to go. "Robert was never like the others." And adds as she helps the frail Angela to her slightly swollen feet, "But I don't suppose that López Rega was either."

Meredith is full of plans. Soon the leaves will turn and dry and fall against the pavement, just something else to be swept away, and the island inhabitants will batten their hatches and turn up their thermostats as another year curls up to die. Soon the season's canning will be done and shelved, the peas and corn and tomatoes and peaches and jars of jam, all labeled and stuck in a cupboard for those months when nothing grows, the knitting will be brought out from the hall closet and the boots will be lined up on newspaper by the back door. Soon even the creatures in this twenty-four-hour-a-day city will hibernate, double-locked and chained behind their reinforced doors, their feet in woolly slippers and ther bodies in shapeless old sweaters; huddled in dark doorways, their feet in old newspapers and their bodies in older pains. It is time for the last picnic, the last swim, the last idyllic weekend, the last sweet summer kiss. But for Meredith everything is about to begin.

"I mean it," says Meredith. "Things are going to be different from now on," and brushes away a curious insect. If the thought intrudes that she has said all this before, she brushes that aside, too.

They are sitting on Will's old plaid baby blanket. The supper things have been packed away, the light has almost seeped right through the sky, and there is only an inch or two of wine left in the dark green bottle. Will himself is a small blue and white figure further down the walk, shaky on his skates. "That's great," says Maggie, tempted to add, as either of their mothers might, "After all, you're not getting any younger," but doesn't have the energy. Jokes are wasted on Meredith. Jokes and irony and evenings like this, the earth so strong and the sky so fragile, the city itself shimmering insubstantially as though no more than a trick of the light or the brain, so inconsequential that the land itself is revealed in all its timelessness and tellurian beauty.

"I've come to realize one or two things this summer," Meredith is saying. "I'm not going to kid myself on anymore."

Maggie brushes the grass at her side with her hand as though stroking something precious. Maggie feels as though she is likely to cry, and moves her cup to her lips.

Meredith pours the last of the wine with an air of assured determination. "It's time I did something with my life." Like what? Mail it to someone else? Meredith's body moves closer with earnestness. "Like you are." Maggie meets her eyes and smiles a smile that could be mistaken for encouragement or even sympathy. "I mean, look at me. Just look at me," wails Meredith, her hands slapping against her thighs. "I'm nearly thirty-five years old, and what have I got to show for it? What do I have for thirty-five years?"

Maggie turns her head toward where the small blue and white figure now sits on a bench, kicking off his skates, but there is nothing, really, to say.

"Well," she answers at last, realizing that the question was not wholly rhetorical. "You make your own way, don't you? You live your own life." A light blinks on and off in Jersey. "What else do you want?"

Meredith takes an audible breath. "Clive says that it's a crime that a woman of my brains and ability should have to live from hand to mouth the way I do. That I should have to deprive myself of so much." Clive is Meredith's new boyfriend. He used to be a history teacher, but now he's a serious playwright, well considered in some circles, though not all that many. Meredith now carries with her a photocopy of a piece that appeared on Clive in the *New York Times*, half a page with a picture, "Look Forward in Anger." "He says it's because no one's ever really encouraged me before."

Maggie looks at Meredith, to see if this might be a joke, but it isn't. "Oh."

"Clive says that as soon as his new play is produced, he'll have enough money so I'll be able to take it easy for a while. You know, concentrate on what I really want."

"And what is that?" asks Maggie, her eyes on the glinting water and her voice from far away.

Somewhere in the distance a steel band is playing. The trees rustling in a random breeze seem almost to be dancing.

"I'm going back to school." Meredith picks up her sweater from the corner of the blanket and puts it on, turning as she does so to wave in Will's direction, yoohoo come on back. "I'm going to finish my degree. I've always really wanted to be a teacher. You know that."

Once Meredith always wanted to open her own shop, and before that Meredith always wanted to do a course in massage therapy, and before that Meredith always wanted to be a wife and mother, and before that Meredith wanted to see the world, and before that ... Maggie turns her head to look at Meredith, and nods, oh, yes, she knows.

"It's seeing you getting your life together that's done it," Meredith says, staring her square in the eyes. That and Clive. And once there was a man named Peter who looked at Meredith's round, opulent, and maternal body and saw a good cook, and immediately after that saw the small, home-style restaurant, pine tables, and diner tableware, that she must always have yearned to own. And once there was a man named Dave who always wore a gold ID bracelet and a three-piece suit (linen in the summer) who believed that job satisfaction was directly proprotional to the salary earned, who, entranced by the perfect alphabetization of Meredith's books, got her to invest one hundred dollars on an introductory computer programming course, more opportunities than the Gold Rush. And, too, there was another man, a man named Stewart, who, inspired by the chaos of Meredith's housekeeping and the frantic stories about her even more frantic mother, insisted on taking Will for a whole weekend while Meredith spent the money meant for a new sofa on a psychotherapeutic weekend on Long Island, meals included. And a man namd Fred, a man named José, a man named Bill, a man named Bob; a job with a mysterious travel company, a children's book and a cookbook, night courses in photography, macrobiotics and the *I Ching*. "Clive says that my problem is I've always been running away from things, you know? I was terrified of turning out like my mother, and at the same time terrified of taking responsibility for my own life. It's a problem a lot of people suffer from."

"And what is it Clive writes?" asks Maggie, her fingers in what's left of her hair.

"Plays."

Maggie presses her breasts against her thighs and hugs her knees. "Not musical comedies?"

Meredith's mother would have sighed like a vacuum cleaner suddenly snapped off, but Meredith snorts. "I don't know what's wrong with you tonight, Maggie," she snaps, more hurt than angry. "You've been bitchy since we met you."

And that is true, or nearly true. Certainly, Maggie has countered Meredith's new mood of enthusiasm and positive thinking with her own old mood of pessimism and doubt. No joyous exclamations, no girlish glee, no warm expressions of support and empathy, I'm so happy for you, it's about time you got what you deserve. "I'm sorry," says Maggie, though far from contrite, "I don't know what's wrong with me tonight."

"Neither do I," and Meredith gets to her feet, flapping her arms at the short, dark shape still yards away. "Will!" she shouts, catching the attention of a couple of dogs. "Will! Come on!" It is impossible to tell if he can see or hear her. "Goddamn that kid," says Meredith. "Why won't he ever do what I tell him?"

Maggie rests her chin on her hands. All day, for days now, she has been feeling nothing. Not a thing. Since the morning Skip woke alone in her bed with one hell of a hangover, calling, "Maggie? Maggie? Where are you, Maggie?" the nerves to her heart have been severed. Severed or frozen. Frozen or simply no longer there. Or, perhaps, it is just since then that she's noticed.

"Maggie?" he called. "Maggie? Are you there?" And she had glided in to the room overloaded with sunshine, still dressed for a party, a pot of coffee and two cups in her hands. "How's your head?" And she brought him juice and toast, and, later, let him pull her into the bed beside him, his dry lips against her warm breasts, her dry lips against his normal hair. And did it all not as a sacrifice but as a gesture, a gesture that had become its own meaning.

It was as they lay, half-dozing, his arms around her, his profile haloed by his pillow, that he told her about his summer. Not about the house or the garden or the spacious accommodations of his new office or the hand-painted tiles for the patio, but about Sandy. Who said there isn't magic in the country air? Who said the human male isn't hunted? Who said an ordinary man might not stumble occasionally? And who said that a man who is uninteresting to one woman is necessarily uninteresting to another? Maggie didn't say anything. How much did she believe him? She lay still against the plane of his body while he talked about his susceptibility (but you seemed so far away), his vulnerability (beginning with his mother, he has always been a sucker for strong women), his innocence (it was nothing he'd planned), his insecurity (what if Maggie had changed her mind?), and his guilt (you have no idea how it was, the hell I've been through). She lay with her body so white against the brown of the sheets. Moments can break; moments can splinter from the body of time and orbit forever within a mind. She will always feel his fingers on her shoulder and hear his voice like a wave breaking against the cliffs of the coast, it doesn't make any difference, that's why I told you, it has nothing to do with us. And so it doesn't. What has it to do with her? With ineffable tenderness, he made love to her again, as though, by memorizing every inch of her body, by setting his heart to the beating of hers, by speaking to her only with his flesh and the rhythms of his blood, he might erase all the damage done by words and their consequential deeds, must make them real once more, must give them, together, personal immortality, he and she and we.

But even as her own body rose to claim him, even as he took her with his own surrender, she felt as she felt when Ben was murdered, as she has felt, it seems, forever—she felt nothing. Though the sensations were sweet, though her body, unheedful of her heart, touched every touch of his, though her mind was quiet inside his sounds, deep within her, there where there is no depth or substance, no shape or form, there were there could be, should be, some joy, some fire, there was there nothing.

Maggie, who did not hear Meredith's sigh or mumbled, "Christ, I guess I'll have to get him," looks up to see Meredith another stranger in the distance. Has she hurt her feelings, too?

Nothing has changed. Meredith, walking toward her now, pulling Will behind her with one arm, waves. Later, when Maggie has settled down at the sewing machine with the first fall order of personalized sweatshirts, Skip will call to tell her that he loves her and what he had for supper, to remind her that he will soon be back to finish tying up all the loose ends, to make sure that she has not changed her mind. Nothing's been lost or fatally damaged. Things are as they were. Nothing has happened that cannot be understood, forgiven, or forgotten. Where would the world be without those three possiblities? Teetering on the crumbling brink of disaster. Where would the world be without the option of compromise? Split into separate cells of sadness and suffering. Any politician will tell you: yesterday's enemy may be tomorrow's ally. Any mother worth her crocheted ducklings for the church's October Fair will tell you: life goes on. And so it should.

There is nothing that the passage of time cannot erase. No passion and no love. No crime, no evil, and no sin whose damage cannot be repaired or obscured, whose wrong cannot be balanced with years. The Romans have been forgiven. The Dutch have been forgiven. The Chinese, the Turkish, the Greeks, and the Corinthians have all been forgiven. The Vikings, the Spanish, the Anglo-Saxons, and the Incas have all been forgiven, too. The English have almost been forgiven. Richard Nixon has been forgiven. Soon, even the Nazis will be forgiven, it's okay, Adolf, we understand.

The drums have stopped playing. Maggie, standing then stooping, gathers their paraphernalia in the blanket, and lifts it like a hobo's sack over her shoulder.

Somewhere in her—there, where there should be joy and should be fire—something says that it is not right that things can just go on. That it is not right that things can be forgotten, that anything may be forgiven. Is everything nothing but a means? Is every step so new? Somewhere in her, where neither heart nor brain can interfere, some thing makes a sound as delicate as the sound made by the rubbing together of an insect's wings, nonono.

It is not the betrayal by others that is important, that is lethal. It is not the defection nor the lies of someone else which pose such threats.

She strides through the landscape of shadows, the empty

wine bottle in her arms. She stops when she reaches Meredith and Will, to distribute the belongings between yours and mine.

As they are straggling out of the park, Will behind them singing what seems to be a song about angels, Maggie says to Meredith, staring straight ahead for any sign of obstacles, "I'm sorry if I've been giving you a hard time."

Meredith makes a face. "Oh, that's okay. We all get moods."

"It must be the moon."

Meredith raises her eyes to the skies. "But there is no moon," she says, as the clouds go skudding by.

They sit in their lawn lounge chairs like space travelers, bodies still but expectant, eyes fixed on the all-enveloping sky, minds fixed on their separate thoughts as they hurl through the cosmos, just as though they are all alone in the universe, far from home and maybe lost, doomed to orbit through eternity for eternity, another nick in the indifferent night. A passing god or alien might well wonder what dreams of home, what fragile memories of love or loss lie behind those still but opened eyes, what wonderings on life and death and time quicken the blood of the hand that rests on the arm of a chair or across a lap as they spin through space.

Sandy is thinking about her new job and the new possibilities it will open in her life. Jack is thinking about the new waitress in the quasi-Japanese restaurant in town and how he'd like to paint her with that here's-a-good-tipper look in her eyes. Edith is brooding about the friends they went to for dinner the night before, the potatoes underdone and the meat overdone, the shower rod looped with underwear and stockings, the living room mined with children's toys, oh, I'm sorry, just throw it anywhere. Skip, who has been worrying about an appropriate present for his youngest daughter's birthday, marked three weeks in advance in his pocket diary to allow time for mailing, is now wondering if he can persuade Maggie to select it for him, women really are better at that sort of thing.

"Well," says Jack, breaking the uncommunal silence. "It'll be winter soon."

"You'd have thought," says Edith, as though Jack's voice were the hypnotist's snapping fingers, "that she could at least have cleared out the living room." She looks at Skip as though explaining. "I never let Sandra leave her things all over like that."

Skip doesn't know what she is talking about. "Yeah," he sighs. "The summer sure goes fast."

"Um," says Jack, already imagining the roads impassable, the trees like skeletons, sparkling in the pure winter light.

"Um," says Edith, thinking that she would never let her children run around half-naked till all hours of the night, and nor would anyone else with any sense.

"I'm looking forward to the fall," says Sandy and raises her head as though already able to sniff the first scent of burning leaves.

Jack, edgy at the thought of all that cold solitude—those short, transclucent days and long hollow nights with no one to talk to but Edith and her less-than-perfect friends, with little more to which to look forward than a couple of self-indulgent holidays and the week in February which Edith always spends with her sister in Miami—is not looking forward to it at all. Nor is Edith, who has enough trouble keeping the world in order when the weather is good, the roads are clear and dry, and everyone is out and about and available for surveillance—if it weren't for her yearly visit to her sister she would probably go mad, cooped up for all those stagnant months with a man who either doesn't talk at all or talks too much.

"Me, too," says Skip, who already has the chestnuts roasting on the open fire. "I'm really looking forward to our first winter up here," and rubs his hands together as though stirring them against the cold.

"Oh, but the autumn," says Edith. "Wait'll you see the trees. I've never known anyone who wasn't amazed by them. Isn't that true, Jack? Aren't the colors just breathtaking?"

"Yeah," says Jack from the depths of his drink. "Breathtaking."

Sandy stretches languidly, a mermaid on a rock. "The summer always makes me feel so lazy," she almost drawls. "It'll be good to get back into things again," and, surprising herself, thinks immediately of Tony, hopping nude through the hallway with a pair of socks over his hands and his hands up around his ears, "Yoo hoo, Sandy, have you seen any runaway kangaroos?"

Both her mother and her father smile at her affectionately,

Skip sighs in agreement. All of them will be glad to see Sandy get back into things.

All in all, though, it's been a good summer, really. A little fraught at times, yes. A little tricky to maneuver in once or twice, that's true. But everything is all right now. Jack and Edith, refreshed by the relief of having someone other than each other to annoy them for the summer, are feeling quite friendly toward one another right now, were even heard giggling together in the shower the night before last. Now the ups-and-downs of the last two months seem far away. All is back to normal. Skip is still getting married, in December and in the Grossmans' living room, and has promised Jack a good deal on an upper plate, and Sandra is still going back to her husband and her home. It was, Edith decided last night, about three minutes before Jack was due to fall asleep, only one of those routine hiccups that beset a marriage from time to time, don't they still laugh about the time Jack was going to move to Santa Monica? "Remember," chuckled Edith, her eyes upon him even though his eyes were closed. "You even had your brother out looking for apartments for you. Remember?" how it seemed as though their lives would be irrevocably changed, how he had pictured himself, soaked in California sunlight, his canvases all marked by that blue that yellow that vibrant and sensual green, painting on a boardwalk with a black umbrella snapped to the back of his chair, how she had imagined herself, released from Jack's demands and needs, entertaining on the weekends all the people he would never allow in the house, how the world of each of them had suddenly seemed turned upside down. "Umber," muttered Jack. "That's all it was," said Edith, apparently unable to recall the raw and swollen texture of those months, the two of them facing each other each morning and night like duelists, waiting to see who would make the first move, waiting to see what that first move would bring. She clicked off the bedside lamp, made out of popsicle sticks by some Indians in New Mexico, and laid her head on her pillow. "Just one of those things." And soon fell asleep, Jack's back just touching hers, safe in her knowledge that all was, as always, all right with the world.

Suddenly in buoyant spirits, Jack jumps up and bustles into the house for another pitcher of Bloody Marys. "Edith!" he shouts as the screen door bangs behind him. "Have we got any pretzels?"

"In the bread bin," she shouts back, and smiles at Skip. "I don't know why he can't just look."

The evening hisses, rustles, crackles, and sighs around them. Skip looks up at the darkening sky, searching, perhaps, for that first lucky star, overcome with contentment. As Jack has said twice since supper, it is going to storm, but Skip wouldn't care if it hailed. Skip wouldn't care if it snowed, tiny icy flakes, each one perfect and each one different, swiftly and silently covering over the lawn furniture and the flower beds, the motorized grill and the bathing suits hanging on the patio rail. Let it snow. Lucky men—lucky men like he—don't give a damn about a little bad weather. For everything is all right again. Everything is just the same as ever it was or ever it was meant to be. Once more has he come close to the edge of the ledge overlooking his most unspeakable fears, and once more has he been hauled back to safety. It does not seem at all strange to Skip that nothing should have changed, that the world should have gone whoop whoosh like a roller coaster and now is just the same again. It does not seem inconsistent or infinitesimally disturbing that he should so casually (without any thought to cause, effect, or retribution) have jeopardized his unwild dreams. Or that, in the end, they were not jeopardized at all. Born to a species with only a partially developed concept of fair play, a species with an apparently hereditary belief in its own rightness, and an indefatigable devotion to getting things its own way, it is little wonder that Skip sees no reason to question himself. Sees no reason for wondering not merely why he shouldn't have what he wants, but why he shouldn't be entitled to everything and anything, without principle or sacrifice, without it ever costing him very much at all. He slurps at the melting ice cubes in the remains of his last drink, and crunches one between his strong, insensitive teeth. He has made a clean breast of things and has been forgiven. He has made an almost-clean breast of things and is willing to let it all be forgotten. And, in a way, things are better now than they were before. Maggie's love has been tested and not found wanting. Her real concern for him has been questioned and proved sure. Throughout history, great men (politicians, painters, statesmen, philosophers, poets, writers, even dentists) have all found comfort and inspiration in the indestructible devotion that only a woman (or two, or several) can give. Great men, and lesser men as well. His father always said, "If it wasn't for Sarah, I'd be nobody," at which recognition Sarah would smile like a queen accepting a compliment from the ambassador of some tiny Third World country. Though it wasn't, of course, exactly strictly true, the point was not lost on any of them: he needed her. Even Jack said the other day—while they were making some tentative plans for a little hunting while Edith is off to the swaying palms and speculative land prices of Florida—"It'll be good to have someone to pal around with. It's funny how lonely it gets here at night." Jack might have been thinking about the annoyance of having to get his own meals and his own coffee, or the luxury of having a live model provocatively posed on the red kitchen chair in his studio without the knowledge that he is under constant surveillance, but Skip knew he knew what Jack meant. That's what Skip wants, that permanence. Yes, all is truly well: Maggie loves him, no matter what, and Sandy is his friend. He turns to her now and smiles.

And she smiles back.

"And you don't think he's having trouble finding the pretzels, do you?" asks Edith, so suddenly that they both jump.

"For heaven's sake, Mom," moans Sandra. "He's almost sixty years old. He can find the damn pretzels by himself." And then relents, her own mood so good, "Do you want me to go and see?"

"Oh, no," says Edith, already banging her thigh on the arm of her chair. "I'll go. Maybe he's having trouble with the ice." Last week he threw the old plastic trays into the barbecue, ranting about the ironies of a technology that can make it possible for men to walk on the moon but not to get their ice cubes out of the tray.

"They're a great couple," says Skip as they watch her bustle away.

"Yes," says Sandy, pleased that she once more feels it to be true. Yesterday morning there was a postcard from Tony, a photograph of John Lennon wearing a New York City T-shirt, the message printed on the back with studied neatness and precision: All lights repaired; Shelves up in study and bathroom; Wood chopped and corded; Larder full; Gingerale in coolerator. She has taken this to mean that he is awaiting her return, eagerly. She has taken this to mean that everyone's lessons have been learned: that he is going to start acting responsibly, and that there will be no more melodramatic madness, surely a man who has been fixing lights and screwing up shelves is not worried about death. And Sandy herself? How is she feeling now, now that she has had her taste of freedom from Rivera, now that she has had enough of Nelson Ellis, D.D.S., to obliterate all memories of the passions and lustful dementia of last winter, her panic and her desperateness? How is she feeling, now that Rivera seems to want her again, now that the indiscretions of the summer seem no more important than a conversation with a stranger on a bus? She feels pretty good. Once more the future looms before her, as solid and as sure as it can be, undisturbed by her temporary abandonment. Jack and Edith emerge together from the light of the house, a fantastical, two-headed, four-armed creature, bearing not jewels nor maps nor coveted trophies but bowls of pretzels and corn chips and a sweating pitcher of drink. Sandy makes a mental note to include a dinner invitation to them in her agenda for September.

"Well, here we are at last," cries Edith. "No. Don't put it on that table, Jack. You know it's unstable."

"Why are you two so quiet?" asks Jack, slapping the pitcher down on the table. "Listening to hear where the rain's coming from?"

Skip helps himself to a handful of chips. "Just enjoying the peace and quiet," smiling as though it is somehow his doing. "Maggie's going to love it up here."

Sandy holds out her glass for a refill. "And I'm going to miss it. But I couldn't live here all the time. After all," she says, turning her eyes toward Edith who is busily waving the gnats away from the avocado dip, "the city needs me."

"It's so muggy," lifting the brown paper bag into his arms. "I thought you might like a beer. Compliments of Larry Parker."

"How did you know where I lived?"

"I remembered from the other night."

"Damn this lock. The only thing that won't open it is the key," jiggling it up and down, down and up. "How long have you been standing there like you're waiting to make a contact?"

"Not long. I couldn't take five more minutes of where I was. So, as I was nearby . . ."

"That was lucky."

The mingled aromas of pot and piss in the elevator, shadows of graffiti on the walls of the hall, someone running up the stairs.

"Do you get paid to live here?"

"I lost a dare."

"You must be glad you'll be getting away from here soon. Up to the tranquillity of the arts-and-crafts belt."

"Oh, I don't know. I've sort of gotten used to the sounds of people bashing each other's heads in late at night."

A paper lampshade, a watercolor of a beach, a charcoal sketch of a huddled man, a clutch of pillows that look like clouds, a black cat with a bent left ear.

"You're not busy, or anything are you? Packing or something?" looking around. "It looks like you're almost ready to move out."

"No. I just never really moved in," throwing her things on a chair. "Here. Give me that. I'll put it in the fridge."

"Who did the pictures?"

"I did."

"You better not let Jack see them. He can't stand any competition. It makes him bad tempered. Edith once took a photograph of a rabbit in the garden and he wouldn't speak to her for a week."

"Maybe he wouldn't like them."

"Oh, he wouldn't like them. But that wouldn't stop him from behaving badly. Jack's one of those people who are never less generous than when they're sure they're in the right," picking up a carved brass bell. "Which is always," making it ring. "Where'd you get this bell?"

"In India. Do you want a glass?"

"Yeah, sure. Do you mind if I put on a record?"

"No. Help yourself. You want something to eat?"

A candle stuck in an old Chianti bottle (whooeee, you don't see many of those around any more), a cheese sandwich, a couple of beers, a few albums spilling sound, the trick the cat does when its stomach is tickled, the story of his first brush with the law (Sophie being called down by the cops because Tony had tried to sneak a girlie magazine from the candy store on the corner, I'd rather be the mother of a boy who stole one of these than the mother of a man who sold them), the story of hers (Kate making her kneel down in the kitchen every night for the next year, praying for Jesus to make Maggie just like her cousin Joan), a stillness in the distance, did she know that he used to be a crack cyclist?

"Carlos wasn't so bad, really. He was just a little crazy, that's all. He thought everybody else was just like him. I've never known whether Sophie left him because she loved him or because she hated him."

"Maybe it was a little of each."

"When she got the letter saying he was dead, she read it off to me like it was a shopping list. 'Está muerto,' she said. 'Loco y muerto.' That's all, loco y muerto."

"One time my mother took me to visit my father's uncle, old man Macauley, in this home in Brooklyn. My father sat in the car. We went down this awful blue corridor, and into this big green room, filled with beds. And in every bed was a little white man in white pajamas. Most of them could barely sit up. And I could only just remember seeing old man Macauley before. My father couldn't stand him. My mother said that it was unchristian to dislike someone when they were weak. So my mother had to do the visiting. And this one time, she took me along. Even though I wanted to stay in the car. She said that old people liked to see children. And there were all these old men in these beds, and they all looked alike. I couldn't figure out how she knew which bed to go to. She kept chatting away, and he just kept lying there, looking at her like he wasn't really sure who she was. And then, just when she started to get ready to go, he suddenly grabbed hold of her hand and started begging her to let him die, tell them I want to die, tell them I want to die."

"What did your mother do?"

"She told him not to talk like that in front of me. And then she dragged me around to every other bed, to say hello to everyone. And when we were ready to go Uncle Bob was asleep. He looked like he was dead."

"Have you ever been to Rio?"

The night shrinking, the night muffled, the cat falling asleep with its head on a cloud, the guitar brought out, the guitar and half a bottle of mescal, some drawings and a paper and comb, she did know the tune to "There Once Was a Union Maid," didn't she?

"This was when he'd just turned five."

"I like the Mother's Day cards," flattening down a piece of paper lace. "Why don't you have an ashtray or a plaster handprint?"

"I threw them away."

"Ah ... Maybe you shouldn't have done that."

"Oh, I didn't want to keep a lot around. I was traveling so much."

"Yeah. You were probably right."

The elevator grinding up its shaft, the candle melted into the neck of the bottle, sunlight beginning to squeeze past the buildings, a voice from a radio plegmatically announcing the disasters of the night, a song he'd loved and she'd loathed in the sixties playing softly on the stereo, and a hand almost touching a hand.

"Listen to this guitar solo coming up. It's fantastic."

"I don't care if he can play the guitar. It's the song I don't like. It's too sentimental."

"It's not sentimental. It has sentiment. What's wrong with that?"

"Listen to that! Isn't that lovely?"

"It's okay. But it's still sentimental. I bet you cried the first time you saw *Day of the Dolphin.*"

"Sentimentality? What sentimentality? It may be a little romantic, maybe, but that doesn't quite rank as a crime. For Christ's sake, where would the world be without romantics?"

"I don't know, either."

"Should I go?"

A kiss, a touch, an awakening of all senses, a kiss, a look, a caress, the possibility of ecstasy, of joy, of knowledge, redemption songs.

TEN

It is not impossible to argue that life is but a series of repetitions. The same motions and the same routines. The same rituals and the same patterns. Air in, air out. Word in, words out. Up the stairs and down once more. Like housewives, washing and scrubbing and cooking and ironing only to wash and scrub and cook and iron again, we bustle through the same days, our heads filled with times and dates, our hands busy at familiar tasks, over and over and over again. Like assembly-line workers, taking the same route to work each morning, always a paper under the arm and always a lunch pail in the hand, along the same corridors and over to the same bench, fingers nimble and minds occupied, clipcloppsstclipcloppsstclipcloppsst, we slouch through our days, each one pretty much like the last.

Just so, once again, he sits on Sophie's sofa, Zorro beside him, bathed in the numinous light of the television screen, the sound turned completely down, the only noises in the room their quiet breathing, an occasional whimper from the dog, an occasional sigh from the man.

"What's wrong with the sound?" asks Sophie, coming into the room like an apparition, her body covered by an improbably colored floral mumu and her hair wrapped up in an old yellow towel. She smells as unlikely as she looks, jasmine, talcum, coconut, and garlic. "And get that dog off the couch. I didn't spend all that money on covers for him."

"Come on, old pal," says Tony, pulling him off by his collar. "You know you're not allowed up on the furniture."

"And what's wrong with the sound?" striding over and banging the side of the set.

Zorro jumps back into his place.

"Nothing's wrong with the sound. It's not turned up."

She moves her eyes off of him for a minute, and onto the faintly flickering screen where a man and woman are pantomiming what is clearly a scene of intense emotion—his hand gripped around her waist, his mouth and eyes looking sculpted, her body pulling away from his but somehow yielding. They might be lovers, husband and wife, assassin and victim, or business partners. They could be arguing about his obsession with gambling, her inability to understand him, her past, or his resolution to take his story to the papers and blow the whole thing sky high. They might even be dancing or about to make love. "I'll be in the kitchen," says Sophie, when in doubt, cook. "In case you're interested in hearing a voice that isn't your own."

But he isn't staying long. He only stopped by because Zorro needed a rest and a drink of water and it was getting near dawn. He only stopped by because they were taking this walk ("Over a hundred blocks?" asked Sophie. "You walked the dog over a hundred blocks?" What was he planning to do, walk to Cuba? "Are you nuts? What are you trying to do? Kill the two of you?" Man walks self and pet to death. "He didn't have a good long walk all summer," explained Tony, though the summer is now just another memory. "He needed the exercise."), and they'd gone further than he'd planned, and Zorro refused to go another step without a break. Which is almost the truth—or part of it. The true part is that he told Sandy he was taking the dog for a walk; the untold part is that he's been out all night looking for Richard. López swears that Richard told him he was going south for the winter, but Vega, whose network of informants spreads the widest, and who, though he might, like López, lie to a friend, would never bother to lie to an enemy, says he heard Richard was dead, stabbed in some scuffle over by the docks. Or something like that. Or something like what?

Sophie stalks off to the kitchen, slamming the glass-paneled door behind her, suddenly missing her own mother so much that she can not only see her—less as a memory than as a vision— young and in sunlight, but can smell her as she was just before she died, a bag of herbs around her neck and a tumor in her throat. Without pause, she heads for the cupboard, pulls out a pot and a pan and bangs them onto the stove, slams the cutting board onto the counter, and starts looking around for a knife.

In the living room, Zorro rests his grizzled little chin on Tony's knee.

They have been all over, to every place he could think of and several they simply found. Down the mean streets, and up the meaner avenues. Into all the darker corners of the city, where he no longer has any reason to go, surprised that he was still remembered, didn't come out with a knife in his back. His feet are killing him. His feet and his mind. Not a trace. Yeah, I know who you mean, big guy, right? Nah, I ain't seen him around for a while. What about the cops? or the loony bin? or the hotels? But he's tried them all, he still has contacts of his own. Not a clue. It is weeks that he's been gone this time. Tony passes by the living-room window at least a dozen times a night, just looking out.

The kitchen is steaming, sizzling, and simmering when he enters. Sophie, with her back to the door, is stirring something in the old iron pot. Wolf hairs? Mare's teeth? Lapwing nests? The blood of an ass, the blood of a wolf, and three sweet gums? Is she boiling up the future, or boiling down the past? Is there anything that she can mix or move, anything that she can whisper or wail, which will secure him his universe—which will save him?

"Wait till you see what we've done to the apartment," he says.

Sophie puts the lid on the oatmeal, slaps the spoon against a ceramic frog whose stomach says Lay on Me. It's not hard to guess who gave her that. "Oh," she says, turning to the slicing of bread. "Now I see. You got me up at four in the morning so you could tell me about your new living-room suite."

"We want you to come over and see it. Sandy's dying to show it off."

The kitchen has been repainted, the stove and refrigerator

gleaming smudgeless and spill-less against its unsubduable yellow glow. The kitchen has been repainted, the living room has had new curtains and its furniture rearranged, the bathroom is in the grim process of customization, soon to be a pastel cavern with a stall shower-bath combination, louvred cupboards and a wooden toilet seat. Most of the things they'd been using just for the time being, until they got something better (the old Indian spread, the parrot shower curtain from Sophie, "I know how much you like the tropics," the lampshade in the hall, stolen by him and Julio one night when they were lost in the Bronx, the art deco table he and Sandy found on the street, painted Chinese Red, and carried home thirty-two blocks in what in Miami would have been a hurricane, all those things and more, all the things he liked best), have been replaced, after all this time, by the things for which, as it turns out, they really were only standing in. New shades, new wastebaskets, new rugs, new bedspread, new toothbrush holder, even new dishes to replace the ones Gene gave them as a wedding present, leftover Green Stamp stock. He will never see those blurred pine cones again. He will never again lie on that spread with its pattern of phallic symbols, remembering the times he and Sandy had lain there in the past, drinking Cuba Libres, eating pepperoni, and reweaving the very fabric of Western society. No more will he bang his head against that lampshade, hung too low and always to be adjusted, soon, and resee Julio vomiting into the tracks of the El, just leave me here to die. They have all been whisked into what looked to him like cadaver bags, and dragged down to the bins in the basement so that Vega and his band of unhappy thieves can go through it before it becomes fair game on the streets. So that they can see what's worth selling, or what they can give to their women as gifts, don't I always get you something nice? If he catches any one of them wearing one of his old hats (you don't really intend to wear any of these again, do you?) he'll murder the son-of-a-bitch. All those things, so valueless in themselves, as Sandy pointed out, have been hustled from the house and in their stead are all new things, costing only money, that fit into the rooms like the pieces in a preschooler's puzzle, C-A-T, D-A-D, M-O-M, B-O-Y, T-A-B-L-E, C-U-R-T-A-I-N, C-O-N-T-I-N-E-N-T-A-L Q-U-I-L-T. As though it had been those old things, carelessly accumulated and carelessly kept, that had held them back, held them apart.

"Why don't you make us some coffee?" says Sophie, now beating five eggs. "I'm fixin' us an omelette."

Obedient son, he does as he is told, filling the old aluminum pot with water and its old aluminum basket with grounds. "I'm not really hungry, Sophie."

She can look at him with only one eye. "It's not a big omelette."

He gets the cups down from the hooks under the cupboard, holding them against his heart for a second like sacred stones.

Mrs. Burkowsky moved out this morning, helped into a beige station wagon that had been to Disney World by her two eldest sons, two cardboard boxes containing all the things she will have room for in the new old-folks' home on Long Island packed into the back. The sons, middle-aged men in slacks and Banlon shirts and fixed cheerfulness, wanted to help her down the stoop, but she wordlessly shook them away with her cane, motioning for Tony's arm. Mrs. Burkowsky has refused to speak to anyone for the past three weeks, ever since the date was set for her evacuation. Sandy says that the staff at the home will know how to deal with Mrs. Burkowsky's attitude. Under the anxious gaze of the sons, It's-For-The-Best and An-Old-Woman-Can't-Live-By-Herself, he helped her safely, if slowly, to the pavement. And kissed her ancient lips, you take care of yourself now, *abuela*, don't do too much dancing. And she patted his hand and reached into her aged purse, holding her half-formed fist out to him as though she were sheltering something delicate or rare, not even saying I want you to have this. Then Vega came rushing up with a bunch of flowers, he at least had no hard feelings, and there was no chance to say thanks.

"So," says Sophie, slapping dishes down onto the table while he leans against the refrigerator with a carton of milk in his hands. He reminds her, posed there—his mouth locked in a smile that might go on forever, his body caught unmoving in a movement—of a cardboard cutout (Ronald Reagan, or Art Linkletter, or Betty Furness), happy among the appliances. He should have a bubble coming out of his mouth, "The name you can depend on for quality." "So what's been going on?"

"What?" In his pocket, still unopened, is Mrs. Burkowsky's grandmother's silver locket. He is afraid to look inside.

"Yeah," says Sophie, slopping porridge into Melmac bowls,

she may not believe in a lot of things but she believes in a nourishing breakfast. "What?"

His life is back to normal.

He has welcomed it back with open arms and an open checkbook. He has greeted it with open smiles and frank discussion. Just as he has taken it back before. Except, of course, that this time is different. There will be no more times. How could there be?

When he left the house last night, Sandy was in her better kitchen, giving Meredith advice about her life. "You should say to him," she was saying, "Clive, I am a person with needs and feelings, and I have a right to know where we stand." He couldn't hear what Meredith answered, but knew anyway. He was standing in the living room, near the window, the leash just fished out from the cushions of the armchair, safe behind the closed glass, staring down on the street. "Forget the cards," Sandy was saying. "It's what you want that matters. It has nothing to do with the cards." He could see López behind his counter, putting yet another quart of milk, can of soup, and loaf of bread into a bag, knowing the way López's apron strings were wrapped twice around his waist. He could see López pull the old black ledger from under the cash register and make a notation, taking the pen from the side of the machine under the card that says: Cash Today Credit Tomorrow—even though it was all a blur from that distance and he only saw it because he had seen it so often before. "Meredith," said Sandy, "Clive is just like anybody else. If you don't make him do things for his own good, he'll never do them." "I just know that this is it," said Meredith, her voice precariously rising above her own established level for conspiracy, unsteady with the force of her conviction. "I won't get another chance like this again." Another chance. And he'd snapped the leash onto Zorro's collar. Another chance. Everything happens but little ever changes. Given another chance, who does more than rearrange the furniture? Given another chance, who does more than replace the old with something new but not-so-different? What difference would it make to start all over—even in a new town or a new country, with a new name or a new persona, or a new person? What difference, indeed? Given another chance, who does more than recreate the past, everything looking different but remaining the same? Given another chance (as each of us is given) who does more than repeat what has already gone before? He has chosen where he is and what he has become—if he chose again—even if he picked a different job and a different woman—what would really change? The color of a room? The shape of a breast? The terminology of the days? The texture of the lies and misunderstandings? "Tony!" called Sandy. "We're going to open a bottle of wine, do you want some?" she speaks to him now in a voice that suggests they have withstood trial by fire and come through whole. "Not right now," he shouted back. "I'm just going to take the dog for his walk. I'll have some later." And maybe they have. They could only go on. "Well, don't be too long." Now, now he is his old self once more, funny again, working hard and always working but still clowning around. He no longer speaks of death. Is afraid of nothing except that the Republicans might win or the Amazon might disappear or the private grant might be cut. Now she listens when he complains about work or complains about the world, no longer sees any malignancy in it (how dangerous can a man be who is committed to buying his own apartment and showing unmistakable administrative flair?), everybody complains. Complains and rolls along. Complains and keeps on going. Complains and shoves the shoulder a little more firmly against the wheel. He negotiated for some sort of salvation, and now he has got it. She has done everything but make projection graphs for the next decade. It was he who told her, yes, come home. He who said, you're right, I'm wrong. Let's celebrate.

"Nothing," he says now.

"Nothing?" snaps Sophie—aware, as she shifts her body, of the age of her bones and her strong and much-used heart. She is no longer young. Spending those weeks with Angela, already middle-aged when a girl, has made her feel all her years, two old ladies still arguing about things that happened forty, fifty years before, only easy with one another when they were bumping around in the past. When Angela dies, and the ever-unique Robert has sold her house and gotten rid of all of her possessions that he didn't want or couldn't use, and there is yet another grave on which she will never put flowers, Sophie will have lost her last link with her self. What do her sons know about her? What does Tony, sitting there with his food uneaten and his hand around his cup of coffee, know about her? When

Angela is dead, all those years of their growing and ageing, all those moments still alive in the light in a room or in the laughter in a voice or in the delicacy of a touch, or in the mostly forgotten and unremarkable past, will be gone. All the things that Angela knows about Sophie—the things never noticed by Sophie, never seen by anyone else—will be as though they might never have happened at all. All gone (their parents and their parents' friends, the occasions and the fights, the dingy apartments and stained hotel rooms, the tantrums and the tears, that red silk dress from Hong Kong, that declaration of fear, that declaration of love, that declaration of despair), all of them gone—except what remains in her own mind and memory. When Angela dies, Sophie will be just another survivor on an empty sea. She wipes her lips on a paper napkin, noticing the getting-ready-to-leave look in Tony's eyes. But she has always believed that there is more than one sea for each of us. "Nothing?" repeats Sophie, making it sound like a threat. "Nothing? What do you think?" waving one hand in front of him. "What do you think? That I'm stupid? That I'm just your stupid old mother who doesn't know shit from Shinola?"

He opens his mouth as though he may speak.

"Nothing? First your wife leaves you and then you go underground. You pop up now and then like you was being hunted by hounds, and when you are home either you don't answer the phone or you pretend that you didn't. You spend the whole summer hanging out with bums in the street. And then, everything's back to normal, like the summer never happened. Your wife comes back, you've got a new suit and you're workin' eighteen hours a day again and worrying about getting a mortgage, and all you can say when I ask what's been going on is 'nothing'?" She leans over and rips the coffee pot from the center of the table. "If that's nothing," she says, banging the spout against the rim of her cup, "then I'd sure like to see what you call something." She doesn't so much pass him the pot as throw it to him.

He watches carefully as he pours himself more, carefully sets the pot back on its raffia mat. When the ritual is completed, they resume their previous postures, poised and facing, gunfighters.

She looks straight at him for several seconds. Searching her target? Checking her aim? Gauging his reactions? "Sometimes I wonder what it is you're frightened of," she says at last, in a voice he has heard before (though he can't remember when), in a voice as far away as the other times he has heard it.

Hay que soñar en voz alta, hay que cantar hasta que el canto eche raices, tronco, ramas, pajaros, astros . . .

He can still laugh. "Frightened?" says Tony. "I'm not frightened. I was just a little depressed." As she fails to alter her expression, he smiles even harder, taking a jaunty sip of his coffee. "That's all. Depression." It sounds so reasonable, he can believe it himself, that's all, just a case of the blues.

Yo sueño con los ojos abiertos, y de día y noche siempre sueño . . .

He is capable of dreams . . . of ecstasy. He can know joy. He can save himself . . . can try.

"Depressed?" hoots Sophie, thrusting herself toward him, the towel on her head slipping slightly, the spoon in her hand gently dripping. "Everybody's depressed. Even the Pope gets depressed. Even Jackie Onassis gets depressed." She leans one elbow on the table, points the spoon at his chest, looking, somehow, like a soldier posing for the cover of *Life*, a plump soldier in a mumu and a yellow turban, Will This Be the Shot Heard Round the World? "Your brother gets depressed every time he bets on the wrong horse."

He hasn't seen Maggie since. Even though he stood in the doorway, his shoulders determining the breadth of his exit, and said, "You'll see me again, you know," this isn't just a one-night stand, I'm not just using you. Even though he was reluctant to leave, to step back through the door and into a world where nothing had happened, knowing whose fault that would be. "I'll call you," he said, so good at lies.

He looks Sophie right back in her dark, determined eyes. "It's not the same thing."

"Bullshit," and drops the spoon into her empty bowl with a clink. "Anybody who doesn't get depressed is out of their minds in the first place. It's the fear that makes it different." And continues to stare into his dark, disguising eyes, she who had never seemed to him to be afraid of anything.

"You mean like whether you're afraid of heights or of spiders?"

"No," says Sophie, leaning toward him as though she is about to grab him by the shoulders and shake some sense into him once and for all. "I mean like whether you're afraid of life or death." She straightens up, suddenly raising her cup to her lips. "What else is there?"

He shrugs his shoulders, how the hell am I supposed to know?

"People who are afraid of death," she says, beginning to stack the plates, "are always busy. Always making things." His plate on her plate, the forks and knives on one side. Bombs and millions and names for themselves. His bowl in her bowl, the spoons stuck into his oatmeal. Wars and plans. Test-tube babies and artificial foods. She piles them all onto the omelette platter. Asserting their importance in a universe whose very existence denies it, in a universe whose continued existence depends on their noninterference.

He waits for her to explain further, but she is busy waddling toward the sink with the air of a woman who believes that, after forty years, some things should be understood.

"And people who are afraid of life?" watching Sophie scrape his meal onto an old aluminum pie pan for Zorro, knowing he will never call her, can never see her again, would only be leading everybody on once again, even more. He has sworn off games.

"They don't do nothing," her voice so steady and her tone so sure. The men Sophie has loved were never afraid of life, and now they both are dead. And soon enough, she will be, too. "They don't do nothing or they just do what everybody else is doing." She begins running water into the sink. "Only they do it slower."

And are Sandy's dreams and feelings so insignificant that they should count for nothing?

In the silence following her words all that can be heard are the separate beating of their hearts and the echo of their voices rolling toward them from over the years.

His hand touches the locket in his pocket. He has never understood before how much it might be that Sophie has willfully lost, how much she may willingly have sacrificed, how enormous may have been her risks and failures, all so that she can be standing here now, her life going on but her dreams all behind her, washing dishes in front of a son who only visits when he can think of nowhere else to go.

"And what if you're not afraid of either?"

And she turns to face him, her hands dripping tears onto the floor. "And who is it we're talking about now?" she asks.

To Sandy, too, even as she sleeps, her hands bunched under her chin and her legs in the place where her husband's legs should be, life must be seeming a bit repetitive. She finally went to bed at midnight, not putting the chain on the door, not angry enough to stay awake. "I thought he was just taking the dog for a walk," said Meredith when the wine was finished and it was time for her to go. "He probably ran into someone he knows," said Sandy, it's a pretty big block. And Meredith shrugged, oh sure, each of them thinking fleetingly of Richard. She cleaned the glasses and wiped off the table. She read two chapters of a book on post-Darwinian theories of evolution and wrote a letter to her mother, I really think we've sorted everything out, I've never felt happier. She took a shower. She set her hair. She drank a cup of tea. And she has felt happier than she has in a long time, has begun to see in him some things new—new or previously obscured. When he throws himself into something he shines, and he has been throwing himself into everything since she returned (work and politics, redecorating and lovemaking), has been shining like a harvest moon for weeks. His energy has been boundless, his enthusiasm contagious. She has been seeing in him all the things she once thought she saw; has rediscovered things for which to love him. She was not angry—this time she was not so sure that he will be back. Even the repetitious is not certain. She is restless in her sleep, not quite sleeping in her dreams. There is an enormous white horse sitting in the middle of a garden, growing up among the flowers. She can see how the green leaves shine in the sun. She hears herself think that's Richard, no it's not, it's a big white horse. She is not quite awake when she hears the rain.

Nor would it be difficult to convince Maggie that life is but a series of replays.

Maggie has been packing again. Just as before (leaving home, leaving San Francisco, leaving Calcutta), heavy things at the bottom, breakables at the top, valuables into the hand luggage. She's gotten pretty good at it, over the years. She didn't have to think as she wrapped and folded, chose what to take and what to leave behind. She's gotten pretty good, over the years, at abandoning her lives.

But nothing can ever be the same.

This time she will take her dishes, glasses, and the second-hand bed. This time Ben's things, usually packed in among her clothes, tossed defiantly into the hands of baggage loaders and fate, you decide whether they're valuable or not, you take the responsibility for their safety or loss, have been put in with her passport and her vaccination record, her birth certificate and her bankbook, her collection of photographs.

This time she will alight neither in Athens in the dead of night, nor in a new hometown in the broadest daylight, her eyes searching the street for the family wagon she can call her own.

It is the middle of the night (or the middle of the morning, depending on how you count these things), but she cannot sleep. She makes her way past the boxes and into the small kitchen, smaller now that it is empty, and boils some water in an old aluminum pan, pours it over a tea bag in a cup without a handle. The coffee pot and three good mugs are in the box marked KIT. "Well," she says to the grimy window, the bulging walls, and the cockroach scuttling along the back of the sink. "I guess this is it." Good-bye old apartment, good-bye old kitchen, good-bye old alley. Farewell old bedroom, farewell old bathtub, farewell old neighbors lurking warily behind your doors. *Adíos* Manhattan and hello Brooklyn.

Behind her already are all the months spent here, all the days and nights of anger and frustration, her mind blind with schemes. Behind her all the days and nights of inflated hopes and manufactured dreams. She has said so long to all that, as well.

Gingerly, Maggie picks up the cup with two fingers and walks back into the living room, still filled with her but waiting for someone else. The cat sits on top of the sewing machine case, his front paws tucked under his body and suspicion in his eyes. Around his neck is a new green collar from which dangles a silver disk containing his new name and his new address, in case he escapes from the van and winds up lost in SoHo. "Well, Cat," says Maggie. "You all set?"

They leave in very few hours. At nine-thirty the utilities will be disconnected; at ten-thirty the mover will arrive. All night they, she and Cat, have sat here among the boxes, like orphans left sitting among the luggage at Pennsylvania Station, name tags pinned to their good coats, but still forgotten, wondering what this all will someday mean. But they have sat here alone. Before, when she was traveling, Ben was always with her, tailing behind and demanding attention, demanding inclusion. Before, when she returned, he was with her still, you should see how they changed the pizza parlor, you wouldn't like what they've done to that spaceship, the old man with the bulldog is gone. All these years he has tagged along—never changing, never aging, never going to go away.

But he is gone now.

She sits on the floor between boxes, and sips her tea.

Ben is dead. Ben is dead, and there is nothing that will ever make that not so. Ben is dead and all that remains of him lies protected by plastic at the top of her satchel, or sleeping in her heart.

And she and the cat are moving to Brooklyn. To Brooklyn where they have shops and theaters and people and public transportation. To Brooklyn where they have bars and restaurants and reasonable television reception. To Brooklyn and a two-room apartment with a fireplace and a landlady who loves cats and who once danced the tango in Buenos Aires. To Brooklyn where no one ever visits you, where you never have to see anyone you don't want to see, where you never run the risk of accidentally bumping into someone you would rather not have seen while you're out for the evening or for a pound of chopped meat.

Later, after there was nothing more to say in words, he asked her if he should go, and she said, "No." And later than that, when they were just lying on the bed, listening to some song on the radio, he said, "No one should live without love," so softly that he may not have really spoken, so softly that she may only have thought it herself, and she'd flattened her hand on his chest, wondering which of them he meant.

But by then she had known (probably had known as soon as she saw him standing outside of the building), had known there would be no winter wedding in the Grossmans' magazine living room, no home for her in the cultivated country, no brand-new child with perfect teeth. She had been thinking, trudging home with Meredith's cries of you'll see you'll see things will be different still ringing in her ears, she had been thinking that to let herself go on, to let it all go on and on and on was like a war in which another thousand dead means nothing, like a world in which another lie, another cheat, another deceit, another hypocrisy mean less than nothing. And, just before she turned the corner, she had one of those moments in which you feel as though you almost understand, in which you feel that you almost know, know everything, when you realize that the universe lies revealed—and then she turned the corner. And he was there.

She got on a bus and went to visit Skip, surprising him in the basement during his inspection of the new storm windows. "Wine!" he cried, as though small, dark waiters with white jackets and amused expressions were likely to appear, we thought you would want the best. "I've got some put away for a special occasion," and loped happily out of the room. She stood at the window overlooking the road and watched the cars go by, imagining Skip's wife, now that she wouldn't be her. Imagining the house transformed into a home—lights left on in empty rooms, and coats and shoes, magazines and books, toys and unwashed coffee cups scattered about instead of carpet samples, paint cards and bits of tiling and wood. She could see what the yard would look like trapped beneath the falling snow. What the garden would look like loose with blooming. She could hear doors slam and voices call out. Could feel the heat from the flames in the old stone fireplace against her face as the wind wound round the walls and the weather knocked on the glass. She could see it all, but nowhere could she see herself. In the jigsaw puzzle constructed by her mind, there was a pair of shoes on the carpet and magazines on the couch, the lights were on, the washing machine shook and groaned, something on the stove was smoking and there were unwashed dishes in the sink, Skip was leaning over the dining-room table, reading something in the local paper, and the telephone in the living room was looking as though it was about to ring—but the pieces that would have composed her (coming up the stairs, perhaps, with something in her hands) were missing, were only a hole in the shapes of the colors, were evermore to be identified only by their absence. Maggie sighed, wishing it were tomorrow, or two years from tomorrow. And then Skip returned, here I am at last, so suddenly that she jumped around as though caught in the arms of another man. He came toward her, bearing a red plastic tray. He walked across the patterns of sunlight on the floor, through the fingers of sunlight that cut into the space of the room, his shoulders broad and his footsteps sure, solid as the old house itself, as solid as the rocks on which the house was built, bringing wine, bread, cheese, reality, and paper napkins, talking about his plans to join a wine club once he got the cellar organized. "Oh, this is nice," she said. "Skip ..." "Jack and Edith belong to one they found in the *Times*. They even have wine-tasting weekends a couple of times a year," placing the tray on the floor and sitting beside it, illuminated in a stream of light as though beamed down from the clouds, a gourmet guru before his humble shrine, intoning Chablis and Bordeaux as though they were minor deities, stepping-stones on the slippery path to salvation. "Jack says they're not as bad as you might think," mistaking the look on her face for skepticism, I wouldn't be caught dead with a bunch of winos from Connecticut. "He and Edith always have a good time." "Skip," she said, her eyes firmly fixed on a scar in the wood of the floor. "Skip, there's something I've got to say." The wine winked and sparkled as he poured it into the glasses. "It's not a big deal." He passed her her glass by the stem. He would have made a good waiter. "The best for less, as they say," he said. "Skip ..."

And what had she thought that he would say? Nothing? Oh, that's okay, I understand? Well, I guess this is so long? How had she imagined he would react, this man who is so sensitive to the sufferings of others that he numbs the gums before administering the novacaine? With a smile? With a hug? With a cheery wave, adieu? Was he supposed to hold her hand gently in his, his thumb against her knuckles, the look in his eyes pained but tender, all I've ever wanted is for you to be happy, that's the only thing that counts? He stared at her, a smile caught on his lips, his eyes blinking, his glass glowing against the skin of his arm like a giant ruby, and all this am I offering you, too. When she'd finished her speech (if only I felt something, anger or horror or something, if only I really cared), he cleared his throat, shifted his body, opened his mouth, and said, "What?" "It's all my fault.

It has nothing to do with you." "What?" "I just don't love you." "What do you mean, it has nothing to do with me?"

And then he went on to explain that people often got the prenuptial jitters, at his first wedding he was so stoned he had to keep asking people afterward if he'd had a good time. Then went on to explain that it was typical of her to think that she was the only one who noticed differences between them, typical of her to think only of herself. "What about me?" he asked. "What about me? Do you think I'm just going to disappear?" Typical of her to be concerned about only the possibility of her suffering, never mind about his. Did she think he couldn't have done better than her? Did she think he wasn't making sacrifices and compromises, taking a chance? No, he had never known anyone more selfish, egotistical, or self-absorbed than she. He knew why she'd never been married before, why she was nearly forty (forty, now that's a big age for a woman) and never had a family. Because she was the most selfish bitch who'd ever drawn a breath, because she was so fucking sure she should have every-thing her own way, he certainly wouldn't want her to have to think about somebody else for a change. The first three times she'd tried to leave, he yanked her back, his grip sure and supple from so much manual labor, and the last he slugged her, I've never hit a woman before but you drove me to it. He kicked the wine bottles across the room and told her that they were made for each other. He said he couldn't believe that after all these years she still thought she was going to make a go of her designing, Jesus, she didn't really think she had what it takes, did she? And then had to blink back a tear as he remembered all their plans. An intrepid alien, wandering innocently into the middle of the argument, would have been forced to conclude that there were actually two women involved: one who was detestable and one who was adorable; one who was universally loathed and one who was selflessly loved. To Maggie it seemed that there were two men: the one she had imagined and the one she had never cared to see. Good old Skip, kissed by the sticky sweet lips of success when first laid in his heirloom cradle, guaranteed at birth that his life would be a pleasant one, he could afford to be a real nice guy; and this other Skip, small, deformed, and mean, kept chained in the basement and fed on scraps and bones, driven only by the demon lusts of humankind.

Afterward he drove her to the bus stop in town, took her for a beer and a bowl of chili while they waited for the Greyhound, told her that all she had to do was call him if ever she changed her mind, if ever she needed a friend. She waved to him through the tinted window, smiling back at her, for all the world like a man who knew she would call.

But she had never intended to call. He called her one night, to tell her how badly it was raining, and how there was a new leak in the basement, and how he'd been waiting for her call. And he stopped by one night and sat on a cushion on the floor with Cat on his lap, looks like you're moving, and she said, "Yes."

With the exception of Kate, she has told no one where she is going—not even Meredith who has gone back to taking in typing, an occupation that Clive feels is more stimulating to, and which offers more opportunities for, a woman of Meredith's intelligence and talents than hustling overalls and pillows that look like snails all over town, what kind of future's in that?

She looks at the cat, looks at the telephone, looks at the boxes and stacks of books tied with string. She gets up and goes to look out of the window at the fading night, though all the windows in this apartment only look out on other windows. In Brooklyn all her windows look out on the street, lined with trees planted in a more hopeful time. In Brooklyn, she can keep going, just as she is, just as she could be. In Brooklyn there will be no distractions, no regrets.

Across the narrow alleyway, through the dimly lit window of the apartment below, two men can be seen in a kiss. In Brooklyn (in Brooklyn or somewhere else) she will be able to grow older gracelessly, another insignificant figure in the pageant of history, another unmarked life in time's graveyard, growing weary of the world but not immune to its strange charms and timeless fascinations. Unthinking, she turns from the window, walks back into the room, and from an open box removes the slightly battered satin heart, its lace just a bit more crumpled, its legend starting to pull off at the edges, surrendering itself, and carries it back to the open window, leaning out so that she can watch it fallfallfall until it's just another shadow on the ground below, just in time for the rain.

◇   ◇   ◇

Out into the cool cool morning steps Tony Rivera, putting his collar up against the rain.

It is not so late, but it is late enough. Late enough, the streets calm enough, for a man to feel his own aloneness, his own smallness against the terrible beauty of the planet—even here where there are no silent mountains to witness the steady trickle of the centuries, no infinite nights with enormous secrets promises and threats. Even here.

Out into the cool, gray morning steps Tony Rivera, out into the land of his hopes and of his dreams, the rhythms of his heart more steady than the rhythms of any one of a thousand of man's creations, braver than the beep and cackle of a voice coming from the moon.

He gives Zorro a come-on whistle, and begins trotting down the block to where there is a liquor store, a Brazilian café, a telephone booth, and a whore drinking coffee from a styrofoam cup.

The phone rings and she jumps, her hand caught rubbing her eye. The phone rings and she watches it, hesitating from across the room, ring and ring and ring.